ROMANCING
ON JEJU

T0130926

ROMANCING ON JEJU

HYUN-JOO PARK

Translated by Paige Morris

AMAZON **CROSSING**

Previously published as *Searching for Honeyman* by Wisdom House, Inc. in South
Korea in 2019. Translated from Korean by Paige Morris. First published in English
by Amazon Crossing in 2024.

Published by Amazon Crossing, Seattle

www.apub.com

Amazon, the Amazon logo, and Amazon Crossing are trademarks of Amazon.com,
Inc., or its affiliates.

ISBN-13: 9781662523564 (paperback)
ISBN-13: 9781662523557 (digital)

Cover design by Laywan Kwan
Cover image: © Moremar, © chrupka, © Tassia_K, © Volha Hlinskaya,
© gomban, © Dashkevich Snezhana, © Moleng24 / Shutterstock

Printed in the United States of America

Contents

SOMETIMES YOUR SIGNALS GET CROSSED

The *Searching for Honeyman* project was born out of a conversation with Do Romi. It may seem cliché to say now, but no one could have predicted then just how dramatically that conversation would change their lives. That day was a special one for Park Hadam, not only because of what it would ultimately come to mean, but because it also happened to be her thirty-sixth birthday. It was the day she distinctly felt she had crossed over that decade's halfway mark and into her late thirties. There was another reason that day was so special, too, but Hadam didn't have time to dwell on it. Right then, she was sitting—alone and anxious—at a table for four in a popular restaurant with a line that went out the door and around the corner.

Hadam's waiter had already come around to her table three times and filled her glass with water, but if he was judging her for taking up the table, he didn't show it. For that, Hadam was grateful. Her seat faced the door at such an angle that the people waiting in line could see how long the other chairs at her table remained empty. To avoid their pointed stares, Hadam studied the menu so hard, she practically memorized it. She had just decided on a salad when a familiar face appeared in the doorway.

"Romi, over here!"

Romi made her way to the table, her long, fanned-out skirt fluttering and grazing other customers in the restaurant as she moved around them.

"Sorry I'm late," she said. "And on your birthday too. I'm such a mess. Sorry! Really."

Sure enough, the look of apology on Romi's face was as pure as 24-karat gold. Hadam knew Romi had a tendency to be late, so she had come to expect as much. But the past half hour had done a number on her nerves—rather than irritation or resentment, Hadam felt more relieved than anything to see Romi come through that door.

"No, no, I'm sorry," Hadam said. "I picked a spot near my place, not yours. It was hard to find, wasn't it?"

Romi waved her hand. "Don't be silly. It's your birthday. Of course we should meet up closer to where you are. I just ended up on the subway headed for Dunchon somehow."

"What? But this is East Ichon-dong."

"I know. When I realized I should be headed toward Ichon Station, I got off and backtracked. Then I got here and realized I had forgotten the name of the restaurant."

"Huh? But I sent you the directions yesterday."

"I know, but my battery died. Earlier, when I transferred to Line Four, I texted you that I'd be a little late. My battery conked out right after. I got off at Ichon Station and kept trying to remember the name of the restaurant. I asked some people on the street whether there was an Italian restaurant called C'est Si Bon nearby, but no one had heard of it. So I was wandering around for a while, looking for the right place."

"This is a French restaurant called Bon Vivant . . . How did you end up finding it?"

Romi opened a menu. "I kept asking random people while I was walking around the area. The fifth or so person I asked was walking their dog and told me there was no C'est Si Bon, but there was a Bon Vivant."

"Right . . ." Hadam had figured as much after a half hour had passed from the time they were supposed to meet up. She blamed herself for not having met Romi at the station so they could walk over together.

"Where's Chakyung, by the way?" Romi asked.

"Ah, she told me beforehand she would be a little late. She has an executive meeting tomorrow. She'll be here after she finishes up her presentation."

Just then, Hadam's phone pinged with a message.

"She says she's here," Hadam said, laughing. "Coming up the street now."

"Oh, that worked out perfectly! Now we can all order together."

As Yoon Chakyung stepped inside the restaurant, she dodged the harsh looks from all the people waiting in the sweltering heat who must have thought she was trying to cut the line. *Don't be mad at me*, she thought. *My friends are already waiting inside.*

Chakyung spotted a pair of familiar faces in the corner. One of them had chin-length blond hair, which she kept tucking behind her ears as she studied the menu. The other had short hair and was wearing jeans, and she kept tapping away at her phone. As Chakyung approached their table, Hadam—the short-haired one—looked up and waved.

"Chakyung, you're here already!"

"What do you mean, 'already'? I'm so late. Sorry about that."

Romi grinned so brightly, her eyes disappeared. She pointed to the seat next to her. "Hey, I was super late too."

Chakyung sat down, setting a white shopping bag tied with a black ribbon down on the table. "Happy birthday, Hadam."

"Oh, are we doing gifts now? I have one too!" Romi rummaged around inside a big bag on the floor and handed Hadam the pink bundle she pulled out.

"Thanks, you two." Hadam seemed flustered for a moment over what to do with the presents. She set them down on the seat next to her. "I'll open them after we eat. First things first, let's order. I'm starving."

Once they had cleared their plates, their waiter brought out tea and coffee. Hadam opened her presents. Romi's gift was a pretty pink wool scarf. Hadam was surprised, considering the current season, but she ran a hand over the scarf and did her best to mask her confusion.

"It has . . . a nice texture!"

"I thought the color would complement you really well. I know it's summer, but the material is a cashmere blend, so you can bring it when you go places with air-conditioning."

The shopping bag held a sample bundle of new cosmetics that Chakyung's company was promoting. In a yellow box, there was a bottle of grain-scented perfume—a new product from a brand Hadam had seen in upscale stores abroad when she was overseas filming last spring. The prices had been so high that she'd barely looked at the items before returning them to their shelves.

"I thought this fragrance suited you. It's not too overpowering, so it should be good to wear for work."

Something flared up in Hadam's chest, but she tried a spritz of the perfume on her wrist, determined to suppress the feeling. The fragrance reminded her of a field in the English countryside, its faint scent tickling her nose. Hadam told herself she was tearing up simply because of the perfume. She steeled herself in preparation for sharing the news with her friends.

"It smells lovely, Chakyung, but I won't get to wear it to work right away. As of today, I quit my production job."

There was a brief silence. It took about twenty seconds for Romi and Chakyung to decide how to react.

Chakyung spoke first. It was in her nature to take the lead on breaking through the awkward tension in such situations. "Good for you," she said. "That couldn't have been an easy decision."

"Yes, good for you!" said Romi. "Now you can take a break and work on something of your own!"

"I'm sorry to come out of nowhere with news like this today. But I realized I'm already in my late thirties—I'm afraid if I don't do my own thing now, I might never be able to." Hadam had been working as a documentary producer for seven years. She had directed photo shoots of all sorts of animals, from elephants to praying mantises, and had been everywhere from the Himalayas to Buenos Aires. She had no fears about going to the South Pole to film penguins, but it was being contracted out to work on the films that made her feel like it was time to step down. She wanted more say in the jobs she took on.

"When I quit, though, something else happened that really made me mad."

"What was it?" Romi asked, already livid on her behalf.

"One of my coworkers, another producer, is getting married this month, and a senior male coworker asked me if that was the reason I was quitting."

"What kind of crap is that? Did he actually believe that would make you leave?" Chakyung narrowed her eyes.

"Well, he said he always thought the two of us looked good together. We're around the same age and started at the same time, so we get along better than a lot of other people at work, and last year when we were filming this documentary on South America, I helped him out a few times when he was getting absolutely nowhere on his own, but I wouldn't say we were close. You know how it is, though—a lot of times when you have a couple of single people around the same age, they tend to get paired up." Hadam sighed.

"Still, it's a good thing you didn't mistakenly think he had feelings for you. I've had that happen so many times," Romi said, grimacing.

"Yeah, but when the coworker who's getting married approached me, he implied that I had done exactly that—assumed he had feelings for me. He said he was sorry I had to find out through rumors that he was getting married, that he should have come to me directly and told

5

me. But I thought, *Why?*" Hadam recalled her coworker's face as he handed her the wedding invitation. He had seemed sorry at first, then relieved to have the upper hand.

"There are so many people going around without an ounce of common sense in their heads. It's good you quit working at a company like that." Chakyung set down her coffee, her voice softening all of a sudden. Deep down, she didn't think retiring or quitting should be taken lightly, but she felt that now was the time to encourage her friend before anything else.

Hadam seemed lost in thought. "I agree, but I wonder if I gave him mixed signals? If I caused him to misunderstand?"

"You're not the type. You're a softy, but you're always clear about your feelings."

"You think so? The whole situation upset me so much, but then I started questioning whether it was my fault."

"It's not. Lots of people mistake kindness for something more than that." Chakyung had a tendency to be blunt, but there were times her no-nonsense style could be comforting. This was one of the reasons Hadam had first wanted to be her friend.

"That's why I almost moved to Jeju Island to become a beekeeper," said Romi.

One of Romi's quirks was tossing out comments without any context whatsoever. This was one reason Hadam had wanted to be her friend too. But Hadam had to admit she was thrown by this particular comment, which had seemed to come completely out of left field.

"You said 'that's why' . . . but how is that connected to this?" Hadam asked.

Chakyung, on the other hand, seemed totally unfazed. "You're saying you were one of those people who mistook kindness for something more, and that almost led you to move to Jeju and take up beekeeping?" she asked.

"Exactly," Romi said gleefully. "It all happened three years ago . . . ," she said, launching into her recollection of events. "If I remember correctly,

I went to Jeju three years ago sometime in September. I'd been invited to take part in a joint trade fair. I'd worked on this project where independent artists and companies partnered up to make and sell goods. They told me to sit at our booth and explain our goods to people. I worked the booth for two of the three days, but since I didn't have to stay the whole time, I thought I'd explore Jeju as a tourist. In the end, I barely got to see anything there. But anyway, I had a ton of Instagram followers at the time, and I posted that I was going to Jeju and wanted recommendations on where to eat, where to go.

"But then this one guy came to the fair to see me. He looked nice—he was wearing jeans and a light summer jacket, and he seemed to be in his midthirties, around the same age as me. He told me he was a fan of my illustrations. He'd been following my Instagram for a long time and came all the way to the fair because he wanted to meet me. That made me happy, you know? He didn't seem dangerous or anything. He bought us donuts and coffee, and we talked for maybe a half hour, forty minutes. He said he was a beekeeper. I'd never met a beekeeper before. Once we made it past the initial awkwardness, we started talking about different ways to revamp the image of the beekeeping industry. I asked him what he thought about using illustrations to create a brand image, things like that.

"Until then, I thought this man was just a fan who came to meet me out of curiosity. You think maybe he just wanted to commission an illustration from me? Sure, that's possible. But hear me out. He came back the next day too. Wearing this nice clean jacket with cotton slacks. His outfit that day looked more expensive. And his hair? I don't remember if his hair was different, but when I think back on it now, he had maybe styled it in a slightly neater way. Anyway, this time, he gave me chocolates. Not the ones you'd get from a mini-mart or department store but, like, handmade ones. Later, I posted a photo on Instagram, and someone commented that they were from this famous chocolatier in downtown Jeju that had won all kinds of awards. That day, we went to a café nearby and talked for about an hour. The day before, he'd come to see me in a big—what do you call that?—right, an SUV. But that day, he was driving a sedan. Had he rented a different car? I was wondering that too. Unlike the previous day, we didn't talk much about beekeeping. We just chatted about life on Jeju—the weather, how he liked the scenery, that sort of thing. The more we talked, the more I felt my heart pounding and my face getting all hot. Was he attractive? I think so—he definitely gave off a much better impression the second day. He was average height and sort of on the tan side, maybe, or maybe not. Either way, he looked good to me! For some reason, I got this feeling. Like what if I married him and moved to Jeju to live as a beekeeper? Why are you two staring at me like that? There are people who know from the moment they see someone that this is the person they're going to marry. That's how I felt.

"When we went our separate ways, all I said was goodbye. We didn't hold hands. We didn't even exchange numbers.

"Why didn't I get his number? Well, I thought we'd naturally keep in touch via Instagram. He could send me a DM, you know? I had a strong feeling we would meet again. He said he was my fan. I came back to Seoul and posted something like, 'Enjoyed Jeju all the more because I met such a sweet person.' I even added a ton of hashtags, like #FunMemories and #SweetChocolates. There were so many hearts and comments on that post. But he didn't leave a single one. He didn't even DM me! I went looking through the #JejuBeekeeping hashtag, too, but I couldn't find him. I was never able to track him down. He hasn't reached out to me since.

"Yes, I've been waiting for him. Even though I may have been mistaken all along."

"Hmm. This seems pretty different from Hadam's situation. Considering everything that happened between you two, I don't think you were mistaken at all." Chakyung bit her tongue to keep from adding, *Even though you were probably rushing into things.*

"I wasn't, right?" Romi's eyes gleamed. "I know I'm not that reckless."

"Yeah. It's risky to make generalizations here, but isn't there usually a certain behavior or quirk that comes out when someone's romantically interested in someone else? Like in a straight relationship when a man is interested in a woman?"

Romi nodded. "That's right."

"Wait. One sec." Chakyung slid her tablet PC and pen out of her bag and opened up a memo app. "Check this out," she began, writing neatly on the screen as if she were giving a presentation. Romi leaned in close to watch while Hadam looked on, too, tapping away at something on her phone all the while.

SIGNS THAT SAY "I'M INTERESTED IN YOU"

1) Coming to see you not just once but twice

It would have been enough to come say hi to you once, since he knew you from social media, but he came by twice. That's not just mere curiosity. Meeting once is fate, but meeting twice is intentional. Besides, if he hadn't been into you the first time you met, he wouldn't have come to see you again. To add to that . . .

2) Dressing up the second time you met

He wore a jacket and jeans that first day and gave off a more casual vibe, but the second day, he dressed up a little. That means he was interested in you. He wanted to look a bit cooler to you—that's a sign that he was in the early stages of liking you.

3) He bought coffee the first day, but chocolates the second

Coffee seems like something you'd buy an acquaintance, but chocolate feels a bit more like a present. If he gives you chocolates on the second date? The kind you can't just buy anywhere? He's giving you a thoughtful gift. This is clearly something you would normally do to show you have an interest in somebody. So you can infer that he liked you on day one and came back to show you that on day two.

4) He switched cars

No one switches cars overnight, right? Doesn't the fact that he changed cars and came to see you the second time obviously mean he planned to take you somewhere and had asked to borrow someone else's car? Everyone knows it's easier to drive someone around in a sedan than in an SUV. And borrowing a car is no easy task—it requires a lot of forethought. Couldn't you interpret that as a sign that he's interested in you? I'm positive you were reading all his signals right.

Chakyung paused to catch her breath. Romi clapped, satisfied, as though she were in the audience at a real presentation.

"That's right—the vibes on the second day were definitely good! We even locked eyes a bunch of times." Romi was soon swept up in her own thoughts. "But I guess I can't really know for sure."

"No way. He was definitely interested in you. He got you chocolates!"

As Chakyung gave a briefing of the points she'd outlined, Hadam studied her phone, muttering to herself. Chakyung and Romi turned to look at her.

"Romi," Hadam asked, "where was that exhibit?"

"The exhibit? Hmm, I don't know the name of the area, but it had lots of hotels—the Shilla, the Lotte Hotel. And there was a big exhibit hall nearby."

"It was probably the Jungmun area, and the place you mentioned was probably the convention center. I found a newspaper article about a trade fair like the one you described that was being held there around that time."

Romi and Chakyung had long admired Hadam's ability to gather information the way a worker bee would gather honey and arrange it in a clear pattern they could see.

"And the chocolatier that makes the chocolates you got as a gift is in the heart of Jeju City, near city hall. Since that guy is a beekeeper, I doubt he would work downtown. But he went all the way there to buy the chocolates and then went all the way to Jungmun to give them to you," Hadam went on. She held up her phone to show her friends the map with a thick blue line drawn from the chocolate shop to the exhibit hall to indicate the route between them.

"About twenty-five miles. As long as a marathon course. It'd take more than an hour to travel this, even by car. Then he'd have to travel the same distance on the return trip. That's a long trek to make for someone you only know from social media. Plus it was the second time he came to see you."

"When you put it like that, I guess he *was* interested in me!" Romi raised her hands as if to clap, but then she paused, thinking deeply. "But why didn't he contact me again? I even sent him a signal of my own when I wrote that he was the 'sweet person' I met."

As far as Romi was concerned, she had definitely given him the green light—the universal signal to approach her. But then he'd simply vanished. Why was that? It was a mystery that was all too common in relationships, a riddle everyone believed they knew the answer to. It often came down to those famous words that had swept the globe for the last two decades: *He's just not that into you.*

Chakyung studied Hadam. Their eyes met. Chakyung carefully weighed her words.

"Maybe something went wrong the second day."

Hadam thought hard. Was it really just that this guy didn't like Romi? After he'd gone to such lengths for a chance to see her a second time, however briefly? Even if he wasn't interested in her, he could have at least been polite about it. Was it too much to think he could have said a simple hello on social media after all that?

"I don't think that's it," Hadam said. "Romi said she was even thinking about marrying this guy. That kind of feeling isn't usually a one-sided thing. It happens when something clicks between two people. Don't you think so, Chakyung? What was it like when you met Chanmin? When you thought, *I'm going to marry this person?*"

Chakyung thought about her fiancé, Chanmin. There had to have been something between them that made her think she wanted to marry him, right? *Was* there something between them? She didn't answer.

"I didn't get the feeling that I messed up or made him lose interest in me," Romi said.

Chakyung cleared the memo on her tablet and started writing a new list. "If we suppose that you did in fact give him the green light," she said, "there are a few possible hypotheses."

REASONS THE GUY WHO SHOWED A CLEAR INTEREST IN YOU MIGHT NOT HAVE CONTACTED YOU AGAIN

1) He likes you but lacks confidence

This is common for most guys. They lack confidence, so they hesitate. They don't even ask you how you feel. Plus you didn't ask for his number, so . . .

2) He likes you, but his job is more of a priority

Same thing as number one. He's hiding his insecurities behind excuses. This is also really common.

3) He's married or already seeing someone

Maybe?

All was silent for a moment. In Bon Vivant, the customers were trickling out one by one, and the lights had dimmed. Candles had been put out. The waiters moved quietly to clear the empty tables. It was almost closing time. The three women sat there, each imagining her own version of this man they hardly knew.

He could have been married. Even earlier, Hadam had considered this possibility. That would explain why he would give off all those signals that could be taken as interest, only to never approach Romi again. There were people like that in the world, after all—people who skirted accountability. But it made her sad to think that Romi had held on to her fond memories of him for three whole years.

"You've made a lot of guesses," Romi said. "But why aren't you considering the most plausible reason?"

"And what would that be?" Chakyung asked.

"He might have amnesia. Maybe he got into an accident that night after seeing me."

It was hard to tell whether Romi was joking—pulling a line straight out of a Korean drama—or whether she was 100 percent serious. Chakyung almost burst out laughing, but she stopped herself at the sight of the sincere look on Romi's face. If a man had completely forgotten about you, maybe it was better to chalk it up to amnesia rather than assume he was married.

"Well, I suppose that's possible," Chakyung said, frowning. "Many things are possible."

Hadam was listening in, but all kinds of scenes kept playing in her head. A swarm of bees, a field of yellow flowers, blue seas and green mountains, people leaving the city and going to Jeju Island . . .

She slammed her hands on the table, rattling their teacups. Romi and Chakyung looked up in surprise.

"Let's find out."

"Find what out?" Romi asked.

"The reason that guy didn't reach out to you again."

"But how?" said Chakyung.

"Let's go to Jeju. To find that man, the beekeeper. Romi, you want to know what happened to him after the last time you saw him, don't you? And, Chakyung, your company's been looking for an eco-friendly project to build a campaign around, right? This could be a documentary, a marketing campaign, and a search for a long-lost love, all in one." Although Hadam hadn't had more than a single glass of wine at dinner, she had forgotten about the drinks she'd had with her freelancer friends earlier that day after quitting her job, so she didn't consider that this all might have been the alcohol talking. But sometimes alcohol brings unexpected gifts—genuine passion, pure curiosity, and artistic inspiration.

Hadam declared, "We'll call it *Searching for Honeyman*."

YOU HAVE TO SEEK TO FIND

Nine Years Earlier, Summer

The flames were getting stronger. The shouts, too, grew louder as the fire swelled. Hadam thought she would lose her mind from all the noise. Her hands were shaking, her heart pounding, yet all she could think about was somehow putting out the fire. The extinguisher she'd grabbed, though, was rusty and not working properly.

"Hadam, stay back! It's dangerous!" Yoojin shouted from behind her, but Hadam couldn't hear much of anything. Someone tried jumping into the fire from the side but leaped back as the flames lunged like a wild beast.

"Ugh!"

Hadam recognized Pilhyun even with his face coated in soot and dirt. He rolled around on the ground, trying to snuff out the flames that had caught on the hem of his pants.

"Pilhyun sunbae, no!" Hadam cried.

Yoojin, Hyunsuk, and Jungmin came running toward Pilhyun, stripping off their own clothes to cover him and smother the flames. Yoojin sat him up and asked, "Sunbae, are you all right?"

Pilhyun grabbed Yoojin's wrist, his face twisted in pain.

"Hadam, get back!" shouted Hyunsuk, shaking his head and gesturing for her to move.

When would the fire trucks arrive? The area was remote, and it would take even longer than usual for cars to navigate the narrow mountain road that led out here. The smoke was growing thicker, making it hard for Hadam to see what was right in front of her. People were coughing nonstop, and she heard shouts and noise coming from every direction, but it was impossible to make out any one sound in all the chaos.

She had to do something.

Hadam peeled off her blouse and tied her hair up with it, then took off, running back inside the building.

"No!"

She heard several voices shouting at her back, but all she could think about was saving the end product of the crew's hard work. What would happen to the camera? The film?

As her hand gripped the doorknob, someone grabbed her and pulled her back.

"Let go! I have to get the camera!"

As she shook off whoever it was and turned back to face the building, a gust of wind swept through and sent the blaze soaring even higher. Before the flames could pounce on her, the person who'd grabbed her whipped around to block them. Next thing she knew, Hadam was being hoisted up into the air, flung over the guy's shoulder, and carried off. She struggled and squirmed in his grip, but the guy kept walking right ahead, taking long, determined strides.

"Hey, Gu Jaewoong! Put me down! I said, put me down!"

He did—on the field about fifty yards in front of the building, and not at all gently. Hadam rolled over on the grass. Jaewoong grabbed a hose and sprayed her down. Only when the water hit her skin did she realize she had burns that made her entire body sting.

"Pull yourself together! You almost died just now!"

Hadam held her hands up against the rush of water. When the stream subsided, she lifted her head to look at her boyfriend's face.

"I have to get the camera and film! What did you do with them?" Water dripped off Hadam as she stood. She pushed her wet hair out of her face to get a better look at the house. The fire raged on, more violent than before. Jaewoong didn't offer her so much as a hand.

"I can go back for them—"

"Hwayoung got hurt!" he shouted. It was the first time Hadam had ever heard him raise his voice like that.

"What?"

"She jumped from the second floor and broke her leg! Are you hearing me? She could have died!"

Hadam hadn't known Hwayoung was still inside. It dawned on her then that she didn't know who had gotten out and who hadn't. She hadn't seen Jaewoong or Hwayoung after the fire first broke out and she herself had jumped down to escape.

"Shouldn't you worry about people first? Is the film that important? You're supposed to be the director!"

The flames shot up from the house, and someone let out a piercing scream. Somewhere in the middle of it all, Hadam heard a familiar sound—the wail of a fire truck's siren approaching.

"Is—is everybody okay?"

She looked up at Jaewoong, standing in the shadow of that massive blaze. His face, too, was smeared with soot, the skin under his temple peeling. Hadam reached for his hand. In that moment, she wanted to hold someone's—anyone's—hand. But Jaewoong flinched, refusing to take it.

In a voice as hard as the look on his face, he said, "Go see for yourself."

For a long time after, Hadam remembered that scene better than even the most unforgettable scenes in her favorite films. The building, scarlet and blazing under the shadows of the mountains, Jaewoong's dark face standing out against that cruel light. His face, full of anger directed at her. And lastly, the feeling of warmth that lingered on her hands, a warmth that also felt colder than anything she had ever experienced. It was a feeling that clung to her long after that sweltering air was carried away on the wind.

◆ ◆ ◆

Project: *Searching for Honeyman*

Day One, Jeju

It had been a long time since she'd been to Jeju. Through the plane's window, Hadam took in the landscape, which evoked a strange feeling in her—"strange" being another way to describe the feeling of fear, or anticipation. People feel afraid when they don't know what sorts of things will happen, but they feel anticipation when things might happen that they don't expect. It was an unusual feeling for Hadam—that sense of anticipation taking shape inside her.

They got on the Rent-a-Car shuttle bus right as it was about to depart from the airport bus stop. The driver checked their names against his list—Park Hadam and Do Romi—and stowed their suitcases. Since this first visit would be more of a preliminary research trip, they hadn't yet arranged for accommodations beyond the first night.

Without plans, there was always a chance for things to go wrong. Earlier at the Rent-a-Car center, Hadam learned that the car she'd requested had been in an accident the day before, so she would have to switch to a different model.

Despite peak season being over, there weren't many other cars left to rent. The employee at the desk said, "Most of the domestic compact class vehicles are already rented out, and none of the remaining models have a rearview camera or a parking system. Besides those, a couple of electric cars are available for a slightly lower price."

Hadam thought it over for a moment, then turned to Romi. "What do you think? I'll be doing most of the driving, but there's the off chance you'll have to get behind the wheel."

"Well, wouldn't the compact class car be the best choice?"

Hadam was slightly surprised by Romi's quick reply. "Oh, do you think so? I mean, the insurance for an electric one would be cheaper—"

"But wouldn't the classiest cars already be in top condition?"

"I'm sorry?" Hadam seemed confused, the conversation having taken a left turn.

"She said the cars are compact class, right? Like first class or prestige class. In that case, wouldn't those be the cars the rental center considers the best?"

"Ah, it's not that kind of class. They mean class as in size—subcompact class, midsize class . . ."

The employee listening to their conversation pressed her mouth shut tight, trying to hold in her laughter. She seemed like a nice person, seeing as how she tried not to laugh right in their faces.

In the end, they went with an electric car. A new car would probably be better if Romi ever had to drive. And, of course, they couldn't discount the cheaper price tag.

The ride was surprisingly smooth sailing all the way downtown. So far, the tourist traffic hadn't been too bad, and they hadn't seen too many of the big tour buses either. Everyone else was probably headed to some tourist attraction away from the city center. Hadam and Romi's first destination was a hotel not far from the airport. They had to check in, set down their luggage, and take care of the next thing on the agenda. Which was . . .

"So it's been a while since you've seen him, then? Your ex. Gu Jaewoong."

Romi's question came out of nowhere. As they were getting off the plane earlier, Hadam had told Romi the simplest version of events. It wasn't like she could avoid mentioning him or that particular item on the schedule.

Hadam gripped the steering wheel. "I haven't seen him since before I graduated, so it's been, what? Eight or nine years?"

"Did you break up right after what happened with the fire at the film shoot?"

"No, it didn't happen all at once. There were some hard feelings on my end, and on his too. I had to go to the police after the fire, and I was having a hard time dealing with everything. Lots of people came out of it with injuries, big and small. I got into a heated argument with the owner of the house over who was at fault. In the end, they found out an old, worn electrical line had short-circuited, so I wasn't to blame, at least not entirely, but . . ." Hadam sorted through her memories. "We fought a lot. I was exhausted and struggling. He was busy with his own stuff and probably just got tired of me in the end."

More than a little while had passed between the fire and their breakup, but looking back on their last days together now, Hadam found it hard to distinguish any one day from the mass of them. Repeated arguments, short-lived reconciliations, resurfaced conflicts. They couldn't continue to see each other, not because they hated each other, but because they each hated the way they were carrying on.

No one could know who had been the first to say, "Let's end this." Whoever it was had probably meant, *Let's end this fight*, but soon enough, it came to mean, *Let's end this relationship*. They finished school and slowly, steadily grew apart, without ever saying so much as a proper goodbye.

I was upset and wanted him to coddle me, but because he wouldn't, I gave him a hard time. Hadam hadn't been able to tell Romi much more than that earlier. Now, she kept her tone intentionally even. "It was nine years ago. That's all in the past. We have no relationship now, either, so—"

"Just because you have no relationship now doesn't mean the one you had doesn't matter," said Romi thoughtfully. "In fact, because you don't have one, doesn't it matter that much more that you're meeting up again now?"

Hadam struggled to think of a reply. But she couldn't quite hide her excitement. "I guess you're right," she said.

"Thank you, Hadam."

"Hmm? For what?"

"You've had to do all sorts of things you didn't want to, all because I wanted to find Honeyman. And I know it must have been a hassle for Chakyung too."

"Not at all!" Hadam couldn't explain it exactly. It may have been possible to film the documentary even without Jaewoong's assistance. But having it would certainly make the process much easier. Besides, if they wanted to find Romi's beekeeper, a local's cooperation was a must. This was the logic Hadam had used to convince herself as she studied the email address Yoojin sent her, typing and erasing several drafts to Jaewoong asking for his help.

Maybe this was all because of Romi, or maybe Hadam was using Romi as an excuse. She didn't think she had any lingering feelings. She just didn't want to avoid him on purpose and risk looking like she did.

Still, when he replied, saying he wanted to meet up with her to go over the details, she was struck by two different feelings. This emotional cocktail was 90 percent relief that they had moved on from the past, and 10 percent emptiness because they really seemed to have no relationship at all with each other now.

Jaewoong offered to come by the hotel after he got off work, but Hadam declined, carefully scouring online maps and blogs until she found a quiet café near city hall and replied that they should meet there. She already felt like she owed him big-time and didn't want to ask anything more of him, not even something so small.

Hadam left the hotel with a plan to get to the café ten minutes early. Most times when she made plans with someone, she felt uncomfortable when the other person beat her there. She was the one who waited for others—every time. If she got tired of waiting, she could walk away first.

But as it turned out, Jaewoong had gotten there before her. Hadam opened the door to the café and stepped inside. When she spotted him sitting at a table, his posture perfect as he pored over a book, her heart leaped. All this time had passed, but when she entered that café, she realized how familiar a sight he was. Romi was right. Whether they had a relationship now or not, she couldn't say their old one didn't matter. Hadam couldn't bring herself to look at him as she approached. The distance from the entrance to the table felt impossible to bridge.

"Hi," said Hadam.

Jaewoong shut his book and set it aside. "Hey." His voice was a little hoarse. "It's been a while."

Only then did Hadam look him in the eye.

"You look exactly the same," he said. "I recognized you right away."

She smiled awkwardly at that. "You too." But she knew neither of them looked exactly the same as they had back then. He hadn't changed so much that she wouldn't have been able to recognize him if their paths crossed on the street—his hair wasn't thinning to the point of baldness, and he hadn't put on a ton of weight or anything. But he was prematurely graying in places, and he must have laughed so often that even his resting face held traces of laugh lines, crow's-feet creasing the skin around his eyes. No matter how much someone's appearance changed, though, they remained the same at their core.

Back in school, Jaewoong hadn't majored in acting, but oddly enough he'd been asked to act in different projects every now and then. On-screen, he managed to blend well into the background. He could make ordinary moments look a little more polished without ruining the illusion of the everyday. Even now, in a white shirt and jeans, he looked a little older but still gave off that impression. Jaewoong didn't stick out, not even in this Jeju Island café. Rather, he was like a natural part of the scenery.

Once their iced coffees came out, they had trouble finding things to say. All the topics of conversation that should have been used to break through the awkward tension had already been discussed over email, so they would simply be repeating things the other knew.

Jaewoong spoke first. "I heard about what happened to Hyunsuk."

"Yeah. He looked so ill in his last documentary. It was hard to see him like that."

"I'm sure it was. I couldn't make it out there for the memorial film screening, so I sent some money and my condolences." The words sounded strangely aloof coming from Jaewoong, who usually made it a point to look after his seniors and juniors, but everyone had been busy living their own lives, it seemed. Hadam awkwardly went on.

"I ran into a lot of our old schoolmates there. They told me you were working here on Jeju."

"Yeah. I haven't been here long."

The conversation came to a brief pause. A piano cover of "The Girl from Ipanema" flowed through the café. The music suited the island well.

"So," Jaewoong said, "I looked into what you told me."

Hadam had mentioned in her emails that she was making a movie about beekeeping and searching for a certain person at the same time. She hadn't gone into detail about the parts of the story that had to do with Romi. All she'd said was that the person she was looking for was an acquaintance of her friend.

Jaewoong took a yellow memo pad out of his bag.

It'll be more comfortable if we just talk business, Hadam thought. *Nothing more.* "Sorry to ask so much of you," she said.

He brushed off her apology, flipping through the notes he'd written and rereading them.

"There are about two hundred bee farms on Jeju in all. And around one hundred sixty of those own more than ten beehives. You can think of those as commercial businesses of sorts."

"I see. There aren't as many as I thought there would be," said Hadam. Her voice rose, excited and determined. The job would be easier than she'd expected. "We should be able to track him down soon, then."

Jaewoong looked at her across the table. The corners of his mouth turned up in a little smile. "You think one hundred sixty bee farms aren't a lot?" he said. "I figure it'd take you a few months to go around to them all. Just the fact that you're considering it shows you've still got that same tireless passion."

Hadam winced. Sure, there were times she could be overly eager. There had been a point in her life when she couldn't distinguish between passion, sincerity, and ambition. "I guess so," she said.

Jaewoong set his memo pad down on the table and folded his hands, looking serious. What he said next made the temperature, which had been mild until then, as cold as the cubes in their iced coffees.

"I can't give you detailed profiles on each and every beekeeper."

Hadam's hand stopped mid-stir of her coffee. The ice cubes rattled in protest. "What?"

"I'm a civil servant. It'd be one thing if this were public information, but I can't give out those details without the consent of all parties involved."

Hadam's face burned red, seeing the situation from Jaewoong's perspective. She couldn't ask this sort of favor of him as if they still had the same relationship they used to. "Right," she said. "I'm sorry."

"That's my official position, though. Not my personal view. It's not like I can stop you from going to these beekeepers and scoping them out for yourself as a director."

Hadam hid her reddening disappointment. Calmly, Jaewoong began to explain.

"A man in his thirties—there are very few people who fit the profile you gave me. Most of the beekeepers are in their fifties at least. Plus, if you consider the ones who came from other regions to farm, the scope narrows even more." He unfolded his hands and picked up his memo pad. Flipping another page, he tore off a sheet and slid it onto the table. "This is the most information about animal husbandry on the island that I, civil servant Gu Jaewoong, can share with you, film director Park Hadam. To aid in the production of a film that will help revitalize the local beekeeping industry, there are three bee farms I would recommend looking into."

Hadam took the paper. It listed exactly three apiaries. Despite the search not even being for her sake, her heart leaped at the idea of finding Honeyman at one of them. She scanned the list of names.

"Much more doable than one hundred sixty farms, right?" Jaewoong's cheeriness was enough to ease the awkward tension between them.

Hadam found herself smiling. She clapped her hands and nodded firmly. "Right!"

Jaewoong pointed at her. "That hasn't changed either."

Hadam looked confused.

"Your habit of clapping when you're happy. You still do it, even now."

Jaewoong's voice also sounded unchanged when he said things like that. Even when he was being mischievous, his voice was so gentle that it seemed like his mood would never sour. When he suddenly brought up the past, his voice was like a wave lapping at the island shore. It was the voice he once used to tease her when she was going on and on about her plans. She used to share these fantasies, like the milkmaid counting her chickens before they'd hatched. Even when he made fun of her for it, he listened to every word. The two of them used to share their dreams about their distant futures. Movies they would watch and make together. Countries they would visit. Countless things they would do. All those dreams forming in her mind like sea-foam on the ocean's waves had been swallowed up, bubbling into nothing, but it felt like they hadn't been completely swept away. Like they might still rise to the surface.

For the first time that evening, Hadam looked at Jaewoong in a real and meaningful way. He looked right back at her. When their eyes met, he grinned.

The first word that came to Hadam's mind was "trouble."

Imagine, just when you think your heart has settled, a wave rips through you, tossing and turning inside you at the mere sight of your ex-boyfriend's smile—there were no other words for such a situation aside from that one: "trouble."

No matter how many channels Romi flipped through, the only thing on at this hour was the Jeju Island local news. Rolling over on the crisp, clean hotel bedsheets, she watched news stories about local industries and what was going on in town. A festival celebrating Jeju's haenyeo was set to start soon, and preparations were underway at one of the divers' homes. The women divers had rescued a swimmer who'd gotten swept away by the rough ocean waves. Upkeep on the facilities along the harbor had begun in preparation for a typhoon that could strike at any moment. Last summer, the number of tourists during peak season had dropped compared to other years. A local commercial came on then, cutting off the news story at the interesting part. It seemed even minor, everyday life events got their own commercials here.

Information on local weddings and funerals appeared on the TV. Lines of announcements ran down the screen—a Jeju City trading company CEO's third son had gotten married at some wedding hall; a distribution center employee had gotten married at another.

"No matter how low everyone says the marriage rate is these days, plenty of people are still getting hitched. Look at that," Romi muttered to herself, reading the list. "There were that many weddings on Jeju this past month alone." Just whom were they targeting with these announcements? Right as the list finally came to an end, Romi's phone rang. It was Hadam.

"Hello? Hi, Hadam. No, no. You two can have dinner on your own. Oh, if another friend is joining you, you three can dine together, then. I already ate."

It wasn't exactly a lie. She hadn't had dinner yet, but she'd had a snack earlier and wasn't all that hungry. It wasn't that she was hoping to give the two of them some space to rekindle those old feelings now that they were seeing each other again. It would be nice if they did, but they were adults who could make that choice for themselves. It was more that another friend of theirs from their college days might be joining them. Romi would have to spend the next few days traveling with other people—she wanted to be on her own, however briefly. It wasn't bad, having the hotel room to herself and being alone for a little while in an unfamiliar place.

Romi ended the call and studied the screen for a moment before grabbing the remote and shutting off the TV. She'd seen something just then that she'd meant to tell Hadam, but she couldn't remember what it was.

Looking out the window, she noticed the sun beginning to set. Could she find somewhere within walking distance to have dinner with a view of the sea? Could she find a scene like that in real life—the sun dipping below the horizon like something in a painting? If she wanted to try, she'd have to head to a beach on the west coast. The evening air on Jeju would be so refreshing, unlike in Seoul. It was decided—Romi would hit the town. This was a tourist city. There would probably be lots of places she could go alone.

As she took the key card from the slot next to the door and stepped out, the feeling Romi had earlier, that she'd discovered something important, completely disappeared from her mind.

◆ ◆ ◆

Many business trips overseas had taught Chakyung the ultimate survival secret—pack light. No matter how little luggage she brought with her, the amount of stuff she had to carry always seemed to multiply on the return trip, so she'd learned to pack things she could simply throw away. She was able to pack all the necessities while keeping things to a minimum. This was a point of pride for her—being the business-trip guru. But it was all too common for her personal principles to fall apart when it was time to be Chakyung, the employee.

As soon as she arrived at the airport in Honolulu, Chakyung grabbed the huge golf bag from the car with the cab driver's help.

"Hey, Manager Yoon. I heard you decided to go straight from Hawaii to Jeju on business. That's perfect. I'm going golfing there this weekend. Bring my golf bag with you to Jeju, would you?" Director Kim had handed this headache of a task off to Chakyung. He'd bragged about the new golf bag he had bought on the trip, but he must have realized how heavy it would be to carry back to Korea and had sneakily given Chakyung the honor instead.

"Wouldn't it be better if you took it home with you and brought it to Jeju yourself? Since it's so valuable," Chakyung had asked through gritted teeth, but Director Kim hadn't seemed the least bit apologetic.

"Ah, well, I bought some stuff here and there while we've been in Hawaii, so I've got too much luggage to take back as it is. They told me I was over the excess baggage limit. But you only brought along your one carry-on, so . . ."

So he'd asked this huge favor of her to save himself a few coins. All because he'd spent so much already just to fly business class. If she'd known he would pull a stunt like this, she would have gone on a shopping spree herself. But she'd had back-to-back meetings all day and had another one in the evening—there'd been no time. Director Kim had suddenly requested revisions on her materials, so she'd stayed up all night in her hotel room working on them. Her pitch to the executive board for a documentary ad campaign centered on local, naturally sourced ingredients had been a success, perfectly timed with the company's plans to launch a new honey-based skin-care line the following year. Still, Chakyung was starting to regret having mentioned that after the business trip in Hawaii, she was planning to head straight to Jeju to get started on the project with the resource extraction team. Knowing Senior Director Kim Jaejin, though, he would have somehow found someone headed to Jeju and shoved this responsibility off on them anyway. Chakyung prayed he would never get promoted—the pairing of his current title and name made it so that she could call him Director Dim to her heart's content.

He'd even lied and said the golf bag would be light. Dragging the bag along on a cart, Chakyung headed toward the check-in counter. She sighed at the thought of having to track the golf bag down again when she landed at Incheon to bring it with her on the next leg of the trip.

Standing in the check-in line, she noticed the person in front of her had a cart with a sports bag as big as he was. He was a young guy, tall, wearing a T-shirt and shorts. The sun had browned some of his hair, but from behind, it was hard to tell what country he was from based on his build. People from all over the globe came to Hawaii. One thing Chakyung could say for sure, though, was that he had an eye-catching physique. People's eyes kept seeking him out, even after they had checked in and were headed elsewhere, their stares lingering a bit longer than usual.

The man put his luggage on the conveyor belt. One glance at his side profile showed that he was smiling. The person at the counter was a Hawaiian local in her early thirties. The man said something to her that made her burst out laughing. He set all his luggage on the belt and made some sort of hand gesture, and the woman held up a loose fist with two fingers raised in return, mirroring him. As the man left the check-in area, he turned his head and locked eyes with Chakyung. He looked East Asian—Korean or Japanese, she couldn't be sure. They'd never met before, but the man nodded at her, still wearing that earlier smile.

He seems friendly, Chakyung thought, but she was wary of him. Regardless of their intentions, good-looking people who laughed a lot always made her feel cautious. If their intentions were bad, she had to be careful not to get hurt, and if they were good, she had to be careful not to hurt them. It was when someone like that had no intentions at all that it was easiest for someone to get hurt. Her wariness stemmed from lots of experience. There were exceptions, of course. Chanmin had given off that sort of vibe when they'd first met—had he laughed a lot, though? Now that she thought of him, Chakyung remembered that she'd only seen him briefly the day before her trip, and he hadn't called her yesterday. She hadn't told him she was going straight to Jeju either, so she made a mental note to call him after she checked in at the hotel.

Chakyung maneuvered her carry-on suitcase through the narrow aisle between the airplane seats. Her seat was toward the middle of the plane. Since she'd been a bit late to change her itinerary, she hadn't had a ton of seating options. She was usually fine with traveling over long distances, but today, she already felt exhausted, and the plane hadn't even taken off yet. Was this some sort of delayed jet lag? A sudden wave of dizziness made the suitcase she usually wheeled along with ease feel incredibly heavy. She strained, even grunting a few times, but she couldn't pull it any farther.

She had to do something quick—she was blocking the aisle. With a sigh, she hunched over to lift up her suitcase and, like a miracle, it rose up into the air. She looked up in surprise, only to see a pair of strong brown arms lifting her suitcase into the overhead bin. A bit dazed, Chakyung bowed slightly, a smile spreading across her face.

"Thank you," she said in English.

"No problem," came his breezy reply.

It was the guy from the counter at the airport earlier, the one who'd set off her suspicions. He studied her for a moment. Then he smiled, hoisted his own backpack into the overhead compartment across the aisle from hers, and took his seat. As soon as Chakyung had sat down and fastened her seat belt, a petite woman—also East Asian—came down the aisle, grumbling and lugging a huge bag with all her strength. The man seemed to realize she must have been assigned to the window seat next to him and stood up again, moving aside so she could sit. He was standing right next to Chakyung now, and when he moved to lift the other woman's bag into the overhead bin, too, he leaned back a little, giving Chakyung a clear view of the broad expanse of his back. She scooted to the side, careful not to touch him. Just then, her phone started ringing— she'd forgotten to turn it off. She hurriedly fished it out of her handbag, swearing internally when she saw the name that appeared on the screen.

"Yes, Director Kim. Yes, yes, I brought your bag with me. Oh, the part that's missing from the materials I gave you yesterday—sure, when I get back to Korea . . . Well, I'm on the plane right now. We're about to take off."

Even after that, Director Kim kept on talking. Chakyung held the phone away from her ear, made a face at it, then spoke into it again.

"Yes, sir. The plane is taking off now. I'll look it over and call you later."

He started to say something else, but Chakyung ended the call. Still, the phone began to ring a second time. The man from earlier sneaked a glance over at her. She sighed. The name on the screen read "Mokdong Mom." Chanmin's mother. Chakyung hesitated for a moment, then slid her finger across the screen to accept the call.

"Yes, ma'am."

"Oh, Chakyung. You're busy, aren't you? Still in America?"

"Yes, ma'am. I'm on the plane right now."

"Oh, it must be a bad time." Still, she didn't end the call. "I'll be brief. It's about the furniture we're getting for your newlywed home. You know, there's that imported furniture dealer I've been looking into."

"Yes, ma'am. But there's still six months to go before the wedding . . ."

"Sure, of course, but the stuff there is really expensive, and they're having a sale next week. So I was looking into it a bit ahead of time—"

"Ma'am, I'm sorry, but I think the plane is about to take off. I can't talk for much longer."

"All right. But how come you hardly ever call? We should talk about these things more often—"

"Ma'am, I'm really sorry, but the takeoff announcement just came on."

"All right, all right. Give me a call when you get to Seoul."

Chakyung ended the call and pressed a hand to her forehead. Chanmin's mother wasn't the kind of mother-in-law who went around sticking her nose in all sorts of business, but she seemed determined to live out her own nuptial fantasies through her son's wedding. Her behavior wasn't unheard of.

More and more people steadily made their way to the back of the plane. Chakyung's migraine began to worsen a little. It felt like a little canary was living inside her head and pecking at the walls of her skull. Chakyung closed her eyes. She heard the scattered sounds of people's conversations, all their words forming one constant hum. Several languages ran together, one impossible to distinguish from another. The next thing she knew, the safety announcements had ended, and she could feel the plane gradually lifting off.

At the sound of the seat belt sign turning off, Chakyung opened her eyes. She felt as if her head and the plane both were suspended in midair, the canary's beak growing sharper and stronger, but first things first, she had to make those revisions Director Kim had requested. She pulled her laptop out of the bag at her feet and set it on the narrow tray table on the seat in front of her. The revisions weren't something she could do in a day or two, even if she worked on them now. The shifts in air pressure were unusually strong, though, and her computer nearly fell twice. Figuring it was just one of those days, she shut the laptop and put it back in her bag, then leaned her head against the window. She couldn't keep her eyes open for long this time.

The sleep she managed to get on the flight wasn't that great. When she woke up, the canary's pecking had intensified. Chakyung looked around, holding her neck as if to keep her head from falling off her shoulders. The flight attendants were bustling around, getting ready to serve the scheduled meal. Chakyung decided to skip it. She raised her hand. A flight attendant hurriedly approached her. She had a baby face but masked her youth with an impeccably friendly smile. It was clear, though, that she still didn't have much experience as a working adult.

"I'll skip the meal," Chakyung said.

As if a switch had flipped inside her, the flight attendant's perfectly gentle smile shifted into a flawless look of concern. "Is everything all right, ma'am? Would you like some fruit or a different meal option?"

"No, I just have a bit of a headache. Could you bring me an aspirin?"

Once the flight attendant left to get it, Chakyung closed her eyes again. To the little bird in her head, she thought, *Please go back to sleep.*

The woman soon returned with water and the pills, cautiously offering them to her. Chakyung took them once she managed to open her heavy eyelids. As the flight attendant moved to leave again, the man sitting on the other side of the aisle called to her in a low voice.

"Jeogiyo."

So he was Korean. Chakyung swallowed the pills and glanced over at him. With a brazen sense of overfamiliarity, the man slipped the flight attendant a folded-up note. And the woman, with that same friendly smile on that same baby face, accepted the note and hurried off.

What had Chakyung just seen? She looked right at the man, but he was chatting calmly now with his wife sitting next to him. Even Chakyung couldn't explain the source of the disappointment welling up inside her. Was she really going to look at all of humanity in a harsher light now because this polite, friendly man had turned out to be the type to chat up a flight attendant? Wasn't this sort of thing common anyway? Lying to your aging wife with a straight face after having slipped a note to a young flight attendant while she was on the clock—where did people find the nerve?

Maybe I'm being too old-fashioned. This sort of thing is probably no big deal; it's so embedded in our society. I guess if you like someone, you don't think too hard about the time or place and just go for it.

The bird inside her head roused itself again, pecking especially hard at her current thoughts. Chakyung furrowed her brow.

As if he could feel her watching him, the man turned to her. She squeezed her eyes shut. Awkward, yes, but she didn't care. Once they got off this plane, she would never see him again. Besides, it could end up being a good thing that he knew someone was watching him. He might not do something as rude as trying to hit on an on-duty flight attendant again.

Counting the feathery shapes floating behind her eyelids, Chakyung once again dove into a dreamy pool of thoughts. Maybe she just wasn't up-to-date on the current methods of approaching someone and getting the green light when it came to dating. It had been three years since she and Chanmin officially started going out, and their relationship had followed the standard path laid out by society to a T. He'd asked her out; they'd gone on run-of-the-mill dates on a regular basis; and they'd introduced each other to their families at an appropriate time. It had been ages since Chakyung bid farewell to the old method of meeting people by chance. Maybe her database was flawed.

It was the same when it came to Romi's beekeeper guy. Even though he'd approached her with what seemed like harmless interest, there must have been some other signal she'd missed if he hadn't contacted her again. But what could that signal have been? Chakyung's curiosity was piqued. Here was a riddle even she couldn't solve—why someone would muster up the courage to approach a stranger and just stop there.

Hadam and Romi were already on Jeju by now. Had they started scoping the place out? If they'd already somehow managed to find the beekeeper guy, this mystery would have been as good as solved. But no. Chakyung didn't think they'd be able to track him down that easily. *Wait for me, ladies,* she thought.

Several thoughts rolled around her mind like a ball of string that had unraveled, its threads tangled in places. A dream formed from the hazy fog of her feelings. She thought she could hear the sound of so many bees' wings beating in her ears.

YOU COULD LOSE
YOUR WAY

The man couldn't believe his eyes at first. In a neighborhood so many people passed through, including tourists from all over the world, this one person's resemblance to the woman on his mind was so uncanny, he had to rub his eyes and do a double take. But once he did, he was certain it was Do Romi. She had dyed her hair blond, so he hadn't recognized her right away. His heart was racing. In a daze, as if he'd been struck in the head, he almost went up and spoke to her before he stopped himself.

Romi was dressed comfortably in a long, flowing skirt and T-shirt, like someone who had stepped out for a walk. Was it really her? It couldn't be. He hadn't looked too deeply into her social media in a while, but there was no way she'd moved to Jeju—right? Romi wandered among people walking down the street, stopping to peer inside the storefront window at a new bakery. It didn't look like she had any particular destination in mind.

The man switched directions, keeping a good thirty feet between himself and Romi as he trailed her. She walked in a zigzag pattern, stopping here and there at different storefronts before moving on, like a bee alighting on flowers. He didn't need to worry about getting caught. There were tourists everywhere in that neighborhood, and if she had the same habit he remembered from so long ago, she would walk on without once looking back.

After she'd been walking for a while, she ended up at a quick-meal spot. It was famous on the internet for its fish cake soup made from Jeju seafood, and the man himself had even heard other people talking it up before. He'd never been there, though.

He waited patiently until Romi came out and started walking again. He was nervous, but not overly so. He'd waited for her before—in the rain, on cold and windy days, while she was meeting up with another man. Now, he followed her back to her hotel. So she was traveling.

When he got home, the man sat down in his swivel chair and stared for a while at the photos of Romi on his wall. Even he didn't know why he hadn't torn them down when he'd come back. He was certain he had predicted this sort of encounter. So this was how they'd been destined to meet again. He opened up Romi's Instagram page for the first time in a while. Her handle hadn't changed. None of her photos featured any recognizably "Jeju" things. The only trace of Jeju he could see was a single photo of the tteokbokki and fried snacks she'd just eaten, and there was no mention of Jeju itself anywhere, only comments saying, "Looks delicious!"

Early the next morning, the man went to the Rent-a-Car center and took out a long-term rental. He didn't know how long he would need it. He parked near the entrance to the hotel parking lot and went in. His guess was that she would be coming out soon. He opened up a newspaper and sat on a sofa in the lobby, watching the front desk.

Determined to wait all day if he had to, he was surprised when Romi appeared in the lobby shortly after. She was with someone else. It might have just been due to shock, but he almost bolted up from the couch before he managed to calm himself down—he couldn't get caught. The two women checked out of the hotel and left. He carefully observed them as they got farther and farther away. He didn't get up; instead, he just sat there thinking for a while. He had confirmed everything he needed to confirm for that day, so there was no need to follow after her right away.

He couldn't have predicted any of this in advance. Running into Romi here after three years had passed, following after her again the same way he had before. Even he couldn't have known it would come to this. Without noticing, he'd been rubbing traces of the past onto his left hand with his right. He couldn't sort out his feelings at all. Things were riskier, since Romi wasn't alone this time. But that could also be more advantageous. Now, he had a string he could grab ahold of that could help him find her wherever she went. He finally had the upper hand. Rather than pursuing her as if this were a hunt, he could lie in wait like someone casting a net. He could follow her without losing his way.

This would be his reward for what happened three years ago, the man thought. A chance to make things right again. The winds of fate were carrying him to Romi.

The man stood up from the sofa and left the lobby. The sunlight on Jeju that morning was strong and bright as was his mood. The sun felt inescapable, even, as it relentlessly bore down on him.

The most important thing—Romi still didn't know of his existence. For now, this was good. It couldn't be helped. But soon she would become aware of him. And once she did, she would never forget.

◆　◆　◆

Project: *Searching for Honeyman*

Day Two, Jeju

The man must have been in his midfifties. His suntanned skin was a sign that he spent a lot of time working outdoors, but he had an intellectual air about him too. From his gentle eyes and the way he carried himself with such an upright posture, Hadam guessed that he'd been quite the charmer in his prime.

"Nice to meet you." The man politely handed Hadam his business card. She accepted it and politely looked it over.

"The Jeju Beekeeping Research Association. You must be the vice president, Kim Manseop. It's nice to meet you too."

Hadam and Romi stood in front of the car they had parked in the middle of the road, bowing deeply. All around them was wilderness, no houses in sight.

"I would give you my business card as well, but my job title changed recently, so . . ."

Still in the habit of exchanging business cards, Hadam was clearly flustered, but the man replied graciously, "I heard a lot about you from Jaewoong, of course. He said you're a film director."

"Yes, that's right." Hadam seemed relieved not to have to explain in further detail. "And this is Romi. She's an artist."

"Hello. I'm Romi, an illustrator."

"Now, what brings two artists all the way out here? What led to such a deep interest in beekeeping?"

Hadam and Romi exchanged a look. Jaewoong had put them in touch with this man, Kim Manseop, who was going to give them an overview of beekeeping on Jeju Island, starting by taking them to the first bee farm on the list. He hadn't given them the full rundown on the bee farm but had mentioned it was hard to get to. It was in the heart of the mountains and had a name different from what was listed on the sign, so it was difficult to find using GPS.

"We're interested in the regional agriculture. We've heard beekeeping draws lots of folks back here to rural Jeju from the big cities, so we thought we'd research some of them."

"That's true. There are quite a few returnees from the city."

The conversation picked up after that. Could Kim Manseop possibly know Honeyman? There was a good chance.

"The bee farm we're going to see today is run by a returnee, actually."

Before Hadam and Romi could ask any other questions, the vice president got back inside his own car, which looked like a white box. "Follow me. Let's head there first, then talk. It's best to go early, since it's in the mountains."

Before they could even ask where they were headed, he was in the car with the doors shut. Hadam reached for the door on the driver's side of their car too. "Let's go. We'll find out where we're headed if we follow him."

But Romi came over to the driver's side and said, "I'll drive. You were at the wheel all day yesterday too. And you'll need to film what's happening."

"But it's not easy to follow someone in a car—"

"Let's see how it goes, and if need be, you can take over. Now hurry. He's already pulling off."

Indeed, the vice president was just about to start up his car and leave. It would have been nice if he'd at least given them the address in advance. Hadam was a bit nervous not knowing their destination, but there was no time to waver now. Kim Manseop was probably not one for talking at length. Romi hadn't had her license for very long, but she approached the driver's seat confidently like someone who got behind the wheel on a regular basis. Hadam got into the passenger's seat, and Romi hurried to start the car.

The morning sky on Jeju was as blue as a picture in a travel guide. Hadam took out her camera and aimed at the sky, wanting to capture its color for the film. They drove for a while along the mountain road nearly empty of other people. As the end of summer drew near, sunlight shone on the mountain and illuminated all the lush greenery at the peak of its bloom. In a little while, all the colors would completely change. Hadam loved to capture the many signs of the shifting seasons on camera.

The car slowly turned onto an isolated road.

"The view is gorgeous," Romi said. "I've been to Jeju so many times, but I had no idea there were views this stunning."

Hadam agreed. "Seriously. When people think of an island, they might picture only the ocean, but the mountains here are so beautiful."

They drove underneath a sign that announced they were entering Seogwipo. *So the bee farm we're going to see is in Seogwipo,* Hadam thought. *I could have sworn he said it was in Jeju City proper.* Doubt wormed its way into her mind, but maybe they were taking a shortcut. Or else he might have been referring to the whole of Jeju earlier. As she filmed, Hadam committed the direction they were traveling—east to west—to memory, for when she needed to do reshoots later.

They had been driving for a while when Romi asked, not taking her eyes off the car ahead of them, "How did your meeting go yesterday?"

Figuring she was asking about Jaewoong, Hadam was careful as she answered. "Oh. I just got the information from him and . . . we had dinner. Our old sunbae lives in the area, so the three of us had planned to grab a bite together, but something came up last minute, and our sunbae couldn't make it."

"Hmm, so it was just the two of you." Romi hummed meaningfully on that "hmm," but Hadam pretended not to hear.

The evening before, after Romi had turned down her dinner invitation, Hadam messaged Pilhyun, hoping to avoid being alone with Jaewoong. Pilhyun said he would come but canceled when something suddenly came up on his end. Hadam and Jaewoong ended up alone at a nearby restaurant that served local Jeju fare, and they'd ordered abalone and rice in hot stone pots. The lingering awkwardness between them slowly melted down like yellow margarine sitting atop warm rice.

Things had been quite natural until that moment—when Jaewoong reached over to brush away a grain of rice stuck at the corner of Hadam's mouth. He'd gestured that something was there, but Hadam kept missing it when she tried to remove it herself, and before he knew it, like a habit, he reached out and brushed it away. Hadam realized what had happened and quickly dabbed at the corners of her mouth with a tissue. When he reached for her cheek, Hadam had seen the faint burn scar that remained on his finger. She thought again about the night the fire had broken out. At the time, she hadn't realized he'd gotten burned. Even though he'd just come out of the fire, she remembered, his hands had felt so cold.

As the events of that evening nine years ago and those of the night before ran together in her head now, Hadam shuddered, trying to shake off the memories that clung to her. Romi studied her out of the corner of her eye as she drove.

"Are you cold? Should I turn off the AC?"

The late-summer sun was glaring down on the two of them through the window. "No, thanks," Hadam answered quickly. "I'm fine." She wanted to change the subject, but Romi didn't give up.

"So, what did you and your friend talk about yesterday? You couldn't have only been chatting about beekeeping the whole time."

Hadam didn't want to replay the entirety of the evening, so she shifted to a different topic, one that had to do with Romi.

"You know—this and that, stuff about the past. By the way, he said he knows you."

Romi's eyes went round. "Me?"

"Yeah. He asked me who I came to Jeju with, and when I mentioned your name and told him you were an illustrator, he said he's a big fan of yours from your blogging days. He even left you some comments."

"Oh, really? I wonder what his username was. Did he say when he did?"

"About four or five, or maybe three or four years ago? He said you probably wouldn't remember."

"Yeah. About four years ago, huh? A ton of people were reading my blog around then."

Romi suddenly went quiet, and Hadam realized this might not have been a safe topic after all. Romi had been quite active on social media, but Hadam knew it had caused her plenty of headaches as well. A few years back, she'd even been harassed by people nearly stalking her. A few days earlier, too, she'd mentioned feeling uneasy when a stranger on Instagram had recognized her but wouldn't reveal their identity. She was fascinated by strangers and wanted them to find her, but at the same time, they had her living in a state of constant fear. To make acquaintances, she had to overcome that hurdle. And not everyone was worth leaping eagerly over that hurdle to meet. Wondering why she'd even brought up the topic, Romi calmly turned the steering wheel to follow the car ahead of them.

"Let me know his username later, so I can figure out who he was."

Before Hadam could reply, Romi changed the subject.

"Oh, could you hand me the sunglasses in my bag?"

Now, as the morning passed and midday drew near, the sun was beating down with even more intensity. Hadam reached behind her for Romi's canvas bag on the back seat, but because of her seat belt, she couldn't grasp it easily. She held out her hand as far as she could, unfastening her seat belt when she realized she wouldn't be able to get it that way. The no-seat-belt signal went off.

Studying the dashboard, Romi noted, "So this is one of those cars with a no-seat-belt signal for the passenger seat." The warning sound continued to ring throughout the car.

"Where in your bag—"

"Oh, there's a pouch inside that inner pocket."

"Aha, here it is. One sec—"

Romi glanced back briefly. Just then at the intersection, a huge truck appeared on their left, coming toward them at full speed. Hadam screamed.

"Romi, watch out."

Romi slammed on the brakes. The rental car came to a precarious stop, the truck recklessly screeching past them and spewing black smoke.

Hadam let out a deep breath, clutching Romi's sunglasses in her hand. "Whew, that was almost a disaster."

Surprisingly unfazed, Romi replied, "There was still a little space between us there."

She started driving again, taking the sunglasses Hadam handed to her. As she put them on, she asked, "Where did his car go?"

"He must be waiting for us somewhere. Should I try calling him?"

Just as Hadam took out her phone, Romi pointed at the car up ahead. "There he is."

Sure enough, on that nearly empty road, there was a white box car speeding in front of them. Romi tried to get behind it. But she couldn't close the distance by much. The car was headed down a road that wasn't showing up on the GPS system. Then it made a sudden turn up a mountain trail where the road itself was hard to see.

"Are we really supposed to go up this road? It feels like we're getting farther and farther out." Hadam sounded somewhat nervous.

"Well, he did say the bee farm was in the mountains. This seems right."

He had said that, hadn't he? Hadam blamed her own anxiousness for how quick she was to jump to conclusions. She was the type who got flustered when something happened that threw off her plans and who was nervous facing a road she hadn't traveled before. Looking over at Romi, she felt like she could count on her friend's calm. Even though it was her first time there, Romi didn't hesitate to follow the other car up the mountain road. It made sense—when you put your trust in other people, you could move forward. With Romi at her side, Hadam felt like she could breathe a little easier.

But the car in front of them didn't seem like it was planning to come to a stop any time soon. Did it really take this long to get there? A quick look at the clock showed they had already been driving for almost fifty minutes. Was Jeju really so huge? As they went up the mountain, Hadam thought they were headed toward the bee farm, but then the car in front of them went downhill again and came back to the main road. Now they found themselves headed down a narrow road with stone walls and fields on either side.

Hadam's anxiety once again reared its head. "Why does it feel like we're going in circles?" she asked.

"I'm not sure. Maybe he's giving us a sightseeing tour of Jeju?"

But the vice president didn't seem so easygoing. Either way, Hadam figured it was time to give him a call. She found the number she had called to reach him earlier and dialed it again. But there must not have been any cell service in the area, or else something was wrong with Hadam's phone, because it rang several times before automatically cutting off.

"What's going on?" she wondered aloud.

"It's all right. I'm following right behind him. If you're really worried, do you want me to try going ahead of him?"

Before Hadam could stop her, Romi began speeding up. But the car ahead of them wasn't easy to catch up to. It sped up the mountain road that cut through the middle of the island. Romi floored it and tried to keep up. Once she had started to close the distance, she eased back, then rinsed and repeated. At first, it was like they were being lured along, but now it looked more like an unwanted chase. Just then, the car came to a road densely lined with trees. The shadows they cast were even darker now. The road was unpaved too. Hadam wondered why she hadn't stopped Romi from coming this way. She thought of those Stephen King novels, the terrible things that happened to people in them when they went following after strangers. If she and Romi turned back now, they could still save themselves—but Romi kept driving, without an ounce of hesitation.

Once she had plowed through the trees, an enormous house came into view on the other side. It was a grand modern home built from concrete that seemed out of place in its surroundings. Each floor was divided into several sections. Hadam was baffled. *What's this? Some kind of hospital?* An elegant gray sign with English and Korean words stood in front of the building. The car had stopped in front of it.

"Is this really a bee farm?" she asked.

Hadam looked around. "I'm not sure," she said. "I don't see any hives."

The moment they slowed down, the driver's-side door on the car in front of them flew open, and someone jumped out. Dumbfounded, Romi and Hadam rolled down the windows.

The other person ran toward their car, screaming, "Who the hell are you two? And why are you tailing me?"

Like one of those old American comedy show duos, Romi's and Hadam's mouths dropped open in unison, the two women speechless. Just then, Hadam's phone pinged with a message.

Where are you?

—Jeju Beekeeping Research Association VP Kim Manseop

Hadam got out, came around the front of the car, and took a good look at the other person. She was a young, petite woman in a gray linen shirt, her short hair tied up and held back with a headband.

"What are you doing following someone?"

"We weren't—"

The woman sank to the ground in front of their car and burst into tears. Hadam looked to Romi, at a total loss for what to do. Romi looked panicked for the first time that day. Right then, Hadam's eyes went to the sign out front.

HONEYCOMB GUESTHOUSE

"How odd. I know they say it doesn't matter how you go as long as you get there, but . . . ," Kim Manseop tutted as he came into the living room, where Romi and Hadam sat cooling off and casually sipping mandarin juice. They stood up as he entered.

"We got your car mixed up with someone else's," Hadam said. "We're so sorry."

The vice president waved his hands. "No, no. It was my fault for not checking on you more carefully. I took the scenic route on purpose to give you two a glimpse of the views around here."

"Oh, so that's why it took a while. It *was* very beautiful, though." Hadam suddenly remembered what Romi had said in the car, about how the VP was probably going out of his way to show them the scenery. So he really was the warm, considerate type. Not considerate enough to have told them that ahead of time, but still. Maybe that was the Jeju way to show friendliness.

"Halfway here, I realized you weren't behind me anymore. I tried to call, but I couldn't reach you," the vice president explained awkwardly.

"I see. So you were calling us. That must have been why our calls didn't go through." Hadam felt like she should apologize, the connection issue being at least partly her fault.

"It couldn't be helped," said the VP graciously. "It all worked out, since you ended up following someone who was headed here anyway."

"We were also shocked by how that turned out," Romi said. But for someone who was supposedly in shock, she looked incredibly calm. She had soothed the crying woman and cleared up the misunderstanding that they'd been trailing her on purpose. Hadam felt deeply sorry and could understand the woman's fear, seeing as she herself had been so anxious about simply following behind a stranger. But the woman said she'd been at least slightly relieved when she saw it was two women pursuing her. As they chatted, they learned that the woman was the owner of the Honeycomb Guesthouse, which she ran with her husband. Once they were inside, Romi and Hadam called the VP and were surprised to find out they had unknowingly ended up at the guesthouse attached to the first bee farm they were set to visit.

The woman, who was around Romi and Hadam's age, introduced herself as Kim Sumi. She brought out new drinks and honey toast for them on a tray. With the horror brought about by the earlier mix-up now behind them, she seemed much more at ease. Sumi set down the refreshments on the table, then crossed the living room to carefully brush the dust off the back of a yellow sheet of paper hanging in the corner. It looked very old and worn, and she handled it with tremendous care.

After dusting it off, Sumi turned to them and said quietly, "I was really shocked myself. I thought I was being followed. I couldn't shake you off on the road either. Even when I changed directions, when I went up that mountain pass and came down again, you were still there. Following me."

"We thought the car in front of us was just going to the bee farm. We're really sorry," Hadam apologized again. Romi smiled in awkward agreement.

Sumi shook her head. "No, *I'm* sorry for startling you. Something similar happened to me in the past. I overreacted."

The VP seemed uninterested in all the chatter about the car chase. Taking a sip of juice, he asked, "Have you had a look around the bee farm?"

"Yes, the owner gave me a tour. I was really grateful," Hadam added, watching the man enter the room now after his wife. He was slim, in his early forties. His name was Seo Jungmoon, a former construction company worker who had moved to Jeju four years ago to set up a guesthouse and start a bee farm there. When she first saw him, Hadam looked over at Romi, who shook her head. It was a relief on all fronts that he was not the man she was looking for.

It was September, and the bee farms on Jeju were preparing for winter. The season of scorching summer heat on the island had already passed, and honey-gathering season was coming to an end. All the hives had been moved to Seogwipo, where the weather was slightly warmer. They had to prepare and store food for the winter. There was a lot to do and then some. *Do you know how taxing it is?* the owner had asked. But the work seemed to be equally as rewarding. Watching the bees, one could learn so much about the fundamentals of society and the profound laws of nature. The owner described all this as he opened the hives and lifted out slivers of honeycomb. Still, he didn't fail to mention how much profit he brought in from harvesting and commercializing Jeju pollen in the summers. He beat a flyswatter at the wasps racing toward the hives, which gave his story an added sense of triumph. The bee farm certainly seemed huge and well run. It must have been a ton of work to operate such a big farm and the guesthouse at the same time, Hadam thought.

"Come on. Quit laughing."

"I'm sorry, but seriously, what kind of Robert Altman comedy were you starring in? I can see if the driver got mixed up while she was focused on the road, but how could *you* not even realize what had happened?"

Jaewoong couldn't stop laughing, even wiping tears from his eyes.

"Romi's always been the type who can't tell similar things apart, but as the person in the passenger seat, I definitely should have been able to see that. I'm such an idiot." Now that Jaewoong was laughing about what had happened, Hadam felt like she could too. The night breeze gently intermingled with the sounds of their laughter.

I have some info to give you, Jaewoong had said when he called her earlier in the day, and he asked if it would be all right to come by that night. *We're a bit far out from you,* Hadam told him. At the recommendation of the owner, Hadam and Romi had decided to stay the night at the guesthouse, far from the city center. The owner seemed exceptionally pleased to have Hadam as an eager audience for everything he had to say. Sumi added that it seemed fated now for them to stay the night. And not just for the sake of business.

Hadam told Jaewoong all this, worried it would be too far for him to drive, but he said it didn't matter. It was deep into the night when he got there. There weren't many places nearby for them to go, so Hadam brewed some coffee herself and brought it out for them to have in the yard. They sat on a bench shaped like a beehive—a cluster of little hexagons.

"And look at this building here. The owner really loves bees, so he had the guesthouse built to look like a hive. You can't even imagine how much he loves them, seriously. His wife said he basically sees the bees as his own children."

"Is that so? I didn't even know a place like this existed."

The two of them looked up at the building, its hexagonal windows glowing in the night. Even though peak season was over, there were a few windows lit up. It was like a beehive full of empty cells that only a handful of bees remained to guard. Quiet bossa nova music flowed from the speakers in the yard. This time, the vocal version of "The Girl from Ipanema" was playing.

"It's huge and gorgeous—it must be really hard to manage."

"Yeah. The husband handles most of the business for the farm, while his wife, Sumi, mostly manages the guesthouse. I think she worked at a bank when they lived in Seoul. Must be why she comes across as so calm and collected. And she seems to run this place well too."

"Someone that calm who's used to a peaceful environment must have been really shocked, then, with a strange car following her and all."

"I felt so bad. I almost got on my knees and begged for forgiveness."

Jaewoong threw his head back again and laughed at the sight of Hadam clasping her hands together, pleading.

"You used to be really good at that. Quicker to apologize than anyone."

"Of course. I'm still that way."

Their laughter drifted up to the sky like musical notes hung from the stars. After the echoes of that sound faded away, as if suddenly remembering that there was business to attend to, Jaewoong handed the file folder he was holding to Hadam.

"These are the monthly schedules for Jeju's bee farms, plus the stats on all the returnees who have set up bee farms on the island. You probably won't need to include all this technical stuff in your film, but it could be good to know. I'm sure your documentary wouldn't just cover beekeeping in general. You'd want to include information on this trend of Jeju natives returning to their hometowns to settle down. Plus the impact of that trend on the housing and environmental conditions on the island."

Hadam was quietly surprised to hear him lay out everything she had been planning. "How did you know all that?"

"That's how I would film it. Plus," Jaewoong said, turning to her, "I know that's what Director Park Hadam would do too."

Hadam felt something like a lump rising in her throat and turned to look up at the sky. For so long, she had worked on films that weren't her own—to hear these words from him was so warmly encouraging. She counted the several stars she saw above her, as if trying to drown out this weird feeling.

Hadam looked down again just as Jaewoong slapped his own arm.

"Damn it, so many mosquitoes." Already, a spot on his elbow was swollen and red.

Hadam touched his arm and studied the bites on his skin. "Oh no. It's not just one or two of them either. Why didn't you say anything? I didn't get bitten at all—I had no idea there were mosquitoes out."

"Really? I guess the swarm decided to focus its attack on me."

"It's always been that way. When we were together, you were the only one who ever got bitten in the summer."

As they recalled those summers, they both smiled. Hadam liked going for evening walks in the summertime. After dinner, the two of them would walk along the river or in the parks. Even in the sweltering heat on tropical nights, they walked together, arm in arm.

"Yeah. You used to say mosquitoes only liked me, to the point where you never needed anything else to keep them away from you."

"Exactly. You were my human mosquito repellent."

They realized they had said too much, touched on too meaningful a memory. Hadam's hand was still on Jaewoong's arm. When she pulled it away, their eyes met. She couldn't remember having looked someone else in the eyes in so long. But she felt like she had spent too much time doing it in the last two days. She had forgotten what it was like to have been so used to it at one point, only for it to feel so strange to her now. Jaewoong looked around suddenly, as though searching for mosquitoes that weren't there. To the open air, he said, "Jeju's mosquitoes are seriously something else."

They fell silent. Hadam thought of something she had learned in school. She had heard it from her instructor in a filmmaking course. In French, there was a well-known saying, *un ange passe*. "An angel is passing." But in English, instead of an angel, you might say a tumbleweed was going by. That was because in old Westerns, whenever silence fell, there went a tumbleweed rolling across the screen. Right now, in this moment, Hadam felt as if all the grass on Jeju would roll itself into a ball and go tumbling past. The premonition of trouble that had loomed in her mind the day before rose up again.

"I should go."

The bench was clean, but Jaewoong brushed his pants off as he stood.

"Oh, okay." Hadam stood up in a hurry. The guesthouse café was closed, and there was nowhere else to go around here, no roads bright enough for a walk. Besides, for some people, the two of them hanging out at this hour of the night would have other implications. Implications were like honeybees. They could be sweet, but they could also be dangerous.

"Probably a busy day tomorrow too," Jaewoong murmured to himself.

For her or for him? "Yeah," Hadam said.

"I didn't get to meet Romi today either."

Hadam looked up at the guesthouse windows. The second-floor lights were still on.

"That's true. Come by a little earlier next time."

Would there be a next time? Hadam wondered vaguely. "Next time" wasn't just some moment that came after the present one. It was a situation you had to intentionally create. It was something that came only to those who took the first step and didn't stop until they reached whomever they were headed toward. In the past, when they were dating, "next time" had always been a given. But it dawned on Hadam now that at some point, "next time" had stopped coming for them.

Before Jaewoong got into his car, he said, "I'll call you." He didn't say when.

Hadam just nodded and waved.

As soon as Hadam returned to the room, Romi looked up from where she lay on her stomach in bed, tapping away at her laptop. "Did Jaewoong leave?"

"He did. He wanted to say hi to you, but it was already so late."

"I wouldn't want to say hi to him like this after I've already washed up for the night anyway." Romi sat up. "Why'd he come by?"

Hadam tossed the file folder onto the table. "To give me this."

"He could've sent that in an email."

Hadam could hear the underlying implications in that comment. "Maybe," she said. "I guess he didn't have electronic copies of the files?"

"Did he say he was coming by again tomorrow?"

"No, he didn't. He has no other business out here anyway."

"Hmm." Romi shut her laptop and slid it into its pouch. Hadam found her toiletries in her bag and headed for the bathroom.

Romi tossed another comment over her shoulder like a dart. "You don't have to worry about our evening plans tomorrow, Hadam," she said. "I'll be perfectly fine on my own."

"Romi, I told you. It isn't like that."

Romi wasn't someone who made an especially strong impression right off the bat. But the more time you spent studying her, the easier it was to see what made her stand out. Something about her made people who met her once keep thinking about her after they went their separate ways, if only for that night. It was probably her smile, which Chakyung had described at some point as a Cheshire cat grin. People had trouble remembering her face without it, but they always remembered that smile. It tended to linger on her lips for a long time because no one could ever find the words to say in response to it. Just like now.

"Right, I believe you," Romi said. "One hundred percent. I mean it."

◆ ◆ ◆

Chakyung mostly trusted her own judgment. She used the word "mostly," humble but nondescript, as a way to entertain the possibility of exceptions without actually accounting for them. But as the situation at hand clearly showed, exceptions happened. Chakyung had made the wrong judgment call in flying straight to Jeju.

She was completely exhausted by the time she arrived at Incheon Airport. The landing had also been rougher than usual. When she remembered that she had to find the golf bag now, she heaved a deep sigh. After that, she had to get to Gimpo and catch her transfer flight to Jeju. She wanted to just listen to her heart and go straight to her home in Seoul, but she couldn't bring herself to change her flight plans now.

Once the plane had come to a complete stop and the seat belt sign went off, she turned on her phone, and a number of notifications began to appear one after the other at the top of the screen. The notification bell kept sounding like a warning signal: *Caution. Caution. You are now entering South Korea.* Chakyung tapped all the messages to mark them as read. When people began to disembark, Chakyung stood up too. She took down her suitcase from the overhead compartment. As she did, a bag fell and struck her on the hand.

"Ow!"

The man who'd sat across from her now stood in the aisle, pulling down his wife's bag from the bins. He turned to her. "Are you all right?"

"Just fine." Chakyung realized her answer was more blunt than usual, but it was hard for her to feign friendliness at the moment. The pain in her hand combined with her headache was making her feel nearly disoriented. Right now, she just wanted to get off the plane—fast.

She started pushing her suitcase forward. The man's wife was coming out into the aisle just then, and Chakyung's suitcase rammed her foot. The woman shouted something in Chinese.

"Oh my goodness, I'm so—"

Chakyung tried to apologize, but someone behind her pushed her forward again. In a panic, Chakyung grabbed on to the woman's husband to stop her fall. Now, she was close enough to see the wrinkles in his T-shirt that stretched over his muscles. She became exceedingly aware of him in that moment.

"Jeez."

Chakyung pressed her palm against him to open up some space. But what she ended up doing was more akin to shoving him. The man looked down at her, flustered. "Sorry," he said.

Chakyung knew it hadn't been his fault, but she didn't have the time to apologize. As the people ahead of them filed out, the man and his wife continued down the aisle too. Chakyung sighed, firmly grabbed ahold of her suitcase again, and got off.

Even though there was an airport line on the subway, the airport bus to Gimpo was crowded today. Chakyung's luggage had been late coming out (that damned golf bag!), so she had already missed the train. As she boarded the bus, a steady stream of other people headed to catch their flights got on after her. She had a long layover until her next flight, but she figured it was better to get to Gimpo early and wait at the airport. She took a seat by the window and looked outside.

It was a rainy evening in Seoul. The rain drew dotted lines on the glass. It took so long to catch a plane. You had to traverse not only distance but time. The rain seemed to be making incision lines through time. Now, a new hour had begun.

The last person to board the bus looked around for an empty seat. Seeing no others, he plopped down in the seat beside Chakyung. She scooted a bit closer to the window to make room for him and caught a glimpse of her new seatmate. A one-time coincidence was a matter of chance, like a stone falling into a pond. But even a stone that fell in by chance still made ripples on the water's surface.

"Oh, it's you! From earlier!" said the man.

But Chakyung acknowledged him with only a brief glance and turned around again. The meaning of the gesture was clear: *I have no plans to pretend a coincidence is a reason to befriend someone.*

Luckily, her phone rang again at that moment. As she hurried to answer it, she caught the man's eye. He had AirPods in his ears. Warily, Chakyung answered the call.

"Yes, ma'am. No, I arrived in Seoul, but I have to go on another business trip to Jeju. I'm on my way to the airport again. Yes, it's for work. Sorry, ma'am, but I'm on the bus right now—it'll be nighttime when I land, so I'll call you later."

It seemed like Chakyung could only ever apologize to her. She sighed. Why did they have to buy the furniture now, anyway? Why couldn't she wait just a little while?

After she ended the call and sent a few hastily typed messages in reply, she put her phone away. The man next to her didn't seem to have been eavesdropping or to really care at all what was happening with her. Chakyung felt even more uncomfortable now, being the one of them who was so overly aware of the other's presence. She closed her eyes. Soon, she was asleep.

When she woke up, her head felt warm. *Do I have a fever?* Her skin stung as if she'd been passed out with her face in the sand, the inside of her mouth rough and dry. She didn't know what had happened. She thought she had felt somebody gently shaking her, but the seat beside her was already empty.

She got out to look for her luggage, picked up the golf bag, and swayed a bit. Once again, she silently cursed Director Kim—no, she couldn't even bring herself to address him by his title in her mind. Just then, the bag was hoisted from her. She felt a sense of déjà vu. Just like he had on the plane, the man picked up the golf bag and loaded it onto his own cart, on top of an enormous bag.

"Hey!" Chakyung shouted, surprising herself.

The man didn't seem startled in the least. "Let me carry it to the airport counter for you," he said, loading her suitcase onto his cart as well. The cart was overloaded with her stuff and his huge bags.

"Do you even know where I'm going? And who are you to do this for me, anyway?"

"Even without knowing where you're headed, I can tell the check-in counter will be the same. We flew in on the same airline. Let me at least help you carry this stuff up to that point. It's not even that far." He pushed the cart forward, his expression never changing. "Besides, I know you're going to Jeju. On the same flight as me. Just think of us as flight buddies."

Chakyung was briefly suspicious, wondering how he'd found that out, but then she remembered her phone call earlier.

"Why were you listening in on someone else's conversation?" she asked. "Isn't that rude?"

The man breezily continued to push the cart along. Chakyung followed hurriedly behind him.

"I wasn't listening in. I just happened to hear you. Anyway, all this is clearly hard on you. You've already passed out three times that I've witnessed today alone. You were even groaning in pain. I thought you were going to slip into a coma, and I almost flagged down the flight attendant to tell her. And just now, you almost didn't make it off the bus."

So he was the one who had woken her up. It was always jarring to hear about your own condition from someone else. And there were people you would be especially mortified to hear this sort of thing from. Chakyung now considered this guy one such person.

Before long, they reached the check-in counter. He gestured for her to cut in front of him. "You go first."

It seemed he was doing her a kindness, since they might be seen as a couple otherwise. Chakyung didn't say so much as a thank-you as she stepped forward. She was worried he might be patronizing her, but that didn't seem to be the case. When her turn came, Chakyung went ahead. She meant to say something to him once she had checked her bag, but when she turned back, he was in the middle of checking in himself and didn't look her way. The back of his head, his close-cropped hair, and long, wide neck were all she could see.

She didn't see him again—not at the boarding gate, not even on the plane to Jeju. Soon enough, the sky outside the tiny plane window had gone dark. As she took her seat, she thought she should at least text Chanmin. But when she pulled out her phone, she saw that her battery was dead. She'd forgotten to charge it at the airport earlier. She wouldn't be able to do it now before the plane took off, so she put it away.

Of course, it wouldn't be easy to bring a trip that had gotten off to such a rough start to a smooth end. Bad luck was exactly that—bad luck. When she arrived at Jeju Airport, Chakyung stood in front of the carousel waiting for her luggage to come around. But while all the other bags came out, she saw no sign of the golf bag. She waited patiently for a half hour, then flagged down an employee who was coming toward the carousel.

"Excuse me. Is that all the luggage for flight 1265?"

The employee wore a grim expression, as though already bracing himself for her complaints. "I'm sorry. But some of the luggage has been delayed. The announcement about it just came on. With different international connecting flights, we get an overload of checked bags. I'm deeply sorry."

It was like a heavy gong had been struck inside Chakyung's head.

"Then when will the luggage arrive?"

"In an hour or two? I'm not really sure. I'll find out for you."

Could something like this really happen on a Korean airline in this day and age? Chakyung honestly wanted to cry. She wavered, trying to decide whether she should leave the airport and come back, but if the bag got lost, she would no doubt get an earful from Director Kim. She couldn't imagine what would happen if he showed up at the airport. She had to charge her phone, and her whole body was weak with exhaustion—she didn't want to take another step. Chakyung sat down on the airport's hard plastic seat and rested her head against a column. If she stayed here any longer, she would fall asleep on the spot. Just then, something soft covered her body. Something that smelled like sunlight. Running her hands over it, she imagined it was a huge towel, a beach towel, maybe.

"Use this. I washed it, so it's clean."

She heard an unnecessarily gentle, low voice. Chakyung squinted her eyes open.

"My luggage isn't here yet either. We may have to wait it out together. You look really pale. You're sweating and shaking too."

Chakyung strained to speak, her voice dry. "I don't need help from a stranger I didn't ask."

"You're right; you didn't ask—and it's rude to approach you like this, I know. I'm being very rude." His voice was surprisingly deep and full, contrary to the playfulness of his words. He sounded like a boy past puberty. There was something familiar about his voice, something she felt she could put a face on. "But still," he said, "I'm only rude to strangers who need help."

Chakyung looked at him. It was that weird guy she had met while traveling. Now her guard was definitely up. Maybe he really was this friendly. But when aimed at a woman, unwanted or unexpected friendliness from a stranger could be a trap. It was sad but true. Just then, Chakyung remembered the man passing that note to the flight attendant. At least it didn't seem like he had that sort of interest in Chakyung. Not when she looked so rough from the exhaustion of traveling and working.

At some point, Chakyung must have fallen asleep again. How long had she been out? Someone was calling her name.

"Yoon Chakyung?"

She woke up, startled. The beach towel slipped to the ground. Eyes open, she could see the owner of that voice kneeling before her. He was looking up at her with concern.

"Your luggage came out. I was rude again and got it for you." He stood and pointed to the bags on his cart. "I had to check your name to make sure it was yours, but I didn't look at anything aside from that. Don't worry. That's the end of my rudeness for today."

With that, he loaded the suitcase next to her onto the cart too. Chakyung pressed a hand against a column as she stood on shaky legs.

"But then I may as well extend the favor out to your car."

It was already after midnight. As they left the airport, the island air cloaked Chakyung like a blanket that wasn't completely dry. The guy loaded her bags into the trunk of a cab that sat waiting outside and opened the back door for her.

Only then did she muster up the words to address him. "Thank you for everything today. Even though I was kind of rude. Ever since we were on the plane—"

"You were rude, yes." The smile never once left his face. Chakyung felt like she alone had suffered the long flight. This guy was like that beach towel that still held the warmth of the Honolulu sun. "But there are times I can empathize with a person, however rude they may be."

A sense of anticipation seeped into the space between each word. Chakyung could feel it coursing through her as he chose what he was going to say next. But when he spoke again, his comment was so simple, even friendly.

"As long as it's someone who can smile brighter than anything when she's not exhausted."

He bowed his head, still smiling. She bowed hers, too, not really understanding.

When the cab pulled off, she looked back one more time. He was still standing there in the taxi pickup spot with his huge bag and the luggage tag that had been attached to it. *Han Sooeon.* She wasn't exactly sure how to read his name—it had so many vowels. Vowels were soft, but they glided by on the sound of the wind, never landing anywhere. His name was like that. She knew it now, but it would soon glide away. It wouldn't stick or last.

Chakyung modified her earlier thought. The odds of a trip that had gotten off to such a rough start ending well were slim, but there were times when such a trip could still be meaningful. This man she'd met in passing had made her trip like a graduation album full of bad pictures. The memory was precious enough not to throw away, but she didn't dare take it out and open it again either.

YOU'LL WANT SOMETHING NEAR AND SWEET

Three Years Earlier

(Phone ringing.)

(Quietly.) Hello?

It's me. Can you talk now?

Yes. No one else is here.

Good. The talks are going well. Looks like the advance will be wired over soon.

(Brief silence.) I see. Things are shaping up, then. In that case—

(At the same time.) So that's why—go ahead.

No, you first.

We have to make a plan on our end. If you lure him out, I'll bring the car around and be on standby.

(Silence.)

What's wrong? Don't think you can do it?

It's just—it's a lot to handle.

Are you starting to panic? It's not too late to back out if you want.

I'm not backing out, but—

But?

I just—I don't know what'd happen if he were to have something so precious taken from him.

Why are you only now telling me this? You think I don't have any emotions? And are you even considering what we've been through? You don't think it'll hurt us if we just keep on the way we've been doing?

I hear you, but this isn't easy, you know? It's—

No, it's not easy. Emotionally or physically. That's why so much money is involved.

(Silence.)

Hello?

I'm listening.

You've got to make up your mind. If you don't, nothing will ever change.

I know.

I'll let you know when everything's all set. Until then, let's be in touch by phone. We shouldn't be too obvious.

Will do. But—

What?

That guy, the one who's paying me. Can we really trust him?

He's putting his own name on the line—do you really think he'd try to con us?

This is a crime we're talking about. If he's willing to do this, what's stopping him from—

Listen to me. If we plan this out in detail, we're not going to get caught. And more importantly, no one will get hurt.

I really hope you're right.

(Emphatic.) Everything will be fine. Are you listening?

I'm listening. I was just thinking it through.

Well, think of everything we're doing as being for us.

(Silence.)

This is all so we can be together.

I know.

Do you?
It's all for us.
Exactly. Which is why we can do whatever we have to do.

◆ ◆ ◆

Project: *Searching for Honeyman*

Day Three, Northeastern Jeju

"Here at Dolmiyong Jeju, we're not only producing the highest-quality honey in the nation—we're currently developing a royal jelly ampoule, honey-infused green juice, and a convenient honey meal replacement powder that contains propolis. We also put out a call for recipes that incorporate honey and are good for skin care, so we have a cookbook in the works as well. Moreover, we're developing more fragrant products made by combining honey with different fruit flavors, such as mandarin honey and grape honey. We have plans to expand into the food industry by 2022 with canned products like honey-pickled fruit, honey snacks, honey vinegar, honey salad dressing, and so on. We're even in the middle of designing a makeup line. This is all what it means to live in the era of the sixth industry."

As the woman—in her fifties at least, as diligent as a worker bee and as brightly dressed as a sunflower—rattled off her spiel as if running lines in a play, they all entered the showroom packed with rows of bottles, large and small.

"Just hearing the description alone, it seems like quite a big project," Hadam noted, her camera bobbing up and down as she nodded along with what the woman was saying. "And you said this is a sixth industry?"

"That's right. We're making our way into every aspect of human life!"

Startled by the woman's sudden, impassioned outburst, Romi nearly dropped the sample of royal jelly ampoule she was holding.

"In making use of the tremendous productivity of the honeybee, we've become a clear front-runner in the sixth-industry sector."

Hadam thought she must have heard that phrase some sixty-six times that day. Just what was a sixth industry? It seemed like just yesterday she'd first heard the term "fourth industrial revolution," so when had people started talking about the sixth wave?

Romi carefully set her ampoule down on the display stand. "In other words, this seems like a honeybee empire."

The woman showing them around was Kang Hyunbok, the director of Dolmiyong Jeju, a bee farm and food company located in northern Jeju. "Dolmiyong" was a word in the Jeju language that meant "sweet." Already, it seemed like she had shown them more than fifty of the company's products. And if they counted all the products the company was in the process of developing, the scale was staggering. Since Vice President Kim Manseop had called ahead and introduced Hadam and Romi as filmmakers, the two of them had a relatively easy time getting to observe the bee farm's many products and production lines. Of course, they also had a chance of finding Honeyman here.

"That's right!" Director Kang seemed to love the expression Romi had used—"a honeybee empire." "Dolmiyong Jeju is a representative company in the sixth-industry sector, which combines the primary-industry element of agricultural products, the secondary industry of manufacturing, and the tertiary industry of tourism. You see, in addition to creating our bee-derived products, we hold workshops where people can experience beekeeping or use beeswax to make candles and soap. On top of that, we offer introductory classes for people who want to run urban bee farms or return to the countryside to become beekeepers."

Finally, the riddle of the sixth industry had been solved: $1 + 2 + 3 = 6$. By adding the primary, secondary, and tertiary industries, you got the sixth industry. Or wait, was it actually multiplication? $1 \times 2 \times 3 = 6$. Whatever the case, the most important thing for Hadam was the latter part of what the director had said. Hadam studied Romi's face. She wore no particular expression. She was still peering closely at the label on a bottle of grape-flavored honey powder. Before Director Kang could launch into another explanation, Hadam quickly cut in with a question.

"So I heard that here at Dolmiyong Jeju, there are a lot of young beekeepers as well. You even have staff overseeing the product planning and marketing. Have you come up with some sort of product mascot?"

The person behind that mascot was one of the candidates Jaewoong had told her about. Hadam thought she should include not only young beekeepers in her search, but also people who did not directly work on the bee farm, like those in product development or those who attended classes. The place that best suited her hunch was the Honeybee School, the workshop and classroom run by Dolmiyong Jeju. Honeyman had told Romi he was developing a character related to beekeeping, so Hadam figured a company like this might be the right place to find it.

"It looks like you already have one," Romi said, pointing to the label on the bottle of grape-flavored honey powder in her hand. "Someone must have illustrated this."

Director Kang squinted at the label.

"Ah, that—Department Head Boo designed it for us. He's quite good with his hands."

"Yes, it's a nice illustration. The image is clear too." Romi set the bottle down and picked up the bottle next to it, a sample of canola honey.

"Actually, Mr. Boo is good at all sorts of things. I think he said he majored in business administration in college. Young guy. He's running one of our beekeeping classes at the Honeybee School too. Oh, careful. The stopper on that one doesn't quite fit, so if you hold it like that, it may spill . . ."

"I see," said Romi, licking at the honey smeared on her left hand. At some point, the front of her black sundress had been stained sticky.

"Oh no, I'm so sorry. I saw it wasn't sealed this morning and meant to switch it out, but things got busy with customers, and it completely slipped my mind. Do you have something you can use to wipe it off?"

Still holding her camera in one hand, Hadam dug out some wet wipes from her bag and handed one to Romi, then used one to wipe the honey off her own hand.

"Would we be able to interview this Mr. Boo today? It would be great to hear about beekeeping on Jeju from a young person's perspective as well. Including the prospects for the future of Jeju beekeeping as, um . . . a sixth industry."

"Oh, that sounds excellent. Let's head to the annex, then. Right now, we have a group visiting from Seoul—they're doing some business related to urban bee farms, so they're probably in the middle of a tour. Wouldn't it be nice to include that too?"

Director Kang led the two of them around to the back of the three-story building next door. Behind the building was a huge vacant lot, where ten beehives were placed close together. The hives were humming with the sound of bees, a kind of background music, and there were ten or so people in protective suits huddled in front of the hives. One man was standing in the middle in a comfortable polo shirt and khakis, no protective gear on except for a beekeeping veil hat. He was a strapping, tall guy, a little on the skinnier side. Was he in his early or midthirties? With the veil covering his face, it was hard to tell.

"Each swarm shares a hive, and there's a chance the swarm will divide into two colonies. Simply put, if they think their home is too crowded, the one group of bees will split into two." The man brought his fists together, then pulled them apart. "One of the new groups will leave the hive and move to another one. New swarms naturally spring up around May or June, but they can emerge at any time, so you have to be careful. If you crowd them too much, you can induce a split, so you should make sure to give each hive its own space. On the other hand, though, the population could decrease around the fall, so in September, you should take a look at each colony, and the bees that don't seem like

66

they'll survive the winter should be consolidated. Meaning you should put them together in the same hive."

The man brought his fists together again. Thinking about how even bees moved out and merged households, and how all animals that had homes were bound to leave them eventually, Hadam suddenly remembered that she didn't have much longer on her lease. She wondered how much the security deposit would increase and whether she would have to move back in with her parents now that she no longer had a job. Hadam hated the mere thought of merging hives—er, households.

The man's voice coming through the veil of his beekeeping hat was calm, a far cry from Hadam's anxious jumble of thoughts. Director Kang pointed him out.

"That man there is Department Head Boo Hwachul. You can watch for now, and after the class is over, you should chat with him."

Hadam gave Romi a look. Romi studied the man closely, but she merely shrugged her shoulders as if to say she wasn't sure. The man had certainly seen the director and the two of them even from this distance, but he didn't react to them in any particular way. Was it just because he was in the middle of teaching?

"We should get a bit closer and take another look," Romi whispered to Hadam. The two of them slowly moved behind the group of students. Mr. Boo carried on with his explanation.

"And then from July to October, wasps will be springing up constantly, with the peak being in September, so you always need to be on the lookout—ah, I see we have some here too. Oh boy."

A pair of wasps circled the man's body and tried to land on his shoulders.

"This is why you should never approach a beehive without wearing your protective gear, everyone. I took mine off earlier when it got caught and torn on one of the hives, but . . ."

The wasps were moving around him menacingly, and Mr. Boo grabbed the bee brush next to him and gently swept them off. The moment he turned his head, Romi moved closer to get a better look at his face. He had just brushed the wasps away when one suddenly darted right toward the huddled crowd.

"Oh my god!"

"It's huge!"

As the wasp flew toward them with a terrible noise, people leaped out of the way. The once-orderly group dispersed. Still holding the bee brush in one hand, Mr. Boo tried to settle the crowd.

"It's all right. You're wearing your protective gear, and as long as you don't excite the wasps—"

At that moment, the man locked eyes with Romi. Well, she couldn't really see much of his face, but it seemed like he did. Before she could form another thought, the crowd that had been shielding her before parted down the middle like the Red Sea, and the wasp headed straight toward her.

"Oh no, it's probably because of the spilled honey from earlier. Aren't they drawn to the smell?" Director Kang leaned against a pine tree, speaking lightly as if nothing out of the ordinary were going on. At first, Hadam had stepped back under the tree in shock, but as soon as the wasp set its sights on Romi, she leaped toward her friend.

"Romi!"

"Everyone out of the way; it's dangerous!" Mr. Boo shouted, approaching Romi as more wasps and honeybees alike appeared. They all began to gather around Romi. The people in the crowd were screaming. In an instant, the bees had Romi fully surrounded.

"Shoo! Get away from me!"

"Romi!"

Because of the bees circling her friend, Hadam couldn't get any closer, could only stamp her feet in front of Romi. Meanwhile, Romi shut her eyes and waved her hands wildly. Hadam looked around, unsure what to do. She spotted a beehive beside the pine tree closest to her, the spare lumber from its construction propped up against the tree. Hadam set down her camera, grabbed a piece of wood, and swung it from where she stood about ten steps away from Romi. She thought maybe if she did that, she could take some of the attention off her friend.

"Please don't do that! You shouldn't agitate the bees!"

Holding a spray bottle in one hand, Mr. Boo slowly approached, gesturing for Hadam to stand down. With her wooden beam high in the air, Hadam moved back. Mr. Boo searched all over, measuring the angles, seemingly trying to avoid causing any harm to Romi with the insecticide. The people standing behind her all looked on, not knowing what to do.

"Ma'am, please hold still and try not to move your hands or your head. All right, I'm going to spray . . ."

The bottle made a spritz sound, and Romi shouted, "Ack!" before dropping to the ground. The moment they were sprayed, the bees flew off in all directions. Everyone in the crowd leaned to one side, screaming again.

"Are you all right?" Mr. Boo went closer to Romi and bent down to look at her. "I think the wasps saw your black clothing and mistook you for a bear or some sort of predator, which got them all riled up. If you could leave . . ."

Romi grabbed ahold of Mr. Boo's arms and looked him right in the face. Afraid she was going to pass out, Mr. Boo grabbed on to her arms too. Romi's lips parted.

"Not you."

His smooth, round face sort of reminded her of the tapioca pearls in a milk tea. Harmless. He looked puzzled.

"I'm sorry?"

"I said it's not you."

Just then, Hadam—who was standing under the tree behind Mr. Boo—spoke up. "Romi . . ."

Still gripping Mr. Boo's arms for support, Romi got to her feet.

"Hadam," she said, "he's not our guy."

But Hadam didn't hear her, instead lifting her hands. "Romi, I think I got stung. My neck burns . . ."

Hadam's hands were hovering in the air, halfway to her throat, when she suddenly fainted. Like a choir, the tour group from Seoul shouted out cries of "oh my" and "oh no." Director Kang, who had been lounging beneath the tree until then, suddenly rushed forward and caught Hadam's head before it hit the ground. Romi ran toward her, too, and took Hadam's face in her hands.

"Hadam, Hadam, wake up. Oh my god. I think she got stung by a wasp! Bad enough that she passed out!"

Mr. Boo came over and knelt beside them. He examined Hadam's face, then turned to Director Kang, who was kneeling beside her, and said urgently, "First things first. I'm going to run and grab some ice and medicine. While I do that, call 119. She needs an injection, fast—"

"Sure, we could call 119, but she's going to be fine."

"What?"

Director Kang spoke calmly, like someone who dealt with this sort of dangerous situation daily. Romi felt a twinge of suspicion, wondering whether such emergencies actually did happen all the time here.

"I think she'll be fine. She didn't get stung by a wasp."

"And how would you know?" Romi snapped. "She's passed out! And even if she wasn't stung by a wasp, a beesting is dangerous too!"

"She wasn't stung by a bee either."

Crouched on the ground, Director Kang gathered up her skirt and slowly brought Hadam's head into her lap, turning it from side to side. "No stings on the back of her neck."

There were no signs of swelling or redness. No signs of any kind.

"But the symptoms of a sting could show up later!"

The moment the words left Romi's mouth, a pine cone fell out from behind Hadam's head and rolled onto the ground.

"I was watching from over there. She was holding up the wood beam when it got caught on the tree, and a pine cone fell on her neck. It must have pricked her, so she mistook it for a beesting and jumped out of the way."

Confused, Romi and Mr. Boo turned to look at Hadam's face. There were no traces of swelling or redness on her face or around her eyes, but . . .

Director Kang plucked out two sharp pine needles from inside Hadam's collar.

"She passed out simply from the shock."

When Chakyung arrived at the Honeycomb Guesthouse parking lot, it was early evening, and the sunlight was coming down at a slant. Several cars, including rental cars, were lined up in the lot. Chakyung quickly parked next to a huge SUV and got out. The moment her hand closed around the handle on the door to the guesthouse, she flinched. The handle was colder than she had anticipated, but even more surprising, there was a man coming out at the same time. He had short hair, like he'd just come back from the military, and a prominent bone structure. He gave off the vibe of a statue you would have sketched for practice in a high school art class. Normally, when someone was said to resemble a statue, that meant they were good-looking, but in this case, the observation felt somehow different. The statue man lowered his head and moved to the side so that Chakyung could pass. She stepped back too.

"You can go."

"No, you first."

Just then, Romi appeared behind the man.

"Oh, Chakyung!"

"Romi."

Romi looked at the man and bowed her head with a little smile. "Goodbye, then."

The man gave a slight bow, also smiling awkwardly at her. "Right, well. See you." His eyes returned to Chakyung and lingered for a moment, subtly taking note of her. In a momentary daze, Chakyung gave him a look of acknowledgment as well.

The man slowly walked over to the SUV next to Chakyung's car. Romi stood in the doorway, gripping the handle. Chakyung watched him all the way to his car, and as he got in, she asked, "Who is that?"

"Oh, one of Hadam's sunbaes," Romi said. She lowered her voice suddenly. "He came by along with Hadam's ex-boyfriend from way back. Hadam passed out earlier."

Though there was no need to whisper, Chakyung also lowered her voice to match. "Is she all right? Did she go to the hospital?"

"She says she's fine. She got a little scratched up from the fall and was in a bit of shock, but she got checked out and was given some allergy medicine just in case."

"Why did her ex come? Better yet, how'd he know about what happened?"

"Honestly, I thought that was kind of strange too. How *did* he know to come?" Romi tilted her head. Just then, the two of them heard Hadam's voice coming from inside.

"What are you two doing over there? It's hot. Come back in."

Chakyung and Romi exchanged a look before they headed in. The guesthouse was larger than Chakyung had expected, large enough to be considered more of a small hotel. The area Romi was showing her now was like a parlor, and there were hexagonal bookcases on the walls with assorted decorations on each shelf, as well as a foosball table set up in one corner. A yellow paper lantern hung off to the side, adding a slightly different element to the otherwise modern vibe. Hadam was sitting on the sofa with her legs up and a blanket draped over them like a sickly young girl in a children's book. A clean-cut man with a sharp nose and creaseless eyelids was sitting upright in one of the high-backed chairs at the table across from her. Hadam reached her hands out toward Chakyung as she entered.

"Chakyung, you made it."

The man stood up. For some reason, Chakyung thought he—mainly because of his jawline—resembled someone printed on paper money. Not the face on a thousand-won bill, but maybe the five-thousand-won face? Less hale and hearty, more fraught and concerned?

Hadam looked up at the two of them standing and offered introductions.

"Jaewoong, this is my friend Yoon Chakyung. She works at a cosmetics company. And Chakyung, this is an old college classmate of mine, Gu Jaewoong."

Chakyung held out her hand. "Hello." She didn't add any unnecessary remarks like how it was a pleasure to meet him or that she'd heard so much about him.

Jaewoong gave her hand a light, awkward shake. "Yes, hello."

When they were all seated again, Chakyung took a good look at Hadam's face. "Do you have a headache or fever at all?" she asked. "Do you feel like you're going to be sick?"

Putting a hand to her head, Hadam said, "I don't think so. More than sick, I just feel stupid." She'd tried to lighten the mood with her joke, but no one seemed to know how to react, and the atmosphere only grew more somber. Then Jaewoong chuckled. Chakyung thought of something funny she had seen on the internet once. If you folded paper money a certain way, you could change the serious face on the bill into a smiling one. With his laugh, Jaewoong's face transformed in the same way. As laugh lines creased the skin around his eyes, his worried five-thousand-won expression softened. *He seems like a nice guy,* Chakyung thought. You had to be nice to laugh at someone else's corny jokes. Either that or you liked them.

"Still, the doctor said if any unusual symptoms appear, you should go to the hospital," said Romi, looking serious, hands on her knees.

"I suppose I should, shouldn't I?" Hadam mused, and Chakyung, Romi, and Jaewoong all nodded their heads like doting parents. Then, as often happens in a group of people meeting for the first time, the conversation died out. Chakyung suddenly spoke.

"Jaewoong, how did you know Hadam had passed out?"

She worried her tone may have come across as accusatory, but Jaewoong answered openly.

"I found out from Pilhyun, our sunbae who came by earlier. He said Hadam had collapsed and suggested we go and see her. Figured she might need help from people she knew, being taken to the emergency room so far away from home. Pilhyun said he heard what happened from someone he knows at the Honeybee School."

"I see. And you went straight to the hospital?"

"At first, we thought she'd been stung by a wasp, so we were really worried. When we couldn't reach her by phone, we checked with the folks at the Honeybee School and found out she'd been taken to the emergency room at the provincial hospital."

"Ah, my phone was on silent in my bag. I must have missed your calls," said Hadam, sounding embarrassed.

"Of course. You were probably out of it at that point."

Chakyung was surprised by how gentle he sounded. It was hard to insert herself into their conversation. Soon enough, silence fell over them all again.

Then, as if a thought had suddenly occurred to her, Romi spoke up. "Jaewoong, you said you visited my blog before, right?"

"Yes, I browsed around from time to time. Someone told me about your site and how great your illustrations were, but I can't remember who it might have been. Anyway, I visited your blog to see the illustrations you posted."

"Did you ever leave any comments? What was your username?"

"I did comment a few times. I doubt you'd know my username, though. I'm not the type to update my own blog a lot."

"Ah, I see. Still, I was curious."

At the end of the conversation, Jaewoong glanced at his watch. It looked like a TAG Heuer, brand-new. The latest model. *So he's the type to spend good money on a watch,* Chakyung thought. She caught herself sizing up all sorts of things about him and felt a bit embarrassed.

Jaewoong calmly reached over and picked up the bag next to him—it was unclear whether or not he had noticed Chakyung's appraising eyes.

"I'll get going, then," he said. As he stood up, so did Romi and Chakyung.

"You're leaving already?" said Romi. "Won't you at least join us for dinner before you go?"

"Sorry. I have dinner plans tonight."

"Sure, of course. Thanks for coming today—I know you must have been busy."

When Hadam tried to stand as well, Jaewoong waved his hand to stop her. "Be careful," he said. "And if you need anything, give me a call."

"I will."

Chakyung and Romi saw him to the door. Sumi, the landlady, was coming in from the garden out back with a heap of laundry in her arms when she ran into them.

"Oh, he's leaving early today," she said. "I was just going to ask you all how many people to expect for dinner."

"I know," said Romi slowly. "So early today."

Sitting at the table after dinner, Chakyung said to Sumi, "It must be so much work, serving dinner in a guesthouse this big."

Sumi had just finished doing the dishes and was untying her apron as she came in from the kitchen. She smiled.

"We don't usually serve dinner, but I heard our guest passed out today and figured it would be a hassle for her to go out and eat, so I just prepared something simple."

"Simple? It was delicious, really. I heard you used to work at a bank, but judging by this meal, I would have thought you were a professional chef."

"Since we have guests to entertain, I did end up taking cooking classes for a bit. My husband loves to go all out when it comes to our work here."

That same husband had disappeared somewhere right after dinner. Throughout the meal, he didn't speak much at all if the topic wasn't related to beekeeping, but he had a lot to say about apiculture. His wife had asked the three women all sorts of questions and come across as a sociable host. Sumi had even shown some interest when Chakyung was talking about the cosmetics company where she worked.

While Sumi brewed tea, Chakyung took a brief stroll, looking around the guesthouse kitchen and dining area. She could tell that everything from the salt and pepper shakers to the cushions had been meticulously chosen to match the mood.

"How pretty," said Chakyung, examining a vase on the dining table. "You can really feel the affection in every corner of this place. It must be nice to see your lifelong dream realized like this."

Without looking up, Sumi said, "This was indeed my husband's lifelong dream."

Sensing some emphasis on the words "my husband's," Chakyung studied Sumi's face. Not seeming to notice Chakyung's eyes on her, Sumi went on, her hands busy working. "I think you three are the ones living your dreams. You can go anywhere you want."

Chakyung waved her hands. "I'm just a regular old company worker. If someone at the top tells me to go, I go, and if they tell me to come, I come."

"Still, your job takes you on business trips to all sorts of places. So does Hadam's work, making films around the world." Sumi stood on tiptoe to grab the teacups from where they sat on the shelves and set them down on the island in the kitchen. "And is Romi traveling to Jeju for pleasure? I heard her talking earlier, and it seemed like she was here looking for someone."

Chakyung was surprised. Had they been talking about their true intentions behind Romi and Hadam's *Searching for Honeyman* project? Of course, there was a good chance Sumi would know some suitable candidates. But even if Romi had mentioned her intentions, it seemed like it wasn't Chakyung's story to tell. She still personally hadn't heard anything more about it.

"Romi's tagging along and helping out with Hadam's investigation," she said.

Sumi nodded, then pointed at the tray on which the teacups and the teakettle sat. "Take this and head on up," she said. "I'm sure you three have a lot to talk about."

Holding the tray Sumi had given her, Chakyung carefully climbed the stairs. The door was open, and Romi and Hadam were sitting on the edge of a twin bed. The room was furnished with another bed, a small vanity, a round table, and a single chair, and the walls were covered with light yellow wallpaper.

Chakyung set the tray on the table and sat down on the chair. "So how's the *Searching for Honeyman* project coming along?" she asked.

"We found two of our three contenders, but as you know, neither one was our guy." Hadam briefly recapped the events of that day and the day before. Chakyung listened calmly and took mental notes.

"So now there's only one man left to find," she said.

"Right. We're planning to track him down tomorrow. We heard he runs a bee farm in Seogwipo."

"Maybe I'm getting ahead of myself, but what are you planning to do if he's not the guy either? Hadam, your ex—I mean, your old college friend—might have missed something when narrowing down the options." Chakyung looked back and forth between her friends. Compared to Hadam, who appeared to be deep in thought, Romi didn't seem particularly concerned.

"I'll continue filming the documentary regardless, so it doesn't matter to me, but Romi . . ."

Hadam glanced over at her. Romi was blowing gently on her tea and taking a sip.

"I'll just stay and help Hadam as much as I can, then head back to Seoul," she said.

"Won't you feel like it was a waste?" Chakyung asked, but Romi's expression remained calm.

"Maybe, but honestly, I've already been through not being able to find this guy. Going home without having found him yet again would be nothing new."

Chakyung brought up the question she had been holding in since earlier. It might have been too late to ask, but the thought had been making her uneasy all this time.

"Romi, did you even want to find him in the first place? I'm worried you've only come all this way because we pushed you."

Romi's eyes widened in disbelief. "Why would you think that? If I didn't want to come, I wouldn't have tagged along. If there was a way to find him, I wanted to try."

Hadam chimed in. "I'd also been wondering whether everything would turn out okay if you did manage to meet up with him again."

Romi peeled the wrapper off a snack on the tray and said, "I'll just have to see. I didn't agree to look for him just because I had some wild idea of our getting together."

"So why did you want to find him?" Chakyung asked.

"I just wanted to know." Romi bit into the biscuit with a crunch. "Years ago, there was that saying that was all the rage, remember? 'He's just not that into you,' meaning he didn't fall as hard for you as you did for him."

Chakyung remembered that saying coming to mind the first time she'd heard Romi's story. It had been the title of a relationship advice book that was a massive hit and had even been made into a movie.

"As the saying goes," Romi continued, "one reason a guy would have failed to reach out to you is because he just wasn't *that* into you—I wanted to know how much *that* was. What it would take for him to be *that* interested. I wanted to ask him."

All sorts of reasons weighed on her mind. These were questions anyone would find difficult to answer. How much did you really have to like someone to try reaching out to them again? Was there any other reason not to, aside from the fact that you simply weren't into them? Until she found him again, she would never know.

"And if I had to name another reason I wanted to join the search," said Romi as she finished the biscuit and picked up the crumbs that had fallen on the floor one by one with her finger, "then I would say because I thought it might be fun."

At that, Chakyung and Hadam were briefly stunned speechless. But when it came to the most important motivating factor in life, what else could it have been if not fun? If something was fun to do, people did it. There was no simpler or clearer motivation than that.

Romi placed all the crumbs inside the snack wrapper and brushed her finger clean. "What about you, Hadam?" she asked.

Hadam, flustered at having the focus return to her, asked, "Huh? What about me?"

"What are you going to do about your boyfriend, Mr. Gu?"

Romi had thrown her a fastball straight down the middle. Her frankness felt like an ambush.

"Well, I—I'm not sure what you mean."

"Come on. Spill what happened when I wasn't here." Chakyung had only guessed at what had gone on based on the mood earlier.

Hadam waved her hands. "No, please don't mention that. We just grabbed dinner together the first day while he was sharing information. That's all."

"But when he heard you'd passed out, he came running to the hospital. Like there had been some kind of major accident or something," Romi said meaningfully, but Hadam waved her remarks away again.

"He just came along with our sunbae, Pilhyun. He probably wanted to see if there was anything he could do to help me as someone he happens to know."

Chakyung piped up. "Is he really the type to be so concerned about others?"

"Yes," said Hadam immediately, "he absolutely is. That's actually one of the reasons we broke up." She briefly recounted the story about the fire at the filming site. That cold feeling she'd had as the fire raged on, and the growing sense of estrangement between them even after.

"It was nice that he was considerate of others, but I guess I felt disappointed that he didn't seem to understand what a big deal the whole thing had been for me too. And then I was so busy dealing with the aftermath of the fire and picking up where I had left off with the film while he was busy with his own things and not reaching out anymore. Even if I had wanted to vent my frustrations to him, there was never any chance to, and I felt like we were constantly out of sync. We didn't have a huge fight or anything—we just naturally drifted apart. And even now, we might be hanging out again, but . . ."

"Since he came to see you at the hospital today, it seems like he still really cares about you. What would happen if he made amends for the things he regrets from the past and said he wanted you to take him back?"

Right away, Chakyung jumped in to say, "I'm thinking about it differently. Usually when you're regretting a breakup, you tend to remember only one part as bad and everything else as having been mostly good. And you think that if only the other person could fix that one essential flaw, the two of you could be together again. But if that one flaw was so crucial that it led you to break up, and if it's part of the other person's nature or an issue of fundamental incompatibility, it'll be hard to fix. Most people who get back together in those cases end up breaking up again."

Hadam nodded. If he had a change of heart, maybe they could get together again. If they decided to make an effort with each other, maybe their relationship could pick back up. It wasn't as though she had never thought about it before. She had, for the three years following their breakup. And even after that, she had mulled over the idea. On the days she didn't want to eat alone, when she read articles about rerun screenings of old films the two of them had loved, when she realized the guy she had dated after him had been secretly meeting up with his old flame, Jaewoong sometimes came to mind. And yet . . .

"The way he sees it, he would have no reason to change himself. He'd see no need to go that far just to be with me again."

Chakyung took a sip of her tea. "Right. Besides, you two live in such different places now. You'd definitely have to be much closer if you were to continue the relationship . . ."

"Oh, wow, do you really think so?" Romi asked, tilting her head in surprise.

"Of course. People usually end up choosing partners from among the people nearest to them."

"You said you met Chanmin through your university's student union, right?" Hadam asked.

Chakyung wasn't the type to divulge much about herself, but Hadam had happened to catch some of the details of her and Chanmin's history before.

"Right, but we weren't dating at that time. He was just someone I saw around. I think there was another girl he liked. And I didn't have the best impression of the friends he hung out with. But when I joined my company, because of our work in developing cosmetics, we had projects where we consulted with the research team so we could draw up plans, and that was where we started seeing each other. As we interacted more often at work, I came to realize he was much more hardworking than I'd thought. Plus he lived in the apartment complex next to mine, so we started commuting together after work and often had the chance to talk on the way home."

Proximity was clearly important. Trying to date someone who wasn't in the immediate vicinity and with a schedule so packed there wasn't even time to eat lunch was bound to be tough. Chakyung sometimes thought the reason they had quietly grown more distant lately was because their current homes were far apart.

"You have a point, Chakyung, but I don't think people hit it off just because they happen to be near each other," Hadam said. "I make films, so there are tons of people I've stayed up all night with, traveled around foreign countries for several days with when we're filming overseas, and never once had those kinds of feelings for. If all it took for people to develop affection was being near someone, I probably wouldn't be single right now."

Hadam shuddered, remembering her former coworkers. They weren't entirely bad people, but they could be insensitive, and they wouldn't hesitate to make offensive jokes using the fact that they were close as an excuse. Of course, they weren't all like that. Not always . . .

"Isn't the most important thing a sense of tenderness? Of sweetness? People with those qualities you can grow to like."

Just hearing the word "sweetness," Romi and Chakyung gave Hadam a look that implied they could relate to that as well. And yet . . .

"What does it even mean to be 'sweet'?" Chakyung sighed. As Romi and Hadam listened to her talk, they had guessed her fiancé didn't quite fit the "sweet" standard. But Chakyung had never spoken so bluntly about such things before.

"Hmm, maybe it means taking note of the other person's comforts and discomforts ahead of time? And then doing things beforehand to help make that person feel at ease?" Hadam wondered.

She thought again about the conversation she'd had with the Honeycomb Guesthouse owner earlier at dinner. Worker bees store honey inside their bodies and regurgitate it several times, the powerful fanning of their wings blowing away the honey's moisture. The honey becomes sweeter as it undergoes this natural ripening process. Showing affection toward others was like that. It was possible only when you gave your all, drawing out what you had kept inside of you for so long. Becoming sweet required the effort of endlessly fanning your wings.

"But no matter how close or how sweet someone is, it doesn't mean everything will turn out fine," Romi declared, grabbing two more snacks. "More than anything, you need to feel a spark. Without that, all the other stuff is useless. It's only when the magnetic field envelops two people," she said, loudly tearing the wrapper off one of the biscuits, "that those two people fall in love."

◆ ◆ ◆

Hoping to get back to the hotel before it was too late, Chakyung left the Honeycomb Guesthouse around nine o'clock, but darkness had already fallen over the island like a blackout curtain. There were no streetlights along the mountain road to Jungmun and not a single other car to be seen. Chakyung drove cautiously, worried that a wild animal would leap out in front of her. A few raindrops began to fall. The windshield wipers, equipped with a rain-detection system, activated automatically. It wasn't her first time driving around Jeju in a rental car, but she always felt nervous taking mountain roads on overcast nights.

Rounding the curve in the steadily increasing rain, she saw a truck approaching from behind. The truck sped up, and Chakyung yielded, allowing it to pass as she felt uncomfortable racing ahead. The moment the truck slipped past, Chakyung glanced over at the driver, but it was so dark, she couldn't make out much aside from the fact that it was a man. What a relief that she had let him go first.

The truck moved into the next lane over for a moment, then went ahead, racing with reckless abandon compared to the speed it had been going at first. The driver seemed to be rushing ahead to keep a certain distance from Chakyung's car. The rain had grown steadier, so he might have been taking precautions.

Through the waving windshield wipers, Chakyung could see the rear of the truck ahead. There was something in the trunk. In the dark, the taillights resembled a pair of glaring red eyes. The driver could simply be speeding. Or could he have other intentions? Chakyung grew nervous, tried not to get too close. She figured she should maintain a safe-enough distance to avoid rear-ending the truck if the driver made a sudden stop. But she wasn't as afraid of the dark now as she had been earlier, so consumed was she with following after those taillights.

The truck gained speed once it came to the main road. Those red eyes soon grew distant before they disappeared entirely. Just then, Chakyung realized that from this point on, the way ahead was well lit by the streetlamps lining the road. Had the driver in the car ahead of her purposely put on his taillights so she could follow behind in the rain? It was impossible to know, however much she wanted to believe in the kindness of a stranger she'd met by chance on the road. But perhaps there were times when dark roads were illuminated by the unnoticed kindnesses of others. Thinking of the people who had been kind to her despite not knowing her, Chakyung wanted to believe this world she lived in was still such a place.

YOU END UP
FINDING WHAT YOU
WANT

Three Years Earlier

The rain grew heavier. The sound of its drumming on the roof filled the car, drowning out the prolonged silence. The man's wife made no move to wipe away her falling tears. The man himself didn't know the reason for them. At the moment, he didn't feel any particular way about them. The rain falling on the windshield seemed to be pounding against his heart, but he felt no pain.

"Honey . . ."

At the sound of his wife's trembling voice, he quietly replied, "Let's go home and talk first." He didn't want to distract his wife while she was driving. This was a road they had been on countless times since they had moved to Jeju, but today it seemed suddenly unfamiliar and dangerous.

Soon after, harsh lights appeared behind them, glaring into his eyes. The car in their rearview must have had its high beams on. Probably because there were no streetlights on this road and the weather was terrible, the man figured, but he still found it grating.

His wife stayed on the right side of the road, leaving room for the car behind them to pass. But the car made no move to do so. Its driver only kept the high beams on, closing in on them enough to raise concern.

"Are they crazy? What the hell is wrong with them?"

It was unusual for him to swear, and the man's wife flinched when she heard it. But she said nothing to scold him as she gripped the steering wheel, knowing it would be hard to respond calmly and with restraint. She picked up speed, but the car behind them immediately followed suit. It stayed right on their tail, evidently with no intention of passing them. They couldn't do anything. Couldn't slow down. All the thoughts that had been occupying their minds just a moment earlier had vanished.

A nervous tension spread throughout the car. The man grabbed his wife's arm.

"Honey, slow down. It's dangerous."

They were going more than sixty miles per hour on a narrow road. His wife tried to shake off the car behind them by switching lanes, but she got the feeling the other driver was relentlessly pursuing them. The rain was coming down harder than before, and she couldn't see well ahead of her. They would probably get into an accident soon if they kept up this speed. The man could feel his wife trembling next to him. A cold sweat ran down his spine.

Suddenly the car behind them swerved into the next lane over and picked up speed. Thinking the other car was finally going to pass them, the two breathed a sigh of relief. The man's wife slowed down. But the car beside them slowed to match their pace and rammed up against their car. The man's wife swerved off the road in surprise, but the car in the next lane doggedly followed after. The car streaked past the branches of the trees, rain-soaked leaves sticking to the windshield. The man could see the trees through the passenger-side window, could feel them tugging at the car like the ghost of someone drowned. His wife rolled down the window and shouted toward the car next to theirs.

"Hey, what the hell! Are you crazy?"

The man had said the same thing earlier, but hearing his normally calm and composed wife shouting like that made something in his chest lurch.

"Honey, it's dangerous!" he said, but his wife kept on shouting.

"What the hell kind of driving are you doing?"

The man leaned forward in the passenger seat to get a good look at the other car. He had never seen this car before. A black SUV. Because of the rain and the dark tint on the windows, he couldn't quite see who was inside—but he had the feeling their pursuer had suddenly faltered for some reason, hitting the brakes on the wild chase he had been giving.

Seizing the chance, his wife sped up and passed the other driver. The trees beside them became a blur as they swept past. The man could only hold on tight in his seat, feeling his soul leaving his body. Just then, the car behind them came around onto their right. His wife swerved to the left and tried to race ahead so she could give them the slip. The man looked behind them, and the moment he turned back around to face forward, he saw an enormous shadow in front of them.

"Honey, the other way!"

A huge truck blared its horn as it came at them from the opposite direction. Their car had crossed over the median strip, and they were speeding in the wrong direction. It seemed like the car was out of control. His wife's screams rang in his ears. He tried to hold her, but she yanked the wheel back toward herself.

The car sped on with no traction for a while and only came to a stop after it crashed into a stone wall surrounding a field, rolled twice, and flipped over. The airbags burst open, the pressure crushing into the man's chest. He lost consciousness for a moment but quickly came to. Some distance ahead, he saw lights. The SUV that had been chasing them had come to a stop. The man opened his eyes and tried to commit the car to memory, but because of the heavy rain and blood in his eyes, he couldn't see it well, and the lights soon disappeared.

"Honey."

His wife didn't answer. Hanging upside down in his seat, he called out for her again.

"Honey . . . are you awake?"

Still no answer. He hardly had to turn his head at all to see that his wife's neck had snapped.

He unbuckled his seat belt and climbed out. He staggered over to the driver's side and tried opening the door. It wouldn't budge. He shook on the handle with both hands.

"Honey, Hyeyoung, wake up! Wake up!"

Sparks jumped from the crumpled hood of the car. White smoke drifted up and vanished into the rain. The man yanked frantically on the door handle, completely out of his mind. The falling rain mixing into the blood running from his head prevented him from seeing clearly. On second thought, the rain had already started to let up—the wetness on his face must have been tears. He kept yanking at the door, calling over and over for his wife.

That was when he heard the first explosion.

◆ ◆ ◆

Project: *Searching for Honeyman*

Day Four, Seogwipo

The rain that had been falling since last night had not let up. Chakyung couldn't have imagined the impact of a typhoon passing through Japan would be felt even here. Outside the hotel window, the horizon was clouded over, blurring the border between sea and sky. It was so early that she hadn't even had breakfast yet. Hair wrapped in a towel, Chakyung looked over the day's schedule on her phone.

That morning, she had to visit a green-tea field to prepare for the promotions of her company's green-tea skin-care line, the main objective of this business trip to Jeju. After lunch, she had decided to have a brief meeting with the documentary team there to film the camellias. It wasn't yet the season for the flowers to bloom, but because the seeds would start being gleaned around mid-September, the film crew had come early. Later on, when the camellias bloomed in the winter, the grandmothers would gather the flowers again. Chakyung's heart raced, imagining how beautifully the documentary would turn out with the gorgeous blossoms.

Her phone rang. The name on the screen read "Yang Chanmin." She'd sent him a message when she landed on Jeju, but this was the first time he'd called. She quickly tapped the screen.

"Hey."

"What's kept you so busy that you couldn't even call?"

"Look who's talking. I called you so many times."

"I had my phone off while I was working on my paper and presentation. When I called back, you didn't pick up."

"Let's just say we missed each other's calls."

"Fine. How's Jeju?"

"Hmm. Rainy."

"It's a shame that it's cloudy out. Still, make sure to see the ocean and have a good time. I'll be there soon."

"You're coming to Jeju?"

"I told you this already."

"Did you?"

When had he mentioned that? Chanmin talked as if they agreed on things well in advance, but in reality, he always made one-sided decisions and just informed her of the outcome after the fact.

"Yeah, next week I'm presenting at a conference."

"Ah. I think I'll be back in Seoul by then."

"That's too bad."

"It is. If you'd told me ahead of time, I would have planned it so our dates overlapped."

"I did tell you ahead of time."

Both of them could have been telling the truth. *Maybe he told me and I didn't hear him, or maybe he told me in a way that made it impossible for me to get the message*—this was how Chakyung tried to make sense of the situation. In turn, she shifted the conversation to a topic that was mutually uncomfortable.

"Your mother has called me several times now."

"Oh, right. About the furniture."

"Yeah. The thing is, I told her I couldn't get to the discount furniture store right away, and she said she would go instead and buy things for us. She'll send us pictures, and we can pick out things we like, then transfer her the money later."

Chanmin said nothing for a moment. When his mother and Chakyung butted heads, he usually opted to stay silent. Until now, Chakyung had considered this a good thing. It wasn't as if she couldn't convey her thoughts to his mother on her own. She would much rather speak her mind directly than go through Chanmin. But his mother had never been this headstrong and insistent before.

"I told her the two of us would take our time choosing the furniture. We haven't even found a house yet, so why buy furniture so far in advance? But when I said that, she just offered to store the furniture for us."

"Yeah."

She hadn't been looking for a short-answer essay in response, but maybe his curt answers were a sign to end the conversation there. Still, Chakyung found herself pushing on.

"I told her it was fine, but she kept insisting, and I told her I didn't want things to happen like this. No matter how big a discount we get on the furniture, it's not as if buying it all will be cheap . . ."

"Right, my mother told me."

Had she really? Or did he just not want to hear what Chakyung was saying? More and more, Chakyung felt like they were dodging these necessary conversations like potholes, one after another.

"Great, so please explain this to your mother in a way that doesn't upset her."

"She's already upset. But you know that's just how she is."

Why exactly was he telling her this? Was he saying they should all be upset together? Chakyung wondered how exactly his mother had spun the story to him. Then she decided there was no reason she needed to know.

"Just text her. Tell her you're sorry. Right now, I need to get to work."

Hearing Chanmin speak as if all this had nothing to do with him, Chakyung had to fight herself to keep from shouting *Why should I?* at the phone, not wanting to upset him when he was on his way to work. She never wanted to be the person who made others feel bad just because she felt bad herself.

"Okay," she said. "I'll call you later."

Chanmin hung up without another word. It felt like everything he'd left unsaid was still hanging in the air.

Chakyung looked out at the ocean through the window. Any thoughts of having breakfast were already long gone. The sky and the sea, the rain, everything was the same gray in slightly different shades, all of it bleeding into one.

At that early hour and because of the rain, the beach was quiet. A few cars were parked nearby, but Chakyung didn't see any people around. She held up her umbrella and went down the road leading to the sand. This was her first time seeing the ocean on this trip. She went to Jeju on business every so often, but rarely did she have the time to relax and take in the views. Her visit to the green-tea fields that morning had been canceled due to the rain, so she found herself with time to spare until the meeting.

She was relieved she had packed flip-flops. Her dress shoes would have easily been ruined trekking across the wet sand. She walked slowly, feeling the sand shift beneath her sandals. Once she reached the shore-line, she began to walk the length of the beach, parallel to the horizon. Waves surged over the sand, tickling her ankles before retreating. The water was swelling higher than she'd expected in the wind. Chakyung passed the middle of the beach and kept walking toward the steep rock cliffs.

At first, she thought no one was there, but suddenly several colorful dots appeared in the water—people. They had suddenly emerged from behind the tall waves and were whirling around in the crests. *They must be surfers,* Chakyung thought. She had seen surf shops in passing, but this was her first time seeing the surfing itself. She hadn't known waves could be ridden in the rain. These surfers had climbed onto their boards even in the downpour and were riding the broad faces of the waves, sliding down and twisting into turns at the bottom before plunging into the water. Chakyung stood on the sand as the waves came in and rushed out, her eyes following the surfers' silhouettes, which was all she could see of them from this distance.

They lay atop the boards on their stomachs, paddling forward with their hands before standing on their feet. They followed the waves, ris-ing and falling before disappearing into the water. It filled Chakyung with glee to watch them slip under one moment, only to resurface the next. People using their immense strength to battle it out in the rain. Facing nature head-on and becoming a part of it. For the first time in a while, she was witnessing something that made her heart feel light.

The surfers carried on like that for a while—riding the waves, crash-ing and falling in time with the sea, rinse and repeat. Once the waves had gotten a little smaller, the surfers rode their boards to the shore again. Realizing she had spent a while watching them, Chakyung made to turn away. She felt like she had trespassed on their time. But as soon as she began walking again, she paused. She'd spotted one of the surfers holding up a hand with his middle three fingers folded down and shaking it from the wrist. The others made the same gesture and burst out laughing. Chakyung could have sworn she'd seen that gesture somewhere before. And the person who had made the gesture too . . .

He was coming up the beach at that moment, holding a yellow board. Even in a wet suit, his angular shoulders and long neck were familiar.

He turned and looked right at Chakyung where she was standing on the shore. She returned his gaze, red umbrella in hand. She couldn't tell whether or not he recognized her. He turned away nonchalantly, running a hand through his hair. Then he laughed and grimaced at the same time and shouted something to his friends. She couldn't hear, but reading his lips, she thought he might have said, *Ugh, it's freezing!* His two fellow surfers laughed also.

They continued walking up the beach with their boards. Chakyung lowered her umbrella to cover her face and stood watching the distant sea. The sound of waves crashing reverberated inside her body. Time seemed to take slower strides.

Then her umbrella began to bob and tremble. Someone was knocking on it. Chakyung slowly lifted the umbrella to see a smiling face. The man was leaning down slightly, looking at her underneath the cover of the canopy.

"Hello there, Ms. Rude-and-Sleepy."

Chakyung wondered if she should try feigning more surprise, as if she'd only just now noticed him, but in the end, she greeted him calmly.

"Hello, Mr. Rude-and-Friendly."

She tipped her umbrella back slightly. Raindrops fell onto the tip of her nose. Some also dripped onto the guy's already-soaked hair.

"My name's Han Soo-eon," he said. It was the first time he'd said his name aloud to her. So that was how it was supposed to sound.

"I'm Yoon Chakyung."

"I know." He grinned again.

"So it was a surfboard." Chakyung pointed at the board he was holding, a yellow swallow-tailed surfboard with red stripes. Soo-eon looked down at it.

"Ah, right. My luggage. I heard this was made by a master shaper, so I bought it in Hawaii and brought it back with me." He said this with the excitement of a little kid bragging about a new toy. "But what brings you here so early on a rainy morning? It doesn't look like you came to surf." He gestured toward the sea with both hands in mock seriousness. "This isn't exactly a good place for golfing either."

He had remembered her luggage too. Chakyung saw no need to tell him the golf bag wasn't hers.

"This isn't good weather to do much of anything in," she said.

"I don't know—seems like decent weather for a conversation, no?"

Chakyung looked at Soo-eon's face in earnest for the first time. Was her sense that he seemed like a little boy based solely on the fact that he looked younger than her? Was it just because she was more tired than he was?

Chakyung shrugged. "I don't think the ocean, the rain, and a conversation are the most harmonious match, exactly—"

Soo-eon threw an arm around her shoulders and pulled her toward him. After a moment of confusion, Chakyung realized someone had nearly decked her with a surfboard.

"Oh no, so sorry."

The person whose huge neon board had nearly hit her was a young guy with a big build. But the guy had just turned away, and the woman with him had apologized instead. Chakyung frowned. Soo-eon let go of her and turned to the shamefaced woman, nodding and warning her, "Be careful. The waves are high right now."

The guy who had nothing to say earlier when he should have been saying sorry turned around and glared at Soo-eon. "Pfft. Who do you think you are?" he sneered.

As he stalked away, the woman with him cast one more look back before trailing sheepishly after him. Still within earshot, the guy grumbled, "So-called locals think they know everything."

Soo-eon watched him go, muttering, "Those aren't waves beginners should be riding, though . . ."

"How do you know he's a beginner?" Chakyung asked.

"His wet suit and board are brand-new. He might have been surfing a couple times, but his stuff doesn't look rented. He doesn't have much of a tan for a surfer. Or look like he's done much paddling. Yet he's using a shortboard."

The two of them watched the man lie stomach-down on the board and swim out into the open water. The woman stood on the shore, watching. The wind was blowing, and the waves were a little higher than before.

"The waves are rough today," said Soo-eon, measuring them with his finger. It was still raining. A few yards out from where they stood, the men Soo-eon had been surfing with earlier stopped walking to watch the other man.

Chakyung wasn't normally the type to interfere in other people's business. She would offer help to those who requested it, but she viewed stepping in any sooner as an intrusion. In her eyes, there was nothing she could do for those who ignored the help or warnings they'd been given. Still, she could already tell Soo-eon was a much different person than she was. It was that difference that unnerved her. She couldn't simply leave the beach now. Not until the rookie surfer made it back out of the water in one piece.

But the waves were high, and the arrogant man's skills were predictably flimsy. He appeared to catch a small wave once, but after that, he kept wiping out on any other wave he tried. He couldn't even stand up on his board properly before he was falling off again. When another wave came in, he managed to get on his feet despite wobbling. He somehow succeeded at catching a wave that looked to be about three feet high. But in the blink of an eye, the wave broke. The man fell forward and was swept under, his board flying up and landing on the water again with a thwack. All the surfers on the beach let out a collective "Ouch!" The man did not resurface.

One of Soo-eon's surfer buddies shouted, "Did the board hit him on the head?"

The beach wasn't officially open yet. It was raining early in the morning, and they were a bit far from the main area—naturally there were no lifeguards in sight. The woman on the shore looked around nervously. Two minutes. Three. The man still hadn't come back up. The woman tapped her foot, anxious, before starting toward the water on impulse.

"It's dangerous!"

Soo-eon ran across the beach. His surfer buddies chased after him.

He pushed past the woman, wading into the water, and threw himself into the churning waves. He was quick to reach the open sea, where that neon surfboard floated, looking like an overturned wreck. The other surfers swam out close behind him.

Then Soo-eon's head went under and disappeared too. Time seemed to pass at a crawl. Chakyung felt like she could hear her blood rushing in her ears. At last, Soo-eon resurfaced, holding the unconscious man, and the other surfers helped him haul the man back to the shore.

They laid the man out on the sand, and the woman who had been with him dropped to her knees beside him. While one of Soo-eon's buddies was attempting CPR, sirens wailed nearby. Everyone turned their heads. An ambulance pulled up, and out came the medics, running a stretcher across the sand. The surfers cleared a path for them as they lifted the man onto the stretcher to carry him out. The woman ran after them. Meanwhile, the surfers seemed to take it upon themselves to look after their boards, bringing them back up and onto the beach.

Soo-eon approached Chakyung. "Did you call the ambulance?" he asked, grinning.

She nodded. "I didn't know what might happen, so I went ahead and called. They got here fast."

"Thanks to you, he'll be able to get first aid quickly. He should be fine."

"If he does pull through, it'll be thanks to you, not me."

They began walking toward the sloping path that led up the beach. Chakyung held her umbrella so that it also covered Soo-eon. He was already soaked, but to let him continue getting battered by the rain didn't sit right with her. She didn't know why they were walking together. They had nothing much to talk about now, nothing to share.

"I guess surfing is a pretty dangerous sport," Chakyung said. Still gripping the umbrella with one hand, she bent down and rinsed her feet under the outdoor shower. Golden sand had wedged itself between her toes. Soo-eon took the umbrella from her. She looked up at him looming over her and getting soaked in the rain he was shielding her from.

"It's not so hard if you follow the rules," he said, "and if you do it with someone who has professional expertise and can help you when it gets tough."

Chakyung finished rinsing her feet, then gathered the hem of her skirt and made to crouch down to wash off the sand sticking to her sandals. "You mean someone like you, for example."

Soo-eon wordlessly returned her umbrella. Without thinking, she accepted it, then watched him get soaked by the rain as he bent down to pick up her shoes. He blasted them with the air hose to get the sand off and rinsed them clean under the running water.

"Yes," he said. "I mean someone like me, for example."

He set her sandals down before her feet. She couldn't see his face as his head was bowed, but she knew he was smiling.

When they reached the parking lot, Soo-eon pointed over his shoulder and said, "The guys I came with are waiting for me, so I'll head back."

He turned to go and had only taken a few steps when Chakyung called out, "Wait."

He turned back around.

"There's something I wanted to ask you," she said.

"What is it?"

Chakyung tried to re-create the hand gesture she had seen him make at the airport in Hawaii and again earlier on the beach. She held up her pinky and her thumb, keeping her middle three fingers folded down.

"What does this mean?"

"Aha." Grinning, Soo-eon folded his fingers into the same gesture, then turned his wrist to show her the back side of his hand as well. "It's called the shaka sign. It's a way surfers greet each other."

"Does it have any meaning?"

"Well, it could mean lots of things. It can mean 'take it easy.' It can mean 'nice job.' There are times you use it to say 'thanks,' or 'hey, hello.'"

"Can you use it to say 'take care'?"

"Sure you can."

"Well then." Chakyung turned her wrist to show him the back side of her hand like he had done. He smiled again, still holding his hand up too.

"What are you using it to mean?" he asked.

Chakyung shrugged. "Could mean lots of things."

She watched him take off running, his hair getting soaked in the rain. To her, the hand sign seemed similar to the one for "call me." This wasn't a gesture you could make to just anybody—they had to have your phone number. Even people who knew your number couldn't always call you. Or else, they chose not to. There were times you might tell someone to call you, yet the call never came. It seemed better, then, not to know anyone's number. That way, there was no reason to ever tell someone, "Call me," to ever wait for a call. That way, there was nothing you could do.

But what if you still wanted to tell someone to call you? Chakyung held up her folded fingers. Soo-eon was already gone, returned to the beach and the company of his friends.

Outside the car window, the ocean was still a dark gray, though bits of blue sky were peeking out over the mountaintops. The rain had stopped, and the view had cleared up.

"It was always a fantasy of mine to go for a drive along the coast."

Romi was behind the wheel today. No matter how much Hadam insisted she was fine, Romi refused to put an injured person in charge of operating a motor vehicle.

"The weather today is pretty nice for a drive," Hadam said. "I'm glad it cleared up."

She aimed her camera at the distant sky and adjusted the focus. Now that the rain was gone, it also wasn't a bad day to meet up with someone. Hadam hoped the third Honeyman candidate they were seeing today would be the real deal. If things went amiss again, she wouldn't know where to start over from at this point. It seemed like Hadam was the only one fretting, though—Romi looked completely calm.

"I like this song," said Romi, listening closely to the music. "Who's it by again?"

The clear trills of birds rang out. Hadam looked down at her phone. "Ah, this says it's by Nohelani Cypriano. The song is called 'Lihue.' I think she's a Hawaiian musician." The song was on a playlist Yoojin had sent along with some other materials when Hadam mentioned she was going to Jeju. "Yoojin said it was great music for listening to on the beach."

"Yoojin—she's one of your old classmates from the film department? Along with Jaewoong and that Pilhyun sunbae of yours?"

"That's right. Pilhyun actually took some time off to work before starting school, so even though he's older than me, we were in the same year. It's kind of weird to call him 'oppa,' though, so I just call him 'sunbae.'"

"What does he do here on Jeju?"

"Oh—well, he was a film major like the rest of us, but he doesn't make movies anymore. He worked overseas for a few years, but I think he said he came to Jeju to take part in a couple exhibitions of some sort at the biennale."

"Is he an artist? What medium? Painting?"

"At the moment, he's leaning toward installation art. A combination of installation and media art. He told me he's videographing installation art that melds the organic with the mechanic, but I don't really know what that means. I think the exhibition starts soon, so we could go and check it out together."

"Sure, I'd like that," Romi said, but she didn't seem all that interested. In that same, even tone, she asked, "So what made Jaewoong quit making movies?"

Hadam shook her head. "I don't know. He . . . was really good at it."

She didn't say anything more than that. The sound of music filled the car in lieu of a real answer.

"Hmm. Well, I suppose everyone has their reasons."

"You're right. We all have our circumstances."

For a while, the car was silent except for the music playing as they cruised along the coastline. The blue of the sky and the sea slowly spread out across the afternoon.

"I'm sure that man has his reasons too," Romi said suddenly after a while of seeming lost in her own thoughts.

"That man?"

"The man we're looking for. The one we'll probably never find."

"Oh right. Of course."

"I was thinking about what I would say to him if I did see him again." Romi waited for a moment, yielding to the car nosing into their lane from the next one over.

"What would you say?"

"Well, I'm not sure. It could be better not to say anything at all."

As the car merged, its driver flashed the hazard lights three times, a sign of thanks. Romi stepped on the gas again.

"Because I don't know his situation," she went on.

"Of course. You'd need to know that before you'd have anything to say to him."

"I don't care about anything else, but I'd really like to know at least that much."

Hadam mulled over these words. Once you knew a person's situation, you could no longer claim to be an irrelevant character in their story. So many things became relevant to you then. For the first time since Hadam had started this project, she felt a slight sense of fear. Of what would happen if they couldn't find Honeyman. Of what would happen if they did.

The third place they visited was at the top of a hill with a view of the distant sea. It was surrounded by grass and gave off an especially invigorating feeling. According to Jaewoong, this place was a shared living space for young farmers returning to their hometowns on Jeju, transplants from the mainland, and long-term travelers. It was more or less a community of various people coming together to live, share information, and help one another with their work. Someone Jaewoong had filmed something for once had given him the address.

"Nol," the community house, was a white, two-story building in the shape of the Korean letter ㄷ, a multi-unit home where each household had its own entrance. In the center was a glass-roofed courtyard garden where people hung out and ate together. The surf-themed café out front had all kinds of surfing gear on display, including boards in all different colors, as well as comfy seating like hammocks and beanbag chairs spread around the space. From the café ceiling hung a sign featuring swelling waves and the name "Dilla" in italics. The owner explained that "dilla" was a word for carefree, laid-back people. "Nol," too, was a reference to the Korean word "nolda," meaning "to hang out," but it was also the Korean word for a giant wave.

Romi thought the café owner resembled Moana, the Disney character. Maybe it was because of her long, curly hair and tanned skin. She seemed as cool and refreshing as the blues that decorated her café.

"You won't find a better place to feature in a documentary about starting a new life on Jeju," the owner said. Fittingly, the Moana of Jeju was named Mo Ayoung. She had greeted Romi and Hadam and offered them a tour of the house.

"Our Nollers—that's what we call our residents—work in all different fields and are all different ages. We mostly host lots of singles or families without children, though. We've got people who work in agriculture or at companies here, as well as artists and surfers. We even have folks who make things like clothes or books. Our kitchen is a huge common area we all use together. And we share more than just food. Every weekend, we host our Mixing and Buzzing event, where we hang out and socialize, and sometimes we invite guest speakers, so we get to attend lectures and performances too. In the summer, we have a surfing class, and in the winter, we offer yoga classes. We're kind of like a Northern European co-op."

Hadam was excited to film all the different areas around the shared house. There was a joy in discovering the perfect shots. The kind of footage she had wanted to include in the documentary from the beginning, back in the planning stages—it was all here. One of Hadam's goals for the film was to show the new kinds of residences that had emerged where no such places had been, as well as how a more traditional way of life allowed for people to live in harmony.

The white walls in the hallway leading from the surf café to the courtyard garden reminded Hadam of a gallery exhibit, showcasing color and black-and-white photos of people who had stayed at Nol over time.

"I would love to turn this space into an exhibition hall or a museum someday," Ayoung explained, breezing past the photos on the walls. "A place to show how the history of the people here is interwoven with the history of the island."

While Hadam captured a shot of the length of the hallway, Romi glanced at the photos, stopping in front of one of the black-and-white images and taking a closer look. She turned to say something to Hadam, but her friend was paying her no mind as she chatted with Ayoung.

"How long has Nol been open?"

"About five years now? Just barely enough time to settle in."

"Then are there people who've been here for a while?"

"We have some who've lived here for more than two years, and some who've stayed for a month. When we were planning the house, my friend who runs it with me and I made it one of our goals to give people flexibility. So we divided the complex into units that can accommodate different household sizes. Each unit has its own parking too."

"Are all the units filled at the moment?"

"Not all of them. We usually have a lot of folks from spring through fall, and then people leave in the winter, so sometimes the units are empty. These days, though, we tend to get a lot of long-term folks who stay at least six months, so I think we'll need to adjust the number of units we have that can accommodate them."

Hadam carefully broached the subject she had come to discuss. "You know," she said, "our film is also going to be about beekeeping."

Ayoung nodded easily. "Of course. I heard all about that from Mr. Kim Manseop. We have a beekeeper staying here as well. I think it would be great for you to meet him. He's really enthusiastic about what he does. And he's been living here in our community for a long time. In fact, he's right outside, so you should be able to meet him soon. But . . ."

In the meantime, Romi had made her way to the end of the hall and now stood before the glass door facing the courtyard. All kinds of potted green plants were placed throughout the space to give it a feeling similar to a real garden. Blue light lingered in the air. In the center of the courtyard was a huge white birch table with long benches on either side.

There was only one person out there at that moment—a man with short hair wearing a plaid shirt. He was sitting at the table, reading something that looked like an academic journal in English.

He looked up at Romi when she opened the glass door.

Ayoung tugged on Hadam's sleeve. "There's one small problem," she said quietly.

Hadam lowered her camera and turned to Ayoung. Just as it seemed Ayoung was about to say something, Romi strode toward the table. Now that the clouds had lifted and the weather had cleared up, the glass rooftop itself was the same blue as the sky. That blue was even reflected in the man's eyes. Romi stood before him, looking down at him where he sat.

"Found you," she said.

Hadam, who had been listening closely to Ayoung, sensed that the atmosphere had grown serious and looked over.

Romi called out to Hadam, louder. "We found him. He's the one."

Hadam watched them—Romi and the man in the plaid shirt, staring at each other in the sunlight that flooded into the yard through the glass.

Quietly but still loud enough to be heard by listening ears, Ayoung whispered, "Three years ago, he lost his memory in an accident."

Hadam's eyes went wide. She turned back to Ayoung. "What?"

In the dignified manner of an emissary, Ayoung recounted the tragedy. "Yes. He can't remember anything that happened prior to his car accident. His wife died that day, and he lost his memory from the shock."

EVEN IF YOU CAN'T REMEMBER, IT'S THERE

The man dragged the chair across the floor with a grating sound. But he made no move to sit down and slammed his fists on his desk instead. He felt a sudden, uncontrollable surge of heat, like a volcano had erupted inside him.

He hardly remembered how he had gotten from the guesthouse in Seogwipo to his own home. He'd almost mowed down the entire guesthouse or surf café or whatever kind of place it was when he saw Romi with another guy, but he'd just barely managed to calm himself down and leave before it came to that. He'd nearly crashed into those two ditzes in the rental car, too, but they had swerved to escape him like a pair of scared little mice.

Romi had come to Jeju to find that damned guy from three years ago. He'd never considered that she still hadn't forgotten him. The mere thought of them together made his blood boil, then go cold, over and over again. He banged on the desk a few more times. The pain didn't even register.

A moment later, once his breathing had steadied and his anger gradually came to settle in the pit of his chest, he sat down in the chair, tilted his head back, and began to coldly, carefully weigh the situation.

First of all, he couldn't stand by and watch Romi reunite with that guy. It had been one thing when he didn't know about the other man, but now that he did, he couldn't allow it. Couldn't just swallow the fact that Romi had come here in search of someone else.

But he had to be more alert. He couldn't afford to make a mistake like last time. He remembered what happened three years ago. While he'd been loitering around the exhibition center and waiting for the chance to approach her, he'd lost the initiative. And then there was the accident. Even after all that, no one had been keeping an especially close eye on him, but now he couldn't be sure. The closer he got to Romi, the greater the danger seemed to grow.

But it was a danger worth enduring. An electrifying thrill coursed through his veins. He stood, picked up the photos on the desk, and stuck them to the board on the wall. They were photos he had taken of Romi while trailing her for several days. In a handful of them, she wore a sunny, utterly unsuspecting smile.

It's true, he thought, tapping Romi's face in the photos with his finger. *You still have no idea. You still haven't found anyone.*

The fact that Romi still didn't know the whole truth was an opportunity for him. *I'll be able to jog her memory myself.* He locked eyes with her in one of the photos. This was nothing to be angry over. He had time. Time to either reward or punish Romi for forgetting about him and finding herself another man.

A chuckle escaped his lips. For a long time, he couldn't stop laughing.

As soon as Chakyung arrived at Nol that evening and spotted Romi and Hadam, she asked breathlessly, "So you mean to tell me the guy actually had amnesia all this time? Like—like in some kind of K-drama?"

"I told you it was a possibility," Romi said. She was lying on a beanbag chair, hands folded over her stomach. Chakyung couldn't see her expression, but she couldn't imagine Romi was feeling all that proud to have correctly guessed this secret.

"And it turns out," said Hadam cautiously from where she sat on the edge of the sofa, casting a glance toward Romi, "he was also a married man."

Chakyung sighed.

"I suppose any of our guesses could be true. He was interested in me. He wasn't interested in me. He was interested in me but had no confidence. And he was a married man. One who also has amnesia." Still staring at the ceiling, Romi spoke as if she were reciting the lyrics to a song. Her voice betrayed no upset feelings. She seemed lost in thought.

Hadam painstakingly relayed the information they had gathered about the guy. His name was Seo Kyungwoon. He was thirty-six years old. He'd studied animal husbandry at a university in Seoul and was working a regular job before he moved down to Jeju with his wife, who was pursuing a PhD. They had been living on Jeju for three years, running all sorts of experiments to refine the traditional beekeeping process, when they got into the accident that killed his wife. The beekeeping work had been left to someone else while he was being treated in Seoul, but a few months ago, he'd returned to Jeju at last.

Chakyung also chose her words with care. "And, Romi, you recognized him right away, didn't you? Even though he couldn't remember you."

Romi unclasped her fingers and tried to push herself up on her elbows, groaning as the beanbag chair shifted. Hadam went over and reached out a hand to pull her up.

"Phew." Romi sat up properly in the chair. "It's been three years, so he's changed a bit. It was hard for me to recognize him right away. His face was scarred from the accident. I wasn't one hundred percent sure at first, but—there was that hallway leading out of the café. With all the photos on the wall."

"It was already evening when I got here, plus I was rushing to check in. I didn't even know there were any photos," Chakyung said.

"There are—of all the people who've ever stayed here. I saw him clear as day in one of them, the way he looked three years ago. Wearing the same clothes he wore the first day he came to see me, that same jacket, and standing in front of the same car he'd been driving initially. And then there he was, sitting in the garden."

Romi remembered the moment she had spotted Kyungwoon earlier that day. Her looking down, him looking up. The two of them facing each other like that, the sun shining on the strands of hair that fell over his forehead. He set down the English journal he had been reading and opened his mouth. His low, heavy voice sounded strange but familiar.

"Do we know each other?"

For a while, Romi couldn't respond. *Has he forgotten me?* She thought she hadn't been expecting anything, yet a sense of disappointment bloomed inside her. There hadn't been a concrete shape to her anticipation, but she realized this disappointment was now taking up the space once held by her secret hopes.

Kyungwoon seemed to pick up on that.

"I'm sorry," he said. "I was in an accident and lost my memory."

His tone was apologetic enough, but there was also a hollowness to his voice that gave away nothing more and nothing less about his own condition. Romi felt his voice like a bass in her heart before she heard it in her ears.

"When I heard his voice, my heart started racing. Not jumping up and down, either, but leaping all over the place. I felt like it was darting everywhere. I remembered. I remembered him," Romi said.

Chakyung and Hadam exchanged a look. It wasn't some complicated thing for a single woman's heart to race because of a single man. But there was still one loose end that remained.

"Romi," Chakyung said, "are you okay with the fact that he was married when you met him three years ago?"

Hadam looked sharply at Romi too. "Right. Aren't you upset?"

Romi lay on her back atop the beanbag chair again. "Hmm . . ." The room fell silent once more as she drifted into her thoughts. After a while, she answered, "I'm not sure."

"What?" her friends asked.

"It's like I'm upset, but I'm also not."

Hadam raised her voice. "Still, this man deceived you. Showing an interest in you when he was already married."

"But we can't know that's what really happened," Romi whined. "He never said he was married, but he never said he wasn't either."

"Was he wearing a ring?" Chakyung asked, raising her finger.

"I didn't notice one three years ago—I don't think he was."

Chakyung studied her own hands, absent of any rings, and considered this. There were lots of married people who opted not to wear theirs. There were also those who intentionally removed theirs before they went out.

"He could have taken it off before coming, since he came from work," Hadam murmured to herself, as if reading Chakyung's thoughts. But Chakyung could detect a trace of dissatisfaction in Hadam's voice.

She felt the same thing herself. Still, this wasn't something she could meddle in. It wasn't easy to meet someone who could set your heart racing three years ago and even now. It suddenly occurred to Chakyung that she had felt that same thrill recently, but she tried to suppress that thought.

"And there's a chance we shouldn't have read his coming to see me as being interested in me," Romi said evenly. "If our analysis of his signals was all wrong, then he didn't lie about anything. I wasn't deceived." She said this last sentence with emphasis, as if putting a period on the whole situation.

Chakyung knew it would be better to believe that had been the case. But she didn't.

Our analysis wasn't wrong. He definitely had feelings for her.

But there was no way to know, because Honeyman in his present state couldn't remember anything. Even if he'd liked Romi, and even if he had been deceiving her, or if he had just been reasonably curious about her, the past had been permanently sealed away in a bog of the unknown.

Were feelings you couldn't remember having no different from feelings you never had? Could you simply say there had never been any feelings now that they'd been completely forgotten?

These were questions to which no one had the answers.

Hadam and Romi decided to stay at Nol for a few days. Hadam planned to gather as much information as she could about the co-op to include in the documentary. She'd asked Romi whether it would be uncomfortable for her to stay there, too, but Romi calmly waved off the concern. Nol didn't usually rent out rooms for such a short period of time, but peak season was over and people were leaving, so there'd been an empty room available.

"Chakyung, you should stay here with us too. This unit was meant for a family, so it has two bedrooms. We heard the previous occupants were a mom and her elementary school–aged kids. The living room is huge too. We could hang out together at night."

Chakyung considered the suggestion. Spending the trip with her friends did seem like it'd be more fun and a boost to her mood, but it wouldn't be easy to share a two-bedroom place among the three of them for several days. She said she needed to think more about it.

Ayoung came to let them know dinner would be held in the courtyard. Folks usually cooked in the shared kitchen and ate separately or else brought out meals to share, but once a week, Ayoung provided a meal, and all the residents helped out.

So this was the sort of space that was worthy of the label "hip," Chakyung thought, looking around the interior of the building and at all the people there. The gallery hall that connected the café to the courtyard, the small door that led through the back of the shared kitchen beside the cafeteria, and the door to the residential complexes—they were all connected by three paths. A grass field spread out from the buildings as a kind of yard with several small benches throughout. In the summer, the courtyard got a lot of sunlight, and in the winters when it snowed, the space transformed into the picture of quaint elegance, but the indoor air-conditioning and heating seemed incredibly difficult to manage. It was a good idea, though, having the glass roof over the courtyard garden so it could double as a sunroom. A new sort of energy was flowing through this place, one that could easily appeal to the public. It was a place a person would want to try living in at least once in their life. Rather than any personal longing for that lifestyle, Chakyung had a practical interest in the space. She could see her company forming a partnership with the co-op later on and making it into a project.

The current residents of Nol—the Nollers—were a couple in their forties preparing for the opening of their bookstore and book-art exhibit near the Seogwipo Maeil Olle Market; two women somewhere in their late thirties to early forties who worked for a company in Seoul but were spending a month on Jeju on sabbatical; a man in his twenties who had quit his job and was traveling—and then there was their Honeyman, Kyungwoon.

As Ayoung came out with that day's meal of grilled salmon over rice, a man in his thirties stood to help her, bending down a bit to take the tray from her and bring the food to the table to share. When he set a bowl down in front of Chakyung, she bowed slightly in thanks and noted the burn marks on his hands. Based on what Hadam had said earlier, this had to be Kyungwoon.

"Thank you," she said.

So this was their Honeyman. As she ate, Chakyung kept stealing glances at him where he sat, diagonal from her. There were traces of the accident on his face, too, but he must have had surgery, and the scars themselves were almost completely faded, so they didn't stand out. Chakyung couldn't tell whether his melancholic expression was due to the accident or his natural disposition. She'd heard he hadn't lost his memory completely, but that he was missing scattered memories of incidents from the year or so before the crash. He didn't seem like much of a talker, but when people spoke, he focused on listening, nodding and even smiling gently as he did. The handful of times he opened his mouth, his voice was calm and unhurried. Chakyung could see what Romi had liked about him. Still, an uneasy feeling spread out beneath her heart like sand.

When Chakyung tuned back into the conversation, Hadam was in the middle of asking about the Nollers' lifestyles on Jeju. What had brought them here, how they felt about their lives on the island. They were the kind of questions you would expect to hear on a show like *Documentary Three Days*, but everyone had their own history.

"This place is pretty huge, but how many people usually stay here? There are probably tons of folks here in the summer, right?"

Ayoung answered, "It depends, but there are lots of people who stay here for two months in the summer. A lot of them come here for marine sports. We also run a surf shop, after all."

"It seems like there's a lot that goes into overseeing Nol. It's amazing you're able to run a shop alongside it."

Chakyung thought of Sumi, whom she had met yesterday at the Honeycomb Guesthouse. She couldn't help but admire the absolute vigor of the people who moved to Jeju.

"A friend of mine runs the surf shop with me," said Ayoung. "I don't know the first thing about surfing. He's in Hawaii at the moment. Meeting surfers and making purchases."

The bookstore owner cut in. "Oh, Taylor went to Hawaii? To surf?"

Kyungwoon, not Ayoung, responded. "Not just to surf, but on business. He said he would stop by Seoul on his way back too."

"Oh, is Taylor the owner of the surf shop?" Romi asked. "Is he American? Does he live in Hawaii?"

The people at the table suddenly burst out laughing. Chakyung and Hadam looked at each other, also confused. A man in his twenties with a goatee said teasingly, "He's not American. That's just his nickname. It's related to his job. But right now, he's running the shop, which has nothing to do with his main line of work. You'll know him when you see him."

Ayoung pointed to Kyungwoon. "He's Kyungwoon's younger cousin. I know everyone's different to a degree, but those two are total opposites."

The man in his twenties chimed in again. "Taylor is Kyungwoon's cousin?"

Kyungwoon nodded quietly. "Yeah. He's my mom's sister's son. That's why our last names are different."

Chakyung silently listened to this conversation. Hawaii and surfing. Two words that reminded her of someone. A sense of foreboding crept up on her like someone approaching her from behind and grabbing her by the shoulders. But there was no way, right? Jeju may have been an island, but it was still an entire province in itself. A big place with tons of people. It stood to reason lots of surfers were there too.

"At any rate, Taylor's still a newcomer to the world of surfing, so he has lots of friends who help him with the work. Depending on the season, they're all roaming the seven seas, but he has another young friend staying here now," Ayoung explained. Chakyung kept trying not to look back at the premonition she felt tapping her on the shoulder.

"Oh, speak of the devil—here he is." The wife from the couple in their forties pointed out the person coming through the kitchen door. This time, Chakyung couldn't resist turning around.

Jeju was huge. But on the map of chance and destiny, nowhere was *that* huge. Jeju was suddenly small enough that you could run into someone you had seen that morning again that afternoon.

The kitchen door was low, so Soo-eon had to hunch over a bit to step through it. Chakyung recognized him at once. Straightening his back, he gave Ayoung and the Nollers a nod of his head and a bright smile. It seemed like an incredibly long time passed before his eyes came to land on Chakyung.

"Oh?" His grinning face briefly took on a look of surprise, but he was soon back to smiling. Chakyung recalled what Romi had said earlier. *My heart started racing. Not jumping up and down, either, but leaping all over the place. I felt like it was darting everywhere.*

If she had understood those words in her head earlier, she now could feel them, palpable, in her chest.

Romi had never thought of her observational skills as being one of her strengths; they really weren't. Nonetheless, she was confident she had a decent ability to read the room—and that ability always went in unusual directions.

Today, her room-reading ability was fully focused on Chakyung and the surfer guy who had just arrived.

First of all, they didn't seem like strangers or two people who'd never met before.

"What brings you here?" the surfer guy asked, taking the empty seat across from Chakyung.

"My friends are staying here. I'm not, though."

Romi remembered Chakyung mentioning earlier that she was still thinking about whether to stay there or not—though it was possible she had made up her mind in the meantime.

"Oh, how do you two know each other?" Ayoung asked, setting a plate in front of Soo-eon and looking back and forth between them.

"We met on the same flight to Jeju, er, well, from Hawaii first," Chakyung answered quickly.

"Ah, so that's the nature of your relationship—crossing the Pacific together," the husband from the bookstore couple in their forties joked with zero subtlety.

The surfer guy picked up his chopsticks right away and dug a piece out of the grilled salmon. "We also ran into each other this morning on Jungmun Beach," he added.

Chakyung spoke up quickly yet again. "Right, by chance."

Before the surfer took a bite of his fish, he glanced up at her and broke into a grin. "Yes. By chance that time."

Hmm. What a strange way to word it, "that time," Romi thought with interest. *Did he plan on their having another run-in—on purpose?*

Second of all, there was a distance between them that didn't seem friendly but also didn't seem like the distance between two people who didn't know each other at all.

Romi knew Chakyung was by nature an adherent to social etiquette. They had been friends for a long time, but even now, she still spoke formally with Romi and Hadam. Despite that, Romi had never thought of Chakyung as being stiff. She could even carry on a friendly conversation with someone she was meeting for the first time. But it seemed like she was maintaining an odd distance between herself and this surfer guy. He was on friendly terms with all the other people staying at the co-op, but with Chakyung, he seemed unusually careful. All throughout dinner, they didn't look directly at each other, chatting instead with the people next to them. But even this didn't seem like how strangers would behave, Romi thought. Rather, if they were strangers, wouldn't they have talked to each other even more, feigning an appropriate amount of friendliness?

"Now that you brought up Hawaii, I remembered—my friend was apparently on the same plane as you, Soo-eon. She's a flight attendant. She asked me if the name of the place where I was staying was Nol and whether I knew you," said the twentysomething guy whose name Romi didn't remember as he stacked his cup of water in his empty bowl. He had that goatee that didn't suit him, so Romi mentally nicknamed him Goat Guy.

"Oh, really? Who's your friend?"

"She's a stunner, the type you won't easily forget once you've seen her. She has something of a baby face." Goat Guy was grinning, clearly insinuating something. It was a look that said, *You get my drift.* But Surfer Guy didn't have the quick wit to play along.

"Maybe it was the person who served the meals on my side of the plane? But how did she know I was staying here?"

"You had to fill out the arrival form on your way back. She must have seen it then. I think she said you had written the Nol Community House."

"Oh, I see."

"A flight attendant shouldn't look at a passenger's personal information like that. And it's especially unprofessional to share it with other people," one of the women who looked to be in her midthirties chimed in, sounding stern. She had her hair tied up in a bandanna and was wearing bohemian-style clothes, but ironically the shape of her mouth made her look somewhat like a teacher.

Another woman at the table in a black-and-white-striped T-shirt with three-quarter sleeves, whose long arms made her look like an elegant spider, furtively elbowed her friend. Romi inwardly gave her the name Ms. Charlotte—the name of the spider in a children's book she liked. Her friend, Romi decided, would be called Ms. Bandanna. She had already long forgotten the names she'd heard earlier.

"She probably just saw the information by chance and mentioned it since he was staying in the same place as her friend," Ms. Charlotte said generously, glancing between Ms. Bandanna and Goat Guy.

"Right, right, you have to understand. I don't know whether my flight attendant friend looked at Soo-eon and took an interest in him. But anyway, she had nothing but compliments for the guy."

"What kind of compliments?" asked Moana—no, Ayoung—as she paused in the middle of getting up to collect the empty bowls. Everyone else at the table seemed deeply interested in this story. Even Ms. Bandanna, who'd criticized the flight attendant's professionalism before, showed keen interest. Only Chakyung seemed not to be paying any attention, getting up and helping to tidy up the table too.

"Apparently, he was way too nice yet again. He saw some poor person in a bad situation and couldn't pass them by. He sat next to a Chinese woman on her way to see her daughter, and this lady had all sorts of different allergies, so she couldn't eat the flight meals. Soo-eon noticed and interpreted all that for her in a note to my flight attendant friend."

"Oh, Soo-eon, you're amazing. You speak Mandarin?" the book-artist wife from the bookstore couple said, hands clasped in appreciation. Surfer Guy shyly scratched at his cheek.

"No, I only know a little bit of Mandarin, so I didn't do a great job—I even had to use a translator app. They're pretty decent nowadays, you know."

"He handed my friend a note, so at first, she thought he wanted something from her," Goat Guy said, cutting a look at Ms. Bandanna as he spoke. "That would have been against regulations, so she felt flutters—I mean, flustered, but when she looked at the note, that was what it said. She was relieved after that and thought, *What a sweet guy.*"

"I guess even that sort of thing happens on planes. Like in the movies," Hadam said, looking at Chakyung.

In a dry, formal tone, Chakyung replied, "I suppose so. I was so exhausted, I kept falling asleep, so I didn't see any of that happen."

At that, Surfer Guy's eyes returned to Chakyung. She refused to meet his gaze.

"Well, it's a relief you didn't see anything. Because it was nothing like a movie. I was just trying to help, and the flight attendant was just doing her job."

Surfer Guy's tone was so firm that it seemed to embarrass Goat Guy. Only then did he stop talking, but who knew whether the conversation would continue later when only the two of them were there?

Romi thought she saw the corners of Chakyung's lips twitch. Was she mistaken? Was she not? But she didn't have long to muse on it, because Honeyman spoke up.

"Soo-eon is a warmhearted guy. If he sees someone having a hard time, he doesn't know how to look the other way. He's scared of bees, but he still helps me transport the hives around my bee farm."

Kyungwoon wore a gentle smile. Romi realized that day was the first time she had seen his smile. It was one that gently swept up the subtle emotions floating around inside her heart like a broom.

Soo-eon shuddered exaggeratedly.

"Ugh, still, I really am terrified of bees. When I was little, I got stung by one on a field trip."

"Oh, come on. Forget about that. And if you're not busy, help me out on the farm tomorrow. We wouldn't be doing anything where you could get stung."

Without thinking, Romi raised her hand. "I'll do it."

The others turned their attention to her, but she stared directly into Honeyman's eyes.

"I'm going there anyway, so I'll help you. I've always been . . . really interested in it."

A suspicious glint shone in Kyungwoon's eyes. "In beekeeping?"

Romi nodded. "Yes. In beekeeping."

Kyungwoon studied her, and Romi suddenly felt like he was a stranger. And it was true that he was, considering he didn't remember a single thing about her. The feeling was strange enough to overshadow her own excitement. She lowered her hand slowly, unconsciously. A moment later, Kyungwoon nodded as if to say he understood something now.

"Sure. Why not? Then let's go there together tomorrow. I'll be heading out around ten in the morning, if that's all right with you?"

"Of course," Romi answered before the question was even fully out of his mouth. She didn't ask what they were going to be doing or where. She didn't even try to comprehend why she was agreeing to tag along with this man. Hadam and Chakyung each shot her a look, but neither of them had anything to add.

When dinner ended, everyone got up and busied themselves with cleaning. The men carried the plates to the kitchen, while the women wiped down the table and cleaned the floors. It was an awkward position for anyone who was left sitting still with nothing to do. The bookstore couple brought out some beer. It was the new brand from a Jeju distillery whose owners they were on good terms with, so they'd gotten it as a gift. Chakyung volunteered to make a few quick snacks to go with the drinks.

"When I was in school, I worked part-time at a bar," she explained.

Romi had already known this, but each time she heard it, it seemed as surprising as it had been the first time. It was hard to imagine Chakyung working at a bar. Chakyung consulted with Ayoung about the available ingredients and decided to make a non-spicy sea-snail salad and some stir-fried bacon and mung bean sprouts.

After three or four rounds of drinks, everyone was red in the face. Their volume in decibels had increased steadily as well, and because of the glass ceiling, their voices reverberated. The first person to pick up on the sound of other guests outside was Ms. Bandanna.

"I think you have customers?" she said. "Isn't the café closed?"

"Yeah, I thought we wouldn't have any customers today, so I closed up the shop, but I must not have locked the doors. I should go out and tell whoever it is that we're finished serving for the day." Ayoung set down her glass and hurried inside to the café. The muffled sounds of conversation followed shortly after.

At first, Romi didn't pay much attention to what was going on outside. What was happening inside was far more interesting. First, she thought, she had to figure out whether the calm expression on Kyungwoon's face reflected his true feeling or whether he was displeased. She was also interested in the scene playing out as Surfer Guy quickly took plates of bar food from Chakyung and locked eyes with her. Romi noticed that Chakyung didn't meet his eyes. But when Ms. Charlotte stuck out her neck to see what was happening in the café, Romi found herself turning toward that direction too.

"Is it a customer for the café?" Ms. Charlotte asked. "Maybe someone looking for a room?"

They could faintly see people at the end of the gallery hallway that connected the café and the courtyard. Romi stuck her head out like Ms. Charlotte had. The customer appeared to be a man. His voice traveled down the hall.

"I was interested, so I wanted to see . . ."

At the sound of that, Chakyung—who had been chatting with Surfer Guy—flinched and looked over. Her senses were unusually sharp. Her ears perked up like a cat's upon hearing a noise in the dark. A moment later, Ayoung and the customer came up the hallway together, the customer's voice growing closer. All the people who had been sitting around chatting turned to look. The voices in the courtyard quieted to a hush.

"If you're not planning to stay here right away, you can take a look around first. To help you decide later on . . ."

Standing behind the petite Ayoung, the new customer was strapping and tall. Romi's first impression was that he looked like a true-blue city guy. Her next impression was that with those glasses on, he looked familiar. Where had she seen him before?

"Oh?"

Chakyung came out from around the table and approached the newcomer. As soon as he saw her, his mouth opened halfway, but no sound came out. He just adjusted his glasses. Like he couldn't believe his eyes.

"Chanmin. What are you doing here?"

Chakyung's voice was dripping with suspicion, which soon spread to the people around her.

As soon as she heard his name, Romi remembered that this guy was Chakyung's fiancé. She had seen his face at some point in one of the photo albums on Chakyung's phone. In the pictures, he'd looked composed and coolheaded, but she was surprised to see that he was capable of the expression he wore at that moment. How to describe it? He looked like someone trying to pretend he hadn't been completely caught off guard, the gears in his brain turning at full speed to figure out how he would explain his way out of this situation.

Romi was curious about what he would say. But she wouldn't get to hear his answer, because at that moment, Chakyung's cell phone started to ring.

SOMETIMES YOU CAN BE DECEIVED

Chanmin hurried to the car. He knew Chakyung and the others were watching him from the guesthouse entrance, but he had no time to delay.

"That was fast—you said you'd be a while." Just as the woman in the passenger seat pushed her jet-black hair over her shoulders and turned to glance behind them, Chanmin snapped, "Don't look!"

Risa pressed her red lips shut, shrugging as she faced forward again. "There's nothing to yell about. Quit acting like you're being followed."

Without a word, Chanmin pulled off. His mouth shut tight, he started turning over all sorts of explanations in his head on the ride up to Sagyebung-ro and for a while after. He could cook up a story to explain the identity of the person in the passenger seat, but as for the reason he'd gone to Nol . . . Should he say he went by to scout out the place where he'd be attending a workshop in the spring? Would Chakyung believe him? She wasn't easy to fool. But he had to come up with a lie she could at least pretend to believe. His blood pressure was starting to rise. He relaxed his grip on the steering wheel.

He cast a sidelong glance at Risa. Her expression looked cold, but she hadn't asked him a single question the whole time they'd been in the car. That was one thing he liked about her—she wouldn't say a word when it was clear the other person didn't want to talk.

"Sorry. I was a little oversensitive back there."

In response to his apology, too, Risa's expression didn't change. She just pretended it didn't matter to her either way.

"It's fine. It's not like I don't know how testy you can be. You must have run into someone you knew in there and gotten yourself all worked up."

Chanmin didn't respond to that. "I should head back east tomorrow," he said. "There's not much to see out this way."

"I'm meeting up with my team in the afternoon—we have to prepare for our conference panel. Didn't you say you had people you'd need to meet with too, Dr. Yang?"

Another good thing about her—Risa wasn't merely some woman he'd picked up on another night out with his friends, but one of the graduate students on his previous project team. When he first recognized her at the club the night before, he'd been taken aback, but at the same time, he reasoned this was probably for the best. He wouldn't need to tell Chakyung a complete lie on that front. All he had to say was that they were taking part in a conference together. Chakyung was on Jeju, and he'd known it would be a risky move doing business here, but the island was huge, and he'd carelessly thought nothing would come of it. His carelessness always made such a mess of things.

"I can just meet up with them briefly. Then again, I might not."

"Then we can grab dinner."

Chanmin didn't think they could, since it would be weird for him not to meet up with Chakyung. But he couldn't explain that to Risa. As he ran through all the items on his schedule, juggling plans in his mind, Risa pointed out his cell phone ringing in the phone holder in front of him.

"Someone's calling you."

Honeyman. Chanmin hesitated, hands gripping the wheel, while the phone insistently continued to ring.

"Should I answer it for you?" Risa asked, but when she reached for the phone, Chanmin batted her hand away.

"No. Hold on."

While he searched for a good spot to pull over, the phone stopped ringing. He saw a sign showing the way to Hwasun Port and turned onto that road.

"Why'd you turn down here?"

"Let's check out the ocean for a bit."

This late at night, even the occasional lights in the raw-fish restaurants seemed tired. The few boats anchored in the port all looked asleep, and only the fishing boats farther out on the water, roaming in the dark like nocturnal animals, gave any sense of life at all to the area. Chanmin got out of the car and held his face up to the salty breeze.

"If you're going to smoke, I'll just stay here."

He felt rather relieved that Risa wasn't getting out too. Chanmin walked toward the dock, an unlit cigarette in his teeth. Once he was far enough from the car, he took out his phone and tapped on his missed-call notification. Honeyman picked up after one ring.

"It's me."

Honeyman seemed to be holding back a lot of anger on the other end of the line. Chanmin didn't know how the news that he'd gone to Nol had traveled so fast, but he was soon badgered with questions about why he'd acted so rashly. As he was being pelted by Honeyman's barrage of words, Chanmin lit his cigarette.

"Look, I just went to scope out the situation. So we can be sure about the trade." He decided to switch from defense to offense. "You're the one who hasn't been great about communication lately, you know. It's like you had a change of heart."

He blew out a heavy cloud of smoke.

"Anyway, I hear you. I didn't mean to leave you out of the loop—I'm sorry. I won't act on my own again."

The light gray trail of smoke suffused with a sea breeze that soon blew away.

"I'll know what moves to make on D-Day. I'm ready on my end."

As he stood on the beach, the wind felt unusually strong to him that night. Like something big was coming head-on.

There was almost nobody in the lobby of the country club hotel. The low lighting gently illuminated the front desk, and it was so quiet that it was hard to believe any guests were staying there at all. The only one speaking up was Chakyung.

"So you're telling me you don't know where the golf bag is? Is this sort of thing even possible at such a first-class hotel?"

The hotel manager, front desk clerk, and concierge wore the same expressions as those dolls in the set of three that had been all the rage back in the day. The manager, a man in his fifties with a lean face, looked slightly terrifying, the clerk in her midtwenties seemed on the verge of tears, and the concierge in her late twenties wore a fixed smile.

The scary-looking manager spoke now. "We conveyed your message to the guest in room 420. Kim Mihye came by, picked up the golf bag, and left."

"I asked you to pass along the message to Lee Mihae, not Kim Mihye."

The manager's tone was polite but firm. "There was a slight mix-up with the names, but you told us she was staying in room 420. She must have assumed her name had been written incorrectly by the person who left the bag for her, so she took it with her and left."

Chakyung was at a loss for words. Wasn't this *his* fault? She tried to compose herself.

"Could you at least let me know her contact information?"

"Because the reservation wasn't made in Kim Mihye's name, she did not provide us with her contact information, and her companion who did make the reservation claimed not to know her number either and ended the call saying we should discuss it later. Therefore, we're not in a position where we can ask any further questions tonight . . ."

The manager trailed off and exchanged a look with the clerk. Chakyung could guess what it meant—they were afraid of others finding out that the person who had booked the room had come to this hotel with Kim Mihye. It was someone they needed to shield. And a hotel shouldn't probe into the secrets of its guests.

Beside them, the concierge listened quietly, looking sympathetic. She had been the one to accept the golf bag initially, but it was the clerk who had handed it over to Kim Mihye in room 420. Chakyung was the one who had brought the bag here for safekeeping. And the person who, after giving her the wrong hotel name in the first place, had suddenly called Chakyung up in the middle of the night screaming for her to go and find the missing bag was none other than Director Dim—er, Director Kim.

Chakyung had done nothing wrong besides show up at the Woonam Country Club Hotel like Director Kim had told her to and pass on the message he'd given her for Lee Mihae in room 420. He was the one who hadn't known the correct name of the hotel where his own wife was staying, and he hadn't given Chakyung so much as her phone number, but not a single word out of his mouth seemed to imply that any of this was his fault. Hadn't he been the one to mix up the hotels?

"Do you have any idea how much that bag is worth? You should have checked properly! Without that bag, tomorrow's golf outing will be ruined! I never thought you were stupid, Manager Yoon, but how could you be so careless?"

Earlier, when he was screaming at her on the phone, Chakyung had wanted to tell him to kindly spare her the BS, but she kept her mouth shut as she had done for her twelve years as an employee. He would find golf clubs to use somehow, she was sure, but he'd just wanted to take his anger out on her.

Now, Chakyung furrowed her brows. "Then are you saying you can get in touch with that person tomorrow?" she asked the front desk staff.

"We will inquire about the matter again in the morning."

"And you can't just give me the contact information directly? Or at least tell me where they're staying now?"

"That's against our hotel's policy," the manager said firmly. Chakyung could understand that. The manager was just doing his job earnestly and thoroughly. Chakyung was in the same position. She respected his professionalism and decided not to press him any further. As she nodded and took a step back, she watched some of the tension leave the corners of the manager's mouth. As if to show that he understood where she was coming from, too, the manager added kindly, "Fortunately, they're still staying on Jeju. We should be able to get in touch with them tomorrow."

Chakyung felt something brush against her and turned around. Soo-eon had placed a hand on her shoulder and was gently telling her, "Let's head back for now."

Chakyung nodded, feeling drained. The whole ordeal had become such a hassle, but she couldn't keep on making a fuss here. If she continued to fight back on this, she would only be a nuisance to all the people who had come here to rest and enjoy some quiet time.

"I'm sorry," she said.

Soo-eon stepped back so she could be the first to leave through the revolving doors.

Once they were outside in the parking lot, Soo-eon called out in the dark for her to stop. "Wait here for a second," he said.

Chakyung didn't even have the chance to question him before she heard the sound of footsteps clicking toward them.

Soo-eon raised his hand. "Over here."

At first, she couldn't tell who it was because they were hidden in the shadows, but once the person came closer, the blue lights in the parking lot illuminated their silhouette. Soon, a woman's freckled face appeared. It was the concierge from earlier.

"I waited for a good time and pretended I was stepping out to take a call." She held up her wristwatch to check the time. It was a new TAG Heuer watch that glinted under the parking lot lights. "I have to get back soon before they notice I'm gone."

"I'm sorry. For asking you for a favor like this."

"No, it was our mistake. The hotel didn't want to get caught up in the middle of this, but it feels wrong to pretend we know nothing." As she slipped something into Soo-eon's hand, she flashed Chakyung a smile. "I hope you find it."

Chakyung bowed to her, surprised.

The concierge waved to Soo-eon. "See you at the surf house next week!" she said, tossing Chakyung another smile before she ran back toward the hotel.

Chakyung watched her go, then turned to Soo-eon. His cheeks were puffed out as he read the note the concierge had given him.

"What is that?" Chakyung asked.

Soo-eon looked up at her and grinned.

"The phone number of a different travel companion of Kim Mihye's, and the name of the new hotel they're staying at."

The truck Soo-eon was driving rattled precariously over a speed bump. Chakyung found herself gripping the handle above her head.

"Oof, sorry. This thing is really shaky. It's a piece of junk, as you can tell, but it's definitely transported some delicate passengers before."

"No, it's fine. I think it's just the beer I had earlier coming back up."

"You didn't drink that much, though," Soo-eon said casually, turning left. As the wind swept through the darkness of the night, a couple leaves fell into the paths of the beams shining from the truck's headlights. Chakyung became newly aware that it was the middle of the night and the two of them were alone in a car of all places. But glancing over at Soo-eon, she saw that his face was completely free of any hint of panic. His skin was as tanned as one would expect of someone who'd spent all summer catching waves in the rays of the sun, but also strangely clear.

"Still, I'm the one who should be sorry. It's because I drank that you had to drive instead." A belated apology, but better than pretending she didn't owe him one.

"Well, it's no problem for me, driving at night. And aside from you, I'm the one who knows that golf bag the best. Actually, I might know it better, no? Since I'm the one who carried it."

He looked like he was holding in a laugh, the same as he'd been earlier. In front of Chanmin. When Chakyung could have easily been embarrassed in front of everyone.

"That's why I'm grateful," she said. *You saved me from humiliation,* she didn't say.

Soo-eon glanced over at her. "It's really no big deal."

His voice was gentle, like a warm wave of ocean water over her skin, but at the same time, it was as firm as a surfboard cutting through that water. She suddenly wanted to cry. But as always, in the face of a crisis, Yoon Chakyung was not the type to let anybody see her tears.

An hour earlier, Chakyung's conversation with Chanmin had been cut short when she answered Director Kim's call. Her face burned with embarrassment as she listened to her boss shouting loud enough that the people around her could hear him through the phone. She managed to squeeze in a calm apology and a promise to resolve the issue right away. With that, she ended the call. Everyone was staring at her, not saying a word, when the owner of the bookstore encouraged them all to finish cleaning up and the crowd dispersed at last.

Chakyung placed her hand over her chest and took a deep breath, then fixed her face and turned to Chanmin.

"I'm not sure how you knew to come here, but I think I need to head out early. Director Kim needs me to take care of something. Can we go together and talk in the car on the way? I was just drinking with everybody, so I'm no good to drive."

Chakyung was the one who had been drinking, but Chanmin's face was flushed an even deeper red. If shame had a color, would it be that shade?

"Well, the thing is . . . it'll be a bit difficult for me to take you right now."

Now it was Chakyung's turn to go red in the face. "Oh?"

"Why is that?" The bold question came from somewhere behind Chakyung. It was Romi. Hadam elbowed her in the ribs, but the look on Romi's face suggested that she'd asked out of pure curiosity.

Normally, she might have let it slide without an answer. Chakyung watched Chanmin's mouth helplessly hang open. But when Romi was determined, there was no one who could avoid a conversation with her. And when she was tipsy? Enough said.

"Oh, um. I came here with someone from the conference, so I should make sure they get back to their accommodations all right." Chanmin hesitated for a moment, then added, "I'll drop them off first and then come back."

"Where's their hotel?"

"About an hour from here."

Chakyung was at a loss for words again. If the hotel was an hour away, it would take him two hours to get back here. Romi cut in again.

"Hmm. Can't you bring that person with you on the way?" Seeing Chanmin growing flustered, Romi quickly added, "Or they can come inside and wait here with us?"

In Chakyung's mind, the scene unfolded with the companion who was waiting outside for her fiancé coming in and meeting everyone. Chanmin's face had gone as red as it could get and was now taking on a bluish hue like an incredibly hot fire. Hadam took Romi by the arm and covered her friend's mouth with one hand.

"So sorry, Chakyung. We've all been drinking, so there's no one here who can drive."

Right then, Soo-eon stepped up. "I can go," he said.

Chanmin looked him up and down, but Soo-eon didn't spare the other man so much as a glance. His eyes were on Chakyung the whole time he spoke.

"I didn't have anything to drink, so I can help you out. I'll go and grab my keys."

In the darkness ahead of them, a small truck emerged from behind a stone wall. It had a rental car license plate, and the driver didn't seem to know the area well, the truck inching slowly up the road. Soo-eon followed, keeping a good distance. Chakyung suddenly remembered the truck that had lit the road for her the day before. Somehow this one seemed familiar.

"Could it be . . ."

The moment Chakyung started to ask the question, her phone rang. The feeling of gentle calm that had been settling over her evaporated in an instant. The name she hated the mere sight of appeared on her screen.

"Yes, Director Kim."

Director Dim seemed a bit calmer now, but Chakyung was still upset just talking to him.

"So what happened?" he asked.

"Right, well, I got the contact information for the person who mistakenly took the golf bag and am on my way to find them now, since they weren't answering my calls. I feel bad, but I figured it would be best to go and see them in person."

Chakyung didn't mention that she'd actually gotten the contact information for an acquaintance of the person who'd taken the bag. She figured she should spare the few remaining hairs on Director Kim's head from falling out in shock.

"Of course. I know you're good at your job, Manager Yoon, so I expect you'll have this all handled for me by tomorrow morning. It took a lot to get this group of folks together, and I already told them about the new golf clubs I bought in the States, so if I show up without them, how do you think I'll look?"

Chakyung tried to tamp down the words threatening to escape her mouth in response.

"Understood. I'm sorry. I'm on it, and I'll contact you once I've tracked down the bag."

"All right. I'm trusting you, Manager Yoon."

Before he could continue blowing smoke up her ass, Chakyung ended the call. She tried to hide her trembling hands, and the moment she let out the deep breath she'd taken, her phone pinged with a message she'd missed while on the phone with Director Kim.

It was from Chanmin.

What happened? Your line is busy.

Rather than call him back, Chakyung fired off a text in reply.

I'm on my way to find the bag. I'll call you later.

Chanmin replied via text too.

Sure, you must be exhausted running around in the middle of the night. Your boss is kind of a jerk. Where are you? Want me to come to you?

Now? Chakyung remembered the sight of him earlier, getting into his car and taking off. She hadn't gotten a proper look at the person in the passenger seat, but their long, dark hair had caught Chakyung's eye. It was impossible to tell anything from that detail alone, but Chakyung couldn't ask him anything about it then. The tips of her fingers had gone cold, but at the same time, people were staring at her, making the back of her neck burn hot.

No, it's fine. I'll handle it. See you later.

Soo-eon must have clearly seen everything earlier when he'd come in through the front door of the café. Then and now, his face gave no hints about what he knew. He didn't ask any questions. Except one.

"Your boyfriend—does he know Kyungwoon?"

Chakyung was putting her phone away in her pocket when she was startled by the unexpected query. She didn't bother to correct Soo-eon about the fact that Chanmin wasn't merely her boyfriend, but her fiancé.

"No, I don't think so," she said.

But when she thought about it, she couldn't be sure. If he hadn't come to Nol to meet up with someone, she had no idea why Chanmin would have been there. What she did know was that whoever he'd come to see hadn't been her.

"Or maybe he does," she said. "I don't even know what he was doing there. It's not like he knew where I was and came to see me. He must have had some other business to attend to."

"I thought he mentioned to Ayoung that he was interested in staying there. And he was asking whether any beekeepers were living at Nol now."

Soo-eon mentioned this offhandedly, but it felt meaningful. Chakyung tried to answer just as casually.

"That's because his work is related to beekeeping. He works in a research lab. But it didn't seem like he knew Kyungwoon. If he did, he would've acted like it earlier."

"That's true. Ayoung thought they might be distantly related. She said she heard you mention his family name was Yang, which is Kyungwoon's aunt's family name too."

Soo-eon made a left, their tiny truck picking up speed. Through the window, Chakyung looked out at the night. Wasn't the truck too small to fit three people? There wasn't enough room for him and Chakyung plus the looming shadow of her fiancé inside.

"Are you a foreigner?"

Now that they'd discussed Chakyung, it seemed only fair to give Soo-eon the space to talk about himself as well. Relationships only began through these sorts of exchanges, through telling someone else about yourself. Chakyung was surprised that the word "relationship" had instinctively come to mind, even in the midst of the dizzying feelings that had been brought on by Chanmin and the woman with him.

"Oh, me?" Soo-eon pointed to himself.

Chakyung nodded.

"Yeah, I'm an American citizen. My father's American. I was born there too."

"But your name . . ."

"I have an American name, but my father thought I should use a Korean one. It's a long, complicated story. You sure you want to hear it?"

Chakyung hesitated. As much as she did, there was another part of her that didn't. If she listened to his long, complicated story, she felt like she might somehow become a part of it.

"Not now," she said. "Next time."

Soo-eon shrugged, one corner of his mouth quirking up. "Sure. You must be tired."

"I am." Chakyung turned away and leaned her head against the window, shutting her eyes. When she was tired, she liked to be left alone. And Han Soo-eon was someone who wore her out. Right now, more so than exhaustion, she felt a headache looming. Though her migraines tended to disappear soon after they set in, they kept coming back like an ex she'd grown tired of, just to be a pain. But a moment later, as the truck must have rumbled over something, Chakyung's head banged against the window and her eyes flew open. The truck had come to a sudden stop in the middle of the road.

"Whoa, are you okay?" Soo-eon pressed the button for the car's emergency lights and turned toward Chakyung, looking concerned.

Rubbing her forehead, she looked up. "I'm fine, but what—"

"Over there."

In the glow of the headlights, Chakyung could see the shape of something crouched in front of the truck, but she couldn't tell what it was right away. As soon as Soo-eon took off his seat belt and opened the door, the realization hit her, and she got out after him.

Soo-eon approached the heap of fluff on the road and knelt beside it. He reached out a hand and said gently, "Poor thing. You must have been so scared, huh?"

Beneath his huge hand, a puppy whose fur was probably white under all the grime was hunched over, trembling. It was barking in a quivering voice when its ears pricked up and it turned to watch Chakyung as she approached. The moment she hesitated, the dog leaped up and ran hobbling toward her, then rested its head against her legs and let out another bark.

"Poor thing must think you're its owner," Soo-eon said.

Chakyung crouched down and examined the dog. It looked all the more pitiful for having gotten wet from the evening dew and the thin mist coming down. Its fur was matted as though it had been wandering in the woods for several days, dirt caked up in places. It must not have been able to find a proper meal in that time, judging from its skinny belly and sunken eyes. But it didn't seem to be a stray.

Soo-eon came up beside her and sat, too, bowing his head to look the dog in the eye. At the sight of him, the dog let out a bark and clung even closer to Chakyung.

"There are lots of abandoned dogs on Jeju these days. Non-locals move here for a little while, adopt puppies, and dump them when they leave again. Before, people would raise them as outdoor dogs, but this little one looks too much like a pedigree pup for that. It might be a poodle?"

Chakyung petted its head. The dog rubbed its nose into her palm. Feeling its cold, moist snout on her hand, she felt so moved that it was like something heavy had smashed into her heart.

"We should take him with us. If we leave him here, he'll die. He might leap out in front of any car he sees, thinking his owner is inside, or else some wild animals might . . . might get to him. I'll take him back to my room for today and see if I can get him to a vet or animal shelter tomorrow."

"Don't you have somewhere you need to go first tonight?"

Soo-eon's dark eyes met hers. The puppy looked up at her as well. She understood what Soo-eon was saying. Scooping up the puppy, she stood. Her fingers buried deep in his fur, she could feel his skinny body underneath. Her heart ached.

"I can look for the golf bag tomorrow," she said. "Besides, it was already rude enough to go tracking down a stranger in the dead of night like this. No matter how urgent my boss says it is. Plus, I don't need to be running around following orders outside of work hours. I wasn't thinking straight. If we can't find his bag, I can just compensate him for the cost."

Holding the puppy to her chest, Chakyung got back in the truck, grinning. "Let's go back. I doubt it'll happen, but I honestly don't care if Director Dim gets brutally humiliated in front of everyone. In fact, it'd be a nice change of pace."

Soo-eon strode toward the truck and climbed into the driver's seat again. Once he was inside, he checked that Chakyung and the puppy were seated safely. The puppy's head rested on Chakyung's chest.

"I guess I was wrong," Soo-eon murmured to himself.

"Hmm?"

"Even when you're tired, apparently, you can still smile brighter than anything."

Chakyung looked over at him. His voice was as calm as it had been at the airport, but he wore a crooked smile, eyes shining with laughter.

"Let's head back, then," he said.

The puppy barked in lieu of Chakyung answering. She told herself that her face was warm because she was tired and tried her best to rein in her smile. The truck had felt too cramped with the two of them inside and the additional person weighing on her mind, but with the two of them and the puppy, it felt exactly right.

◆ ◆ ◆

Project: *Searching for Honeyman*

Day Five, Seogwipo

Just as Romi was sliding the fried egg she'd made out of the pan, Kyungwoon entered the kitchen and stopped short at the sight of her.

"Hello."

Startled, Romi spun around, the fried egg falling onto the plate with a thunk. "Ack!"

Kyungwoon approached the counter where she stood. "Are you all right?" he asked.

"No!"

At her frantic response, he worriedly examined her hand. "Are you hurt? Is something wrong?"

"Yes! The yolk broke!"

"I'm sorry?"

"I made the yolk look so pretty by soft-boiling the egg first! And the color came out so nice too!"

"I'm sorry . . ."

Kyungwoon seemed unable to find the words he was looking for and so was left with no choice but to repeat the same ones. Romi used a spatula to neaten up the egg on the plate.

"It's not working. You'll just have to eat this ugly little thing."

"I'm sorry?"

"We agreed to get up early this morning. To go to work."

Smiling sweetly, Romi sat a flustered Kyungwoon down at the dining table in front of a plate of toast, the fried egg, sausage, and tomato. "Let's eat together," she said.

Kyungwoon didn't seem to have as much of an appetite as Romi would have guessed. She watched him pick at the food on his plate. Yesterday afternoon, evening, and this morning as well—each time she saw his face, it looked strange. That might have been due to the traces of the accident. And she didn't mean the physical scars. It was as though he had a thin film over his face like a veil. Was it because he didn't remember her? Kyungwoon looked up, meeting Romi's eyes. As a reflex, she brought her mug of coffee closer.

"Romi. Do you know me?"

"Ah—sorry?"

She nearly burned her mouth on the hot coffee but tried to play it off.

"Yesterday when we met, you spoke to me like you knew me, but you never answered when I asked if you did. Even Ayoung said that was how it seemed."

Romi paused, wondering what to say. Should she tell him they'd met three years ago? Honesty was the best policy, as her mom had been telling her since she was a child.

"No, I don't know you. I must have been mistaken."

She had never been a close follower of her mother's teachings. That was how she'd ended up living the way she did. But she didn't want to say something that might needlessly upset someone who couldn't remember her. She'd heard before that she lacked self-respect, but at times like these, she wanted to protect the little she did have.

"I see." Kyungwoon raised his eyebrows slightly but said nothing more. Instead, he asked an unexpected question. "The man who came to see your friend yesterday—does he know me?"

Romi cocked her head. "No, I don't think so."

Romi and Hadam hadn't given much thought to the reason Chanmin had come to Nol. Chakyung had come back quietly in the dead of night, so there hadn't been a chance to ask her about it. Besides, it was clear the overall atmosphere still wasn't quite right for that conversation.

"Why do you ask?"

"Oh, it's just—I thought I'd seen him somewhere before. His name rang a bell, so I thought maybe he was someone I knew."

"Yang Chanmin? I heard his work is related to beekeeping, but if he knew you, wouldn't he have said so yesterday?"

"I guess you're right. But since I can't really remember . . ."

Just as Kyungwoon seemed prepared to accept her reasoning and move on, Romi asked, "But why did you think you knew him?"

Kyungwoon was about to answer when another man came into the kitchen through the entrance to the gallery in the hallway.

"Oh, hello."

The man wore a white T-shirt and bowed to greet Romi as soon as he spotted her, but she didn't recognize him right away. "Hello," she said. "But, um . . ."

His round face reminded her of Taiwanese milk tea, for some reason. Why was that?

"Oh, what brings you here? And so early too? No class today?" Kyungwoon asked, standing up and holding out his hand. He seemed to know the other man, who shook his hand with a bashful smile.

"Yep, no class today, and I had some business in Seogwipo this morning that I'm just getting back from. I decided to drop in to see you, of course—and to check that the guest who came to our school the other day and fainted is doing better."

The man politely gestured toward Romi with his hands, and only then did she realize who he was. The tapioca pearl guy with the smooth, round face from the Honeybee School. *That* was why the milk tea had come to mind. He was grinning at her good-naturedly—or so Romi thought. He was, in fact, looking at someone over her shoulder.

Hadam came in through the door that connected to the residences, her hair still wet and her eyes widening at the sight of Department Head Boo.

"Oh? Hello."

Department Head Boo bowed in greeting, smiling sheepishly. "Hello."

"What brings you here?" Hadam asked with some suspicion. The Honeybee School was in the opposite direction from Nol. It was a long way to have traveled this early in the morning.

"It was weighing on my mind, how you collapsed that day. And knowing I was to blame for it. Are you all right now?"

Hadam waved her hands, emphatic. "No, no, it was my fault. You didn't do anything wrong. And I'm completely fine, not a scratch on me."

"Still, I should have been better at keeping the bees under control. I meant to come and see you yesterday, but by the time I had finished up with work, it was too late. I'm sorry."

"It's my own fault for worrying you. I heard you carried me and ran all the way to the hospital, and I didn't even get the chance to thank you."

"Oh no, it wasn't all the way there. I just carried you into the building . . ."

When it became clear they had the energy to continue this back-and-forth game of apology catch for even longer, Romi raised a hand and called out, "You two!"

Hadam and Department Head Boo both turned to her. Romi spread out her hands, smiling benevolently like someone in a cable TV commercial.

"Why don't you both have a seat while you chat? Have you had breakfast yet?"

Seated at the dining table and nibbling on a piece of toast, Department Head Boo introduced himself as Boo Hwachul. He knew Kyungwoon through a beekeeping group they were both in, and they were close enough that they had an older brother/younger brother dynamic. He'd heard from Sumi, his sister-in-law at the Honeycomb Guesthouse, that Hadam and Romi were staying here at Nol now. And Director Kang at Dolmiyong Jeju was the one who had told him they'd stayed at the Honeycomb Guesthouse prior to that. It was like a honeybee network, how they all seemed interlinked. Romi didn't remember mentioning to Sumi that she would be coming to stay at Nol, but if she thought about the network within the co-op itself, it made sense that Sumi had somehow found out. Kyungwoon and Department Head Boo continued to chat, friendly enough that they did seem to know each other well.

"When did Taylor say he was getting back?"

"I think he said his flight gets in tomorrow or the day after. He's in Korea now, but it seems like he'll be in Seoul for a bit first. I wonder if he's goofing around on the mainland because he knows I'll ask him for help at the bee farm once he gets back."

"If I don't have any work to do, I can help you out. I learn a lot from seeing how you keep the bee farm in order. I'm curious about the nursery too. And I heard you bought some new mobile and electric honey extractors."

"They haven't gotten here yet. Come by tomorrow. When you get a break at the school."

It was refreshing to see Kyungwoon so talkative. His easy smile seemed to lessen the weight that had been pressing on Romi's heart. As if suddenly noticing the two women's eyes on him, Department Head Boo turned to Hadam and apologized.

"Oh no, I'm sorry. We got so caught up in our own conversation."

"No worries. I also happen to be doing some research into beekeeping, so I find it interesting."

While Department Head Boo and Kyungwoon resumed their discussion, Hadam listened attentively and nodded along. Now and then, Department Head Boo even made eye contact with her and thoughtfully answered any questions she had. As the beekeeping conversation went on, Kyungwoon sent apologetic glances toward Romi, but she simply continued to smile and watch Department Head Boo and Hadam as they chatted. *I was the one who almost got stung by the bees, but he only apologized to Hadam, and even now he doesn't seem to care much about my opinion,* Romi thought. She felt the urge to tease him a little, but she was enjoying the moment playing out in front of her, so she said nothing. Kyungwoon and Department Head Boo sat side by side, while Hadam and Romi sat across from them. The morning light shone on the men's hair, and the apples on the table gleamed exceptionally bright. In reality, the morning was dark and overcast, so Romi knew the sunshine and the luster on the fruit were nothing more than a filter her eyes had applied on their own. Nonetheless, the day was bright enough to Romi. Two couples having breakfast—she was delighted by the composition of the scene, like something in a drama. At least, she was for about fifteen minutes.

"Hadam."

When she heard that somewhat familiar voice, Romi got the feeling that she had somehow predicted this situation. Things had been peaceful for far too long, hadn't they? Romi slowly turned around.

The man who had come into the kitchen through the café had a hand raised and was looking at Hadam. Did no one have to go to work today? Romi wondered. It was a weekday, she was fairly sure.

"You're here earlier than I thought," said Hadam, her face brightening.

Jaewoong, however, wasn't smiling. Romi could sense his eyes on Hwachul where he sat across from Hadam. Jaewoong bowed to greet Romi, too, pointing a thumb over his shoulder. "Pilhyun sunbae's here too. I asked for his help reviewing the rough cut of your film. Figured it'd be best to get another set of eyes on it."

A tall guy—Hadam's sunbae, apparently—appeared in the doorway behind Jaewoong.

"Yup. Jaewoong knows things are busy for me with the exhibit, but he *insisted* that I come and check it out. He must've been too shy to come alone."

Pilhyun let those words hang meaningfully in the air, glancing over at Hadam with a look that suggested he was in a tight spot. Soon, though, as if noticing the other people in the room for the first time, he turned to bow to the rest of them. The men at the table hesitantly returned his greeting. Hadam looked at Romi, as if wondering whether to introduce them. Kyungwoon and Hwachul were strangers to Hadam too. They had only just barely met. Meanwhile, Pilhyun and Jaewoong were people she had known in the past. As she did not know how they would factor into her future, would it be socially appropriate to introduce them to the others? Romi was no help at all in a situation like this. She hadn't properly heard Department Head Boo's full name earlier, and she already couldn't remember whether she'd caught the name of Hadam's sunbae just now. Several awkward seconds ticked by.

But there was no need to worry for long.

◆ ◆ ◆

There was a passage in a book Chakyung liked about how impossible it was to imagine the world without certain things in it. What would the world be like without the music in our hearts, the flowing rivers glittering with sunlight, the green and tender grass swaying in the wind? What would the world be like if it weren't for dogs?[1]

Chakyung couldn't imagine such a world, but she was sure the people in it would be even more awkward with one another than they were now. This was the conclusion she drew as she watched the group in front of her looking flustered, at a loss for what to do at the sight of a dog leaping around.

Her exhaustion and sadness from the night before were fading. She had bathed the dog as soon as she got back last night, and he looked well groomed and healthy. And now he was darting around the six people in the kitchen, barking boldly and leaving them no room to be shy around one another.

Hadam's ex-boyfriend held out his hand, but the dog ignored him and dashed over to Romi. She bent down to scoop up the puppy, but he must have been uncomfortable, sticking his legs out of her arms and writhing around. Kyungwoon quickly reached out to support the dog's legs as Romi handed him over.

"Geez, this little guy. How can he have so much energy this early in the morning?"

Kyungwoon's voice was friendly and affectionate. A round-faced man Chakyung had never seen before stood beside him, scratching behind the dog's ears while the dog happily perked up his head.

---

1   From *Dog Songs*: Poems by Mary Oliver, Penguin Books, 2013.

"He's still a baby," said the stranger. "Where'd he come from?"

"I'm not sure," Kyungwoon said, looking at Romi. She shrugged and looked at Hadam, who mirrored the gesture and turned to look at Chakyung. Everyone's eyes found Chakyung then.

"We found him wandering around lost on the streets last night and decided to take him home," she said calmly. "Me and . . . Soo-eon."

She had debated whether or not to add that part, but she wanted to stress the fact that she hadn't taken in the dog on her own whim. They had done it together.

"He's cute. I want to hold him too."

The moment Hadam reached her arms out to the dog, he easily moved from Kyungwoon's embrace into hers. As Hadam looked down at him, the dog licked her face. She turned her head, laughing. "Hey, cut it out," she said.

"He doesn't look older than a few months. And there are no stray dogs in this neighborhood." Hadam's sunbae spoke up from where he stood in the doorway at a bit of a distance from the others. Romi approached the dog, bent down, and brought her face close to his.

"You're right. He looks like a family pet—do you think he was abandoned?"

The round-faced man bent down beside Romi and did the same thing, leaning in close. The two of them looked like a mommy and daddy dog gazing at their baby.

"I'm sure of it. He looks like a purebred too."

The dog, perhaps excited by the sudden crowd of people gathered around him, began to wriggle in Hadam's grip. When Hadam tried to adjust her hold on him, the dog stuck out his hind leg and—

"Oh my god!"

"Ugh."

The round-faced man quickly pulled the dog away from Hadam, who narrowly avoided the yellow stream of pee that soaked a dark line onto the man's blue sweater. Kyungwoon pulled Romi to his side so she could also avoid a golden baptism.

"Oh no—I think I saw some towels around here earlier," said Chakyung. Even though the dog wasn't hers, she felt her face reddening as if she were indeed his owner. She went around the room in search of the towels. A dishrag caught her eye, but it seemed like a bad idea to use it.

As the man who had been christened in the dog's pee set him down with a pained smile, the dog bolted off as fast as lightning, leaping between people's legs and coming to hide behind the folds of Chakyung's skirt. It seemed like even he could sense he had done something bad.

Hadam grabbed the sleeve of her own cardigan and tried to wipe the man's sweater clean. "Oh no, Department Head Boo, this was all my fault," she fussed. "Your clothes are completely soaked."

"Hold on." Jaewoong cut in between the two of them to stop Hadam. He took off his own shirt and balled it up. "I'll do it," he said.

"What?"

Hadam looked up at Jaewoong in utter bewilderment, but he stood his ground and repeated calmly to Department Head Boo, "I'll clean the dog pee off."

Department Head Boo looked flustered but obediently craned his neck and allowed Jaewoong to wipe off the pee with careful dabs of his shirt. The two of them were close, with only a gap the size of a fist between them, and Department Head Boo's face slowly began to turn red.

"Uh, you really don't have to do this."

"Jaewoong, you're . . . really too kind."

This wasn't what Romi had originally been planning to say, but she gulped down the words she'd held back. Kyungwoon's hands were still on her shoulders.

"Right? Seems like you're hell-bent on being especially nice today for no reason." Pilhyun had taken a step back and now stood by the window, watching them all, arms crossed. The corners of his mouth were quirked up slightly, either holding in a laugh or biting down his displeasure.

Ayoung came into the kitchen, holding a tray, and almost tripped in surprise at the sight of Jaewoong and Department Head Boo mere inches apart. "Holy crap, you scared me," she breathed. There was nothing wrong with the two men being so close, but it wasn't the sort of thing she saw every day.

"What's going on this early in the morning?" Ayoung scanned the room, spotted the dog, and seemed to be trying to assess the situation. "Did the dog take a leak?"

No one answered, but they all turned together toward Ayoung, then fixed their eyes again on the two men. Hadam tried to take the shirt from Jaewoong.

"I'll do it," she said.

"It's fine. You should go and wash your hands."

While the two of them bickered, Department Head Boo waved his hands.

"You've done enough, really," he insisted, his round face still red. "It would be better if I went and cleaned myself off."

"I'll show you where the showers are," said Ayoung, carefully setting the tray down on the counter by the sink.

Just then, Kyungwoon seemed to realize how close he and Romi were and let go of her shoulders, taking a step back. "I'll go and find some clothes for you to change into."

As if in reply, the puppy let out another bark. Everyone dispersed and went off to where they needed to be. No one paid Chakyung any mind. She sighed, exhausted from being an audience to all that chaos, and looked down at the puppy.

Do you have any idea what you've done?

The dog looked up at her with clear, dark eyes.

She wasn't sure whether dogs could detect things like subtle competitiveness, jealousy, and anticipation among humans. But if dogs did sense these things, they were capable of putting on an innocent face and pretending they didn't. That might have been what made them so lovable.

WEDDINGS AND FUNERALS MUST BE ANNOUNCED

The car was parked in front of the hotel entrance. The headlights shone on the signboard that read "Maison Prunier." It was a newly constructed boutique hotel with huge windows and an enormous swimming pool out front. In order to avoid drawing too much attention, the person behind the wheel had come to this hotel at dawn and now felt a bit on edge. Anger transformed into nervousness, burning a cool, steady blue. The driver cut off the engine and headlights and waited.

A tall man came walking out into the pale darkness of the early morning. It was the first time the driver was seeing him in the flesh. Before, he'd only been viewable online through a search for the name Yang Chanmin. Now, perhaps because it was still dark, he looked like a different person from the man in his staff photo on the research lab website. The driver had no desire to get out of the car and opted instead to roll the window down a crack.

After he'd been thoroughly grilled about why he had gone against the plan and cased out Nol on his own, Dr. Yang's excuse was simply that he'd wanted to check the place out for himself. There was no point in having a long, drawn-out conversation about this. It wasn't clear whether he'd gone there to steal something, but he certainly wouldn't be able to find what it was that he wanted so easily. Only one person in the world knew the passcode to the safe in which it was being kept. At one time, there had been two people in on the secret—and then there was one.

Yang Chanmin spat out one last remark as he walked away from the car. "Don't mess this up. Let's be in touch by text message between now and the conference."

The driver watched him disappear into the hotel through the front door. He moved at a pace that was not quite a walk, not quite a sprint—something was obviously making him uneasy. Maybe it was because he was involved in this furtive little scheme, but that couldn't have been all there was to it. The driver looked up at the hotel. The building itself was small, but the aesthetic interior and its location right on the shore made the place a nice, private spot. Still, it was expensive—not a place just anyone could readily choose to stay. He must have come with someone else—someone he didn't want anyone to see. But as long as it didn't disrupt the task at hand, the driver figured, it wasn't something to be concerned with.

The driver started up the car and pulled off. This was especially not the time to draw attention. Not here, not now. The driver turned back onto the narrow road that had led up to the hotel, passing by a black SUV. What was a vehicle doing there of all places? It looked like someone might have been in the car, but the engine and headlights were off. The driver felt that something was amiss but didn't have time to think too much about it.

Stopped at a traffic light, the driver saw something floating up ahead. Something round that glowed white like the cosmos, studded with constellations. It wasn't clear what the object was, not at first, but the moment a person's arm came into view, lit up by that glow, the driver knew. It was one of those LED balloons that were popular lately because they looked great in photos. The light swayed from side to side in the wind. The woman holding the balloon looked to be in her twenties and wore a blue gingham dress. Beside her stood a man in a white T-shirt and jeans. They were walking hand in hand, and when the woman looked up at the man and laughed, the sound seemed to seep into the driver's car despite the windows being up. The spirit of late summer clung to the couple's arms, bare feet, and disheveled hair like beads of dew.

The sight of them brought forth a memory from a long time ago. Another birthday had come and gone without anyone seeming to have remembered. Late that night, the driver had gotten a text saying to look out the window. Outside, a bright light was coming closer, shining through the glass. A woman appeared beneath the window, smiling as bright as that glow, the folds of her blue chiffon skirt swallowing her legs. With one hand, the driver covered a sudden, surprised laugh and rushed down the stairs to meet her. When they were both outside, the woman carrying the light smiled and said, *Happy birthday. Here, I brought you a paper moon.* She added shyly, *I made it myself from paper and LED bulbs.* Hyeyoung was that sort of woman. Remarkably bright, capable of discoveries that would rattle the world but also able to find amusement in making little things. The two of them held up the paper moon together and burst out laughing. Underneath the glow of the paper moon, with the chirps of crickets resounding in the stillness of the night, their laughter still remained an unforgettable birthday present.

Now, the light changed, and the driver pulled off, leaving the summer lovers behind. It had been a while since that woman, too, had left, and whenever she suddenly came to mind like this, the driver's heart ached. But it might have been inaccurate to say it was sudden. "Suddenly" described things that came to mind unexpectedly after a long time of not thinking about them. The memory of Hyeyoung, though, had never once stopped weighing on the driver's mind. It was the reason behind the resolve to carry out this task, the plan they'd made as a pair but couldn't fulfill. The plan that would have seen the two of them end up together, but at the last minute, Hyeyoung changed her mind. Then she'd left the world of the living entirely, and the plan never had a chance to come to fruition.

There was a time after Hyeyoung was gone when the driver watched a movie on cable called *Paper Moon*. The driver had never heard of the movie but found it surprisingly absorbing after watching a few scenes. *I brought you a paper moon.* The driver suddenly wondered whether Hyeyoung's present could have been a reference to this film. The story was about a woman who works at a bank and falls in love with a young man who is not her husband, and all the lines she crosses to be with him in the end.

No—as much as their story matched the plot of *Paper Moon*, it was painful to imagine theirs having the same ending. *I'm different. I'm going to make it.* Even if that meant using Yang Chanmin and deceiving perfectly good people. The driver would probably have to go around and do some observations later in the morning. It was important to make sure Chanmin's appearance hadn't drawn any unwanted attention.

Looking through the windshield at the pale moon and LED balloon glowing in the distance, the driver gripped the steering wheel. The time to act was drawing ever nearer.

The dog was fast asleep at Chakyung's feet. Despite his accident earlier, he looked peaceful and content.

Chakyung sat alone under the glass roof in the courtyard garden. Once the early-morning commotion had died down, there'd been time for more formal conversation. The men introduced themselves and exchanged business cards. The mood was less awkward than it had been, but at the same time, no one had really grown that much closer.

In the end, everyone had scattered off to do their own thing. Hadam went to review a cut of her film with Jaewoong and Pilhyun, and Romi set off for the bee farm with Kyungwoon. They'd had the good sense not to ask Chakyung about the night before. They didn't even ask whether she'd spoken to Chanmin. It seemed like they were waiting for her to tell them herself.

The other residents had also left to see about their own work. The couple who owned the bookstore said they needed to drop by their shop to prepare for the global beekeeping conference. Other guests had decided to spend their short-term stays relaxing to the fullest and had taken off for the hills or the sea. Ayoung left in a hurry, mentioning something about a meetup for locals in the surf café. Seeing as Sumi from the Honeycomb Guesthouse was coming, it seemed like a gathering of people around the same age who lived nearby.

Chakyung also had things to do. She had to take the puppy to a shelter, and she had to track down Director Dim's golf bag.

She knew she had to get both tasks done as soon as possible. But the truth was, she didn't want to do either.

She reached out to pet the dog. He seemed to be deep in a dream, startling a bit in his sleep at her touch but not waking up.

There was one more thing she didn't want to do, and that was talk to Chanmin. She couldn't put it off forever. Their relationship wasn't one where they could slowly drift apart without a word and simply hope things faded out naturally. It may not have been set in stone just yet, but they had a kind of contract to uphold.

A heavy torpor settled over her in the stillness. Her head hurt thinking about what she had to do. Soo-eon came to mind then, as if summoned by the headache. He'd been notably missing from the crowd earlier that morning. She wondered where he might be.

Had the pain in her head traveled down to her chest? She felt a sharp, cold prickling sensation as if her heart were being pierced by a needle of ice. A few days ago, Chakyung hadn't even known he existed. He had no reason to tell her where he was going. She could have asked Ayoung, but she had no real reason for wanting to know.

Her heart sank at the sound of someone else coming into the courtyard. Chakyung slowly turned around. All the while, she felt her blood turning to ice.

She guessed it was Chanmin from the familiar smell of his sandalwood cologne. Until then, she had liked the scent, but here it seemed out of place. He gave Chakyung a cautious smile as he came to stand in front of her.

"How come you haven't been answering your phone?"

The dog suddenly looked up and started barking at the sight of Chanmin. He looked like he might lunge at any moment. Chanmin took a step back.

"Hey, what's going on? What's with the dog?"

Without answering, Chakyung patted the dog's head and scooped him up in her arms. "It's okay, no need to bark," she shushed the puppy. While she was comforting the dog, she could talk to Chanmin without having to look at him. "My phone's on the charger in my room," she said. "I forgot to bring it when I came outside."

Forgot to bring it, her foot. She just didn't want to answer Director Dim's calls. Plus, she hadn't guessed that Chanmin would be trying to call her.

"I was worried," he said. "I wanted to know how everything went with that issue you were having yesterday."

Only then did Chakyung look up at him. They stared at each other in silence for a moment. Chanmin didn't avoid her gaze. He was that composed.

"I didn't find the bag. Not yet."

"Is that so? That's too bad. I figured if you'd handled it already, we could go for brunch or something. What'll we do now?"

Chanmin was trying to act natural, like he would on any other day. But now everything about him seemed off.

Chakyung bent down and set the dog on the ground again. "I have to find it. I'd better get going soon."

They came to an impasse again. Though Chakyung refused to meet his eyes, she could clearly sense Chanmin trying hard to pick up the cut cord of the conversation. He was looking for a way to shift the uncomfortable mood. He leaned back against the table, holding himself up on his hands.

"What's the matter with that company? What kind of director makes his staff run his personal errands? Isn't this workplace mistreatment?"

If it had been a mere few days earlier, Chakyung wouldn't have felt one way or another about Chanmin getting angry on her behalf. Now, she was seething with irritation. She knew he hadn't genuinely considered the situation from her point of view and thus wasn't genuinely upset. He wasn't the type to get worked up over anything that wasn't related to his own personal benefit.

"Yeah," Chakyung murmured.

"Can't you report something like this to the internal audit team? He may be an executive, but he's still a contingent employee. If he's accused of misconduct, he would be the one in hot water, not you."

Chakyung clapped her hands and stood up. The puppy leaped around in front of her.

"It's fine—just drop it," she said curtly. "I took on the responsibility, and I need to sort it out. I made the choice, so I should be accountable."

"It's because you keep taking on these kinds of things that you're being used at work. You're becoming a doormat. If it's too hard for you to report him yourself, do you want me to do it?" In the middle of his impassioned speech, he stood up and reached into his pocket for his phone. "Should I call Myungjin? He knows a lot of the execs there."

Myungjin was one of Chanmin's rich chaebol friends—Chakyung didn't like the guy one bit. The first time they met, she'd gotten goose bumps from the feeling of his eyes scanning her from head to toe. But she never said a word of this to Chanmin. She didn't like the thought of his hanging out with those types, but she figured it was his personal life and she couldn't interfere. Had their relationship soured while she was pretending not to notice these minor annoyances? She thought they were walking the same path together, yet all the while she'd been ignoring the signs that they were fundamentally different people. In retrospect, everything seemed like a mistake. That was when she realized the relationship, too, had gone all wrong.

"Forget it," she said quietly.

I'm already a doormat, according to you. Chakyung stared at him coldly. He was still trying to maintain a cool expression, but the act of remaining composed always betrayed the effort that went into it. The harder you tried to appear as if you had it all together, the clearer it became that you did not.

"But if your superior at work is abusing his power, you have to teach him a lesson." Chanmin really seemed like he was going to make the call. Chakyung felt there was no need for her to watch this performance of his for too much longer.

"I said forget it. It's my business, and I'll handle it."

"Just hold on a second. I wonder if Myungjin's awake yet—"

"Give it a rest, Yang Chanmin!"

Both the puppy and Chanmin looked absolutely floored. Since she and Chanmin first met and the whole time they were dating, Chakyung had never raised her voice like this. In fact, she'd never shouted at anyone like this since the day she was born.

A shadow appeared by the door that led to the café. It seemed like someone had been peeking in on them, but the shadow just as quickly disappeared. Chakyung composed herself. This was a public space where anyone could walk in at any second.

"Give it a rest. We've never meddled in each other's business before, right? There's no need for you to handle anything concerning my work."

Chanmin stood his ground, getting loud all of a sudden too. "I'm trying to help you!"

Chakyung shook her head. "No. We've never helped each other like that when it comes to work. If you start doing things like this now all of a sudden, I can only assume there's another reason for it."

Chanmin's face was red, he was so livid. "What? Another reason?"

The hotter his blood boiled, the more the flame in her heart subsided. She didn't respond. Growing restless, Chanmin hurled the question at her again.

"What other reason would there be?"

Chakyung drew in a deep breath. It took some courage to tell the truth. "We both know why you're acting like this, Chanmin. What happened yesterday—we've been together long enough for you to know I'm not that blind. That's why whenever you've wronged me, you've done this—taken out your anger on someone else."

"Chakyung, why do you insist on taking things the wrong way? I must not have explained things properly yesterday . . ."

He took a step toward her. She took two steps back.

"We need to talk about what I saw yesterday, as well as what it is you're hiding from me. But let's not have this conversation now. We both came here on business, and we both have things we need to deal with first."

For the first time that day, Chakyung looked him squarely in the eyes. Until now, she'd thought just the two of them looking out at the same spot was enough. She'd thought that was how they could become a family. But that wasn't the case. People who wanted to be together in the long term had to face each other, too, even if that meant seeing things they didn't want to see. When Chakyung looked at him now, though, Chanmin's gaze wavered, and a moment later he turned away.

"I can explain," he said, sounding somewhat drained.

"Of course you can. I know you can," said Chakyung. But an explanation given when he couldn't even look her in the eyes was nothing more than an excuse, she thought wearily. "Not right now, though. We'll talk after you finish your work and I finish mine. That way, we'll have some time to gather our thoughts about what we want to say."

Chakyung took off the gold chain around her neck. Her engagement ring hung from it. She hated having clunky things on her hands, so she'd taken to wearing the ring on a necklace, which Chanmin had understood. He didn't wear his ring either. Chakyung never found it strange. She'd thought keeping some distance between them, even when they were walking around together, was good for maintaining a comfortable relationship in the long term. But now being close to each other had become a burden.

Chakyung took her ring off the chain and set it down on the table. It hit the wood with a dull, hollow sound.

"Take the ring," she said. "Let's talk things through later."

"What?" All of Chanmin's earlier efforts to appear calm had completely disappeared. His face was screwed up in anger. It was the first time Chakyung had seen him like that. She didn't know he was capable of such a menacing glare.

He took another step toward her, lowering his voice. "Why do you have to go this far?" he said.

In turn, Chakyung stood firm. "Trust me. I still haven't gone nearly as far as I should."

Chakyung went upstairs, sat down on her bed, and released the breath she had been holding. She'd needed to say what she said, but it hadn't been easy to say it to his face.

The puppy struggled and squirmed, trying to climb onto the bed.

"No, sir." Chakyung raised a hand to stop him. "Hold it right there. You really must have been spoiled rotten by your last owner."

As soon as she said it, her heart ached. How could a little one that clung to people this easily have been abandoned? She felt so sorry for the puppy that she scooped him up again and set him on her lap.

Being abandoned was something that happened because you loved someone. The first one to leave couldn't be abandoned.

The puppy tried to lick at Chakyung's hand. She opened her clenched fist. The ring had left an impression in her palm from where she'd been gripping it too tight. Chanmin had refused to take the ring with him and just walked off. He must have wanted to believe that as long as Chakyung had the ring, there was still room for reconciliation.

But the token of an empty promise may as well not even exist. Chakyung wrapped the ring in a napkin and stashed it in her makeup pouch.

Her phone pinged with a notification on the table. She had a message. She'd completely forgotten about Director Dim. How many of his texts and calls had she missed? It had been about an hour since he'd told her he was headed to the golf course. Chakyung sighed and checked her phone. Just thinking about reading all the unread messages he must have sent made her feel sick to her stomach.

The newest message from him was a selfie. Who the hell would want to see a picture of their boss in their inbox? He must have been out of his mind from the moment he woke up that morning—his head was probably spinning like a top. Chakyung cursed him under her breath with enough venom to startle the puppy.

"Sorry," she said.

The selfie didn't paint the picture Chakyung had imagined. There was a golf cart parked in front of a lush green course. Beside the cart,

Director Kim was in sunglasses, posing next to a brand-new golf bag, his stomach and face puffed out triumphantly.

—good work manager yoon guess I could have cut you some slack yesterday you were more than capable all along

The selfie was too much, and he was missing punctuation in several places. Chakyung didn't know whether to laugh or cry. She had no idea how this had happened—then, a moment later, a single face appeared in her head. There was only one other person who knew where the golf bag had ended up. Chakyung bolted from the bed and rushed downstairs to the café.

There were no customers except for a couple sitting lovingly side by side at one of the tables. It looked like all the people who had come for the neighborhood meeting had left as well, and now the place was quiet. Ayoung turned around from where she was washing dishes and regarded Chakyung with a strange look.

"Is something wrong?" she asked.

Breathlessly, Chakyung asked, "Have you seen Soo-eon at all today?"

Ayoung's eyes widened. "He left really early this morning, I think. He usually goes surfing in the morning. Maybe he went to the beach?"

"Do you happen to have his cell phone number?"

"I do, but if he's surfing right now, I doubt he'll pick up."

Chakyung didn't think he'd gone surfing, but like Ayoung said, he wasn't answering his phone. Ayoung mentioned he would probably be back around lunchtime, but Chakyung couldn't sit still and kept pacing around in front of the café.

Clouds were spreading throughout the sky like streams of ink in water. Chakyung's skirt, hair, and heart fluttered in the blowing wind that was tinged the color of the rain.

A familiar truck was coming through that wind and pulling up in front of the café.

The truck door opened, and out leaped Soo-eon. Chakyung's heart pounded with every step he took—as if they were in sync.

"Oh, hey." Soo-eon smiled, eyes crinkling when he spotted Chakyung. Once he was close enough, she could see that the white T-shirt stretched over his square shoulders was soaked with sweat. As was his hair. It was an overcast day, to be fair, but he looked like he'd come back from a solo trek through the tropics.

Looking up at him where he stood about three feet away, Chakyung was made aware once more that he was a real, living person. When countless people passed you by, most of them didn't even register, transparent as the air. But every now and then, there was one who left a vivid impression, one who felt like a real, flesh-and-blood human being. To Chakyung, Soo-eon was that kind of person.

"Were you waiting for me?" Soo-eon asked far too casually, not seeming to pick up on Chakyung's mood. She didn't answer him right away. She couldn't tell him she'd been waiting for a while.

"I got a message from my boss. You . . . Why didn't you ask me to go with you?"

"There was no need for two people to go. I figured I'd be fine on my own. And besides, I was the one who had the contact information."

"Was it easy to track down?"

"Oh man, not at all. I found out the lady who took the bag had already left for the golf course, so I had to go all the way there and find her, then head all the way to an entirely different golf course to deliver the bag to your boss. I just barely got it to him in time. I've been running around like crazy since early this morning."

His hair fell into his smiling eyes again. The hair that was now drenched in sweat. Chakyung caught herself wanting to reach up and brush it out of his face, but she knew she shouldn't and instead balled her hands into fists and let them fall to her sides. Soo-eon didn't seem to notice as he swept his own hand through his hair.

"I guess now I'm just showing off, huh?" he said, eyes shining like a puppy hoping to be praised.

Chakyung matched his eagerness with intensity.

"It was my business to handle. My responsibility, not something for me to dump on someone else."

Soo-eon gave a light shrug. "I know," he said. "And I know I was rude yet again with my meddling. It was presumptuous of me."

She didn't want to hear his answer, but at the same time, she couldn't help wanting to know. "Why did you do it?"

Scratching his temple, Soo-eon thought hard. "Hmm. Well, I wanted to help you. It seemed like you were having a hard time yesterday."

Chakyung was struck by a blend of disappointment and shame. Of course, good people were hard to come by, but they were everywhere. People who would see a struggling, exhausted woman betrayed by her boyfriend and feel sympathy for her.

"Thank you. And sorry," Chakyung said quietly, "for making you do something pointless you didn't have to do."

Soo-eon frowned. It was the first time Chakyung had ever seen him do so.

"Don't say that," he said.

"What?"

"I didn't want to hear that sort of thing. That's why I went on my own."

"What sort of—"

"Don't say you're sorry, or that you apologize." He looked her straight in the eye. "I always hated saying those things. Constant sorrys, constant apologies. Did you know you've been apologizing like that to people nonstop ever since we met?"

Oh. Chakyung felt the heat spreading over her face. He was right. All she'd done was apologize—to Director Kim, to Chanmin's mother, at the hotel, to Soo-eon. From Hawaii all the way to Jeju, she hadn't been able to stop. Saying she was sorry had become routine, something she never gave much thought. It even seemed like part of her job. If she could avoid souring someone's mood with one simple word, she would do it as often as she had to. But the person who was left unsatisfied, who had at some point started feeling more and more hurt by this, was Chakyung herself. And she hadn't even realized it.

"I figured if you'd seen any of those people today, you would have bowed your head yet again and apologized," Soo-eon said. "I didn't want that to happen. Just this once, I thought it would be better to go in your place so you didn't have to say you were sorry."

Chakyung felt a tingling pain, not like sadness but heartache.

"And if I could keep you from apologizing," he added, lowering his voice, "then it wasn't something pointless I didn't have to do."

Chakyung looked up, holding in the words threatening to spill out. "Thank you."

The smile returned to Soo-eon's face. He put his hands in his pockets and said teasingly, "You don't have to say that either."

Chakyung's heart was pounding. "What should I do then? When I feel grateful?"

Still smiling, Soo-eon gave the slightest quirk of his eyebrows. "Just don't forget it," he told her. "Don't forget that feeling."

They walked up the steep road and came to a vast plain surrounded by trees. Beyond where the land dipped again into a slope, the ocean was spread out wide. The weather that day was cloudy, and the dark sea and gray sky seemed to have been painted in a single stroke by a brush wet with black paint. Dozens of beehives throughout the area stood overlooking this colorless canvas.

"This is so cool," Romi said admiringly.

Kyungwoon's expression was a blend of pride and regret.

"It would be even cooler if the weather were nicer. Still, I'm confident this honey farm boasts the best views in the country."

It was nice to see Kyungwoon so full of energy. Romi followed him into the gray container building behind the hives. It was unexpectedly modern for a place nestled in the mountains at the end of a winding road.

"Here, I conduct research on bees and develop products as well."

The place was so huge that it was hard to believe he ran it alone. The first thing that caught Romi's eye was the honey tree, reminiscent of a Christmas tree, decorated with bottles of honey. At one end of the container building was a room that looked quite a bit like a lab, with pieces of electrical equipment Romi didn't recognize, as well as microscopes, beakers, and other tools. At the other end was what appeared to be a shop full of fancy, high-end goods. There were bars of soap and candles on the wooden shelves, as well as small wooden trinkets and little bottles lined up in rows.

"I'm developing my own products using honeybees," Kyungwoon said, scratching his head. The tips of his ears went slightly red. Romi picked up the yellow and green papers on the desk in front of her. "What are these?" she asked. "Napkins?"

"Ah, that's wrapping paper I'm trying to make out of beeswax. The idea is you'll be able to use it to wrap sandwiches and store other foods. You'll even be able to wash it and reuse it several times, so I'm trying to make it eco-friendly too."

"It's beautiful."

Kyungwoon frowned a bit and picked up some of the paper. "I wanted to develop this into something that could be sold as well, but the more expensive the product, the nicer the design has to be. In other countries, they have all kinds of commercial designs, but they're still hard to come by here in Korea."

"Hand that to me for a second, please."

Romi took the paper from him. She sat down on a chair and laid the yellow sheet on the table, then took out a pen from her bag. The paper was coated in beeswax, so the pen didn't write well on it, but Romi managed to draw a smooth design nonetheless.

"Rather than basing the design only on bees or hives since it's beeswax gift wrap, maybe if the personality of the product came from nature more broadly like this . . . it'd feel cleaner. More refreshing."

Flowers and trees bloomed fully formed from the tip of Romi's pen. Kyungwoon watched her hand move swiftly across the paper in awe.

"Wow. I should've known something designed by an expert would be on another level. This definitely has a luxury feeling to it. And the design even looks vaguely like a honeybee—not at all like something you just came up with on the fly."

Still drawing, Romi said lightly, "You asked me for help with this before. I've had some time to think more about the design."

Immediately, she wished she hadn't said it, but Kyungwoon seemed to have already guessed as much based on his reply.

"So we *have* met before."

Romi pressed her mouth shut and held out the finished illustration. She looked up at him. "Yes," she said, "but you can't remember."

Kyungwoon accepted the illustrated wrapping paper and studied it for a long time. After a while, he slowly began to speak. "I don't remember, but I had a feeling."

"A feeling?"

"How can I explain it? You look at me the way you'd look at somebody you knew. And seeing this design now, I'm sure I've seen your illustration style before."

"I see . . ."

That feeling that had pooled inside her dispersed as if carried away on the wind. What had she expected? For him to say that seeing the drawing had made him think of her? Those were the words she *least* expected to hear from him.

While Kyungwoon neatly stacked the sheets of wax paper, Romi wandered around the container building, not looking for anything in particular when she found her way over to the window, craving some fresh air.

Outside was the row of beehives with the dark sky and sea and the grass field as a backdrop. Even from here, the views were gorgeous. Only then did Romi realize there was something slightly different about the beehive closest to the window. She squinted, leaning forward to get a better look.

Though it had been faded by wind and rain, she could clearly see a black ribbon dangling from the hive.

Kyungwoon came to stand beside her. He realized what she was looking at.

"I heard that in Europe and the United States in the old days, when some major event occurred in a household, it was the custom to tell the news to the bees," he explained. "When there was a wedding, the bride and groom would pay the bees a visit. And when someone in the household passed away, the bees also had to be informed. People would cover the hive in a black cloth, since the bees were also in mourning."

His voice made her listen closely. As Romi mulled over what he'd said, Kyungwoon pointed outside.

"I think that hive was the one my wife fussed over the most. She marked it with a drawing of a bee. So that was the one I put the ribbon on." He lowered his finger. "I wanted to try to remember her death, even if only through that kind of gesture. Because otherwise, I have no memory of her."

Romi's heart sank. Kyungwoon turned to her.

"If we have met before, it would have been three years ago. I lost my memory right after the accident. It's spotty in places."

But it wasn't what he said that made Romi so flustered. It was the fact that he bowed to her then, deeply, at the waist.

"Oh—what's all this for?" Romi said.

"I'm sorry."

Romi couldn't make any sense whatsoever of his apology. "For what?"

"For not being able to remember you. But if we knew each other three years ago, that would mean—that would mean that I was married at the time."

What he said stirred up complicated emotions. Romi began to doubt everything between them in the past. This person in front of her now seemed unlike the person she had known then. But could she say she had ever genuinely known him? The two of them had merely brushed by each other in passing, had always been strangers. She didn't know him—didn't know why he'd come to see her, why he hadn't searched for her, or even how deep his feelings for her had been.

"I'm the one who should be sorry," she said, bowing deeply as Kyungwoon had done. She was sorry for having sought him out. Sorry for not having been able to forget him. Sorry for still holding out hope.

For the rest of the day, Romi took her time filming and photographing Kyungwoon as he roamed the grounds of the apiary and worked. She had promised Hadam she would get a bit more footage in her stead. Kyungwoon was developing products using beeswax and even selling honey. But he said he had no plans for a big business like Dolmiyong Jeju.

"This is a small-scale place. Instead, I'm thinking of creating products that will draw in young people too."

"What's this model house for?" Romi pointed out a miniature model sitting in a corner. At a glance, it looked like a toy.

"Ah, that's a beehive. It's going to be featured at the beekeeping conference. I saw on YouTube that there's a beehive in Sweden built to look like a tiny McDonald's. I tried to make something similar. A model of a traditional Jeju stone house."

"Wow. It's gorgeous." Romi photographed the hive from several angles. Kyungwoon continued his sort of guided tour of the bee farm. He spent a while explaining the ecology of bees and their assorted by-products, then revealed he was thinking of relaunching a breeding experiment that had been halted for a while now.

"What's a breeding experiment?" Romi asked.

Kyungwoon pointed to yet another container building behind the one they had come out from. "Experiments to develop new varieties of bees. There are breeds that can withstand environmental pollution and ones that are especially good at producing honey. It's illegal now to privately import queen bees, but we can develop breeds using the sperm from drones . . ."

When he talked about beekeeping, his voice got higher. His energy overflowed, racing like the buzz of bees' wings. But as he spoke now, he seemed to be losing strength.

"My wife was really smart and passionate about research. She was the one who . . . The breeding was the area I was most passionate about, but . . . Now, I can't really remember. How much work we'd done . . . And after the accident, the first thing I did was quit the research."

There were shadows of the past all throughout the bee farm. Romi was suddenly reminded of that. But at the same time, that was what made the place strangely fascinating. Romi liked when other people spoke passionately about their own work. She always loved the feeling of warmth she got as someone else's excitement spread to her. It was a similar feeling to the one she had gotten from this man before, the thing that had drawn her to him.

There was a history behind a person's passion, and it was inevitable that other people might have played roles in that history. Still, it was hard for her to decide what to think about what had happened three years ago. Even if his past had been severed by the amnesia, that history didn't completely disappear. Try as you might, it was impossible to meet someone who truly had no history.

"You can start over," Romi said.

At her serious remark, Kyungwoon's eyes widened slightly.

"No matter what's happened, you can always start over. You still have a chance." Romi felt her chest swell with emotion as she spoke. She had always tended to deeply feel even her own words.

Kyungwoon studied her in silence. She looked at him straight on. Then she felt something moist on her face. *What is this? Are these tears? Have I moved myself to tears? Am I crying?*

Kyungwoon held out his palm. Without thinking, Romi reached out to place her hand in his.

That was when he said calmly, "It looks like it's starting to rain. I'd better break out the tarp."

Romi, who had already lifted her hand by two inches, quietly lowered it again.

Hadam clicked the rewind button. The scene on the screen quickly wound back and stopped, a green field rolling forward and dropping off sharply into a cliff.

"I think there should be an overhead shot here. I'll check the Ready to Fly app to see if this area is cleared for filming with drones and try to get some aerial footage. If I can, I should be able to showcase more of Jeju's views and give some context to the scenes."

There was a huge table in the room Hadam and Romi were sharing at Nol. A laptop and camera had been set up on it, which was where Hadam and Jaewoong now sat, going through her footage. Pilhyun had offered to review the footage with them for up to an hour, but he had to leave early to see about something with his exhibit. Jaewoong had stayed behind and was working with Hadam to meticulously comb through the scenes.

"Sounds good. But on Jeju, even if you get permission to film with drones from the land ministry, you could still be restricted from filming near Hallasan National Park, so you'd need to double-check."

"Really?"

"I'll find out for you. There's a department in charge of that."

Jaewoong's hand moved naturally to the mouse. He played through the footage again, lost in thought.

"I think showing this footage of the ocean when people are talking about their reasons for moving to Jeju is a bit too similar to shots in other works. It could come across as derivative."

"Yeah, I was worried about that. It would be great if I had another clip that gave off a bit of a brighter, cleaner feeling. I looked into all sorts of locations . . ."

She took out her phone and opened her photo album. She had searched online and saved several pictures of different places.

"These sorts of ocean views or shots of wind power plants are really common, I guess. If I put in something like the pink muhly grass so many people love these days, I could film some shots like the ones I've seen in a lot of European commercial films, but I think that could also come off looking too much like an Instagram picture."

Jaewoong nodded. "And it's not the right season, so you'd have to film that separately later on."

The thought crossed both of their minds that it would be hard to conjure new scenes here that looked completely unlike the landscapes they could see in any of the travel vlogs from Jeju, the most popular tourist destination in the country over the last several years. They continued to scroll through photos, but none really stood out.

"Wait," said Hadam, her finger stopped on one particular photo. "Why did I save this?" At a glance, the photo appeared to be of a pitch-dark forest. Between the trees floated several tiny green spots as if the photo had been overexposed.

"Let me see that for a second." Jaewoong took the phone from her and studied the photo. At last, he said, "These look like fireflies."

"Ah!" Hadam snapped her fingers. "I think I saved this because I thought filming the fireflies would give me that clean, pure vibe I'm going for."

"I think that's a good idea. There are tons of them on Jeju in the early summer."

"Really? There are fall fireflies too. I'm pretty sure that time we saw them way back when was in the early fall, no?"

Her words had outrun her thoughts. Luckily, Jaewoong took her comment in stride.

"You're right. I remember that day. The fall semester had just started. You were so adamant about needing to get a shot of the fireflies that the two of us went all the way out to Muju to film it. We rode the train and lugged around our bags."

"Only to get there and not see more than a couple of fireflies!" Hadam said, playfully hitting his arm.

"Hey, how was that my fault? It was because of the weather or something. Even then, you were so upset about not getting that shot. You basically threw a fit."

Jaewoong laughed, grabbing the hand Hadam had swatted at him. The moment his hand caught hers, it was like he had pushed a play button on her fingers that made the scenes from that day come to mind. Hadam's face flushed red.

Jaewoong had laughed just like that back then, even though they had been crouching for ages in the early-autumn woods as Hadam rattled off complaints. And then . . . though the darkness of the forest was unfamiliar, that day it was like a dewy flower petal. The fireflies began to appear between the trees, one or two, then three or four at a time. Among all the faintly glowing pulses of light in the air, the two of them shared their first kiss. It was hard to tell whether the softness of that moment was from the forest air or each other's lips.

Until that day, they had been friends, and from then on, they were lovers.

Now, they held hands, looking into each other's eyes. The places where their hands touched and where their eyes met felt hot.

Had Hadam merely imagined that Jaewoong's face had grown similarly red? The more time they spent together, the more the memories tied to him came rising up like bread in an oven. Hadam couldn't say for sure whether she enjoyed this or not. Continuously locking eyes with her old flame, sharing laughs while immersed in past memories, this intense surprise at the mere brush of a hand. Was it always this awkward for lovers who crossed paths again? What was there at the end of that awkwardness? Hadam couldn't stand to be in this state of limbo for too long. It would be best for them both if she addressed and dealt with these feelings in the moment. She decided to tell him now.

"Jaewoong, we—"

"We can see fall fireflies in the village of Yerae here," Jaewoong said, quickly letting go of her hand and taking control of the mouse again.

Hadam's hand dropped onto her lap, and she looked over at his. She was familiar with each one of the fingers on that hand. His long pointer finger. The square nail of his thumb. The familiar burn marks on the back. He'd gotten them from pulling Hadam out of the flames when that fire broke out nine years ago. Just holding that hand she knew so well was enough for a stream of memories to spill out like a reel of film, but at the same time, she knew she shouldn't have held that hand in the first place.

"If the weather were nicer, we could have even seen some today," Jaewoong murmured.

Hadam absently ran a hand through her hair and looked out the window. "It looks pretty overcast outside."

"Yeah. It'll be hard to see anything today."

If it were a sunny day, could we go together? Hadam thought but couldn't bring herself to say aloud.

They continued to look through footage for more than another hour, deliberating over the parts that would need editing. Once the conversation returned to the film, it was like peace and safety had been restored.

"I think here, like Pilhyun sunbae suggested earlier, you can add in some voice-over narration. Something that shows the present state of beekeeping on Jeju."

Hadam squinted at the screen, trying to run a simulation in her head.

"It might be awkward if I add in the voice of a professional voice actor. It could make the whole thing feel like an ad."

"What about having one of the local beekeepers do the voice-over directly? Is there no one who would be good at it out of the people you've met so far?"

"Hmm. There was the woman who serves as the director at Dolmiyong Jeju. She's a really eloquent speaker, plus she's an expert on the sixth industry. But I still think the film might seem like one of those commercials where a CEO appears for comment if she were to do that. It'd be like an ad saying, 'Camellia seaweed, good for your skin!' or something."

"What, eating that seaweed is actually supposed to clear up your skin?"

"Listen—it's just an example."

Jaewoong's smile shifted into a serious look. "Doesn't the man who came by earlier work at Dolmiyong Jeju too?"

Hadam had her head bowed over the script and was intently scribbling something on it in pen, so she missed the look on Jaewoong's face and didn't seem to pick up on the sharp edge to his words.

"You mean Department Head Boo Hwachul? That's right. And he runs a class at the Honeybee School too. Oh, man, he was so embarrassed after the puppy's little accident."

"What brought him here anyway?"

Hadam set down her pen and suddenly looked up. "What do you mean?"

Jaewoong seemed taken aback by her abrupt reaction. "I just mean—well, are the two of you friendly enough that he'd come all the way here to see you so early in the morning? That's all."

"So you thought so too!"

Hadam clapped her hands, and Jaewoong frowned at her sheer delight.

"What, is there really something going on?"

"I picked up on the same thing earlier," Hadam said proudly. "Department Head Boo is interested in Romi!"

Jaewoong felt the tension leave his neck and shoulders. One corner of his mouth quirked up. "So that's what you think."

Hadam twirled her pen. "It's so obvious. Otherwise, why would he have come? Plus, when he looked at Romi, his gaze was so gentle. And he spoke so warmly too."

A single line once again creased Jaewoong's forehead down the middle, but Hadam went on, seeming to think he was simply considering what she was saying.

"To be honest, I think Hwachul would make a better beekeeper guy for Romi than Kyungwoon, but . . ."

"A beekeeper guy for Romi?"

Hearing Jaewoong's surprise, Hadam regretted saying that aloud. She hadn't wanted to mention the stuff about the beekeeper guy to other people just yet. She'd been taking great pains to figure out how she would naturally work the storyline about searching for him into the script, but now she'd just unwittingly blurted it out. Quickly, she went for a change of topic.

"Anyway, it looked like Pilhyun sunbae was also interested in Romi—do we have ourselves a love square?"

Jaewoong looked completely stunned, as if the thought had truly never crossed his mind. "What? Pilhyun sunbae?"

"Didn't it seem that way to you?"

"I think your hunch is way off the mark there," said Jaewoong, unnecessarily stern.

"Really?"

"Yeah. Pilhyun sunbae's interested in Chakyung."

Once again, the conversation had landed on a fact Hadam had never once considered. She tried to recall the expression on Pilhyun's face when he had been looking at Chakyung, but she couldn't imagine his interest being aimed in her direction at all.

"What makes you think that?"

"It seemed like he was paying close attention to her earlier this morning. And he asked me about her, random stuff. Like whether she has a boyfriend."

"Sunbae asked you all that? Pilhyun sunbae?"

Hadam had her doubts, but she realized she didn't know enough about Pilhyun's personality to be able to speak on this or that aspect of it. It had been nine years since they had consistently moved in the same circles and spaces. Since then, she hadn't heard much from him aside from news she learned through other people. Nine years was enough time for his personality to have changed from the one she used to know. The same was true for Jaewoong. No matter how well she had known him when they were together, she couldn't say he was the same person now. Hadam suddenly felt Jaewoong becoming a bit more unfamiliar to her. He didn't notice this shift and went on with what he was saying.

"He didn't ask a single thing about Romi, so I got the feeling his main focus was Chakyung. Besides . . . doesn't Chakyung look a little bit like Hwayoung?"

"Which Hwayoung? You mean Jeon Hwayoung, our hoobae from college? The film editor?"

Jaewoong looked taken aback. If Hadam had been looking in a mirror when she had inadvertently brought up the beekeeper guy earlier, she would have seen this same expression on her own face. Like Jaewoong had also let slip something he hadn't meant to reveal.

"Pilhyun sunbae liked Hwayoung? I had no idea."

"No, I mean—it's not that he definitely liked her, but more that he likes that type . . ."

His vague attempt to dodge the question only confirmed the truth. Hadam rummaged through her memory. Once she recalled Hwayoung's face, which she had seen recently, the first thing that came to mind afterward was the small white ribbon tying up her black hair.

"Even when I ran into her at Hyunsuk sunbae's memorial film screening, I didn't get that impression. Maybe it was because she and Hyunsuk dated before?"

"What? The two of them dated? That's ridiculous!"

This time, it was Hadam's turn to be shocked by Jaewoong's reaction. It was her first time seeing such a vehement response from him. The fact that two people had dated shouldn't have warranted that much surprise, and Jaewoong had never shown an interest in other people's love lives like he seemed to be today. In the past, he'd been the type to mostly respond woodenly to whatever was happening around him. But then again, nine years was a long time.

"Is it really so ridiculous?" said Hadam seriously.

The question mark still hadn't vanished from Jaewoong's face. "Hwayoung and Hyunsuk sunbae? No. No matter how long it's been—"

"What does that mean? Hyunsuk sunbae was a good person. And besides—"

"A good person, my foot. You can only say that because you have no idea. You trust people so easily."

"What are you saying? What don't I have any idea about?"

Jaewoong swallowed hard, as if trying to swallow the words welling up in his mouth. "Forget it. He's dead now. It's in the past."

"But why did you bring it up in the first place? And since he's already dead as you mentioned, why would you say something like that about him?"

Talking about someone who was no longer in this world in this context made Hadam seriously uneasy. But not talking about him felt just as bad. Still, Jaewoong seemed lost in his thoughts again and didn't say another word. Even with Hadam staring at him, wide-eyed, he seemed to hesitate. In the end, he shook his head and raised his hand to say, "Let's stop this. I'm tired just talking about it. And it has nothing to do with us anyway . . ."

The words Hadam had been holding inside for so long burst out all of a sudden. "You said something like this before too."

"What?"

"After what happened nine years ago. When I was going around dealing with things related to that fire, you never once asked me what was going on. You were busy, too, so you were never there for me. When I asked you what was wrong, you said you were tired, said we shouldn't talk about it, since it had nothing to do with us."

Jaewoong clenched his raised hand into a fist. "No, that's not . . ." He seemed to be trying to say something, but at the last moment, he changed his mind.

"You're right," he said, conceding to her. "Everything you're saying is right. That's how I was then. That's how I still am now. There's nothing I can say about it. But that's not all there is to it. The truth is . . ."

Hadam slammed her laptop shut. She worried briefly about having damaged it, but it was more important now for her to maintain some of her dignity. She composed herself, ironed out the expression on her face. "You're right. Let's stop this," she said.

"Hadam . . ." Jaewoong reached out to rest a hand on her shoulder. She lightly shrugged him off.

"I'm tired. Especially today." Hadam tried to mask the trembling in her voice. She slid her laptop into her bag, not meeting his eyes.

"Hadam," he tried again, "even if we couldn't talk about things before, we can at least try now—"

Just then, a notification pinged on his cell phone, which was resting on the table. It looked like he'd gotten a text. Jaewoong quickly snatched up the phone and tucked it into his pocket before Hadam caught even a glimpse of the screen. He lowered his head.

"All right, let's stop here for today. I'll get going."

"Bye."

Even as Jaewoong stood up and headed out, Hadam stayed where she was. He paused at the door and said, "I'll call you."

Until the door closed behind him, Hadam didn't say a word. Once the sound of his footsteps had gotten far enough away, she finally looked up and out of the window. She could see Jaewoong retreating across the yard. He stopped once and looked up at the second floor where Hadam's room was. The wind was blowing hard, and his hair fell over his eyes. Hadam couldn't tell whether or not he knew she was watching him.

On the ride back down the mountain road, the black clouds had crowded together again in the sky and were swarming without a sound. It was silent inside the car too. Neither Kyungwoon nor Romi said much. It was comfortable with Kyungwoon whether they were talking or not, but that wasn't the only reason Romi wasn't speaking. Like the insatiable itch of a sneeze tickling her nose, certain thoughts would poke their heads into her mind and then hide away again.

Romi felt the gears in her head slowly turning in time with the wipers that moved only now and then to clear the raindrops falling on the windshield.

"What was it that you said earlier?" she asked. "About the bees?"

"Hmm?"

"You said something earlier. About the black ribbon, the bees."

"Ah, you mean that custom? Telling the bees when something important happens?"

This had been constantly weighing on Romi's mind since earlier. It nagged at her like a wisdom tooth that badly needed pulling.

"What did you say more specifically? Tell me again."

"Hmm, what *did* I say?" Kyungwoon mused, scratching the side of his head in confusion. "Well, when they planned to hold a wedding, the bride and groom had to pay the bees a visit, and when there was a funeral, people covered the hives in black cloth. There's a poem titled 'Telling the Bees' by a nineteenth-century American poet that describes the practice well. For the young speaker of the poem . . ."

She had to inform someone of something. But what was it? She'd thought there was something she definitely had to announce, but as Kyungwoon continued to talk, Romi felt whatever it was sinking deeper into her memory rather than rising to the surface. She shook her head, blinking her eyes. It wouldn't be polite to fall asleep beside the person driving, but the one place in the world that made a person the sleepiest was the passenger's seat. At some point, Kyungwoon's voice had become like a lullaby.

"The young speaker of the poem only finds out in the end that the young woman he loves has died . . ."

Romi's head slowly began to lean to the side. Kyungwoon, so absorbed in the story he was telling, startled when Romi's blond head fell near him with a thump, and he used one hand to prop her upright again. Carefully righting her head so that it lay back against the seat, he murmured, "You must be tired after waking up so early today."

He sounded perplexed, but there was laughter hidden in his voice too. With that laugh, Romi fell deeply into a dream that may have been a real memory or merely something she'd imagined.

She had quickly crossed a stream. There were flowers she encountered as she walked through a green meadow: red poppies, yellow daisies, white lilies of the valley. She gathered them into a bouquet and walked along a stone fence. The sound of bees buzzing around her made her heart quicken, and she broke into a run. Where was she? Where was this place? But the only thing she could see was a long black ribbon, not tied around a young woman's long, beautiful, braided hair, but instead fluttering in the wind.

Romi came to again and for a short while had no idea what had happened. Had there been an accident? Had the car suddenly flipped over? Her head swayed with a sound like roaring waves, and the moment she was about to hit the window, a large hand came around her head. Romi swung back to the left, bashing her nose into Kyungwoon's shoulder. She thought she saw green grass pushing up against the passenger-side window when the car stopped.

"Romi, are you all right?"

Kyungwoon was still holding her head with one hand, looking concerned. Romi looked up slightly, head still heavy from having been half-asleep when the car lurched to a sudden stop.

"I'm sorry. I made a rough turn." His eyes were fixed on the tail end of a black SUV disappearing up ahead, which he watched through the windshield. "Some car suddenly switched lanes. It looked like a rental car, too, so I'm not sure why the driver was being so reckless."

Kyungwoon lowered his head to look at Romi's face. "Are you really all right? You're not hurt anywhere, are you?"

"I'm fine, really."

Romi pushed herself to sit upright, and Kyungwoon let out a deep sigh.

"That's a huge relief. It really is."

Romi turned to him and was startled by the sight. His face had gone completely pale.

"Are *you* all right?" she asked. After all, she wasn't the one who had been in a car accident before. Romi felt embarrassed now that she had been leaning on him insensitively.

"I'm fine. I'm fine too . . ."

But contrary to what he was saying, sweat was beading on his temple.

"You don't look so good." Romi quickly fished out some tissues from her bag and began to dab them on his face. He flinched but relaxed as Romi continued to wipe his face dry. Still, maybe because she was in such a rush, white bits of tissue were sticking to his skin.

"Oh no." As she reached up to peel away the sticky bits, he leaned forward, his upper body hovering above her hand. Then he quickly sat up straight, pressing his own hand to his forehead.

"Sorry. I suddenly thought of something. The car from before . . . an accident, like this one . . ."

As Kyungwoon murmured a series of disjointed words, Romi didn't hesitate. She held the back of his head with one hand, then pressed the other against his back to pull him toward her own shoulder as if hugging him.

"You can lean on me," she said. "It's all right. This accident wasn't so bad."

Kyungwoon was surprised, but he didn't lift his head from her shoulder. He murmured, "I'm sorry. For letting you see me like this—so weak."

"It's all right," Romi replied lightly, as though she had this sort of encounter every day.

"Just a little—I'll lean on you for just a little while."

"You can lean on me until you feel better."

She patted him lightly on his back. Kyungwoon pressed his forehead against her slender shoulder and briefly closed his eyes. In life, you only sometimes, on somewhat rare occasions, came across a shoulder you could rest your head of jumbled thoughts on. It was a small comfort in the aftermath of a minor accident.

BEES DON'T GET CAUGHT IN THE RAIN, BUT . . .

"The interaction between the twenty-second tropical storm of the season, Learon, and the once-northbound twenty-third tropical storm, Cham-mae, has caused a Fujiwhara effect, strengthening the storm and rerouting its course so that it will now pass over Jeju Island . . ."

A man in his thirties in a Hawaiian-print shirt sat in the front row, watching the TV and hugging his enormous backpack to his chest. His eyes and ears were trained on the weather forecaster, but he couldn't fully concentrate due to the middle-aged man talking loudly on the phone beside him.

"That's what I'm saying! All the flights are canceled! They don't know when the planes will take off again! Are these assholes at the airline telling me to just lie on the floor at Gimpo Airport? That's what I thought!"

It seemed like the older man was fighting with someone on the other end of the line. Right in front of him were a couple in their forties and their elementary school–aged children who had spread their clothes out like mats on which they sat eating cup noodles. Beside them, a college-aged couple stood leaning against a column, noses scrunched at the smell of the ramen, but they didn't take their eyes off their phones. And beside them was a group of tourists in their fifties wearing hiking gear, who were glancing at the man in the Hawaiian shirt, dropping hints like, "Oh, my legs hurt. Looks like there are no seats." But the man had no desire to move from his spot. Then he would have to stand there until whenever they could depart with no promise of being able to find a seat again. He looked up at the board of departures. Each row for the flights to Jeju had "Delayed" blinking at the end. He let out a deep sigh.

The other passengers were griping loudly and endlessly at the counter.

"So when is the flight leaving now?"

"Don't you have to tell us what measures are being taken? What are the measures?"

The man in the Hawaiian shirt knew from years of travel experience that there was nothing the airport employees could say. What could they say when the destination airports were all closed down due to natural disasters or sudden inclement weather? Lots of people who lived in Seoul went back home, and those who had been trying to make a connecting flight and groups of tourists had no choice but to simply wait there. The Korea Meteorological Administration had to be the most-cursed organization of the day, but all the forecasters in the Korea-China-Japan region had been wrong. No one had predicted that the midsized tropical storm forecast to pass over the Korean peninsula would suddenly cross paths with another storm, sharply changing its course and becoming a supersized storm.

The man sighed again and glanced at his KakaoTalk messages. The number "1" hadn't disappeared from beside the message he had sent earlier, indicating that it was still unread. He didn't know whether it was because the recipient had been too busy to check or whether there had been some problem with their phone. He dialed the number for the landline at the Nol Community House. Just when he was about to hang up after the phone rang about ten times, a breathless voice answered.

"Hi, is this Ayoung?" he asked.

The voice on the other end of the line sounded extremely hurried. "All the flights got canceled. I thought you might be worried. Is everybody holding up all right over there? How's Kyungwoon hyung? He went out? In this storm? And the roof blew off? People are missing?"

Ayoung shouted something, but it was hard to hear her properly. The call was breaking up.

"All right, I'll let you go now. Be careful."

Having heard her sounding much more serious than he'd expected, he started to feel nervous. But there was nothing he could do for her when she was so far away. Until the typhoon passed, he had nowhere to go. He was trapped inside the airport.

Still, luckily for him, he would have to wait a little longer to find out what had happened on Jeju and what would happen next.

◆ ◆ ◆

Project: *Searching for Honeyman*

Day Six, Seogwipo

Hadam rarely went to bed late. She had an internal sundial, so she didn't sleep long when there was sunlight coming in through the window. Still, on cloudy or rainy days, there were times she couldn't help it and failed to wake up on time. In her dream that day, there had been people running around screaming. Hadam didn't know why, but she had cut into the crowd and begun running desperately too. Why was she running? The fire wavered in front of her eyes. Was she being chased by the fire? Her entire body burned with heat. Just then, a stranger's cool hand took hold of Hadam's.

"Hadam, please wake up. Hadam."

At first, her vision was blurry. She couldn't tell who had been the one to wake her up just now. *Am I still a student? Who is this person— Yoojin? Hwayoung?*

"Hadam, come have breakfast."

Chakyung's face came into focus. Now fully awake, Hadam sat up in bed. She had been dreaming about what happened nine years ago and couldn't quite grasp the reality she had woken up into now. It was like she was still a university student, like she was stuck at that tender, vulnerable age.

Hadam asked blearily, "Is it morning right now? Not night?"

Chakyung pointed out the window. The sky was faintly gray. Hadam couldn't believe she had been sleeping even as the window rattled so hard in the wind.

"Yes, it's morning," said Chakyung. "It's already almost noon."

Right around when they finished eating, the glass door to the courtyard garden shuddered violently. The tremors ran out as if the wind were shaking the entire house at once. The guests gathered in the cafeteria exchanged nervous looks.

"You don't think the typhoon will strike directly here, right?"

As if Hadam's words had been a sign, the kitchen suddenly lit up and a thunderous noise resounded throughout the area. People cowered, gasping in surprise.

"It's all right; it's all right. This sort of thing happens. I heard on the weather forecast that the typhoon is heading north and is supposed to stop over Japan and miss the Korean peninsula entirely, so it should peter out somewhere along the west coast." The bookstore couple husband feigned calmness as he spoke.

"Why are you talking as if you weren't the first one to jump up in surprise? Besides, that news is over an hour old. Stop telling us what we already know and check the updates on your phone."

His wife had poured some coffee and was chiding her husband, jutting her chin at his cell phone. The young guy with the goatee held up his phone, already in his hand, and studied the screen.

"I'm looking at the updates constantly. They're saying it's possible the typhoon changed its course. Something about a Fujiwhara effect. It collided with another typhoon and created a bigger storm. But they're saying we're still in a safe zone."

Kyungwoon stood at the window, watching the powerful winds with concern.

"Still, I'd better go out and secure the beehives. They're covered in tarp right now, but if the wind keeps raging like this, the hives could fly off. Usually after mid-September, I transfer them from Seogwipo to Jeju City, but . . . I can't move them now. I'd better hurry."

Ayoung, who had been clearing away the bowls, turned to him. "Right now? Alone? Shouldn't you call up someone who can help you?"

"I have to go now. Before the rain starts coming down hard. Everyone's probably busy, so I don't have anyone I can call. And you should put up newspaper on all the windows here just in case. This building has so much glass."

Ayoung looked around, her face slightly pale. "Right—I said from the beginning all the glass in the design was a bad idea. Sangwoo, could you give me a hand?"

The goateed young man nodded.

"I'll help too," Chakyung offered. "It seems like way too much work for two people."

The women staying at Nol said they would paper the windows in their own rooms. The bookstore couple said they had to head to the construction site for their store. There were things they needed to take care of before the rain started up.

"I'll help with the beekeeping tasks," Romi said, raising her hand as the others' eyes found her. "Since I went yesterday. Plus, I like bees." Looking at all the people around her, she added, "We can't just leave the bees to die."

No one seemed to care all that much what Romi's excuse or reasoning was. There was a lot to do ahead of the sudden shift in the weather forecast. It was simply a relief that the guests could help one another.

"I'll go with you," said Hadam. "Hopefully, I can get some footage and help out as well."

It might have sounded a bit insensitive to mention that she was hoping to film, but one did not get many chances like this. She wanted to see how the bees prepared ahead of typhoons. Kyungwoon seemed to understand.

"I have some things in the car, so it'll be hard for the three of us to ride together. How about you both follow me in a separate car?"

"No, you and Romi should head out first. I have to pack my film equipment, and I might have to stop to film one or two scenes on the way. But I'll follow right behind you."

Kyungwoon turned to Romi somewhat shyly. Contrary to the weather outside, she wore a bright smile as she met his eyes. He nodded.

"Then let's get ready and head out together," he said. "Make sure to bundle up. It's cold out there."

People immediately began to file out of the shared kitchen, and only Ayoung, Chakyung, and the goateed young man, Sangwoo, remained like the debris left behind after the wind had swept through.

"Well, where should we start?"

Chakyung rolled up her sleeves and turned to Ayoung, who was thinking, one hand holding her elbow and the other on her cheek.

"First, we should close up the café and take down anything that might break easily from the cupboards, then cover the windows in newspaper and tape them up, and then put away everything that might blow away or become a hazard out in the yard. We can also check whether the water is draining with no issue."

Sangwoo stared at the door that led from the kitchen into the courtyard. "But where's Soo-eon? Is he still not back from going to the beach this morning?"

Just hearing his name, Chakyung felt her heart drop to the pit of her stomach. She asked before she could stop herself. "He went out in this weather?"

But the others didn't seem to notice how her face had paled, and went on chatting.

"Surfers love going out in this sort of windy weather," Ayoung explained. "The waves around here usually don't get that big, and you can ride the tall waves that come in before the typhoon touches down. You can even catch barrels, the waves that look like tubes."

"Soo-eon is the best surfer on this side of the island, so of course he's out there. Taylor hyung would have wanted to see the waves today too."

"Taylor's still a rookie—no way he could ride these waves."

Chakyung was hardly paying attention now that the conversation had shifted to Taylor, whom she had never met. The groaning outside the window had heightened to a roar. The three of them quickly tidied up the kitchen and left the café. They stood outside in the wind and saw people off as they all headed their own way. Romi, dressed in white rain gear, climbed into Kyungwoon's SUV with him, and Hadam got inside the rental car. Chakyung suddenly felt a spike of worry and wondered whether she should follow after Hadam, but she decided she would be more help at Nol than at the bee farm.

When they had first arrived, the ocean as she could see it from the café had resembled a long, blue band, but now it was thrashing about like a living thing. The wind steadily grew stronger, and the rain grew heavier. Chakyung went back inside to help Ayoung, but she couldn't stop her eyes from shifting toward the sea from time to time.

◆ ◆ ◆

Despite wearing protective gear, Romi felt like her face was being pummeled the second she stepped out of the SUV. The rain that had been falling thinly like small-appliance cords until they'd left the guesthouse was now falling in ropes as thick as construction cables. Kyungwoon leaped out of the car as soon as he cut the engine. Romi staggered about, struggling to find her balance in the raging rain and wind, and Kyungwoon quickly grabbed hold of her arm to help her stay upright.

"I knew it. We should have turned back earlier."

"What?"

She couldn't hear him over her rain gear and the storm. Romi held her hands to her ears, and Kyungwoon shouted louder, "I said we should have turned back!"

Romi grabbed his hands and shook them. "Right, let's do our best! Good luck!"

Kyungwoon looked dumbstruck, but Romi didn't seem to notice as she took off, racing through the rain. Kyungwoon could only watch her go with a smile on his face.

But there was no time for smiling. He had to find a cart so he could bring in the beehives in danger of mountainside trees falling on them. After that, he had to secure the hives in place and make sure to stack tires on the ends of the tarp so it wouldn't fly off. The ever-changing weather had become even more dangerous. Romi's clothes were damp from the sweat and rain soaking through them at the same time. Kyungwoon shouted to Romi as he moved about, knotting ropes.

"Romi, get inside! The weather's really bad! I'll finish up here!"

Romi nodded and pumped her fists. "Yes, we're finishing up fast!"

Kyungwoon gave up and simply worked faster. As clumsy as she was, Romi focused hard on the task at hand. She almost slipped and fell as she was rolling tires out from a pile and grabbed on to Kyungwoon's back to stop her fall.

"Careful," he said.

Romi nodded, then leaped back to her feet and hoisted up the heavy tire she had been holding. She obviously couldn't carry it on her own, so Kyungwoon had to lend her a hand.

The rain and wind erased the passing of time. They couldn't take out their cell phones in the storm, so they had no way of checking what time it was either. After however long it had been, they finally completed the necessary tasks. The ends of the tarp were flapping wildly in the wind, but the tires were holding them down, and it didn't seem like the tarp would fly off. Now, there was nothing more to do but pray that the bee farm made it through the storm intact. Kyungwoon pointed to the SUV again, signaling to Romi. She nodded and took off, bounding toward the car.

As she climbed into the passenger seat, she removed her hat and said, "The car's going to get drenched. What should we do?"

Kyungwoon quickly started the engine. "It's fine. It's more important that we get out of here before the typhoon gets worse."

The car struggled to move over the wet ground when he tried to reverse it. At some point, the sky around them had gone dark enough that it seemed like night had fallen.

The branches of the trees in front of them were snapping off in the rain. The car rolled forward a few yards, then stopped. Romi turned to Kyungwoon in surprise. He spoke calmly as he looked out ahead, but there was a flash of distress in his eyes.

"I don't think we can go any farther like this. The road could give out. It might be better to wait inside the workroom until the wind and rain let up."

Kyungwoon parked the car on the road, and the two of them quickly opened their doors and leaped out.

"Run!"

Romi nearly slipped again as she was running and holding up the hood of her raincoat. Kyungwoon reached out his hand.

"The wind is getting stronger. Hurry."

Romi took his hand. In the rain, his hand felt warm. She could hardly see in front of her, but holding his hand in that moment, she thought she would have been happy even if the distance the wind was chasing them across to get to the container building was even bigger.

But Romi was the first one to let go of his hand. As if she were lost in the cold rain, she suddenly stopped. She turned to Kyungwoon.

"What's wrong, Romi?"

She shouted urgently, "I thought of something I'd forgotten. Until just now."

Rain beating against him, Kyungwoon shouted back, "What is it?"

Romi looked around. "Why are we the only ones here? It's been a long time. When we left the café . . ."

Behind her, they heard the sound of a branch snapping. Kyungwoon quickly took Romi by the shoulders and pulled her close to him as the branch fell. The leaves and rain falling together obscured the view ahead.

The café door opened and the bells overhead chimed, everyone's head turning toward the entrance. Ayoung, Chakyung, and Sangwoo were inside, sitting at a table. The dog that had been sleeping at Chakyung's feet suddenly looked up and let out a single bark, but seeing as the newcomer wasn't a stranger, the bark seemed more like a greeting than a threat.

Rain dripping off him, the man asked worriedly, "Is everyone all right?"

Chakyung stood up. "We're fine here, but as for the people who went out—has anyone heard from Hadam?"

As he shook the rain from his hair, a look of doubt arose in the man's—Jaewoong's—eyes. "No, she wasn't picking up her phone. That's why I came. Where is she?"

It had been more than two hours since Hadam, Romi, and Kyungwoon had left, and the wind had grown downright ferocious in the meantime. The clearer it had become that the people who'd gone out had no intention of turning back around, the more the anxiety had swelled for the people waiting in the café.

Chakyung handed Jaewoong a towel. "Hadam, Romi, and Kyungwoon went to the bee farm, but we haven't heard from them. We thought they would be back soon."

"They went to the bee farm?"

"To help Kyungwoon round up the hives in preparation for the typhoon, and to film some more. Just a little while ago, they had no idea the weather would get this bad. And now, the Wi-Fi here is out and our cell phones aren't working, so we can't get in touch with them."

There was no way to get any news about the current weather conditions except through the TV. The two women guests who were on sabbatical at Nol had been watching the news and racing downstairs to let the others know each time the weather forecast changed. The remaining three in the café were on standby. It was Ayoung's opinion that they shouldn't be too hasty to move out with the weather in its current state. But seeing as the people who had gone out still hadn't returned, their patient waiting soon turned to fretful anxiety.

"The situation with the typhoon isn't looking so good. It suddenly got way stronger, and the reports are saying it might hit Jeju full-on. If this isn't the full-on storm now, what'll happen when the typhoon strikes in earnest?" Jaewoong's voice seemed lost in thought as he held the towel he'd been handed, forgetting to do so much as blot the rain from his hair.

Chakyung clasped her hands together, wringing them nervously. "What can we do? The bee farm is in the mountains on the way to the Jungmun area of Seogwipo—but as for whether they can get back from there safely or not . . . Should someone go out there to check on them?"

The sound of the phone behind the counter ringing broke through the anxious silence that had weighed on the café. The piercing sound was like the wail of an emergency siren. Ayoung jumped up and raced to pick up the call.

"Hello?"

Their cell phones weren't working, but it seemed the landline was still functional.

"Sorry? You want me to put Chakyung on the phone?"

At the sound of her own name, Chakyung looked up. Ayoung held the phone with one hand and gestured to her with the other. Chakyung approached the counter and took the call.

"Hello? Oh, Romi. Right, she's still not back. We're all waiting here. Wait, what did you say? All right. We'll look for her."

She hung up and turned around, her face even paler now. She looked right at Jaewoong.

"Romi and Kyungwoon are at the bee farm, but Romi says Hadam never made it there. She said she would meet up with them, but they have no idea where she went. While they were handling things at the farm, they forgot Hadam was supposed to be there too. Romi just called when she realized Hadam hadn't shown up."

Jaewoong gripped the towel in his hand even tighter. "After she left, something might have . . ." He swallowed his own words. "If she couldn't find the bee farm, she would have turned around and come back."

Just then, the goateed guy, Sangwoo, slammed his hands on the table and shot up. "What are we going to do?"

"God, you scared me. What's the matter with you!" Ayoung snapped, loosening her crossed arms, the somber expression on her face smoothing out in surprise.

"That lady came here in an electric car," Sangwoo went on. "There's nowhere around here where she could charge it if she needed to!"

Ayoung's mouth fell open. "What are you talking about? Why wouldn't there be?"

"I heard from a customer here at the café that the chargers here haven't been working for a day or two. So I told them where the next closest charging station was. I wonder if they made it there okay."

Chakyung tried to think. It was possible that on her way to follow after Kyungwoon and Romi, Hadam had taken her car to the charging station. Then from there, what if she had gotten lost because the navigation system wasn't working properly? And what if, to make matters worse, her cell phone wasn't getting service in the storm and she ended up stranded in an unfamiliar area as the typhoon struck?

Chakyung picked up her jacket from where it was slung over the back of her chair. Her voice was strained with worry. "I should head out there. I'll be able to take shelter at the charging station or somewhere else nearby."

Jaewoong held out a hand to stop her. "I'll go," he said. "It'll be hard for someone from out of town to get around in this wind without a working navigation system. And anyway, I know the area better, so I should be able to find her wherever she is."

Chakyung studied his face. The first time she had seen him, she had gotten the impression that he was someone who hated to show others how he was feeling inside. She'd thought his tendency not to reveal his emotions, and the fact that his defining trait was the sense of indifference he gave off instead, made up the underside of his overall spotless first impression. She'd thought he was the sort of man who might appear as a character in a foreign indie film, one whose inner life no one knew. Now, she could see genuine worry and anxiety in his face. Chakyung briefly wondered about the nature of his feelings for Hadam, but now was not the time to dwell on that. His concern itself was one of those feelings. The feeling that when the rain was pouring and the wind was blowing, someone else's well-being became his own problem. That in itself was meaningful.

"All right. Then I'm entrusting Hadam to you."

Jaewoong hurried out the door, and then there were three again. As Chakyung moved to sit down, the puppy started to hop around like he wanted to climb into her lap. Chakyung held the puppy for a short while. He looked up at Chakyung with his black eyes. The puppy felt warm, and his fur was soft—somehow, this made Chakyung want to cry. But she pushed the feeling aside. After gently setting the puppy down with a pat on the head, she stood up again and put on her jacket. She turned to the other two.

"I'm going to head to the beach and look for Soo-eon. It's strange that he's still not back either."

Ayoung shook her head. "No, Chakyung. If anything, Sangwoo should go instead—"

When he made a move to stand up, Chakyung shook her head. "No, no, I'll go." She was already heading out the door.

She knew the others were watching her leave with odd expressions on their faces. But she didn't care. The typhoon had already drawn too near for her to just sit around and worry.

When Hadam turned her phone back on, she still had only one signal bar. She tried to make a call again, but all she heard was the message that announced, "Your call could not be connected . . ." Letting out a heavy sigh, she tossed her phone aside. She tried to push the button to start the car, but it didn't come on. She didn't know how far she was from the charging station. Setting out despite not having enough of the battery left on the car. Not following after Romi and Kyungwoon right away, but instead wasting her time stopping to film the black clouds that were gathering overhead. Her navigation system shutting off before she could get to the charging station and not being able to find her way there. The bad judgment that always came along with her bad luck. If only she had made good judgment calls. But she'd thought it would be wise to wait for the typhoon to pass here in the highlands, since she might end up stranded in a flood zone if she went any farther. Hadam sighed again. The rain was falling harder and heavier, slowly muddying the windshield. The water and the noise made her feel as if her car were submerged in a lake. A subtle fear permeated the air inside the car like steam.

This wasn't the first time Hadam had encountered bad weather. She'd gotten caught up in a sandstorm in the Namib Desert back when she'd been filming a nature program in Africa. When she'd been subcontracted to go to the Philippines and work on the making-of film for an entertainment program, she'd been trapped in the country during a super typhoon. Compared to those times, the powerful lashing out of nature that she was facing now seemed relatively tame. But she'd never been alone like this before. She'd always had a team with whom to share the adversity. Perhaps what people feared was not so much the tremendous force they were up against and could do nothing about, but rather having to summon the strength to face that force on their own. She felt somewhat sad to be experiencing such a crisis on her own, but now she had to manage even that sadness alone.

Watching the water surge around her, she racked her brain, wondering what she ought to do. Should she abandon the car and get out? She wished she could look it up, but her phone wasn't working, so that wasn't even a possibility. Her ability to research things was the one asset she had been confident about, and being without internet access was also enough to make her anxious. Just as she felt certain that all she could do was trust her gut decision, the car shuddered violently.

"Ack!"

She was embarrassed by how loudly she'd shrieked, but there was no one else around to hear. She put her hand on her chest and sighed in relief. She would be all right. She had been in worse situations over the course of her life. Plus, most pressingly, the typhoon was passing through. Hadam combed through her mind for steps she could take. Either way, it would be safer to stay in the car—though if she didn't, she could grab her camera, get out, and find a place where she might be able to get a cell phone signal. She regretted having left her rain cover for the camera in Seoul. Maybe she could wrap her camera in her clothes . . .

"Ack!"

Hadam cowered over the steering wheel. The wind pounded the windshield like the devil coming to steal someone away. The car rocked violently. If it was swaying like this, what if it slipped and rolled downhill? The car would end up somewhere else. As the fear materialized, it began to accumulate. Hadam became aware once again that she was on her own. That meant she had to be the one to make the decision about what to do. She shut her eyes.

The sound of the rain scratching against the windshield and her own anxiety grew in concert. *No. If I stop here* . . . Hadam bent down and picked up the camera from the seat beside her. Then she made up her mind once and for all. Sure, she had no idea what would happen, but she needed to try to film at least a little of it. She lowered the windows. Just then, something came flying at the window on her side.

"Ack!"

Someone's hand and face appeared behind the glass. The sound of someone shouting reached her through the open window.

"Hey! What took you so long to open the window? Do you know how scared I was, not knowing what was going on with you in here?"

What she had mistaken for the sound of the rain pummeling the car had been the sound of Jaewoong banging on it. As soon as Hadam opened the door, his hand reached in and grabbed ahold of her. Hadam felt herself being pulled out and into the rain.

"How did you get here?"

Jaewoong was standing before her with no umbrella, already drenched from head to toe. Hadam remembered that his hair tended to sag into a half-curly, half-straight mess when it was wet.

"You're already soaked . . . ," Hadam started, but before she could finish what she was saying, Jaewoong pulled her closer. One hand came around her back, and the other around her head. He held on to her tight.

"You had everyone worried sick about you!" he said.

The first thing that came to mind was the feeling of being so taken aback, she couldn't breathe, but she quickly pushed him away and soon felt a sense of relief come over her. The danger hadn't vanished, and the wind was still slamming into them. But now, she didn't have to make the decision alone.

◆ ◆ ◆

Chakyung couldn't remember having ever seen an ocean that looked like this one—she mostly remembered having seen the sea glittering calmly as it lay beneath the sun. But the waves Chakyung was driving by as she sped along the coast were rearing up and roaring. She headed west. She'd heard there was a surfing hot spot along the road that ran from Hwasun Port to Moseulpo Port through both Sanbang and Songak Mountains. The waves she was passing lunged fiercely at the shore, just narrowly coming up short of the road before being dragged out to sea again.

There among the waves churning white foam, she caught a faint glimpse of a familiar sight from the shoulder of the road—the two stone islets, "sibling" stones, known as Hyeongjeseom. Chakyung had nearly driven right past them when she slammed hard on the brakes. The tires skidded as the car hydroplaned, but the road was otherwise empty, so she slid forward a few yards before coming to a stop. The familiar sight she had spotted on the road was none other than Soo-eon's truck. Chakyung turned her car around and pulled up beside the truck, opening her umbrella over her head as she stepped out. She leaned out over the railing that separated the ocean from the land.

She saw a black speck inside the mouth of a curled-up wave. Someone was riding on a surfboard. The fierce winds had sent the wave soaring up such that it formed a tunnel twice the height of the person surfing, and it looked like that person was being pulled inside the wave as if by a magnet. Chakyung gripped the railing hard. It took no more than a few seconds for the board to be swallowed up again by the wave, but it felt like much longer. Chakyung didn't even notice that her umbrella had been turned inside out by the wind.

The person on the board that was swallowed up by the tunnel fell backward into the ocean and disappeared under the surface. Chakyung's heart sank along with him. But a few minutes later, his head resurfaced above the water, and he climbed back on top of his board and lay down flat on his stomach. When another wave came surging in, he leaped to his feet on the board and bowed over at the waist, riding along the wide face of the wave as it stood up in the water. As the wind grew fiercer, the wave soared up even higher than the previous one. As it curled into a barrel once again, white foam spraying like an avalanche, the board channeled the wind and raced along the wave, leaving a white trail in its wake as if it had an engine.

Chakyung had never seen anything so dangerous and, at the same time, so marvelous in her life. Her heart was hammering so hard, it hurt and felt like it was going to burst out of her chest, but she couldn't be sure that she hated the pain. After that pain came rage. A rage brought about by seeing someone do something so dangerous as ride that board as though it were no big deal. She watched Soo-eon plummet into the ocean like that and then climb back onto his board and lie down on it, then start swimming back to the shore. Chakyung whipped around and started bounding down the stairs that led to the shoreline overlaid with black rocks.

Right when Chakyung made it down the staircase and was about to step onto a slippery stone, she ran into Soo-eon, carrying his surfboard under his arm. He gestured to her not to step down onto the rock. "It's dangerous," he said. "What are you doing . . ."

Before he could even finish his question, Chakyung shouted, "Did you not hear that there's a typhoon warning? It's dangerous for you to be out here! What are *you* doing?"

Even the pouring rain and winds couldn't wipe the laugh lines from the corners of his eyes. "I didn't know how bad the winds would get, but opportunities like this don't come around often, so I came out to try my luck at catching these waves. I didn't check the storm warnings. Earlier, I'd heard the typhoon was headed somewhere else. I guess I was this close to getting fined for being out here, huh?"

Even his nonchalant tone wasn't enough to quell Chakyung's anger. She shouted back at him even louder. "Regardless, do you know how scary it is to go out into the ocean in this weather? You could die!"

A wave extended its evil reach toward the spot where the two of them stood, then drew back as if in anger. The wind blew fiercely, whipping Chakyung's hair across her face to the point where she couldn't see in front of her. Soo-eon set down his board and reached toward her, tucking back the strands of hair that had been blown into her face.

"Anyone could die at any time," he said.

With the rain coming down as hard as it was, Chakyung couldn't tell whether it was a smile or a frown pulling at the corners of his mouth. He dropped his fingers from her hair.

"But I'm not dead right now," he continued. "In this moment, I'm truly, undoubtedly alive."

With the hand that was not holding her umbrella, Chakyung grabbed Soo-eon's hand and stepped down. The sound of the waves loud enough in her ears to split her drums, Chakyung let her voice drop.

"I was engaged," she said.

The gleam in Soo-eon's eyes briefly clouded over like the sky. "I know."

Chakyung swallowed hard. She spoke louder so the words would not be drowned out by the waves swelling in the wind. "But I broke it off. I'm not going to marry him. It's not only because of you. But it's also not like you had nothing to do with it."

Soo-eon took another step toward her. Chakyung imagined the heat emanating from his rain-drenched body was wrapping itself around her like a hug. Soo-eon bent slightly at the waist and brought his face too close to hers. He was close enough that their noses were nearly touching. He whispered, "Does that mean I can kiss you?"

The umbrella fell from Chakyung's hand and tumbled away in the wind. Like an offering made to the Dragon King in the olden days, it was devoured by the sea, never to be seen again.

"No," she said.

Their eyes met. Chakyung took his face in her hands.

"It means I want to be the one to kiss you."

Soo-eon flashed her a brilliant smile and closed his eyes again. Still holding his face, Chakyung stood on tiptoe and brought her lips to his, still smiling. Their noses, cheeks, and mouths were already drenched in rain, but in that moment, there was not a sliver of space between them for the rain or the wind to break through.

The ocean surged toward them again. For that moment, though, they heard nothing, not even the roar of the waves, as if the entire world had been swallowed whole.

YOU MIGHT VEER
OFF COURSE

The "Conference on Eco-Friendly Bee Farming for the Advancement of the Global Sixth Industry" banner that was going to be hung across the front of the Jeju International Convention Center had been set aside due to the typhoon. People in the area had learned of the typhoon warning and swarmed the convention center to take cover. Not a single package of triangle kimbap nor anything else to snack on was left in the convenience store on the third floor. Most of the refrigerator shelves were empty. Boo Hwachul roamed around the store in search of a snack and ended up purchasing only a bottled coffee. He paid just as two men dressed in black came storming in. They looked like foreigners and gave off a strong, imposing energy. Hoping to avoid bumping into them, Hwachul quickly squirmed his way out of the store.

He ran into a familiar face at the entrance to the hall on the first floor.

"Oh, Jungmoon hyung. Are you taking part in the conference too?"

The man, lean-faced and in his forties, raised his hand in greeting. He was the owner of the Honeycomb Guesthouse who also served as the chair of the Jeju Society for Returnee Beekeepers. Hwachul found the term "society" overly grandiose and thought its meaning was unclear, but the chairman insisted, and there was nothing Hwachul could do about it.

"Department Head Boo. I am—there's a section on returnee bee-keepers, so of course I had to drop in. We're busy with our bee farm, but the host extended such a sincere invitation that I couldn't refuse. Have you already had lunch?"

"No, sir. I went to the convenience store, but all the food's been snatched up. I think all the tourists in the area flocked here and cleaned the place out. The reports said the storm would miss us entirely, but I guess folks didn't know how it would turn out, so they all came here."

"This is why people should check the weather forecast when they travel. So many people these days just don't think. Come have lunch with us. My wife packed us some food."

"Sumi noona? Whew, she must have been hard at work this morning preparing that."

The two of them walked toward the booths set up on one side of the lobby. The owners of the various returnee bee farms recognized Hwachul and greeted him. Most of them had attended the Honeybee School at Dolmiyong Jeju at some point, so they were acquaintances.

Sumi had just finished stacking lunch boxes on a white plastic table when she spotted her husband with Hwachul and waved. Hwachul marveled at the sandwiches and rice balls and beautifully peeled fruit inside, but even more surprising were the hexagonal lunch boxes. They were clearly Jungmoon's design. Hwachul had wondered before whether the Honeycomb owner wasn't overly obsessive. No matter how much consistency a person valued in their life, wasn't it too much to have a house shaped like a hexagon and lunch boxes shaped like them too? Hwachul thought Sumi was remarkable for silently putting up with her husband's intractable disposition.

Just then, someone spotted Sumi and greeted her awkwardly.

"Hello."

Sumi didn't recognize the person right away. Her eyes had a wary glint in them. "I'm sorry, but who . . ."

Hwachul turned to where Sumi was looking. A man with a strong jawline looked up from bowing to Sumi and made eye contact with

Hwachul, who could have sworn he'd seen this man's face before. The man seemed to recognize Hwachul too.

"Hello," he said again. Hearing his low voice, Hwachul remembered who he was.

"Oh, you're the one who came by Nol that time. With that guest who knew Kyungwoon hyung . . ."

A light bulb seemed to go off in Sumi's head as well. "Ah, Hadam's sunbae!"

That was where Hwachul had heard this man's voice. He'd forgotten his name immediately because of all the commotion with the dog.

"I'm Ha Pilhyun. I wasn't able to properly introduce myself last time," Hadam's sunbae said evenly, not seeming to address anyone in particular.

Sumi offered him a seat. "If you haven't eaten yet, would you like to join us? I'm not sure how many people will visit our booth, so I packed plenty of food just in case."

Jungmoon frowned. He didn't seem too fond of his wife's sociable tendencies. Hwachul thought Pilhyun might turn down the invitation, but he readily accepted, taking a seat on the plastic chair Hwachul brought over for him.

When Pilhyun accepted a sandwich, the Honeycomb owner asked him, "Are you in the beekeeping industry, Mr. Ha? We've never seen you at any of our returnee beekeeper gatherings."

"Oh no, I'm not a beekeeper." It took Pilhyun a few seconds to realize the intention behind the question. "I'm here because I'm supposed to be exhibiting my work at the global beekeeping conference. I was commissioned to create a piece with bee colonies as a motif, so I'm here as an installation director."

"So you're an installation and media artist," Sumi clarified, but the Honeycomb owner and Hwachul were both out of their depth here. Hwachul remembered seeing a monitor and what looked like a pillar of beeswax being installed near the entrance.

"Well, well, hello, everyone." Waving, the bookstore couple from Nol approached the crowd around Sumi. The small table was now packed with people.

"I thought you were at the bookstore—what brings you here?" Jungmoon asked, just as the husband turned to Hwachul.

"Department Head Boo asked us what we thought about opening a pop-up store for books on beekeeping, so we came by to drop off some books before the typhoon got worse, and now we're stuck here. The storm is apparently coming over the ocean toward us now, so there's no way for us to get back."

Jungmoon shrugged. "The storm was really sudden this time. It grew so strong without any warning. We're always prepared for them ahead of time, so it won't be a big issue for us. What about at Dolmiyong Jeju?"

"Oh, we have people there today since I can't be, and they should be working on storm preparations now." But Hwachul was worried about something other than the bees. "How's everyone at Nol holding up?"

The bookstore couple wife took out her phone. "I don't think anyone's cell phones are working over there. We tried the landline in the café, though, and apparently the community house is holding up all right."

That wasn't quite what Hwachul had wanted to know, but he couldn't ask for any more detail than that.

The husband turned to look at something in the distance. "I'm worried about Kyungwoon. Whether his bee farm is all right. And the newcomers to Nol, the ladies who went to help him."

Everyone's chopsticks stopped except the Honeycomb owner's.

Sumi asked, "Oh, you mean Hadam and her friends? All three of them?"

The wife said, "No, just two of them went. Who were they again?" She turned to her husband. He was busy checking whether the lunch boxes contained his favorite side dishes as he answered absently, "I think the pretty one was the one who stayed behind . . ."

His wife frowned and elbowed him. The Honeycomb owner chewed a bite of a dried squid rice ball and murmured, "Then if Chakyung stayed behind, Romi and Hadam were the ones who went out."

Sumi's voice rose sharply. "You shouldn't judge people's appearances like that."

Even Hwachul could feel the mood shifting with rising tension. "They're all beautiful women," he said. "They just each have a different personal style."

He felt all their eyes shift to him. Pilhyun's gaze was especially sharp. Hwachul guessed he had somehow misspoken. As Sumi had said, it wasn't right to cast judgment on people's appearances. And if he wasn't careful, the others might uncover his inner feelings.

"Hey, isn't that guy over there the one who came to Nol the other day?" said the bookstore couple wife.

Everyone turned in unison again, this time in the direction she was pointing. A tall, strapping man in glasses was standing by a booth for a honey cosmetics business. His face was radiant with the glow of success.

"Hmm, who's that? A guest?" the Honeycomb owner asked, seeming uninterested.

"Who are you talking about?" The bookstore couple husband adjusted his glasses and squinted to get a better look. "Ah, him. Isn't he the pretty one's boyfriend?"

"Yeah, that's how it looked," said the wife. "Though I'm not sure he's her boyfriend anymore." The way she lowered her voice, it sounded like she was divulging a major bit of news.

"I mean, the atmosphere that day said as much. After all, he showed up with another woman at the place where his girlfriend was staying."

The husband enjoyed gossip a surprising amount, as did most people. The crowd gathered here was no exception. In an instant, the group was humming with excitement.

"That was a bit strange. He came with another woman in his car but had no idea his girlfriend was there—does that make any sense? Plus, the next day, he came by again." The wife was addressing the rest of the group with urgency. The other four, besides the bookstore couple, appeared indifferent, but all their ears were pricked up and listening.

"Did they fight?" asked the husband, to which his wife nodded.

"They had to have fought. But honestly, it seemed like Chakyung's heart was elsewhere anyway . . ."

Hwachul didn't know the bookstore couple that well. He felt uncomfortable engaging in this level of gossip with strangers. It wasn't that he was uninterested. But his sense that he shouldn't be listening to this conversation only continued to grow. Still, there were bound to be people who were impervious to such concerns. People like that thought other people's failed relationships made for fun public-conversation fodder.

"So were Chakyung and her boyfriend cheating on each other? And her boyfriend is that guy over there? Is he a beekeeper too?" the Honeycomb owner asked loudly.

The bookstore couple frowned and brought their fingers to their lips in unison.

It seemed the man in front of the cosmetics booth had heard, or else he had felt their gazes on him, because he looked around before his eyes landed on the group. Everyone averted their eyes, feigning innocence. Luckily, or perhaps unluckily, the sound of something clattering to the floor drew everyone's attention. Sumi had been tidying up the table and accidentally hit a lunch box while she was trying to keep her hands busy.

The Honeycomb owner completely blew up. "Is it so much to ask for a person to be careful? Is the lunch box broken? Do you know how hard those were to find?"

For someone so concerned about the lunch boxes, the Honeycomb owner merely sat still and watched the scene unfold from a distance. Chakyung's boyfriend had been looking in the direction of their little crowd for a moment but had, out of boredom, turned away.

When her husband lashed out at her in front of everyone, Sumi's face went completely red all the way to the tips of her ears. It was bad enough that the other people around her grew embarrassed too.

Hwachul tried to get a sense of what would be best for him to say in this situation.

In a turn of events, relief came from an unexpected source.

"Oh, this was made in Finland, it looks like. But a design shop I know sells this same brand, so even if it breaks, you should be able to find a replacement." Pilhyun held up the lunch box, turning it this way and that to examine it before he handed it to Sumi. "This one isn't broken, though, so you should be fine."

The stiff expression on the Honeycomb owner's face relaxed. Sumi's complexion also returned to normal. The bookstore couple exchanged a look. Even Hwachul quietly sighed in relief.

The bookstore couple turned to Pilhyun.

"So have you known Sumi for a while?"

The mood, which had been warming up, went uncomfortably cold again at the bookstore wife's out-of-left-field question.

"No," said Pilhyun calmly. "I just met Sumi briefly the other day when I went to see Hadam at the Honeycomb."

"But yesterday morning, you both came by Nol, and you're here together now too—it seemed like you two must have known each other."

This time, the husband elbowed his wife. The bookstore couple really seemed deserving of the title "a match made in heaven." If one of them accidentally blurted out a comment that could be seen as rude, the other would give a warning. That was how they kept each other in check, but it was also how they created rumors together.

Sumi looked genuinely surprised.

"Yesterday? I went because of the neighborhood meeting, but Pilhyun, you were there too?"

"Yes, I stopped by briefly with Jaewoong. But I didn't see you there either."

Pilhyun's voice was still the same as ever, so it was impossible to tell what he was feeling. But Hwachul could sense that the Honeycomb owner wasn't pleased with this conversation. He wasn't the sort of person who would enjoy hearing his wife's name come out of someone else's mouth. Even so, what Sumi and Pilhyun were saying must have been true. Sumi hadn't even recognized him earlier.

A lively woman's voice relieved the tense atmosphere among these relative strangers.

"Hello!"

The woman looked to be in her late twenties and was wearing a hotel concierge uniform. Her tanned face exuded a bright, healthy energy. The bookstore husband raised his hand.

"Hey!" the woman greeted him.

"Oh my goodness. What brings you here, Minsun?"

The woman in the concierge uniform pointed to a group of foreigners in black beekeeping gear on the other side of the convention center. "Our hotel also has guests participating in the beekeeping conference. But because of the typhoon, not all their interpreters could make it, so I came running."

The bookstore wife whispered in a low voice, "I guess the beekeepers in that country are really buff types. Their physiques—they must work out."

The hotel concierge's nose, lightly dusted with freckles, crinkled a bit as she frowned. "Well, beekeepers come in all different shapes and sizes. But those guys are probably the bodyguards."

The bookstore husband's mouth formed an O before he murmured, "Why do they need bodyguards?"

The concierge replied cheerfully, "I'm not sure either. And even if I did, I wouldn't be able to tell you more than that. I'm just the hotel concierge. I can't give out information about guests at our hotel."

Hwachul got the impression that as lively as she was, the concierge took professionalism seriously and made sure to draw clear boundaries with others. It was surprising, then, when she turned to greet Pilhyun as well.

"Oh, how are you?" she said.

Pilhyun seemed not to recognize her at first, but he bowed. "Ah, yes. Hello."

So it really was a small world, one where everyone could come to know one another by crossing a single bridge, Hwachul thought. And, of course, the island was even smaller than the world. Small world, small island. Even he happened to know all the people here.

At that moment, a message alert pinged. Everyone checked their own pockets and phones.

"It's mine," Pilhyun said. "My . . . my hoobae messaged me. Hadam got caught out in the typhoon because of some issue with the battery in her electric car, so my hoobae went to get her." As he relayed the message, Pilhyun sneaked a glance at Minsun, the concierge. She didn't seem to notice, but Hwachul found himself bothered by all these looks, gestures, and emotions he had no way of understanding.

"I heard Hadam went out earlier with Romi and Kyungwoon hyung. But I guess she must have fallen behind. It's a relief your hoobae is going to get her, but . . . ," Hwachul trailed off.

Sumi picked up where he left off, sounding deep in thought. "If Hadam got caught up in the storm on her way there . . ." Rather than a brief pause, there seemed to be a long silence between this thought and the one that followed. "That would mean right now Kyungwoon and Romi are at the bee farm alone."

The typhoon that had inundated the island wasn't merely raging outside. At that moment, the storm was brewing in several people's hearts. And where that storm was headed was different for all of them.

"Is your arm okay?" Romi asked, pointing.

Kyungwoon held up his arm, wrapped in thick bandages, to examine. The bandages were still tight and intact.

"I don't think it's broken. You didn't need to do all this."

Romi earnestly shook her head. "It's better to be careful. Besides, you got hurt because of me."

Earlier, Kyungwoon had shielded Romi from a tree toppled by the strong winds. A dark blue bruise immediately formed on the skin of his arm, but the bigger concern was whether the bone had fractured. Romi had offered to bandage his arm for him. Fortunately, there was a first-aid kit inside the container building.

"You're good at this," Kyungwoon noted. The bandage, patterned with dense clusters of barley plants, was securely wound around his arm.

Romi shrugged, smiling. "It's because I used to make and sell knot artwork. I'm pretty confident with binding things." She pointed again. "Is your hand okay?"

Kyungwoon clenched and unclenched the hand with the burn scars. "It is. I burned my hand in the accident, but it still works almost just as well as it used to. An injury this minor I can handle."

Raindrops continued thrumming on the roof of the container building, and the two of them felt like they were inside a drum. From time to time, a gale strong enough to rattle the container blew past.

Romi approached the window with caution and looked outside.

"I think the wind has calmed down a bit. We just have to stick it out a little longer."

She returned to her seat and checked her phone. "Still not working," she said. "Do you think Hadam's all right?"

Kyungwoon spoke calmly as if to put her at ease. "She'll be fine. When I got through to the landline earlier and talked to Ayoung, she said Hadam's friend from college would go out to get her. It's probably an issue with her car. The two of them are likely on their way back to Nol right now. Ayoung said she would call us when they got there."

"Yes, her friend. She must be with Jaewoong now." Romi sighed, fidgeting with the glass of water on the table. Right now, listening to the rain, she felt there was nothing she could do but wait. In silence, like a bee inside a drum.

She looked up when Kyungwoon broke that silence.

"Three years ago . . . ," he began, resting his injured arm on the table and holding his chin up with the other. "How did we first meet?"

Romi hesitated. Did it mean something that he was bringing up a past he couldn't remember? He wasn't responsible for the feelings that had brought her here. She considered lying, saying she didn't remember.

But for Kyungwoon, that was vanished time. So much of our time lives on in our own memories, while the rest lives on only in the memories of others. For Kyungwoon, those moments from three years ago were preserved only in other people's minds. Time unaccounted for in one's own memory, time that exists solely in the memories of others—who was the owner of such time, such memories?

Romi shared a little about those two days from three years earlier. Kyungwoon listened intently.

"What did I tell you about myself?"

"You didn't say much. You didn't even tell me your name, just that you were a bee farmer. You mentioned wanting an illustration related to beekeeping, and you said you'd seen me on Instagram—we talked about the illustrations I'd uploaded and even my cat. And you talked about beekeeping. How you'd ended up relocating to Jeju, and even how you wanted to keep building on what you had done. And on the second day, you told me how much you loved Jeju, how you adored the views here, things like that."

"I'm sure it was all just as boring to hear back then as it is now." He wore a faint smile. Romi slowly shook her head.

"I thought it was really interesting."

"Hmm?"

"I liked hearing you talk about beekeeping. I guess back then, I was—how can I say it? It was a time when I was sick of my work and plagued by fear, so meeting and talking with someone who was so passionate about what they were doing for the first time in a while gave me a renewed energy. The next day when we met up, too, and talked about this new place and new life of yours, I think it gave me some hope for my own aimless existence."

Whether because they were in the eye of the storm or because the storm had passed, the drumming of the rain against the container had quieted. While they listened for a moment to the sounds outside, silence fell between them again. Or perhaps they were only listening so intently so they didn't have to say as much to each other.

"Are you all right now?" Kyungwoon asked.

"Sorry?"

"You said you were going through a rough time, feeling sick of your work and plagued by fear. So I'm wondering if . . . things are better now."

His eyes were full of sincere worry. Romi felt a sense of unfamiliarity in his gaze. The sense that they were strangers. Even though they had technically met three years ago, he was still a stranger to her. More than that, because of his accident, he'd grown thinner and been left with scars. There was nothing strange about the fact that his face was quite different from the one she remembered. They had met only in passing and were seeing each other again after a long time apart.

But that unfamiliarity was waning now that they were showing concern for each other. Even if she hadn't known him in the past, Romi could feel that the person here with her was not such a stranger anymore.

"I'm all right now," she said. "Honestly, my life got surprisingly better after that trip. One of the reasons for that is . . ." Romi paused. She hadn't told this to anyone aside from Hadam and Chakyung. But she wanted to tell him. He watched her with light, unwavering eyes.

"Before that, for a long time, I was being stalked."

When was the last time Romi had been this serious? She hated bringing this up, so much that she didn't dare repeat this story even around her friends. Kyungwoon didn't seem particularly disturbed. He simply nodded.

"It was really so long ago. Maybe five or six years now? At first, I thought it was just a neighbor, someone who'd found my website and blog. I liked that he left me kind comments. And I posted friendly replies. But at some point, things got more intense. Suddenly, his comments got longer, and he was talking to me like he knew me. He knew what I'd been wearing that day, where I'd gone. His comments sounded like things a lover would say. It got to the point where I worried other people reading them might misunderstand. If other men left me comments, he would tell them to back off from his woman."

"Did you report him to the police?"

"I did. It was such a complicated, exhausting process. I went from this division to that division, tried filing a cyber-crime report and a general police report, but since the guy never revealed himself to me, and since none of what he'd said to me had threatened me with physical harm, I was told I couldn't report him. They couldn't give me specific details about him either. They wouldn't even confirm his real name."

So Romi shut down her website that allowed anonymous comments. She stopped blogging, but continued to post on Instagram. He sent her DMs there, but she blocked him. Even so, thousands of emails flooded into her Gmail account, but as there was nothing about the emails that she could report, she just ended up sending them all to spam. She never read them, had no idea what they said. Still, she felt anxious that someone was always watching her. She got messages from an unknown number. Saying that he missed her; he read the book she'd mentioned; he remembered walking the same streets she had. None of the messages were threatening, but they were enough to fill her with sheer terror. And yet . . .

"I still loved meeting new people," Romi said. "I loved having people tell me they liked my illustrations, or that they liked me."

Even though she was afraid of the dark side of strangers, she was drawn to the vague kindnesses she received from others. Even when she was drawing pictures that made her no money, that kindness was what made her feel less anxious. She believed she could carry on that way.

"So three years ago, when you came to see me, I didn't feel anxious. On the contrary, I felt at ease. I thought, *Not all strangers are a threat.* And you didn't act like you knew me excessively well either."

She hadn't been certain what this feeling was back then. Many memories were formed after the fact; many emotions were felt for the first time only after they'd been named out loud. Fearfulness, hesitance, a fluttering of the heart, the feeling of liking someone. Romi's own conviction was the same way, but she was certain now. This person was not scary. She felt at ease with him watching her like this, listening to her speak.

"That was what made me want to work—I got back from Jeju filled with all this energy. But that was also when the stalking suddenly stopped. No more messages, no more emails. So I was able to return to normal. I thought about you from time to time, but I had no way to find you again."

Kyungwoon nodded. "I'm glad things got better."

Romi pressed her mouth shut for a moment, thinking. Then quietly, she said, "Actually, I never told my friends this, but after I got to Jeju this time, I got another strange text message."

Kyungwoon seemed quite surprised compared to how calm Romi was. "What did it say?"

"'Don't think that I forgot about you.' It was from a strange number, too, like the ones you get automated texts from. I don't know if it was sent by that same stalker, but I had a bad feeling."

Kyungwoon's mouth was a hard line. "You should report it to the police."

Romi shook her head. "The police won't listen. It could have been sent to a wrong number, and there are no threats made in the text."

"I guess . . ."

"But I'm not as afraid this time. Whether this message is from my old stalker or from someone new, whoever it is would *want* me to be scared. That's how they intend to control me." Romi's voice wavered slightly, but her face was firm with resolve. "I promised myself I would never let that person manipulate me or force me to cut myself off from people and hide away again."

Their eyes met. Romi found encouragement in the look on Kyungwoon's face.

"I think that's because when I met you three years ago, I realized that meeting a stranger could lead to meeting a good person. That gave me strength."

Kyungwoon was quiet for a while. "That's a relief," he said at last.

"I just feel bad . . . that what was such a lucky day for me turned out to be such an unlucky one for you."

Romi sincerely meant it. This was time the two of them had shared. But time could always be interpreted differently. For Romi, that day had been so pleasant that she wanted to return to it and live it out again, while for him, the day had been marred by tragedy. Kyungwoon seemed to be deep in thought for a long time before he spoke again.

"Aren't you upset that I lied to you?"

"It wasn't a lie." She wasn't simply saying this to justify her feelings. She genuinely believed it. "Neither of us mentioned whether we were married. I'd just assumed. You didn't have on a wedding ring, but lots of people don't wear theirs. And it's not like you came on to me. You didn't promise me anything. All you did was tell me that you liked my illustrations." She swallowed. "Deluding myself is just one of my specialties."

She wasn't expecting him to respond either way. But it didn't matter what he thought—she had to take responsibility for her own emotions.

Even if it had started off as a delusion or an unintentional deceit, all she could do was hold him responsible for his actions. She couldn't deny that she'd developed feelings for him first.

Kyungwoon had been listening to her quietly when he suddenly stood up. He went over to the window and looked outside. It was raining so hard that he couldn't see anything, even though he was standing in the same spot Romi had been earlier, where she had noticed the beehive with the black ribbon.

"After my wife died, that was the most painful thing for me," said Kyungwoon, his back to her. "Not knowing how I was supposed to feel about her death. Of course I was sad, but at the same time, I didn't know enough to feel anything. Because I couldn't remember the time I had spent with her much at all."

Confessions always felt like two-way exchanges. When one person revealed something, the other would reciprocate. Now, it was Romi's turn to listen.

"But a few months after my wife died, I noticed her laptop screen showed she was still logged into the blog where she poured out all her feelings."

Romi wondered whether she was the intended audience for his innermost thoughts, or whether he was addressing them to the black ribbon he couldn't see in the rain.

"My wife was a brilliant person with a kind heart. That's how I remember her. She was so smart, she even went to university abroad. But she ended up following me here to Jeju. I was grateful to her for that, and I thought she was satisfied with her choice too. In my memories, our life here was wonderful and fulfilling. But that wasn't the case." He paused, took a breath, and went on. "I tricked myself into thinking that satisfaction was there. If she was content, that would mean our marriage had no issues. But all the while, she was agonizing over this betrayal she was keeping from me. There was someone else. It seemed like she was deeply in love with this person but didn't want to hurt me. According to her blog, I had no idea. And in her last post, dated the day before the accident . . . my wife wrote that she needed to tell me. She was planning to leave me, but she couldn't just disappear without a word. She was probably going to confess to everything that day, the last day of her life. After I saw that final post, I just logged out."

The conversation had shifted course more suddenly than Tropical Storm Learon. Romi was in shock, but she continued to listen.

"I started to think: Was that why I couldn't bring myself to feel deeply sad about my wife's death? Had I known about this before my wife died? Was that why I lost my memories, because I didn't want to think about it? Was that why her death didn't make me feel sad at all compared to the betrayal?"

Romi couldn't respond. She didn't know the answers. She couldn't even fathom all the time he had lost along with his memories.

"But I've realized something from talking with you, Romi. Maybe I didn't lose my memories to spite my wife, but because I didn't want to hate her. Maybe I wanted to keep only the good memories I had of her. And another thing . . ." He turned to face Romi again. "I realized that if I didn't cross the line with you that day, it was probably because you were too good a person to allow that—not because I was so innocent. So it's gotten easier for me to forgive my wife. Because I know there may be things I've done that would require forgiveness as well."

Still seated, Romi looked up at him, staring into his eyes. The wind had quieted, and the beat of the rain had slowed. Kyungwoon turned back to the window.

"Looks like the rain will die down soon. When it does, let's head out."

Romi got up and went to stand beside him. Sure enough, the rain was lightening up. She nodded. "It does seem like it'll die down soon," she said.

She couldn't see the black ribbon tied around the beehive. She couldn't tell whether that was because it was covered by the tarp or because it was whipping around in the wind. It didn't matter to Romi, either way. For now, it was fine where it was.

"It would be nice if we had a TV or radio," Kyungwoon mumbled. "We could have checked the news."

It suddenly occurred to Romi—memories, black ribbons, funerals. What had he said before? You had to tell the bees about funerals and weddings. TV, news, weddings. The local news she had seen that first night in her hotel room. Funerals and weddings . . .

"Ah!"

Kyungwoon whipped around, startled by her sudden outburst. "What's wrong? Did something happen?"

Romi spun toward him, grabbing him by the collar. "Yes, something happened."

"What is it?"

"I just remembered something I saw on the news."

"Didn't you mention that earlier? How there was something else you'd forgotten?"

Romi nodded once, wetting her lips. "I remembered something even more important, though."

Hadam had heard that even with the battery at 0 percent, an electric car would still be able to get to the nearest charging station. She didn't know if that was true, but even so, she would have found herself in this same situation, unable to get there because she had no idea where to go. Once the wind and rain had let up a bit, she was able to find the station by following Jaewoong's car, which had a navigation system. While they were each driving in their respective cars, the storm of emotions that had suddenly enveloped them began to dissipate. But Jaewoong suggested that Hadam wait with him in his car while hers was plugged in to charge—not the most ideal arrangement, but she didn't want to make things more uncomfortable by refusing his offer. The only place to look was straight ahead, through the windshield. They were crammed too close together to look at each other.

"Should we listen to some music?" Jaewoong asked, trying to shatter the awkward tension.

"It's up to you."

Jaewoong used his phone to put some on, the sound of something like city pop coming through his Bluetooth speakers and filling the car. It was the first time Hadam had heard this song, but the singer was famous enough that she recognized his voice right away. A song of his about meeting up with a past lover and asking how they've been had even climbed to the number one spot on the music charts. The song playing now sounded less sentimental than his other ballads, though, including that hit song. The opening lines of Yoon Jong-shin's "Welcome Summer" breezily claimed that the hardships of the moment would not amount to even a grain of sand in the grand scheme of things.

The two of them listened for a moment to the lyrics that conjured memories of beautiful summer nights, of welcoming the summer and being in love.

Would there come a time when this day and this storm became memories too? When the rain stopped and the sun came out again, would their worries melt away like the song said they would?

"I'm sorry about earlier," said Jaewoong quietly. "For shouting at you."

"What's with you?" Hadam had grown tired of this sort of back-and-forth, the way every conversation became a game of twenty questions. Remarking on the awkwardness, apologizing. Of course, things would be awkward, meeting up with someone you had dated for a long time after an even longer time had passed. But it was also bizarre, being this close. She didn't want the strange burden of this relationship that was neither one of old lovers nor one of current friends.

But Hadam knew that before she could ask him what was with him, she needed to ask herself what was with *her*. People were always asking others the questions even they hadn't yet answered.

The inside of the car began to fog up. Jaewoong turned on the air conditioner. When Hadam started to shiver a little, Jaewoong reached behind him and grabbed a jacket from the back seat. As she silently put it on, she felt his gaze lingering on her, persistent.

"As of right now, I don't know," he said with a sigh. "I was just so worried. About you being out there alone. I didn't even stop to think, *What should I do now?*"

It was as she'd expected, but she still felt disappointed.

When Hadam didn't answer, Jaewoong spoke to fill the silence again.

"I can't tell you what's going on with me now. Once I sort things out—once I get my thoughts in order, I will. But I wanted to help you. That's the honest truth. Because I couldn't help you all that time ago. Like you said."

"There's always so much you can't tell me," Hadam snapped. Even she was surprised by the reproachfulness in her tone. But to be reproachful, she must have had some sort of expectation, right? What could she have expected from him? Did she even have the right to expect anything?

For a moment, there was nothing but the sound of the windshield wipers clearing away the thinning rain. Like those wipers, Jaewoong's quiet voice pushed away the silence that pooled between them.

"The thing I couldn't tell you about nine years ago wasn't my secret to tell. The reason I didn't have the time to look after you back then was because I thought someone else needed my help more. That was my fault, for making a bad call."

"What?" Hadam half turned to him. She hadn't at all expected him to say that.

"It was our hoobae, Jeon Hwayoung."

"Hwayoung? The same Hwayoung we were talking about yesterday?"

"You know—she got hurt that day. Falling from the second floor. But she didn't jump because of the fire. It broke out after Hwayoung had already leaped."

"What are you saying?"

Jaewoong bit the inside of his lip. He spoke slowly. "After I left yesterday, I called to check with her. I asked her if I could tell you the truth, and she gave me the go-ahead."

"What the hell? I mean, if it wasn't because of the fire, then why did she jump?"

"That day . . . she was being sexually harassed. You know how we'd been drinking a bit. Hwayoung was alone in a room on the second floor, and she said someone came in. To escape them, she jumped out the window."

"What? Who was it? I had no idea." Hadam's face had paled. She hadn't known something like that had happened in such close proximity to her. On top of that, she'd been the person in charge at the filming site and had failed to look into it properly.

"Hwayoung didn't want anyone to know. I convinced her to file a report and get an investigation started, but the fire broke out that same day, and she knew you would have a hard enough time with all that."

The truth she was learning after all this time rattled Hadam even more than the typhoon had. As if he understood exactly what she was feeling, Jaewoong said, "It's not your fault. And honestly, I don't think that was the only reason she didn't say anything. She told me it was dark, so she hadn't gotten a good look at the person's face, though she seemed to have an idea about who it was. But because of the fire, there was no evidence."

In her head, Hadam ran through the conversation they'd had not long ago.

"And you thought it was Hyunsuk sunbae, right? Why?"

His expression hardened. "Because I saw *him* jump from the second floor that day. And until then, I had trusted him too. I thought that was the reason Hwayoung didn't want to tell me who it was."

"No way. If he'd done that to her, she wouldn't have dated him later on."

Jaewoong nodded. "You're right. I misunderstood. When I talked to Hwayoung about it, she said she was sorry for letting me carry on thinking that when it wasn't true. She also said she had the facts and evidence to share now, so the perpetrator would be revealed soon."

There was always some confusion mixed in with long-buried truths. But as dizzying as they were, these truths couldn't be avoided.

The wind that had shaken them as it passed through was growing more and more distant. A new landscape had been left in its wake.

Jaewoong looked at her seriously. "Hadam."

It had been so long since she'd heard someone say her name with such familiarity.

"I'm sorry. I was so busy thinking there was someone else who really needed my help that I wasn't able to look after you when you were going through so much. It was a long time ago now, I know, but I truly am sorry."

A surge of emotion welled up inside her. She knew what had happened in their relationship and how it had ended were no one's fault in particular, but it meant a lot to receive such a sincere apology.

"I'm sorry too," she said. "I didn't know what you were going through either, so all I could do was feel upset. I resented you for so long."

The feeling that someone close to her had treated her as unimportant, as well as the feeling that she had been misunderstood, had settled at the bottom of her heart like sediment and hardened like stone over time. Nothing could grow from such impenetrable ground. Neither affection nor compassion could sprout. Hadam realized this at last.

Could something bloom inside her heart now, as scratched up as it had been by those shards of stone?

"Hadam, there's something I want to tell you."

In that moment, she couldn't solidly grasp the shape of it, but she felt an anticipation that could shift into anything surging from deep within her heart.

"But I can't tell you now," Jaewoong stressed. "Tomorrow. I'll tell you tomorrow."

Her anticipation folded. All she could do was cover it up so it didn't wither away completely. "I understand. I'll wait. Until you're ready."

"For now . . . for now, let's just stay like this." He reached out his hand with hesitation. Hadam grabbed ahold of it firmly. Their fingers intertwined. Their relationship was already so far in the past, and the shape of it had changed. Even the texture of his hands was somewhat different. They seemed rougher. More calloused. But they were still the same size as they had been before, big enough to cover hers. Hadam realized she had never forgotten that detail. She hadn't completely forgotten any of it. The feelings lingered the same way a body left a faint imprint on even the springiest bed.

Jaewoong squeezed her hand. Electricity slowly began to course through Hadam's heart as if it were an appliance that had been plugged in again after a long time left sitting dormant. She rested her head on his shoulder.

But in that moment, she was forgetting something she had always kept in mind. The fact that, like the typhoon they hadn't known was coming even a day before, it was impossible to know today what winds would blow in tomorrow.

◆ ◆ ◆

"In here."

Rain pouring down, Soo-eon used his key to open the wooden door that had been painted pink and blue, and Chakyung rushed inside. Before the wind could catch up, Soo-eon hurried in, too, and shut the door behind him.

This small surf shop, run by one of Soo-eon's hyungs, faced the ocean near Sagye Beach. The shop was temporarily closed. Its owner had entrusted Soo-eon with a key before taking off for Bali. Rather than driving all the way back to Nol, Soo-eon figured it would be quicker to take cover inside.

"But the shop is really small, so we just used it more like a storage space, which is why there's nothing here." While Soo-eon, bag slung over his shoulder, went to change out of his wet suit, Chakyung took a look around. Long and short surfboards in a variety of colors hung on the wall to the left of the entrance. On a wooden shelf on the opposite wall were several small cans alongside surfboard fins and ankle leashes. Chakyung picked up one of the cans and read the label: "Sea Wax." She couldn't get a clear idea of what was in the can based on that. Several surfing magazines were scattered on the hammock-like net hanging from the ceiling. Beside the net were a wooden table and an old, worn fabric sofa, on which Chakyung took a seat.

Now wearing a T-shirt and shorts and carrying a towel, Soo-eon came back into the shop through the back door. He repeated what he'd told her earlier, almost like an excuse. "The shop is really small, and no one's been in here for a while, so there's not much to eat or do."

"That's fine."

Seeing Soo-eon all freshened up, Chakyung became all the more unpleasantly aware of her own appearance, her rain-soaked hair sticking to her face. But she had no clothes to change into, and she didn't want to shower here. Soo-eon seemed to have picked up on what she was thinking and didn't suggest it either. Instead, he sat beside her on the sofa and wrapped her hair in the towel he'd grabbed from his truck.

"I look ridiculous, don't I?" Chakyung reached out clumsily to take the towel from him, but Soo-eon didn't let go. He continued to towel-dry her hair, one section at a time.

"No," said Soo-eon, not hesitating for even a moment. "You always look nice."

Chakyung couldn't help but laugh. "Liar. You've always thought I looked pathetic since the first time we met."

"Huh. I never once thought that." He covered her forehead with the towel. While she couldn't see his expression, he asked, "Why do you say that?"

"Hmm. Because from the start, you always tried to help me. Because you only ever saw me at my most exhausted." The line between sympathy and interest had always been thin, and perhaps that was why Chakyung had felt so anxious all the time. But the edges of every emotion always ended up touching in that way.

"I never thought you were pathetic. I just wanted to help you. I think that's a different emotion. One I don't feel toward everybody."

The wind outside still hadn't stopped rattling the surf shop's window frames. Meanwhile, inside, these passionate emotions had swept through like a storm and left the whole place briefly suspended in a lull. Having dried Chakyung's hair, Soo-eon laid out the towel to dry on the arm of the sofa, then turned back to her. Chakyung felt like she had been rendered completely awkward, not knowing where to rest her eyes or hands.

"There's no telling how long the typhoon will go on," she said.

Soo-eon briefly shifted his gaze from her to the window. "You're right."

"We have a lot of time." Chakyung clasped her hands, pretending to be studying a hangnail as she added unaffectedly, "Want to tell me the long, complicated story you mentioned before?"

"Hmm?"

"When . . . when we were in your truck, the night we went to look for the golf clubs."

"Oh, right." Soo-eon stood and went over to where he'd set down his bag, took something out, and returned to the sofa. He handed the item he'd gotten to Chakyung. It was a leather frame with a photograph inside.

"This . . ."

"It's a family photo. My family. Me, my mom, and my dad. Isn't my mom beautiful?"

Chakyung silently studied the three faces in the photo. Soo-eon's mother was an Asian woman with a long neck and elegant bone structure. And his father was gray-haired and ethnically hard to pin down.

While Chakyung examined the photo, Soo-eon pulled his legs up on the sofa and crossed them, facing her.

"My dad was always like that. Always friendly, always trying to help the strangers he met on the street who seemed to be in a bind. It's like people say—even if someone isn't an angel in disguise, they may still be fated for you in ways you haven't realized yet."

Chakyung looked up. Soo-eon and his father looked exactly alike when they smiled, their eyes folding and disappearing.

"That was how my dad met my mom," he said slowly. "That long, complicated story starts here. Do you still want to hear it?"

Chakyung returned the picture to him and answered sincerely, "Yes. I want to."

Soo-eon's eyes softened as he regarded the photo. "When you showed up at the airport looking exhausted, I thought of what my mother must have looked like back then. She was all alone in the Boston airport when she collapsed. I was still in her stomach. My mom . . ." He traced a finger lovingly over her face. "She was studying abroad. Her boyfriend, my biological dad, was in the same situation. I don't know all the details. The two of them dated. My mom got pregnant with me. Then she went to Boston, where he was studying, to tell him. But when she rang his doorbell, another woman answered. My mom sussed out the nature of her relationship to him and left. She didn't even mention her pregnancy, went right back to the airport, and collapsed. She was about four months pregnant at the time, and things were looking bleak. The person who ended up taking care of my mom and escorting her back to San Francisco, where she was living, was the man who became the dad I have today. My mother thought it was a stroke of good luck that the two of them had met and happened to be going to the same place. My father thought it was fate."

There are people who think of the coincidence of crossing paths in a world of several diverging roads as destiny. Sometimes when you meet such people, even by mere chance, that encounter becomes fate in their eyes.

"But my mom and dad didn't get married until I was ten," Soo-eon went on. "My mom said she didn't want to accept my dad's feelings for her because she thought he pitied her. And she hated depending on him because she'd grown weaker. She wanted to wait until she loved him too."

"They seem so strong. Your mother, of course, and your father, who waited ten years," Chakyung said quietly.

"My mom is a really strong person. She had me, quit school to find a job, and raised me all on her own. My dad also had a really strong heart. He didn't know my mom well, so he kept circling around her all those years. I guess he was like a father to me ever since I was young, huh?"

Chakyung covered her face with both hands and lowered her head to her knees.

"What's wrong? Are you hurt?" Soo-eon leaned forward, gripping her shoulder and studying her with concern. "I'll get you some water."

But when he moved to stand, Chakyung reached up and grabbed his wrist with one hand.

"I'm fine," she said. "Just stay."

With his wrist still in her grip, Soo-eon sat back down. Chakyung's hunched shoulders fell. After a moment, she lifted her head and took a deep breath, then turned to look at him.

"That was so moving, I needed a second to calm down. My head is spinning, trying to figure out what I should do, and I feel ashamed now that I've heard your mother's story."

He understood. He nudged Chakyung's fingers around his wrist loose with his free hand and interlocked their hands once again.

"Chakyung," he said.

Outside, the lurching ocean seemed to suddenly subside. The window frames that had been rattling earlier seemed to have hushed and perked their ears up to listen. Chakyung's heart began to pound anew at the sound of his gentle voice calling her name.

"You don't need to do what my mother did. To wait to confirm that my feelings for you aren't pity. Or to spend a long time waiting around for someone who's not worth it."

Chakyung shook her head but kept her hands in his.

"I'm not waiting for either one," she said, painstakingly choosing her words. "It's just—I want to sort out my feelings to the point where I don't need to hesitate, where I'm able to face another person head-on." She couldn't bring herself to tell him that by "another person," she meant him, not yet. That was her own self-consciousness.

Soo-eon brushed his thumbs over the back of her hands.

"I am my father's son, so I can wait." Then his hands fell from hers. Yet she didn't feel the gesture was cold. "But I can't guarantee you ten years."

Chakyung remembered why she had first developed feelings for him. There was always a smile at the end of his sentences like a period, one that couldn't be erased. Chakyung lowered her head until it came to rest firmly against his chest.

They decided to leave Soo-eon's truck where it was in the surf shop's parking lot and go back in Chakyung's car. They didn't say anything in particular, seeming to understand each other's desire for their own space on the ride there. They didn't know how their relationship would change under the constant gazes of the folks back at Nol. But they both knew it would.

The raindrops falling on the windshield quickly ran off the glass and vanished. The rain seemed to have thinned. The storm was moving farther away from the island.

At the entrance to the road that led up to Nol, someone's KakaoTalk message-alert sounds began to ping in rapid succession. All the messages that had come in while the internet was out were coming through at once.

"It's me," Soo-eon said, taking his phone out of his pocket. He scrolled through with one hand and chuckled at the messages on the screen, using his other hand to scratch at the back of his head.

Chakyung worried about what that meant, but she pretended to be focused solely on driving.

"This group chat I'm in is full of messages from people asking everyone if they're okay. Some people messaged that I'm nuts for staying out so long in this weather—they were cursing me out, saying it must be no skin off my back to pay a fine."

"Don't do that again." Chakyung looked and sounded stern. When she thought about how her heart had been racing as he was surfing those waves earlier, she felt angry that she couldn't speak any more firmly than that.

"Of course—I really had no idea. That's why I was out there. If I'd known a typhoon was coming, I wouldn't have risked it. But it was because of those amazing barrels I rarely get to ride. Still, you're right. I shouldn't have done it."

Soo-eon kept checking his Kakao messages and tapping out replies.

"I got a message from Taylor hyung too. Saying he caught his plane. Seems like he should be landing soon."

"I feel like I've heard this Taylor person's name several times in the last few days. You said he's not an American, right? That his name had something to do with his line of work?" Chakyung turned the wheel and rounded a curb. Soo-eon nodded.

"Right. It's from when he worked as a garment cutter in Seoul."

"Ah, a tailor. So that's where Taylor comes from."

"Right, there's that, but also—oh, wow."

With some taps on his phone screen, Soo-eon zoomed in.

"What's wrong? Did something happen?"

"Um, it's Minsun. You know, my friend who works at that hotel. The one who told us where to find the golf bag."

"Oh, right."

"It looks like she's getting married, and she sent me a message with the invitation. I'm just seeing it now."

Chakyung vaguely remembered the face she had seen in the shadows of the hotel parking lot. She had been half out of her mind then, so she hadn't gotten a proper look at Minsun, but she remembered the other woman had seemed cheery and kind.

"She seemed friendly. So she's getting married. I didn't even get to really thank her."

"I know. Her wedding dress looks pretty."

At the sound of the words "wedding dress," Chakyung felt as though her heart had tumbled down several flights of stairs. But she was determined not to let that show in front of Soo-eon. "Is it?" she asked.

"You want to see?"

They were already almost at Nol. Chakyung made a wide turn and studied her side mirror as she tried to back the car up to park. Then she sneaked a glance at the screen of the phone Soo-eon was holding up for her to see. She couldn't read the words in the message, but she could see the image right away. The car screeched to a stop. Chakyung had pressed too hard on the brake. Soo-eon lurched forward in his seat.

"Oof!"

"Oh no, I'm so sorry. Are you all right?"

"It's fine. You were parking and I was bothering you with something else." Soo-eon made the okay sign, pressing his fingers into a circle.

"Wait a second," Chakyung said, suddenly reaching out her hand. "Can I see that wedding invitation?"

Soo-eon seemed puzzled as he handed her the phone. Chakyung zoomed in with two fingers and studied the picture closely, a serious look dawning on her face.

"Is something wrong?" asked Soo-eon.

"No, it's just . . ."

Someone's car pulled up beside them. The passenger window on the other car rolled down, and Chakyung looked up. It was Romi. She was shouting something. Chakyung rolled down her window as well.

"Chakyung, there's something important I have to tell you! It was something I forgot and just remembered again, something I need to tell Hadam too—"

Chakyung held up Soo-eon's phone. "I think I know what it is."

By the time Hadam arrived at Nol, the rain had stopped, and the clouds had dispersed. Her hair whipped around as she got out of her car and walked over to Jaewoong's. He opened his car door and stepped out too.

"I'll get going, then," he said.

"You're going to leave, just like that? You should go inside, have some tea, at least. Your clothes haven't even dried yet."

"No, it's fine. I think I should head back first."

Hadam frowned slightly. "You can't stop by just for a little while? I'll feel awful if I send you off like this now."

"Well . . . I guess I could stay for a bit? I'll go find an actual parking spot and meet you inside."

Hadam didn't cross through the café but instead traversed the garden to the shared courtyard with the glass roof. Chakyung and Romi were sitting at the table, looking at something together. Hadam didn't see the other people there with them.

"Hadam!" Romi stood up. "Are you okay?"

Hadam saw Chakyung furtively lower the phone they had been studying, but she thought nothing of it. She was just embarrassed about having caused such a mess for her friends.

"I'm sorry for worrying you both. I'm fine. Just an idiot—I should have checked that my car had charged properly before I went out," Hadam said.

"No one knew the weather would take such a sudden turn," said Chakyung, her face full of concern.

"I know. Everyone else is okay, right? Still, I'm so glad the storm is past us now."

The other two women hesitated for a moment before Chakyung spoke again.

"Yes, everyone who went out earlier says they're fine. But did you come back alone? What about . . . ?"

"Oh, Jaewoong? He's—"

Right then at the mention of his name, Jaewoong appeared in the courtyard. Hadam turned to him with a brilliant smile.

"There he is," she said. "I convinced him to have some tea before heading out."

Romi and Chakyung exchanged a look. Just as Romi opened her mouth, Chakyung grabbed her hand with a subtle shake of her head.

"Right. Let's have some tea together. I was looking earlier and saw they had a good variety here." Chakyung stood and headed toward the sink, Hadam following after her.

"Ah, I'll do it," Romi said, gesturing to Jaewoong. "Please, sit here."

Chakyung sneaked a look at Romi over her shoulder, but Romi turned away and focused her attention on Jaewoong. Hadam missed this little pantomime act while she was washing her hands.

"Thank you for going out to get Hadam," Romi said.

"No problem," Jaewoong answered curtly.

"Don't government workers have a lot to do when there's a typhoon coming?" Chakyung asked, sounding incredibly calm as she flipped on the switch for the electric kettle. "Seeing as you came all the way out here to Seogwipo, you must have been really worried."

Jaewoong didn't respond, wearing that trademark look of light concern, like that on the face of Yi I on the five-thousand-won bill.

"What about you, Chakyung? Were you here the whole time?" Hadam asked.

At her question, Chakyung's hand stopped in midair as she was spooning tea leaves into a mug. "Oh, I went out for a bit," she said.

"In this wind?"

"Well, I thought someone was in danger—or, I knew they were in danger, so . . ."

That someone's voice now came from the direction of the entrance, leaving no room for any questions as to who it was.

"Oh, you all were in here." Soo-eon bowed his head a bit and swept his hand through his soaked hair as he came over. Chakyung didn't turn around, but Hadam saw the pinkness that spread across her cheeks.

Soo-eon's attention, though, was not on Chakyung. He had been passing in front of the table, but stopped when he spotted Jaewoong and pointed. "Oh! You!"

Jaewoong looked at him in surprise. "Sorry?"

"It's you, right? With Minsun."

"I beg your pardon?"

Mug in hand, Hadam turned toward them. Soo-eon was smiling as if he'd run into someone he was happy to see, but Jaewoong had a strange expression on his face. He seemed a bit taken aback, as well as confused. Romi shrugged with both her hands up, eyes widening. From behind Hadam, Chakyung let out a noticeable sigh.

"You're the one Minsun's marrying, right? I saw the wedding invitation. Minsun's a friend of mine. We surf together." Soo-eon took out his phone and opened the KakaoTalk app, tapped a few things, and held the phone out. "Congratulations."

Chakyung just barely managed to catch the coffee cup wobbling precariously toward the edge of the table. It was the mug Hadam had set down unconsciously.

Hadam held her hand out to Soo-eon. "Can I see?"

Once Soo-eon handed her the phone, looking perplexed, Hadam zoomed in on the picture on the screen.

The woman beaming in her wedding dress looked seven or eight years younger than Jaewoong. On the e-invitation, the caption "Two people who met on the blue island, now bound to each other" appeared boldly along with the names of the couple: Gu Jaewoong and Go Minsun.

Jaewoong stood up. "Hadam."

She quietly returned the phone to Soo-eon. "Thank you."

Soo-eon looked at Chakyung as he accepted his phone, but she was just frowning.

Jaewoong grabbed Hadam's hand. "Hadam."

She coldly shook him off. "Forget it. You should get going."

"Hadam, I was going to tell you."

Jaewoong grabbed both her shoulders, trying desperately to get her to look at him. She spun around and stared straight into his eyes.

"You."

Soo-eon took a step back from them, overcome by an unidentifiable feeling. He must have had uncanny intuition, because right then Hadam's fist struck Jaewoong's jaw with a sound like a clap of thunder. Jaewoong fell back, dropping to the floor.

"Don't touch me, you asshole! What is this, the plot of *Architecture 101*?"

Neither Romi nor Chakyung had ever heard such words from Hadam's mouth. They'd had no idea her voice could even reach such an impressive volume.

Jaewoong's cheek quickly swelled up. Soo-eon, still baffled, looked to Chakyung and mouthed, *What's going on?* But she couldn't tell him, even though she knew.

Hadam spun around, intending to stalk off, back toward the café. But immediately she bumped into someone in a checkered shirt.

"Hi, everyone—"

Kyungwoon lifted a hand to greet the others but noted the serious tension in the air and stopped himself partway. He looked around the room. There was a man with his head bowed and his cheek swollen bright red. There was Soo-eon, standing behind the other man like a cowering puppy watching a fight from a distance. There was Chakyung, leaning against the sink and fiddling with her hair. There was Romi by the window, hands pressed flat against the table as she stood. And there was Hadam in front of him, rubbing her shoulder.

A moment later, a man in a Hawaiian-print shirt appeared behind Kyungwoon, grabbing his shoulders. "Hyung, how come you're standing here blocking the doorway?"

The man peeked around Kyungwoon and spotted Soo-eon, eyes going round. The green palm trees on his black shirt looked bright and blissfully unaware.

"Soo-eon, what's going on in here?"

Soo-eon looked up at him and lifted a hand. "Oh, Taylor hyung."

Chakyung thought the newcomer somewhat resembled Kyungwoon. Of course he would. They were cousins, after all. More so than in their facial features, they bore a striking resemblance in height and the general impressions they gave off. The man they called Taylor stepped around Kyungwoon, who was still standing there blankly in the doorway, and as he entered the kitchen, he waved in the direction of the window.

"Do Romi? What are you doing here?"

At his cheerful greeting, Romi turned to him, her eyes wide and her lips pursed. "Um. Who are you?"

Kyungwoon gave the two of them a pointed look.

The guy in the Hawaiian shirt wore a broad, friendly smile and strode right up to Romi. "You don't remember me?" he said. "We met three years ago when you came to Jeju for an exhibit."

Hadam whipped around. Romi's mouth had fallen open, but no words or sounds were coming out.

"You? You're the one who met Romi three years ago?" Kyungwoon asked.

The guy in the Hawaiian shirt turned to his older cousin and smiled. "Yeah, I told you all about it. An illustrator I really liked was coming to Jeju, so I wanted to meet her. I even showed you her art." He immediately looked contrite, as if he'd completely forgotten about Kyungwoon's amnesia for a moment.

Kyungwoon made eye contact with Romi. "Right," he said slowly. "So the person Romi spoke to that day must have been you. A garment cutter. Not a bee farmer."

Romi didn't say a word. All she could do was look back and forth between Kyungwoon and the Hawaiian shirt guy, Taylor—no, *the* tailor.

A piercing sound rang out through the kitchen. The mug Chakyung had caught on the table's edge earlier had dropped at last, shattering into pieces.

WHAT YOU DON'T HAVE, STEAL

Darkness was spreading like squid ink in water over the windswept sea in the distance. It was noisy inside the seafood restaurant where the company dinner was being held, but no one was engaging in any real conversation. It was a place that gave the illusion of communication even as each person there was preoccupied only with what they personally had to say. Chanmin maneuvered his chopsticks, feigning like he was reaching for a piece of raw rockfish, but he had no appetite. After taking only the tiniest nibbles, he set down his chopsticks and shifted slightly to get up. That was when Professor Min from K University, who was seated next to him, drunkenly grabbed the hem of Chanmin's pants, trying to pull him back down.

"Dr. Yang, where are you going? You didn't even have that much to drink."

Chanmin wiped the weary look from his face and put on a polite smile. "I'm just going to get some fresh air. I'll be right back."

He could only get out by crawling past all the old folks who had gotten unpleasantly tipsy. Here and there, people with familiar faces waved at him, and each time, Chanmin bowed his head and greeted them.

They all had used the conference as an excuse to shirk their work, and from the moment their flights from Seoul landed on Jeju, they had been holding all-day bacchanals starting early in the morning. This was nothing new, so Chanmin didn't even feel jaded by it anymore. They would probably carry on like this tomorrow, and the day after that too.

He crossed the street outside the seafood restaurant and came to stand before the black rock beach. He took out a cigarette and tried to light it, but he had a hard time because of the wind. He gave up and was about to toss the cigarette to the rocks before he changed his mind and put it away again.

He took out his phone and checked Chakyung's message again. All she'd written was Let's sort this all out once you're done with your conference presentation. I'll contact you afterward that evening to meet up somewhere near the convention center. When the typhoon had cleared up earlier, he'd sent her a message asking if she was all right, to which he'd received this reply. The words "sort this all out" weighed on his mind, but this was a problem that could be resolved once they got back to Seoul. Chakyung was a person who meticulously planned out her life path, and Chanmin believed she wasn't the type to change those plans at the drop of a hat. OK, let's do that, was all he'd written in his reply.

But before that, there was something else he needed to handle. It wouldn't take long. If he managed to wrap this up well, things should be smooth sailing with Chakyung too. He searched for the phone number he needed, then pressed the call button.

As if the person on the other line had been waiting for his call, it was answered right away. Chanmin tried to tamp down the anger welling up inside him and spoke in a calm, collected voice.

"What were you thinking? Acting like you knew me in a place with so many people around. What would you have done if someone had caught onto us?"

The person on the other end firmly stated there had been nothing overly familiar about their interaction. On the contrary, hadn't Chanmin drawn other people's attention by bringing that woman with him? The voice on the phone was ice-cold. It occurred to Chanmin that the owner of said voice might want to call off the deal.

"All right, I understand," he said quickly. "That aside—I'll do as I promised. You're all set on your end, right?"

Almost everything was ready, the person on the other end said, so Chanmin had better just worry about upholding his end of the bargain.

He didn't like this change in attitude, that domineering tone.

"Almost? What do you mean, almost?"

It was because the last thing to obtain couldn't be kept for too long. If it was stolen too far in advance, it would be easy to trace. To Chanmin, this seemed reasonable enough.

After the call ended, Chanmin stared out for a while at the rolling sea. The thoughts inside his head were churning much like the ocean. He could borrow from Myungjin part of the money he would need to pay Honeyman. After he'd roughly explained the plan and mentioned he was doing business with global funding sources, Myungjin was able to pull together the money in advance. He had seemed interested in the product, too, and had asked if he could get a cut. He was the type who had cash in abundance and was pouring Dom Pérignon daily at the club. As soon as Chanmin received the product, he could directly wire the money from Myungjin's paper company in Western Samoa, keeping him safe and completely out of the equation. He would hate having to see the haughty look on Myungjin's face for doing him a solid, but he could tolerate that much.

It was a foolproof plan. According to what Honeyman had said, their guy still didn't know about the existence of the product. Or, he once knew, but now he couldn't remember. Having come down to Jeju to see for himself, Chanmin had determined that Honeyman was right.

He just needed to erase all evidence of his involvement like a typhoon that had swept through and vanished. He also couldn't let Chakyung find out. Maybe he could use her to build his alibi. Chanmin grinned. Everything would work out. Just like it had been.

A rowdy burst of laughter and voices erupted from the seafood restaurant. Someone shouted an outdated toast "to grace, godliness, and intelligence!"

It was probably Professor Min. Chanmin remembered having seen him make the same toast at another company dinner. He'd felt like he had to laugh and remark on how funny it was. What a depressing, pathetic, and tiresome life Professor Min must have led, content with his worthless academic job. *I won't live like that anymore,* Chanmin decided, watching the waves crash over the rugged black rocks.

"Dr. Yang? What are you doing here?"

The voice behind him pierced like a dagger. He turned around.

"How long have you been out here?" he asked.

Risa pulled off her hair band and shook out her jet-black mane. "For a while. You seemed like you were on a phone call, so I didn't want to interrupt."

An unpleasant itch crept over him. She couldn't have heard what his call had been about, could she?

"Did you follow me when I stepped out?"

Risa raised her eyebrows. "Well, you were acting like you'd dusted your hands of me. Are you worried other people will see?"

He knew she caught on quickly and was good at piecing things together, but at present, that talent of hers annoyed him. "You know nothing good could come of any of the professors here seeing that you and I know each other. It's best to be careful."

He took out the cigarette he'd put back in his pocket earlier. He knew Risa hated when people smoked, so he lit it intentionally and exhaled, long and slow. Her face crinkled in distaste. She took a step back.

"For someone who's so good at being careful," she said, "how could you not notice when you're being followed?"

Even his cigarette smoke seemed to pause in midair. "What?"

Risa took out some lip gloss from her pocket and applied it, pursing her mouth. "From the time you left that surf café or whatever, someone was following you. A black SUV."

It was unthinkable. Had someone found out about his plans? Even if they had, could they figure anything out from that? The formula he'd so carefully devised began to waver.

One storm had passed, but the ocean was always holding yet another wind.

Risa smoothed out her hair, then turned on her heels, glancing back over her shoulder to toss one more comment his way.

"My extremely cautious friend. Be sure to always watch your back."

Then she crossed the street, not at all concerned about the cars racing down the coastal road.

After dinner, Chakyung knocked on the door. Even though she was also staying in the room and had the right to waltz in as she pleased, she felt that now was the time to be considerate. There was no answer, so she quietly entered. The room was dim, not a single light on. Romi lay face down under the blankets on the bed. On the opposite side of the room, Hadam lay wrapped in blankets on the floor. They were two big anguished lumps crammed into one space. Chakyung didn't know whose situation she ought to address first. She carefully flipped on a light switch and set a tray of food on the table.

"I brought up some curry," she said. "Ayoung made it, and you both need to eat."

There was no response from either of the lumps. Chakyung sighed. She knew it would be best to give it a rest and leave them alone at the moment, but at the same time, they couldn't stay here forever. The wisest thing to do would be to leave their problems on the island. But could they accept leaving with these loose ends untied?

"Romi, it's all right. No one else knows."

Romi sharply tossed her blankets aside. "But Kyungwoon knows!"

Chakyung couldn't grab on to the stream of her own thoughts. She approached the bed and sat down beside Romi.

"I know. But he probably won't think worse of you because of it."

"He'll just think about how stupid I am! I can't hear the difference between 'garments' and 'farming.' I can't tell two people's faces apart. And I don't even have amnesia, so why can't I remember things? He probably thinks I'm crazy."

"No way." He wouldn't think that. Not if he had gotten to know Romi. He would know it wasn't unusual for her to mix up words and faces. Of course, this was a higher-stakes situation now that she'd mistaken someone for the man she thought she'd fallen for, but this was Romi—it would have been more shocking had she recognized the right person from the start. "There's no way he would think that." Chakyung shook her head. "People's memories aren't perfect. Especially not memories from three years ago. Also, the two of them are cousins, and Kyungwoon's appearance changed a bit in the accident. He has no memories either. It's no wonder you were mistaken."

"But what kind of person makes that big a mistake? The guy tells me he hems jeans and cuts garments, but somehow I hear that he keeps bees for farming."

"They're near rhymes," said Chakyung, recalling what she'd learned during her college years in a class on Korean semantics. "I can see how someone could mix them up."

According to Soo-eon, the real Honeyman that Romi had met was embarrassed about his Korean name—Yang Boknam—because of how old-fashioned it was, so he had a habit of mumbling his way through self-introductions. That was why he asked his friends to call him Taylor when he'd started working as a garment cutter. When Chakyung asked why he hadn't corrected Romi when she'd misheard him, Boknam said he didn't like correcting others. Chakyung could understand that. Especially if he'd thought he would never see Romi again.

"He's at fault, too, for not clearing up the misunderstanding. It's not like you did anything bad—"

"It was bad that I misheard him in the first place. And that I couldn't tell him apart from his cousin. How humiliating. I mean, dogs have an uncanny ability to recognize people—even a dog wouldn't have made the same mortifying mistake." Romi covered her face with her hands again and sniffled.

Chakyung resisted the urge to laugh, knowing that doing so would risk their friendship. No matter how absurd the things she was hearing seemed at the moment, she knew she had to respond in all seriousness.

She took Romi's hands in hers. "There's no need to compare yourself to a dog, Romi," she said. "They're superior to most humans when it comes to things like sincerity anyway. But that doesn't mean you're no better than a dog. It just means you're like every other human being who makes mistakes."

The same way I have, she thought bitterly. *I made a huge mistake.*

"We all have different ways of perceiving the world and remembering things," she went on. "You have your own way that's unique to you. And because our ways are different, there will be times when we make mistakes or fool ourselves, but if we never allowed that, we would never fall in love."

Romi looked up, her face stained with tears. "Do you think so?"

Chakyung couldn't tell whom Romi had in mind at that moment. Honeyman? Or his older cousin?

"It's better to have fooled yourself. Rather than be fooled by someone else."

A voice muffled by blankets spoke up from across the room. Hadam's face was hidden where she lay curled up on the floor.

"Even though I was continually being lied to, I had no idea. I mean, it was stupid of me to assume he didn't have a girlfriend from the start, wasn't it? At his age, in these times. Maybe before he got married, he wanted to see his ex from ages ago and have his fun with her while she was in town. And I must have wanted to feel like the main character in a movie or book. I must have wanted to believe he hadn't forgotten me."

Chakyung and Romi stared in her direction.

"Of course, what Jaewoong did was wrong," Chakyung began cautiously, "but he said he was going to tell you."

She remembered his new wristwatch. From the first time she saw him at the Honeycomb Guesthouse, that TAG Heuer watch had caught her eye. It was a more expensive model and clearly brand-new, but she hadn't thought too hard about it, just assumed he was interested in watches. She had seen the same model on the wrist of the concierge at the hotel, but she hadn't drawn the connection. She'd thought it was an unusual coincidence, but not one worth mentioning to Hadam.

Chakyung caught herself wondering why she felt compelled to consider the situation from Jaewoong's perspective.

Hadam tossed off the blankets and sat up straight. "If he was going to tell me, then what was stopping him? He didn't say a thing! Why was he so worried about the typhoon? And why, why did he hold me like he did? Why make me the other woman to someone else's fiancée?"

Chakyung and Romi exchanged a look. So he'd even held her . . . In that case, it made sense that Hadam was furious, but then again, given how often men and women hugged each other in modern society, a simple embrace may not have been such a big deal. Even something more than that wouldn't have been strange. But the two of them did their duty as her close friends and kept their mouths shut.

This all had gotten especially complicated for Chakyung. When she spoke about other people's situations, it was hard not to interject her own point of view. Any other time, she would have been able to offer a more level-headed assessment of the situation. But at the moment, she wasn't sure where she stood on anything.

"I've seen so many movies like that," Hadam went on, murmuring to herself more than anyone else. "So many men like that, chasing after a bit of fun with another woman before they get married, looking for assurance that they're still the kind of men it'll be a shame to see taken off the market. I thought things would be different. I believe my stance is always clear. Even knowing that I have a hard time telling excitement apart from love when I'm traveling, I fell for the act anyway. Having someone encouraging me when I was feeling anxious after quitting my job made my heart waver yet again . . ."

Chakyung thought back to Hadam's shouting about the movie *Architecture 101* and decking Jaewoong in the face, but she knew now was not the time to laugh.

"If you look at it that way, I was the biggest fool of all," she said instead. "With no idea what kind of person the man I was going so far as to marry was. Or maybe I did know, but I just closed my eyes to the truth. I knew he went to clubs, and there were times I had a feeling he was talking to other women. But I didn't ask him about it because of my pride. I thought it was enough that he seemed like a decent guy on paper, that he wasn't so bad when he was with me. I thought that kind of pattern matching was the same as love, that letting the unforgivable things slide was the same as compromising. That was the most foolish part."

Hadam was silent as she listened to her friend's self-disparaging remarks. Chakyung hadn't mentioned Chanmin once since the day he came by Nol, and Romi and Hadam hadn't spoken to each other about it either. They all acted as if nothing had happened.

"Well, you couldn't have done anything about that," Romi assured her. "It's hard not to be fooled by someone determined to fool you!"

Hadam reared up, clenching her fists. "Exactly. Who could win against an expert liar? You can't call someone a fool for believing in lies."

Chakyung wondered whether this wasn't a sudden and complete attitude shift for two people who had been curled up under the blankets just moments earlier, but she took comfort in their words nonetheless. Still, she couldn't simply ignore the reality.

"I don't think it was *their* lies that pulled the wool over our eyes," she said.

Hadam brought a chair over from the table and placed it next to the bed. "What was it, then?"

"Could it have been that we all had our own expectations for what a typical romance should be? Meeting your perfect match by chance, going on an appropriate number of dates like you see on social media, getting married and starting a so-called normal family. Weren't those fantasies also lies?"

They were all silent at first. Then Hadam spoke up, sounding glum.

"I guess even I can't say I didn't harbor some version of those expectations. I think I got caught up in the narrative of two lovers reuniting after a years-long misunderstanding. Maybe it was because we share the same passion for movies. I must have dreamed up a beautiful ending for us, like some kind of romance novel."

"Getting swept up in delusions has to be a patented Do Romi trademark," Romi said. "I managed to come up with a fantasy about a guy I saw once three years ago and couldn't even remember. Clearly, I've seen way too many dramas about meet-cutes while traveling."

Romance lies to us. The countless love stories of our generation deceive us. They cover our eyes and turn us away from the obvious truth, passing off relationships that would require endless compromise to maintain in real life as love. Romance has the same bitter taste as betrayal—a false belief from the start. This was the painful truth the three of them had discovered on this trip to find love.

"What is this, a self-reflection session: Jeju Island edition?" Chakyung said with a slightly bitter smile. "Are we each coming clean about where we went wrong?"

Romi waved her hands. "No, let's not go down that path. None of this was our fault. In the end, it was our expectations about romance to blame."

"You're right! To hell with romance!" Hadam banged her fists on her lap. But her friends said nothing. "Oh, come on. What's up with you two?"

Romi leaned back against the wall and closed her eyes. "I know it's stupid, but I can't give it up."

"What?"

"Romance. I know it's stupid, but I can't give up on it. Because when I do manage to find it, I like it too much."

The sound of barking came in through the window. Chakyung crossed the room and opened the curtains. Someone was in the yard petting a dog. A man in a baggy T-shirt was on one knee, but he wasn't hunching; his shoulders were ramrod straight. Chakyung could only see him from behind, but she could tell from a glimpse of his side profile that he was laughing. A tingling sensation ran from the tips of her fingers through her veins until it reached her heart.

"To hell with romance, all right," she muttered.

Romi and Hadam couldn't see the expression on her face, but there were moments when certain emotions exuded from a person's back alone.

She spoke quietly, her hand pressed against the window. "You might know full well what a shitty concept romance is, but you still can't abandon it. Even when you end up getting fooled again, you can't cast it aside. You know it's wrong, but you fall for it time after time. Because you can't help dreaming that you'll find the real thing."

Just then, the puppy barked toward the window. Soo-eon looked up, shielding his eyes with his hand. Chakyung didn't know if he could see her, but he grinned. Even in the dark, she could see his beaming smile.

"So I guess romance really does screw us in the end," Chakyung said softly.

Lingering vestiges from the typhoon swept through the night, rustling the trees.

◆ ◆ ◆

Project: *Searching for Honeyman*

Day Seven, Seogwipo

The traces of the wind had disappeared, leaving the sky perfectly blue and clear as glass. On sunny days on the island, everyone wanted to get out and go somewhere. Chakyung went to a traditional teahouse in Seogwipo with its own green-tea fields for a marketing research meeting about the company's green-tea cosmetics. Hadam wanted to wrap up the rest of her filming and said she would be wandering around the area close by. Romi spent the entire day holed up in the apartment, drawing on her tablet. She didn't want to see anyone. Even in the midst of heartbreak, a person had to work.

She may have been able to withstand the hunger—she'd wolfed down the curry Chakyung had brought up to the room the night before—but it was hard for any human being to endure without so much as water. She thought about getting some from the tap and cooking up something on the stove. She could even make barley tea or green tea. But the fridge in their room was empty. She waited until she thought there might not be anyone downstairs and sneaked into the kitchen through the courtyard. If she played it cool, no one would notice her. She was filling her jug with water from the purifier when a man in a black long-sleeved shirt and slacks came in through the door to the café, a coffee mug in his hands.

"Oh, Romi! You're here."

Even without looking up at him, Romi knew it was Boknam.

"Yep, I am." She bowed her head, hurriedly clamping the lid back on her jug and heading out of the kitchen.

"Romi, wait up!"

The jug was too slender to hide her whole face, but Romi held it up anyway and shuffled out to the courtyard. Boknam followed, awkwardly calling after her, but she pretended not to hear him.

"Romi! Romi! Just because you cover your face doesn't mean I can't see you!"

He rushed in front of her, blocking her way.

"Romi, please—let's talk."

She gave up and lowered the jug. Boknam led her toward the table in the courtyard. He folded his hands and placed them on the table. Now that she was getting a good look at him for the first time, the only similarities between him and Kyungwoon were their slim faces and their heights—their facial features themselves were quite different. Romi had chalked these differences up to the accident.

"I heard you mistook me for—I mean, you thought the person you met three years ago was Kyungwoon hyung."

Romi's jaw dropped. "Did Kyungwoon tell you that? What did he say?"

"No, I heard from Ayoung and some of the others. They said . . . it seemed like you came to Jeju to find the person you'd met back then."

Romi said nothing in reply.

Boknam chose his words carefully. "I went on talking to you like I was involved in bee farming, and I caused you to misunderstand."

Head bowed, Romi fixed her gaze on his folded hands. Quietly, she asked, "Why did you do it? Why did you lie?"

He seemed taken aback by her question. "I—"

"You came to see me, but were you afraid I would recognize you later? Were you hiding your identity?"

"No, I wasn't thinking about all that. It was because you'd misheard me first. I thought about correcting you, but you kept wanting to talk about bee farming."

"I see. Well, my hearing is clearly terrible, but still—you could have told me."

"I mean, it was honestly sort of funny—"

Romi slammed her hands on the table, rattling the jug next to her. Boknam hurriedly reached out to stop it from falling over.

"It was funny? Making a fool of someone was funny to you?"

The smile on his face vanished. He drew back his hands and lowered his head. "I'm sorry. At the time, I didn't think we would see each other again."

He didn't think they would see each other again. No matter how Romi thought about it, this hurt more than if he'd simply deceived her. While she'd been dreaming about moving to Jeju for him, he'd been thinking the two of them would never again cross paths.

Romi thought back to Hadam's birthday, the day this *Searching for Honeyman* project had begun. She remembered the guesses they'd made that day as to why she hadn't been able to find him—because he was married, because he'd lost his memory. They thought all their predictions had turned out to be correct, but they hadn't. The true answer, in the end, was that the real Honeyman simply wasn't interested. He just wasn't that into her.

"Then why did you come back the second day? Why did you change your clothes and switch cars?"

"Because I had so much fun the first day. The second day was fun too—I enjoyed the time we spent together. The clothes I wore that first day were hyung's clothes because I'd come straight from helping him with his work, but the second day, I went more with my style. It was the same with the car. I borrowed hyung's truck the first day and his wife's car the second. I was still staying at their house at the time, so I didn't have a car of my own."

Romi was at a loss for words. His response was so innocent. She realized why she'd been so certain Kyungwoon was the one when she first saw him. On day one, Boknam was dressed in the same sweater Kyungwoon was wearing in the photos in the gallery, and his truck was identical to the one Boknam had driven. She thought she would remember him, but in reality, all that had remained in her heart were these faint impressions. Weren't such impressions all that memories of a person were? The clothes they wore that day, the car they drove, certain specific moments. Faded memories she'd believed were crystal clear.

Ultimately, the blame lay with human memory and romanticism. To hell with romance, as she and her friends had declared the day before—she had once been so immersed in the love-story narrative that she dreamed of that sort of ending, where a pleasant time spent in the company of another person would lead to an intimate relationship. But he had never promised her anything of the sort, had never shown an inkling of interest in that at all.

"I get it now," Romi said, mustering all the poise she typically lacked. "You enjoyed meeting me. But not enough to go to the trouble of seeking me out again once I left."

Just a few days earlier when her friends asked her why she was going to search for Honeyman, she'd said the same thing. She thought it would be fun. But it was different in Boknam's case. For him, that fun wasn't enough to want to see her again, while for Romi it had been enough for her to come back to find him.

Boknam waved his hands. "It's not like that," he said. "I really did like you."

If she'd heard those words the first time she'd come to Jeju, Romi would have been thrilled. But timing could change things, and the same words now took on a different meaning.

"I see."

"The reason I came to see you twice wasn't because I was plotting anything, but because I really wanted to talk to you." Boknam poured some water from the jug into his coffee mug. Romi thought that would make the coffee taste stale, but Boknam didn't seem to mind. Romi tasted a faint, secondhand bitterness in her mouth.

"You don't have to say that just because," she said.

He seemed to deflate at that, fidgeting with the handle on his mug. When Romi first met him, she thought he was older than she was or else around the same age, but looking straight at him now, she realized she'd been wrong.

"I'm sorry," said Boknam, resting his hands on his knees and bowing his head in apology. "I shouldn't have lied like that, whether I was kidding around or not."

"It's fine," she said.

When Boknam looked up again, his voice was so quiet as to seem foreboding. "But part of me feels so glad we were able to meet again like this," he said.

"What?"

"I didn't know you'd been thinking about me so earnestly for three years. If I'd known how you felt, I probably would have thought about you the same way."

"I'm sorry?" Romi couldn't properly answer him, seeing how his eyes had softened with so much sudden affection.

"Even now, our fates have brought us together again."

Romi bolted up. "What are you saying?"

Was this some kind of hidden camera prank? It felt like the exact scene she had dreamed up coming into this trip. Reuniting with the beekeeper (who'd turned out to be a tailor), confessing her true feelings. But was this really what she'd had in mind?

Someone cleared their throat. Kyungwoon stood in the doorway with a cup in his hands. Romi panicked. Had he heard their conversation? How much of it? Could everyone hear them all the way from the kitchen?

"Did I interrupt something? I was just heading out, so you two can continue your private chat."

"It's not like that!" Romi shouted, surprising even herself.

Boknam caught on and stood up, too, awkwardly pointing toward the exit. "I'd also better get back to the café. I'll talk to you later, Romi. See you tonight."

She could see a signal that was impossible to misunderstand in the glint in Boknam's eyes. A green light.

"But—but—"

Boknam vanished without hearing her reply.

For a moment, an uneasy silence lingered between Kyungwoon and Romi. He gestured toward the exit with his cup, too, turning to leave. "I should also get going."

"Wait!" Romi called.

He stopped and turned around again.

"Um." What should she say? That she was sorry for mistaking him for someone else? That she was wrong for needlessly causing him so much confusion, for having fallen for someone else? Should she ask him to forget everything that had happened? Her head was a tangled mess of thoughts.

Kyungwoon was watching her, waiting.

"I'm sorry! For being so weird!" Romi bowed a full ninety degrees. Then, worried he would see her roots growing out as it had been a while since she'd dyed her hair, she snapped upright again.

Kyungwoon continued to study her. "You're not weird," he said. "And everything turned out just fine. You found the person you were looking for."

He'd heard them! Romi felt her throat close up. She poured herself a glass of water from her jug and gulped it down. As she did, she remembered how parched she had been.

"No," she said. "Or, you're right, I did, but—"

"The person you met who inspired you three years ago was Boknam, and Boknam is interested in you too. Seems like a great outcome. And you don't have to worry about me. I won't tell anyone what happened."

Romi felt like each of his carefully chosen words had stomped on her heart and kept walking. "Why are you saying that? Like you don't know how I feel—"

"How *do* you feel?" Kyungwoon asked. He had always moved at a slower rhythm, waiting until others finished speaking to chime in, so to have him interrupt her now left Romi speechless. Even she didn't know exactly how she felt. Whom did she have feelings for? The person she had known back then? This new person she had just met? Where did feelings born out of a misunderstanding eventually land?

"I . . ."

What about you? Don't you care that the person I fell for in the past wasn't you? Romi wanted to ask, but in the end, she said nothing. It would be too shameless.

Kyungwoon stood there for a moment, seemingly waiting for Romi to continue. Time slipped by unnoticed.

At last, Kyungwoon spoke up again. "I lost my memories, so the only Romi that I know is the version of you standing here in front of me. But the version of me that you know isn't actually me." He paused for a moment, looking at Romi. "I guess sometimes having amnesia is more convenient."

With that, he left the courtyard. Romi plunked down onto her seat. It occurred to her that she ought to drink her fill of water now and grab a few barley tea bags to bring back upstairs. That way, she wouldn't have to leave the room for a long time.

Perhaps because the weather had cleared up, a bunch of young surfers in their wet suits were there dripping water onto the floor of the café well into the late afternoon. The energy they exuded left a deep impression on Hadam. She made a mental note to film something focused on surfers next.

Hadam didn't cut through the café but instead went around the building and through the yard. Though not to the same extent as Romi, Hadam also didn't want to see anyone. She wanted to get back to the room, and fast.

She was treading carefully over the grass when she spotted a black figure moving in the shadows in a corner of the yard. She almost dropped her camera in surprise.

"Geez, you scared me."

The shadowy figure also took a step back, seeming startled, but her voice was quiet when she spoke. "Hadam? It's me."

"Sumi? What are you doing here?"

Sumi, whom she had only ever seen wearing linen shirts in natural colors and wide-legged pants or long skirts, was dressed in a black hoodie and jeans, gripping a black backpack in her hands. Maybe Sumi was actually a really sporty person, Hadam thought. The other woman hurriedly slung the backpack onto her shoulders.

"I came to talk with Ayoung about our meetings. We're holding the next one at our place, the Honeycomb. I was wondering what I should prepare." Sumi looked behind her as she spoke, her voice somewhat high-pitched.

"I think I saw Ayoung inside the café."

"Oh, right—I just got here. I was going to head to the café through the kitchen, but I saw Romi and Kyungwoon talking in the courtyard."

Following Sumi's gaze, Hadam could see Kyungwoon leaving. She only caught a brief glimpse of him from a distance, but she thought his face looked serious.

"Did something . . . happen with the two of them? Was Kyungwoon the reason Romi came to Jeju in the first place?"

"No, not at all!" Hadam said, probably too quickly. Sumi didn't seem to believe her, but she murmured "All right" anyway. It seemed some doubts about their relationship had already firmly taken root in her mind. Or she might have been genuinely uninterested. Sumi coolly adjusted the straps on her backpack and started to walk away.

"Well, then—ack!"

Hadam whipped her head around at the sound of something rustling behind her. When she realized what it was, her heart resettled.

"Pilhyun sunbae? What brings you here again?"

"Um."

When he didn't answer right away, Hadam suddenly had a hunch. "What, did Jaewoong tell you to come by and check on me?"

She must have hit the nail on the head, because Pilhyun pouted slightly. "Well, he didn't say those exact words, but . . ."

"Go back and tell him to mind his own business."

"What?"

"Tell him I said to mind his own business!"

Startled by the outburst, Sumi staggered back a couple steps. People in the courtyard craned their necks to see what all the noise was about. The bee farmer—no, the tailor—as well as Sumi's husband and Department Head Boo all appeared at the window. Department Head Boo looked like a Messenger emoji with his round face and round eyes. Why were all these people here every day? Hadam wanted to know. Were they that close? Did they have nothing better to do? Either way, they always seemed to be the audience for the drama Hadam and her friends couldn't seem to escape. She felt embarrassed now for shouting.

"Sorry, sunbae. I'm really tired today. I think I'd better turn in."

"Sure," said Pilhyun curtly. He seemed to be in a sour mood.

Hadam couldn't quite interpret his expression. But she didn't have the energy to lend much thought to how he was feeling at the moment. She was upset, too, and there were all these people watching.

The three shadows cast by the afternoon sun intersected on the grass. As Hadam passed by Sumi and Pilhyun, she saw the two of them exchange nods. Did they know each other? Hadam wondered. It wouldn't have been all that unusual. It was a small world. The island was even smaller. Jaewoong and his fiancée, the young surfers—they were all linked in a chain of mutual connections. Were the mainlanders the only ones not in that loop?

◆ ◆ ◆

The first one to hear Chakyung's footsteps in the darkness and come running was none other than the puppy. It hadn't been more than a few days since she'd found him, and already the thought that this creature remembered her made her heart ache; it was so adorable. He leaped around excitedly as Chakyung sat down with him and scratched under his chin. She caught a pleasant whiff of the smell coming from the dog's sun-warmed fur. She could immediately tell without looking whose fresh shower-gel scent it was.

"You're back late today. Did you have dinner?"

She looked up, her heart lifting before her head fully had. Before their eyes even met, she knew his would be gleaming with a smile.

"Yes, I had dinner with my coworkers after our meeting wrapped up."

"Something tasty?" Soo-eon plopped down across from her. The dog let out low, contented sighs, loving the additional attention.

"Well, since we're all visiting Jeju, everyone just wanted to have raw fish."

She could have come back earlier, but she purposely hadn't. She knew when she did, she'd have to face Soo-eon, and as much as she wanted to see him, she was afraid too.

He didn't ask her anything else, just continued to gently pet the dog. "Were you bored today, Gnarly? You were all alone, weren't you?"

"Gnarly?"

"That's what I named him. G-n-a-r-l-y. It's surfer slang for 'amazing,' 'daring,' 'cool'—that sort of thing. I want him to live big even though he's little."

"I see. It's a nice name."

Time flew by just doting on the puppy. Gnarly must have been in a good mood, resting his head on Chakyung's palm. She beamed at him. Watching them, Soo-eon suddenly asked, "What are you going to do?"

"About what?"

"Gnarly. What would you like to do with him?"

"I should figure that out. I . . . have to head back to Seoul tomorrow." Chakyung realized how silly she sounded. She must have seemed so irresponsible.

When she'd contacted the pet shelter, they told her no one had reported a white poodle missing. When she'd first taken him in off the streets, she had the vague notion that she'd keep him for a day or two and then send him off to the shelter. So that he could find a new owner. Chakyung looked into the dog's eyes, black like baduk stones. Would he be able to find a new home? There were nearly six thousand abandoned pets on Jeju alone.

"I can keep him here with me at Nol for now," Soo-eon said, reaching out to scratch between Gnarly's ears. The dog leaned his head back. This was, as Soo-eon had said, a "for now" fix. But Chakyung was the one who'd taken the dog in. It was one thing to cross paths on the street and offer help. But it wasn't often that a chance encounter like this ended up coming home with you, becoming part of your everyday life. Could Chakyung care for a dog? Technically, she needed to work only the standard hours at her company, but in reality, there was a lot of voluntary overtime. She lived with her parents, but her mother was allergic to animal fur. More than that, she couldn't be sure what they would say once they found out she wasn't marrying Chanmin.

"But the problem is, I'll probably only be able to keep him for a couple months. It'll be hard to bring him with me to Bali," Soo-eon said.

Chakyung's heart sank at that unexpected announcement. "Did you say Bali?"

He had said it casually, but with the certainty of someone whose plans had already been made.

"I did. I'm headed there this winter. To run a surfing camp. It's been in the works since last year."

"How long will you be there?"

"At the moment, I'm under contract for the season. Until February."

"And after that?"

"I'm not sure yet," he said evenly.

"I see."

You said you would wait, Chakyung wanted to say. The words sat on the tip of her tongue, but she ultimately tamped them back down. She was old enough to know that waiting didn't mean you wouldn't go anywhere or do anything, that you would have eyes for only one person all that while. Still . . .

After yesterday's typhoon, after what happened with Romi, after seeing Hadam in a rage—Chakyung had to reflect.

Even if meeting someone on a trip could be considered fate, it was still nothing more than a chance happening. Even if you believed it would change your life, the reality was that you could still be mistaken. She couldn't be sure that she wasn't feeling that way now. Because they had fatefully crossed paths in an unfamiliar place, because her fiancé had betrayed her, because Soo-eon had treated her with such warmth, she now found herself wavering. But would this feeling remain after she returned to her old normal?

Soo-eon could sense her hesitation. "But when you're undecided," he said, "you can decide anything."

Still seated, Chakyung looked up and locked eyes with him. His gaze wasn't forceful, but it was intense.

"I can come back. Doesn't matter where. But . . ." He held out his hand. "Will you come back too?"

If she took his hand—then what? Chakyung knew she had to give him an answer. But was she ready to? Could the two of them meet again in Seoul or Jeju, or Bali, or anywhere else?

For the person hesitating, time moved quickly, and for the person waiting, time dragged on. While Chakyung wavered, Soo-eon lowered his hand.

"I'm sorry for keeping you waiting," she said.

Soo-eon stood and stepped away. "You said you're headed to Seoul tomorrow, right?"

Chakyung stood up without his help. "Right."

"Safe travels," he said, as if they were parting ways here and now. And she supposed they were. If she didn't say what she wanted to do, then all they *could* do was say their goodbyes for now.

She needed to answer him, but in that moment, Chakyung could bring herself to say only, "Soo-eon, I'll—I'll think about it. Seriously."

He smiled. Even with that hint of forlornness in his smile, he was still a bright, positive person. "I know you will," he said. "You take every moment of your life seriously." He turned toward the dark courtyard and added, "But you know something?"

Chakyung studied his back. Broad, strong, and always warm enough to lean on—but now it was out of her reach. She wanted to go closer to him, to assure herself that he wasn't as far away as he seemed. But her feet wouldn't move.

The last thing Soo-eon said fell over her like a blanket of fog descending on the island. "If you take the future seriously but not the present, this moment right now? You won't be able to move forward."

When Chakyung opened the door to their room, she didn't see Romi but could hear her voice coming from the bathroom. Hadam was at the table in the common room, her face dimly lit by the one small light she had on overhead.

"Hadam, why are you sitting in the dark?"

Hadam blinked, snapping out of a daze. "Oh, right—I don't like when it's too bright."

"Well, can I put on a bit more light in here?" Chakyung's hand found the light switch.

"Go ahead, I suppose," Hadam said, getting up and heading to her room.

Bright light filled the apartment, but that did nothing to brighten the mood. Chakyung followed after Hadam, who was sitting in front of her open suitcase and winding up her computer adapter cable. Neat stacks of clothes sat beside her.

"Are you packing now? I thought you weren't heading back until the day after tomorrow."

Hadam didn't look up, keeping her answer curt. "I decided to leave tomorrow night too."

"Why?"

"Hmm. No particular reason."

Hadam was acting different. She usually welcomed questions about what she was doing and would explain her reasoning down to the letter. Chakyung didn't press her on it, though, as she took a seat beside her.

"Can I help you pack?"

When she picked up an unfolded white T-shirt, Hadam snapped at her, "Just leave it. I'll do it myself."

"It'll be faster if we work together."

Hadam snatched the shirt back. "I said leave it."

Many conflicts tended to pass if you held back and waited a little while. Three hours or so should do the trick. Three hours without asking why the other person was angry, without getting angry in turn. That was usually how Chakyung handled such clashes. But seeing as they were in this confined space and this conflict had arisen while they were on a trip, it was hard for her to let this slide.

"Hadam, have I done something to upset you?"

Too quickly, Hadam replied, "It's not that."

"You've been talking to me for the past while as if I have."

Chakyung noticed that Hadam had been winding and unwinding the same cable over and over and was now unwinding it again. In the end, she tossed the cable aside.

"I'm just a little bit disappointed in you, Chakyung. I thought this thing with the surfer was a diversion, but it must be pretty serious."

Chakyung could guess what Hadam was talking about. She would have had a clear view of the yard from their window, and though she wouldn't have been able to hear their conversation, she could have gotten a sense of the vibe from watching.

"Hadam, I know how it looks. But it's not like I intended for this to happen—"

"It's never the sort of thing that happens intentionally," Hadam cut in, picking up the cable again. "Sure, you might find yourself drawn to someone else ahead of your marriage. Maybe even before you've sorted out your relationship completely. Either way, it's up to you to pick a side."

It's up to you to pick a side, she'd said, but there was an undercurrent to her words, as though it were possible to choose wrong. Chakyung knew she must have seemed no different than someone like Jaewoong in Hadam's eyes. And it wasn't only Hadam. Lots of people would see things that way, regardless of Chanmin's egregious faults. She couldn't always offer excuses. She knew she'd have her share of criticism to endure.

"Hadam, I—I don't think I should have to explain this, but regardless, this isn't some simple phase I'm going through before I get married." She didn't need to, but she at least wanted to explain to her friend the emotions she hadn't even been able to explain to herself. "The relationship between me and Chanmin is our problem. We have to resolve it on our own, the two of us. Soo-eon is a whole other issue. I can't just put him in the middle of things—it's not his place."

Hadam yanked on the cable hard enough that Chakyung worried it might snap.

"Plenty of people say that. But the new relationship can wait until the old one is figured out. It's not like it's so hard to control yourself." Hadam paused to catch her breath. "I'm sorry, Chakyung. I know the situation with Jaewoong is different. But if Chanmin hadn't come by that evening and you hadn't found out he was cheating . . . would things have turned out differently?"

That was one of the thoughts that had been continuously gnawing at Chakyung's mind. Was she simply using the fact that Chanmin had come to Jeju with another woman as justification for breaking off her engagement to someone she already had doubts about marrying? If she hadn't found out, would she never have developed feelings for Soo-eon?

"I don't know," she answered honestly. "But that's what happened, and I did find out, and now I can't imagine going in any other direction."

Emotions flowed like water that might change course when it ran up against rocks but could never flow back in the direction from which it had come. Chakyung realized there was nothing that could be done about feelings that had already flowed elsewhere.

"Well, it's your life," Hadam said with a shrug. It felt like the air between them was riddled with tiny thorns, sharp enough to pierce them both. Just as the words Chakyung had been holding in were about to leap out, a scream came from the other room.

"*Aaaaaah!*"

Hadam and Chakyung exchanged a look, then leaped up and raced out of the room.

The overhead lights shone on the towel wrapped around Romi's wet hair. She must have just gotten out of the bath. Her face was pale, and her entire body was shaking. She was holding her tablet in both hands.

"What's wrong?" Hadam asked urgently.

Chakyung took the tablet from Romi. Hadam wrapped her arms around Romi's still-trembling shoulders.

It was hard to decipher the message written on the tablet. The screen was filled with red, and there were roughly scrawled words on the image. It was a crude sketch, but still clearly meant to be blood. Chakyung tried reading the message.

"What does this say? 'Do Romi, get yourself together and go home. If you don't want . . . to end up like her.' What does that mean?"

Hadam and Chakyung turned to Romi, but she shook her head. "I don't know either. But I'm getting chills imagining someone coming in, writing this, and leaving."

"Shouldn't we report this to the police?" Chakyung looked serious, setting the tablet down on the table. She glanced at Hadam, who was pulling out her phone.

"Should we?" Romi's face had lost all its color. "This time, too, there's no clear threat. It doesn't say anything specific. If the police decide it's just someone's scribblings, they'll probably give up there."

"This time? What do you mean?"

"Actually, I got a message when we first landed on Jeju. From a stranger." Romi took out her phone and showed them the text. "I don't know if it's the same person, though."

As she read the message, Chakyung's tone shifted into analysis mode. "It's a possibility. For one thing, this message also sounds weirdly like the lyrics to an old-timey pop song, and for another, the writing style is similar. So it seems possible these are from the same person. But this message may have also been sent by mistake. Still, it's upsetting, so it should be reported."

Hadam opened a browser on her phone. "If this started after you came to Jeju . . . maybe things will be okay once you leave? Which jurisdiction should we report it to?"

Chakyung screenshotted the message on Romi's phone and forwarded it to herself. "I think we should look into this ourselves for now. But there's a more important issue we have to deal with first."

The silence between saying one thing and another was always meaningful. The other two watched and waited while Chakyung chose her words.

"Whoever left this message on the tablet must have come into this room."

A shiver ran down all their spines. When and how could someone have gotten in? When Romi was alone in the apartment? Or while Hadam and Chakyung were having their little war of nerves?

"Romi, when did you last look at your tablet?" Chakyung asked.

Romi put her hand to her head, trying to remember. "Earlier this afternoon, I was doing some work on the tablet . . . then I went downstairs to get some water . . . and after that, I had a headache, so I lay down for a bit, and then Hadam came and we had dinner. That whole time, I didn't look at the tablet."

"So there's no way to know when this person came in," Hadam said. "I got back around five o'clock. I don't think they could've come in after that."

Truly anyone could have entered the café or the courtyard. Each of the houses in the residential area had steel padlocks on the doors that required a passcode, but someone who knew the code would have been able to come inside anytime. The passcodes at Nol didn't change until the residents came and changed them. Additionally, if there was a property manager, they could have used their key card. Who could have done this? One of the residents here? Or one of the customers at the café? While they turned over all the possibilities, a tense quiet hung in the air.

"What's scarier," began Chakyung, her low voice cutting through the chilling silence, "is that this person somehow also knew the passcode to unlock Romi's tablet."

Romi clamped her hands over her mouth to cover her scream. Hadam's eyes widened. Chakyung looked over the scrawled message on the tablet again, then went to the door and examined it for a moment too.

"I'm going to look around outside for a bit," she said. "I'll be back."

"No!" Hadam and Romi shouted.

"Chakyung, it's dangerous," said Hadam. "What will you do if someone's out there?"

A sense of darkness had descended on the room. Even the small shadows in the corners of the apartment seemed unsettling now. Chakyung opened the door a sliver, looked around, then closed it again, pointedly sliding the latch shut.

Romi hugged herself. Goose bumps had risen on her arms. "I have a really bad feeling right now. Could this be the stalker from before?"

Hadam hugged her. "The security here should be fine. If you're really scared, do you want to move to a hotel?"

Romi pressed her mouth shut, thinking. She shook her head. "I think it'd be better not to leave. It's not a good idea to go wandering around at night either."

After Chakyung had finished checking their surroundings, she said, "The coast is clear. For now, I'll call Ayoung and ask if there are any CCTVs or anything we could check. It could be a thief, so we should let her know right away. I'll tell her to file a police report."

Romi didn't have anything to add, but she didn't think this person was some random thief. The intruder even knew her name. The reality of the situation was dawning on the three of them. After Chakyung ended the call, she took Romi's hands in hers.

"Romi, it's all right. We're here for you."

Hadam's hands joined theirs. "You're okay," she said. "We'll protect you."

Romi studied her friends' faces. They wore the same fear. But there were fears that grew bigger as more people shared them and fears that grew smaller when they were shared with others. With all of them together, they could protect one another. Tonight, she would be able to put aside at least a little bit of her fear.

CHASE AFTER WHAT'S BEEN TAKEN

June 20, 2018

One summer afternoon, a call came into the fire station in the city of S.

CALLER: Right now, there are bees swarming, a huge swarm—it's pure chaos.

Firefighters were quickly dispatched to the scene, where they found twenty-three thousand bees swarming over the road and darkening the sky.

A beekeeper who happened to be passing through gave the hapless firefighters a helping hand.

FIREFIGHTER: The most amazing thing was how the beekeeper rounded up all those bees into a hive. He was like—what's it called? From that old children's book. The guy who played the flute and led a horde of mice away from—was it Hamong? Hamel? Anyway, just like that guy with the flute, he led all those bees away.

BEEKEEPER: Ah, it's not like I used some sort of magic on them. Their queen had died, so they were stranded on that road. I didn't know where they came from, but maybe they were trying to find a new hive . . . In any case, they gather when they catch the scent of a queen bee. So I put a dead queen inside a hive and brought that with me, and the bees followed the scent. I think it took about an hour for them all to be rounded up.

The only victims were a handful of bees that perished in the early stages of these suppression tactics, and no people were hurt. May the queen bee rest in peace.

The afternoon session at the Conference on Eco-Friendly Bee Farming for the Advancement of the Global Sixth Industry was slowly winding down. The conference participants' drive had been on a steady decline since lunchtime, and right around now was when they began to drop off. Several of them, when they finished their own presentations, set off on leisurely strolls around the conference hall, sampling honey creams and the like and chatting with their fellow beekeepers. Boo Hwachul was taking turns with other staffers to hand out pamphlets about the beekeeping education course at the Honeybee School. In the morning, there had been quite a bit of interest, but perhaps because their trial program was now over, the booth had quieted down. Hwachul took a bite of one of the jumbo honey macarons Director Kang Hyunbok at Dolmiyong Jeju had ambitiously set out in an attempt to appeal to the youth. There was an excessive amount of filling, which made the macaron overly sweet for his taste.

Hwachul decided to show off the spirit of exchange and distribute the macarons far and wide. He carried the tray of them around the conference hall, imagining he was promoting samples. Since it was the afternoon, when people felt especially low on sugar, several of them welcomed the macarons. Hwachul slowly made his way down to the first floor, headed out through the back door, and started down the walking path.

He walked for a while, passing tents selling goods related to local beekeeping, and eventually came to a spacious, open lot at the start of the road that led to Jusangjeolli Cliff, where beehives of all different kinds and colors stood in a line. Beekeepers had set them up to show-case the local bee-farming industry. It must have been a suggestion from one of the know-nothing higher-ups on the conference organizing committee. The idea was that setting up the beehives someplace with an ocean view could double as a way to draw people out to the newly renovated walking path, which would show off the nature-friendly aspect of the conference hall and simultaneously make for a nice visual. Jeju natives who were bee farmers were generally unhappy with the plan, wondering who would bother leaving the conference hall to come all the way out here when hardly anyone, even the tourists walking the Jeju Olle Trail, ever came this far. Yet despite the unfavorable location, several bee farmers who had moved to Jeju agreed to participate to show their cooperation with provincial policies.

Wherever Hwachul went, there were bound to be tons of people he knew, but there were certain faces that especially stood out. He spotted Kyungwoon by a beehive shaped like a traditional Jeju house, talking earnestly with a gray-haired foreign woman. She nodded as if in agreement, handed him a business card, and left. Hwachul waited a moment before he approached, glancing over at the woman as she walked away.

"Hyung, who's she? And what were you talking about so seriously? In English, at that."

He offered Kyungwoon a macaron, but the other man held up a hand to decline.

"She's a professor at the University of Minnesota in the US. She noticed that our bees appeared to be a special breed. I think she wanted to know more about the results of the breeding experiment—whether there was a report or something on the findings, or whether I could send her a sample for her to study in her own lab, along with an analysis on the components of their honey or royal jelly."

Hwachul carefully lifted the lid of the hive, which resembled a roof. To his eyes, the bees didn't look markedly different from any others, but it was possible these bees were a bit more active.

"Is that so? I know you and your wife started focusing a long time ago on experiments to improve the breed. Didn't you contact some American universities back then?"

"Right, Hyeyoung and I were working on the research together, but honestly, after the accident, I couldn't really manage it. She'd always been the one leading. I was more like her assistant, so even if I'd come out of the accident with my memory intact, I'm not sure I would have known enough to do it alone. Either way, it's amazing these bees haven't died and are hanging in there. I guess Hyeyoung raised them to be tough little creatures." Kyungwoon smiled slightly as if he'd told a joke.

"Your wife—I remember even in graduate school, there was talk that she was a genius. I heard she was invited to lecture at an American university but decided to follow you here instead."

"She did . . ."

Seeing the shadows darken around Kyungwoon's eyes, Hwachul promptly shut his mouth. But upon closer inspection, it was clear the deep dark circles under Kyungwoon's eyes weren't only from feeling downcast.

"Are you feeling tired today? You're looking a bit rough."

"Yeah. I didn't get any sleep. Is it that obvious?"

"Why didn't you sleep? Did something happen?"

The gloom spread over Kyungwoon's entire face. "Seems like there was a thief at Nol yesterday. A thief, or a stalker."

Hwachul nearly dropped the macarons.

"What? Is anything missing? Was anyone hurt?"

"Well, I heard someone broke into Romi and her friends' room and left some kind of threatening message. And . . . there were signs someone had broken into my room too."

"When? I was there yesterday afternoon. No one said a word about this."

"It seems like it happened at some point in the afternoon when the rooms were empty, but it's hard to know exactly when."

"Sounds like a petty thief who targets guesthouses. Was anything missing?"

As the number of places offering accommodations on Jeju increased with the rise in tourism, so did the number of places plagued by petty crime. Transplants from the mainland were easy victims as many of them ran guesthouses, and they were also easy suspects as they were outsiders.

Kyungwoon frowned. "I'm not sure."

"What? How could you not know?"

"My wife—she had a box with some things inside, but it was locked. I didn't know the passcode, so I just left it as it was. But yesterday, I found it open, and I'm not sure what, if anything, was taken from it."

Hwachul regretted having asked so thoughtlessly. Of course, a person with amnesia wouldn't be able to tell whether anything was missing. The same thing could happen even to someone who hadn't lost their memory.

"Is everyone in Romi's room okay?" Hwachul hesitated briefly before adding, "Were, um, her friends unharmed? Like Hadam, for example?"

"They filed a police report, but the security cameras were destroyed in the typhoon, so they couldn't check any footage. There were lots of people in the café yesterday too. Romi and her friends seemed anxious, so I stood guard outside their room all night. Around dawn, Soo-eon came to switch places with me."

"So that's why you look so tired."

"I guess." Kyungwoon sounded nonchalant, running a hand through his hair.

"Should I head over there today? Do you need my help?" Hwachul asked in all seriousness, but Kyungwoon pursed his lips and shook his head.

"No need—their flights leave later tonight, from what I heard."

"Really? I'd wanted to at least say my goodbyes before they left."

People on a trip always left. That much wasn't new. But when someone left a place, naturally, they left people behind too. People who had always lived there, who unwittingly ended up being abandoned by the mere fact of someone else coming and going. Kyungwoon and Hwachul had the same thought at once—that they were being left behind.

"Well, no time like the present." Kyungwoon gestured toward the conference hall. "Hadam and Chakyung are inside right now. Hadam said she wanted to film, and Chakyung is running a booth for her company."

"What about Romi? Is she alone? Is she all right?"

"It's daytime, and there are plenty of people at Nol. Taylor's with her too."

"Hmm." Hwachul didn't think that man, who'd cast aside his perfectly good name and insisted on being called Taylor, was to be trusted, but as Kyungwoon said, lots of people were there, and he agreed nothing that dangerous was likely to happen at the surf café in broad daylight.

"Well, are you going to head inside and say your goodbyes? Want to go together?"

"Sure, let's do that," said Hwachul, following Kyungwoon.

They walked for a while back up the path they had come down, and as they were about to enter the conference hall, they ran into one of the on-site staff members coming out. The staffer gave a simple nod of greeting and was half running away when Kyungwoon asked, "Oh, are you taking down the beehives?"

Distractedly, the staffer replied, "Yes, I'm tidying up. The chairman is about to wrap up the event soon too. Then we'll be dining here with the association members. I heard we have to close the outdoor area earlier than the indoor one, since it's so far out."

With that, the staffer hurried off toward the exhibition area.

Kyungwoon shot Hwachul a cornered look. "I guess I'd better start packing up, then. I came in someone else's truck."

Hwachul preferred not to have to find Hadam and say his goodbyes alone. He didn't want to be remembered as someone so awkward and bumbling that he couldn't even properly bid someone farewell.

"Then let's say goodbye first," he suggested. "It'd be more of a pain for you to go all the way out to the beehives again and then come back. I'll help you take down your hive. Our truck from Dolmiyong Jeju should be able to handle the load."

Just then, someone else—a familiar face, this time—came out of the convention center. It was the owner of the Honeycomb Guesthouse.

"Hyung-nim, are you heading over to take down your hive too?" Hwachul asked.

"I am. I am," said the older man, eyes darting around, unfocused. "But, Kyungwoon, I heard you're not supposed to?"

"Sorry?"

"You had some people wanting to get a closer look at yours, so I heard you were supposed to leave it up. That's what my wife said. That someone from the conference committee will deliver it to your bee farm later."

The Honeycomb owner rattled off the news like an indifferent messenger, then took off toward the hives. Kyungwoon wanted to ask for more details, but before he could even turn around, the other man had vanished. Dejected, Kyungwoon turned back to Hwachul.

"Who would want a closer look at my hive?"

"Right? I wish we could have asked." Hwachul shrugged. "Oh, well. It worked out for the better. Let's go."

Kyungwoon cast a nervous glance behind him, but Hwachul hurried off so quickly that Kyungwoon had to rush to catch up.

The beekeepers who had taken part in the outdoor exhibition were zooming around like dutiful honeybees with their hives loaded up in carts. A few bees lagging behind the rest of their hives hovered over the cleared-out exhibition area in the early-evening light. Some of the stragglers eventually caught on and took off sheepishly. Little by little, the people who had been on the walking path disappeared into the distance too.

As night fell, the island winds picked up, and the number of people coming and going dwindled. Only one beehive remained, and now someone was slipping quietly into the vacated exhibition area. After pulling a protective hat out of a backpack and putting it on, the person took a look around, slowly approaching Kyungwoon's beehive. At this hour, the hive was hard to see, hidden in the shadows of the trees, but this person moved toward it without hesitation, then opened the hive slowly, carefully, with gloved hands. Once it was open, the sound of the bees' low humming poured out. The person reached in and grabbed the prize, placing it inside a small container. Then off came the protective hat and gloves, which were stuffed into the backpack again. The job was done. Now all there was to do was get out of here. The person zipped up their hoodie.

Turning to leave, though, the person was hit square in the face with the beam from a cell phone flashlight. The light slowly moved aside, revealing two people standing where it had been.

One of them grinned at the person in the hoodie. "Hello. What are you doing here?"

That smile was infinitely bright and infinitely troubling.

◆　◆　◆

Project: *Searching for Honeyman*

Day Eight, Seogwipo

After having an earlier dinner than everyone, Romi went up to her room to finish packing.

Whenever she traveled, she liked to buy little souvenirs—key chains and refrigerator magnets, of course, as well as strange bracelets and local snacks that no one really ate. Because she hadn't gone to many tourist spots this time, there wasn't much to add to her suitcase aside from what she'd brought in it. Had she come on this trip to find something? It seemed more like she'd come to lose things—her fantasies about the person she'd met briefly during her travels; her useless expectations about a life-altering romance.

She heard a knock on the door paired with the sound of someone clearing their throat. "Romi?"

She opened the door a crack with the chain still attached. She could see Taylor's—Boknam's—suntanned face in the gap. Romi undid the latch and stepped outside.

"I have something for you," he said.

They went downstairs and took a seat on a bench in the yard. After the typhoon, the days had grown chillier. It was hot during the daytime, but in the late afternoons, the summer pulled away like a tide going out, leaving behind the chill of autumn. It had been hardly a week since they'd arrived on Jeju, but in that time, it felt like one season had been folded away and a new one had been laid out.

Boknam handed Romi a yellow shopping bag.

"Kyungwoon hyung asked me to give this to you. He had to go to the beekeeping conference today, so he figured he probably wouldn't be able to catch you in time. He said to wish you safe travels back to Seoul."

The bag was heavier than Romi had expected. It was the royal jelly and beeswax wrapping paper.

"It's from his harvest this summer. It was the first thing he did when he got back at the start of the season and tried to restore the farm to how it used to be. It's like proof that he's returned to normal."

Romi hugged the shopping bag to her chest. "It's a really precious gift. Thank you."

Her heart ached at the fact that Kyungwoon had delivered his goodbyes to her through someone else, but a part of her thought she wouldn't have wanted to face him anyway. Besides, from his perspective, this may have been the best farewell he could give.

"Do you think we'll be able to see each other again sometime in Seoul?" Boknam asked, stretching his arms and taking in the breeze.

Romi didn't have an easy answer to that.

"I know I pretended to be a bee farmer," Boknam went on, "but it wasn't like I spun all the things I said out of thin air. I based them on Kyungwoon hyung and echoed things I'd heard from him. His dreams of beekeeping, starting a new life, and working toward a dream. To be clear, I did lie to you, but for him, none of that was a lie."

Romi studied Boknam's face. It had been just a couple of days since she'd learned of his existence, but only now did she feel she was truly seeing him. Until yesterday, she hadn't thought of him as anything other than a guy who reminded her of Kyungwoon. But Boknam was slightly shorter than Kyungwoon and had a sturdier build. His cheekbones were more pronounced, and he had a stronger jawline. As she was getting a proper look at him at last, Romi felt she could now distinguish the two Honeymen inside her heart.

"I know what you mean. Thank you for telling me that. I understand now."

Before the words left her mouth, she wasn't certain, but as she said them aloud, her thoughts became clear.

"Boknam. The person I came here to find—it wasn't you. I think I was searching for someone I made up in my head. I'm really sorry. For getting lost in my own fantasies." She brought her hands together and bowed her head. "But thank you so much for coming to see me three years ago."

Boknam seemed to read the message she was sending him correctly. "No problem. I'm really sorry for misleading—no. For lying to you."

"Yes, well. That was wrong of you, but still."

Boknam had been scratching his head as if he were thinking when he suddenly gasped, eyes going wide.

"What is it?" Romi asked.

"It may be weird for me to bring it up now, but . . . I was going to tell you this yesterday and didn't get the chance." His tone had grown serious. "Given what happened last night, it didn't seem right to hide it."

"What is it?"

"On the second day I came to see you three years ago, when I was leaving, there was a strange note or something on the windshield of my car."

The shock hit Romi hard, flashing right before her eyes. "What did it say?"

"'Don't get involved. If you don't want to die.' Something like that." Boknam shuddered, and Romi felt his shivers in her own body. "It upset me, so I crumpled it up and threw it away, and then later that night, Kyungwoon hyung and his wife got into that accident, so I kind of freaked out."

A sense of foreboding came over Romi. "Do you think the note and the accident might have been connected?"

Boknam tilted his head. "I didn't think about that at the time, but looking back on it, they could have been. The car I drove the second day—the one I found the note on—was Kyungwoon's wife's sedan, but I met up with the two of them for dinner that evening and we switched cars again. Kyungwoon hyung drank at dinner, so he couldn't drive them back, and his wife said she'd be more comfortable driving her own car. So I took Kyungwoon hyung's SUV, and they rode back in her sedan. Later, I heard the cause of the accident was reckless driving, so I didn't even think to make the connection back to that note. Also, it turns out the dashcam in the car hadn't been working at the time, and Kyungwoon lost his memory afterward, so no one knows the details or the full story behind the accident. But now, I don't think I can rule out a connection. Someone might have gotten me and Kyungwoon confused. Just like you did."

Romi's mind was a tangled ball of thoughts. She had always been so bad at these sorts of logic problems. *If Person A takes Person B's car, then A and B switch vehicles, what would happen?* But not knowing for certain whether she had played even a small role in Kyungwoon's misfortune was enough to strike fear in her heart.

"When I told him about the message you got yesterday, Kyungwoon was really worried," said Boknam. "That's why he spent all night standing guard outside your room."

"What? Kyungwoon did that? All night?"

"Yeah, until the break of day. I guess you had no clue."

When she went back to her room, Romi felt an eeriness seeping in through the cracks around the window. She took out the things in the bag Boknam had given her to pack them into her suitcase. Something else fell out besides the royal jelly and beeswax wrapping. It was a letter that had been folded once in half. Romi opened it.

This is royal jelly I harvested myself. According to the people I let sample some ahead of time, it's a really effective energy booster. I recommend a small teaspoon in the morning and the evening on an empty stomach. Once it's opened, you'll need to refrigerate it. In the future, even when times are hard, I hope you can find the strength you need to power through. And I'll keep working hard until the day I'm able to formally request your illustration services. Hoping you're always in good health.

The note was concise. It couldn't even be said to be a personal message. It was very much on brand for him. Not offering any other pointers, not patting himself on the back—this was the writing of a man who was focused, always, on his work. That was enough. Romi bolted up, grabbed her wallet, and raced downstairs.

The smell of coffee lingered inside the café, but there were no customers in sight. Ayoung was collecting plates of leftover cake from a table where a group had been eating earlier. When Romi came running in, Ayoung's eyes went wide in surprise.

"Ayoung—sorry, but I'm trying to get to that beekeeping conference. Do you think you could call a car for me?"

"I think everybody there would have left by now. I could take you myself, though I've still got some cleaning up to do here. Can you wait?"

Romi wasn't sure she could wait another moment. "Would a taxi come out here?"

"It might take a while. And it would be an expensive trip . . ."

Ayoung and Romi turned in unison toward the tinkling bells above the door as it swung open.

"Is the café already closed for the day?" asked a man with a low voice and a familiar, chiseled face. "I was thinking about having a cup of coffee."

"Oh, hello," said Ayoung. "Please come in. We're still open."

Romi greeted him as well. "Hello."

Pilhyun nodded, returning the greeting. "Is Hadam here? I have something I'm supposed to give her."

"No, she's at the bee-farming conference. She should be back later tonight." Romi tried to be as helpful as she could, but she was in a hurry. To Ayoung, she said, "I'll try calling a taxi. Do you happen to know where Kyungwoon might be?"

"I heard he's at an outdoor event area behind the convention center, going toward Jusangjeolli Cliff. Maybe a taxi could take you straight there."

While Ayoung searched for the number on her cell phone, Pilhyun casually cut in.

"Would you like a ride there? I have my car."

"Oh? Really?"

"I'm headed in that direction anyway, and I can do without the coffee."

Romi had no time to hesitate. Besides, it wasn't like this was a complete stranger. She had no reason to turn him down.

"Sure, I'll take you up on that."

Pilhyun held the door open for her. Romi followed him out to his black SUV, matching his pace though her heart was already racing far ahead.

Filming the beekeeping conference was going smoothly. Hadam had expected a boring academic gathering, but not only had there been all sorts of different talks on sixth-industry product proposals and the development of apps for managing bee farms, there had even been events like a panel featuring beekeepers from around the world. Kim Manseop, whom she'd met at the start of filming, had taken part in the panel, which would be helpful for structuring the narrative of the documentary. The participants had all left, and the conference was now clearly coming to a close. The vice president invited Hadam to a dinner gathering afterward, but she politely declined. She was pleased enough to have gotten so much good footage, and she had to head back and get ready for her flight later that night.

The feeling of satisfaction from her work having gone well didn't last for long, though. Hadam had been heading toward the Dolmiyong Jeju booth when she spotted Director Kang Hyunbok chatting with Jaewoong and immediately turned back around. She tried to act calm as she maneuvered her way through the crowd, but she heard Jaewoong behind her, calling her name.

"Hadam!"

She pretended not to hear and kept moving forward with robot-like strides. He caught up and cut in front of her, stopping her short.

Hadam maintained her composure and said in a low voice, "What are you doing? You can drop the act now, you know."

Now that she was facing him again for the first time in a couple days, she could see the tired, sunken rings under his eyes. One side of his jaw was noticeably swollen. The regret about having resorted to needless violence had actually begun to sink in the night before. Hadam forcefully rewound the very slender thread of guilt that had started to come loose inside her. She had to hold off on apologizing until she received an apology first.

Jaewoong held out a huge, bulky backpack. "Here," he said. "It's the camera drone we talked about. You said you might need it for filming.

I rented it from a director hyung of mine on the condition that I get it back to him soon."

All her life, Hadam had believed that someone remembering her needs was akin to love, and she'd always been easily moved by even the smallest show of consideration. But she knew every such action couldn't possibly hold some greater meaning. People might remember things about each other for the sake of furthering their relationship, but remembering alone didn't make a relationship genuine. If she needed a drone, she could have borrowed one herself, and at that moment she didn't need one anyhow.

Hadam tried to sound firm. "It's fine. I'm going back to Seoul tonight anyway."

She knew she would have to come back again while she was working on the documentary, but she didn't want to be reminded of that fact. No matter how many times she returned to Jeju, she would refuse to see him.

Jaewoong's shoulders slumped as if the bag with the drone had suddenly grown ten times heavier. Hadam remembered how she used to find him somewhat cute when he was exhausted. Her memories had terrible timing. They came back to her at the most inappropriate moments. Now was the time to kick and stomp those feelings down.

"Hadam, I really was going to tell you," Jaewoong said. "But I thought—I thought the right thing to do would be to tell her first."

"If you were so concerned with doing the right thing, wouldn't you know not to bring up personal matters like this in a place swarming with people?" Hadam snapped, shoving past him. He stepped back in front of her.

"I already told her that it would be hard for me to go ahead with the marriage when there was still someone else I hadn't moved on from."

She felt like hot lava was coursing through her heart, which had once again hardened to stone. But she strained to suppress those feelings and keep them from erupting.

"Your decision to call off your marriage is a problem for you to take up with her, not me. Leave me out of it." Hadam found herself echoing Chakyung's words. "And you shouldn't have sent Pilhyun sunbae to spy on me or do the talking on your behalf either."

Jaewoong looked like this was news to him.

"What are you talking about?" he asked, frowning. "Me? Sending Pilhyun sunbae?"

Hadam raised her voice, fed up with the lies. "You sent him to Nol yesterday. To see how I was holding up. Did you not send him to ask me to consider hearing you out?"

Jaewoong's expression was gravely serious, as if he'd forgotten for a moment that he wasn't the one in a position to be upset. "Why would I send him to do that? He and I didn't even talk yesterday. I did get a call from him today, however. Asking where you were. Whether you were with Romi."

"What?"

The suspicion and anxiety came in brief but tremendous flashes like lightning that cut through Hadam's heart. *There's no way*, she thought, but her intuition was nagging at her. In her head, she recalculated the time she had spent talking with Pilhyun the day before. The time Romi had been alone before Hadam returned to Nol.

A sudden sound brought her out of her complicated thoughts. It was the ping from a cell phone. At first, she tried to ignore it, as they were in the middle of such a critical conversation. But the pinging continued, relentless. For the modern person, there were times when the ping of a text message could not be ignored. You could ignore the ringing of a phone. You could choose not to answer. But it was impossible not to take even a glance at a message you'd received. It was a conditioned reflex in humans of the smartphone generation. Hadam found herself looking down at her phone. Floating over the lock screen image was a banner notification of a message filled with exclamation points and question marks. It was from her friend Yoojin in Seoul.

"One sec," Hadam said.

Jaewoong looked anxious, but he nodded. There were times a modern person also had to wait for others to read their texts.

Hadam's expression grew somber as she read the message. She clicked the Facebook link in the text. After she had read the entire post, her piercing gaze returned to Jaewoong.

"How'd you know to come to the emergency room the day I passed out from seeing the bees?"

"I already told you. Pilhyun filled me in on what happened."

"And how did he know?"

Only then did Jaewoong's expression shift into one of bafflement as he tried to remember. "Well, he . . . he said he knows someone at the Honeybee School, so he must have heard about it from them."

"But when Pilhyun and Hwachul from the Honeybee School saw each other, they barely talked. If they knew each other, they'd know how to carry on a conversation, at least."

At the mention of Hwachul, Jaewoong frowned again.

"Really? I wasn't paying close enough attention when they were talking."

Hadam tried piecing together the different fragments of her memory. At the time, she hadn't suspected a thing. It all seemed like a natural sequence of events. But now, homing in on the stitching that had appeared so seamless, she could see the crooked parts.

Jaewoong pointed over Hadam's shoulder. "You should probably ask the Honeybee School guy yourself," he said.

When she turned around, she saw Kyungwoon and Hwachul walking over. Hwachul spotted her and raised a hand to wave, but he awkwardly lowered it when he saw Jaewoong.

Before greetings could be exchanged, Hadam cut in.

"Department Head Boo. I have a sunbae whom you've met before. The other morning. Does he know anyone at the Honeybee School, as far as you know?"

A giant question mark loomed over Hwachul's round head. "He didn't mention it? I told him about the Honeybee School, but it seemed like his first time hearing about it. Later, he said he'd seen the school a couple times in passing. But nothing about knowing anyone there."

Jaewoong stood off to the side, listening in, eyes narrowed. "What the hell? What's up with him?"

"Hold on." Hadam took out her cell phone and called Romi's number, but even after however many rings, Romi didn't answer. "Jaewoong, can you try calling Pilhyun?"

Still not fully understanding why, Jaewoong did as he was told. "His phone's off," he told her.

Hadam fretted. "Ayoung, I should try calling Ayoung," she said. "If I call the café, she should be able to put me through to Romi."

"Don't do that—call Ayoung on her cell phone. Here."

Kyungwoon found the number on his phone, pressed the call button, and handed his phone to Hadam. When Ayoung answered, Hadam jumped right in with her request. "Is Romi there, by any chance? What? She went out? With Pilhyun? How long ago?"

After she ended the call and returned Kyungwoon's phone, Hadam's hands were trembling slightly. "She said the two of them left together. About twenty minutes ago."

There weren't many cars on the road running out from Sanbang Mountain. Quiet classical music was playing on the radio. Romi knew this song, Rachmaninoff's Piano Concerto No. 2. It had been in a refrigerator commercial. Once she started thinking about refrigerators, it seemed to grow chillier inside the car. She wanted to check her phone, but she remembered it was in her room. Her dress had no pockets, so she'd left it on the table—bad decision. In hindsight, she was regretting having rushed out so frantically. She sighed. Pilhyun glanced over at her.

"Why are you headed to the conference hall so late in the day anyway? Are you meeting up with Hadam?"

The sudden question caught Romi off guard, but given the tight, closed space they were in, she knew she couldn't get away with not answering at all. Plus, she was no good at making up cover stories.

"There's something I need to tell someone," she said, "before I leave Jeju."

"Is it that beekeeper? Kyungwoon?"

Romi was surprised. He'd zeroed in exactly on the situation. How did he know? Then again, she could guess that several people had already figured it out.

"It is," she said. "There's something I really have to tell him."

"You two seem to have gotten really close, and fast. Or did you already know each other before?"

At some point, Pilhyun's tone had changed, but Romi was so wrapped up in her own thoughts that she didn't notice. "Yes . . . I mean, no."

An even longer silence stretched between them. Pilhyun handed her one of the yogurt drinks in his cup holder. "Have some."

She wasn't thirsty, but it would be awkward to refuse, so she took the drink and set it in the lap of her sundress. "Thank you."

"I really like your older illustrations," Pilhyun said suddenly. "Especially—what was it called? The *Vegetables with a Story* series?"

For the first time since they'd gotten in the car, Romi's full attention was on him. "Oh—you know my work? How did you find it?"

"I saw some of it a while ago on a forum online. The URL to your site was there, so I clicked it and found more of your illustrations."

"I see. I'm a little embarrassed, knowing you've seen those."

"I liked them. Are you not planning to publish them as a book?"

Vegetables with a Story was an illustrated essay that assigned human personas to vegetables like a cabbage, a tomato, an eggplant, and others. Romi had a soft spot for the project and had serialized it on her blog and social media, but publishers had turned it down.

Whenever she met people who were familiar with her work, Romi felt several overlapping emotions. She was overjoyed and welcomed the attention, but she was also embarrassed and even afraid at times. It felt like other people could remember all her failures.

"I'm thinking of publishing them later," she said. "By the way, did you ever leave comments on my website or blog?"

"No, I just browsed every now and then. I told Jaewoong about your work too. He probably became a super fan of yours. Maybe left you comments too."

"He told me."

"His username was 'cameralucida,' I think."

"Ah." A completely perfunctory reply, but she had nothing more to say. Because she didn't remember any of it. And as of recently, she couldn't even trust the things she did.

"You don't remember, do you?" They rode past an elementary school cloaked in the quiet of evening. Romi shuddered at the sight of the empty grounds, feeling a sense of dread. Schoolyards void of children always seemed so lonesome, as if they had been abandoned.

"I don't," said Romi. "It's really too bad."

Pilhyun glanced at her, but he shut his mouth and didn't push the subject.

Days and evenings had especially different appearances when you were traveling. The places around you were unfamiliar even in the day-time, but at night, that unfamiliarity took on an added depth. Romi thought about what unexpected things might happen as she passed through here. Her mouth went dry from sudden anxiety. She twisted the cap off the bottle of yogurt in her hands and took small sips, nearly spilling it on herself.

The most flourishing area at the conference on something-something global sixth industry—in other words, the beekeeping conference—was the cosmetics booth. This was largely because prototypes of nearly finished products such as face masks, hand creams, lip balm samples, and nutritional creams made with honey were being given out there. The event involved spinning a wheel and winning the sample the spinner landed on, but because there were people who insisted on taking just one more spin, Chakyung had been busy managing the booth all day. Someone was already assigned to run this event, but in the end, Chakyung had been left with no choice but to take on the role of middle manager.

As six o'clock drew near, Chakyung began clearing away the remaining face masks and helping to box them up, doling out orders to the other staffers.

"It's time to clean up. There aren't that many products left. Let's finish up quickly and call it a night!"

The color slowly returned to the worn faces of the staffers who had been hounded by people throughout the event. Chakyung had felt sorry seeing them work themselves to the bone all day and decided to send them home a little early before the conference officially wrapped up.

Just as a staff member was about to break down the prize wheel, a huge ruckus broke out in the conference hall.

"Oi, this where they're giving out the free makeup?"

"Looks like it, but is it already over?"

"Didn't somebody say it's going till six? We've still got time."

Upward of forty older women, mostly in their sixties and seventies, had suddenly swarmed in front of the cosmetics booth. The staffers who had been in charge of the prize wheel looked around at a loss, unsure what to tell the crowd. One of them looked to Chakyung for help. She stepped forward.

"I'm sorry, everyone. Our event is over. I know we said it would run until six o'clock, but we're going to have to end early."

A younger-looking woman in her fifties made her way to the front of the crowd. She looked strong, her face tanned copper brown.

"Sorry about that," she said. "Looks like we're all too late. We were at the Jungmun House of the Haenyeo rehearsing for the festival, and one of our old diver ladies who stopped by here earlier came back, showing off her haul. We wrapped up rehearsals and rushed over, but it looks like we missed out."

Her explanation was calm, yet tinged with regret. Chakyung could see where she was coming from. Only then did she notice the faint impressions on the ladies' wrinkled faces where their goggles must have been. Among the younger people in the crowd, she also noticed the occasional set of thinly tattooed-on eyebrows or artfully applied blush. They had the faces of women who had lived their lives in the rough ocean and under the harsh sun.

Chakyung turned to the other staffers. They were young workers who had been hired solely for this one-day event, and they were utterly drained from interacting with guests all day. Even their shoulders were sagging. Chakyung couldn't ask them to work overtime. She turned to the manager who had come with her from the team at headquarters.

"Manager Park, I'm sorry. I'll run the event if you could help set up the products. You may have to open a new box."

Manager Park nodded his understanding and quickly got to work.

The leader of sorts among the event staffers who had been exchanging looks behind Chakyung all the while stepped up. "We'll help too. We don't mind a bit of overtime."

Their only tie to one another being work, they had no obligation to go above and beyond. But they weren't merely being considerate or performing a simple act of kindness—they were in agreement as a team about what would be the most effective approach. In that moment, Chakyung felt assured in her work.

"Thank you all. Anyone who has other commitments is free to go, but if you can stay and help run the event, I'll make sure you receive overtime pay."

Morale was higher now than it had been for the last half hour. The staff members spun the wheel with vigor, and each time the arrow landed on a prize, the crowd of haenyeo cheered. Chakyung rounded up the spare samples and made goody bags to distribute to the winners.

They opened their prize bags on the spot, comparing and swapping products.

Just as Chakyung was wondering when the long line would start to shrink, a pair of men in familiar checkered shirts rushed past her and the booth. Before she could ask herself who they were, someone in a red windbreaker went whizzing by right after them. *Isn't that Hadam?* Chakyung hardly had time to form the question in her mind before the windbreaker was gone. She wanted to run after Hadam, grab ahold of her, and ask what was going on, but she had to deal with all the guests in this line first. There were still so many people waiting.

Once the line had slowly begun to dwindle and the last two people were about to spin the wheel, Chakyung heard a lot of noise coming from the direction Hadam and the other two had run off in. More people were barreling past the cosmetics booth. Chakyung recognized one of the men running at the front of the crowd as the owner of the Honeycomb Guesthouse.

The fuss spread throughout the conference hall. Chakyung knew from experience that something serious had to have caused this level of commotion, which made her anxious. She didn't seem to be the only one. Some of the staffers went to the next booth over to investigate and were bombarded with questions from the others once they returned.

"What did they say? What's going on?"

"Is there an ambulance here? And police cars?"

But the staffers who'd asked around didn't have the full answers.

"Sounds like someone passed out. Over by the cliff. No one else really knows either."

It was impossible to feel satisfied with such a response. The more unfortunate the incident, the more graphic and exciting the details had to be. Another staffer rushed over to the booth across from theirs to do a second round of reconnaissance.

Now it was really time to wrap up the event, Chakyung thought. Whispers and anxiety had even begun to spread among the haenyeo gathered there. If something had happened that warranted the police showing up, it seemed better for them to disperse quickly, since leaving the conference hall could take even longer now. And if something unsavory were to happen on-site, it would be bad publicity.

The staffer returned from that second round of reconnaissance with slightly more concrete information. The others gathered around, brimming with curiosity and the urge to meddle.

"The person who passed out is a woman from Seoul, apparently," the staffer informed them. "They're saying she's unconscious."

"What in the world? You don't think something bad happened to her . . ."

Chakyung fixed the other staffers with a terrible glare. Startled and not used to seeing such a look on her face, the younger workers drew back. Chakyung felt someone tapping her on the shoulder and whipped around. Soo-eon was standing behind her, looking as deadly serious as she had ever seen him.

A Little Earlier

When they arrived at the outdoor exhibition area, the evening sun was setting in the west, and the sky was an array of orange hues. Pilhyun drove around toward the back of the convention center, and Romi looked out the window at their surroundings.

"Where are we?"

"Earlier, you said to go around the back. To the outdoor event area going toward Jusangjeolli Cliff."

"Oh, right."

Pilhyun stopped the car not in a parking lot but in a vacant one. The streetlights weren't on yet, and they were surrounded in every direction by the light of dusk. The car was obscured by the dark shadows of the trees. While Romi looked around, Pilhyun got out. "I don't think we'll be able to drive past this point, so we'll have to walk from here."

Pilhyun was coming around to her side to open the door for her, but Romi opened it herself and stepped out. The occasional passerby glanced their way, but any attention paid to them never lingered long. It wasn't shocking to see a couple wandering around some secluded part of Jeju.

Romi was walking with short, quick steps. "I'll be fine on my own," she said, looking up at Pilhyun. "I know you're busy, so I hope this wasn't too much trouble."

"It's all right. I'm headed that way too," he said firmly, leaving no room for discussion.

Romi's steps became more hurried. She wanted to get off this desolate road and go somewhere that was at least slightly better lit. She was growing breathless and dizzy. She felt Pilhyun's eyes on her, subtly watching, but she kept walking, pretending to be calm.

Dusk had fallen by the time they reached the outdoor event hall and, disappointingly, there were hardly any beehives left to see. No other people were around either. The area looked so much like a vacant lot that Romi had to wonder whether they were in the right place—if it hadn't been for the sign in one corner that read "Local Beekeeping Exhibition," Romi almost wouldn't have recognized it. She really regretted not having brought her phone. She was growing worried she wouldn't be able to find Kyungwoon. If they missed each other here, she knew she wouldn't be able to tell him later what she had decided to say. If she missed the timing, she would lose her nerve.

"Oh, look. Someone's there."

Romi spotted a familiar beehive at one end of the exhibition area. It was the hive she had seen at Kyungwoon's bee farm, the one modeled after a traditional house. She could see a dark figure ambling around in the shadows by the hive. Romi started walking in that direction, Pilhyun following behind and ruthlessly shining his phone flashlight into the stranger's face.

In that beam of light, they could see the face of the person underneath the hood. Romi recalled the first time she had seen that face, several days earlier. Tears had come spilling from those eyes, which had gone wide with fear. Those slender legs had lost their strength and seemed on the verge of collapse. Now, those same eyes were covered by the hood, so it was hard to tell, but there seemed to be something more in them than simple fear.

"Hello. What are you doing here?"

At the sight of someone she knew, Romi flashed a huge smile.

Sumi hurriedly placed something on top of the beehive, but Romi didn't get a proper look at what it was. As Sumi stepped out of the shadows and into the open area over which twilight was falling, orange lines banded her face.

"I came to help take down the beekeeping exhibit and saw that Kyungwoon's hive was still here, so I was taking a quick look," she said. She pulled back her hoodie a bit, then adjusted the backpack hanging from her shoulder.

"You didn't happen to see Kyungwoon himself, did you?" asked Romi urgently.

"I didn't," Sumi answered, too quickly. She gripped the strap of the backpack with one hand and looked the two of them over. Her eyes moved from Romi to Pilhyun, a subtle expression forming on her face. She seemed surprised, as though faced with something unexpected, and there was a look of disapproval in her eyes as well. She approached them with slow steps. Once she was in front of them, though, she said only, "Bye, then."

Not fully understanding what was happening, Romi replied, "Okay." Pilhyun stepped aside to allow Sumi to pass. She lowered her head and started to walk, then looked up. She and Romi locked eyes. For a moment, Romi's vision went blurry, so she shut her eyes and opened them again. Sumi's eyes, meanwhile, never left Romi once.

Romi's mouth twitched in confusion.

Sumi suddenly grabbed her arm.

"Oh?"

Even then, Sumi seemed to be hesitating. Was she trying to make a run for it, or . . . ? Her grip was strong, fingers surprisingly powerful as they dug into Romi's skin.

In that moment, she made her decision. "Romi, you're coming with me."

"What?"

"Let's go."

Sumi shut her mouth and pulled Romi away. Sumi's face—flushed red not even a moment ago—seemed to have paled to a cool blue now that Romi was seeing her up close. She found herself following Sumi, taking a few steps forward. But then Pilhyun reached out and ripped Sumi's hand away. Romi's arm tingled with pain, but there was no time to dwell on that.

"What are you doing?"

Pilhyun's voice was engulfed in darkness. A sudden chill ran down Romi's spine. She tried to step in between the other two, but Sumi was busy struggling to pry her hand free from Pilhyun's grip.

"Let go!"

"Ugh!"

Sumi swung at him, fingernails scratching Pilhyun's face. Blood welled on his cheek, and beads of red began to dribble from the cuts. Romi was startled at the sight of blood, but the moment she moved toward him, Pilhyun muttered, "Shit. I was going to turn the other cheek, but it looks like I can't do that now, can I?"

He struck Sumi in the face, hard. She fell to the ground. The backpack slid off her shoulder and landed on the grass a few feet away. For a moment, Romi was in such a state of shock that she couldn't move, but she quickly returned to her senses and rushed to help Sumi up. All of a sudden, though, a dizzying sensation ran through her head and caused Romi to falter. Pilhyun, meanwhile, was one step ahead. He ran to Sumi, grabbed her by the arm, and hauled her up onto her feet. With Sumi still in his grasp, he turned to Romi, a vicious glint in his eyes.

Romi staggered backward. The moment Pilhyun let go of Sumi and started moving toward Romi, Sumi lunged at him and grabbed his arm.

"Romi, take my bag and run! Call the police!"

"You bitch!"

Pilhyun made to shake Sumi off him, but she doggedly held on.

Romi thought she ought to save Sumi, but her body wouldn't move. The sound of Sumi's desperate struggle felt muted somehow, like it was coming from a radio far, far away.

"I saw you!" Sumi shouted. "Going into Romi's room! Constantly hanging around that guesthouse!"

Romi lifted her cloudy eyes and stared at Pilhyun. The image of him wavered, doubling and then quadrupling before overlapping into one again. She didn't know whether her vision was blurring due to fear or something else.

Pilhyun looked down at Sumi. "You're not the only one who saw something," he said. "I saw you too. I know you're plotting something. With that asshole from Seoul."

Sumi's eyes went wide, all the strength sapped out of her grip. Pilhyun clenched his teeth and yanked his arm from her grasp. She fell onto the grass again.

Pilhyun sneered, voice dripping with sarcasm, "When I kindly let you go, I want you to pack your things and get out of here, fast. Keep your mouth shut. I don't care where you go, but you'd better not tell anyone you saw us. If you do, I'll blow all your plans open too."

As soon as he turned his back to her, Sumi reached out again and grabbed his ankle. "Romi, run!"

Pilhyun kicked Sumi in the shoulder. She cried out in pain but didn't let go. He shook his leg to get her off him. She held on a little longer before wearing herself out and letting go.

Pilhyun whipped around. Romi and the backpack were gone.

"Damn it!"

That was when he heard it—something simmering in the dark of the evening. Was it the sound of his own mind seething? No. This was different. Something was happening here. It sounded like the winds of change were coming.

While Sumi knelt, defeated, on the ground, Pilhyun searched her and found her phone. He pocketed it, stood up, and kicked her again in the ribs. At this point, Sumi couldn't even cry out in pain.

"Stay put," Pilhyun said. "Don't try anything funny."

He scanned his surroundings. Where had Romi run off to? The route she would take was obvious to him. She suffered from night blindness. He spotted some movement coming from the direction of the road leading down to Jusangjeolli Cliff. He grinned. At this rate, he'd be able to catch her soon. The absolute darkness of night would work to his advantage. He took off running toward her.

Sumi, left alone in that spot, didn't move for a while. The sound of humming grew louder and louder around her, like the wind right before a storm. She lay there for a moment, surrounded by that sound, barely moving as she crawled forward on her stomach. When she reached the beehive at last, she hoisted herself up and removed the lid. As all the bees inside soared out, she lost consciousness and passed out on the spot.

FLY, EVEN IN THE DARK

The audience applauds as a woman wearing glasses and a wireless mic steps onstage.

On the large screen behind her is a photo of a swarm of bees in a beautiful orchard, a group of people smiling beside them.

The speaker begins. "The bee is an essential creature in our lives. Without bees, honey isn't the only thing that would disappear. Nor would we just lose some flowers to admire. We would lose the vegetables we eat every day, and fruits would become scarce too. There would be no more feed for livestock, dealing a massive blow to the ranching industry. Ultimately, a world without bees is a world without human beings."

The bees in the photo vanish one by one. Then the people disappear too. The audience stares blankly at the dark screen. After regarding the crowd somberly for a moment, the speaker continues.

"I've given several lectures about why bees are disappearing. Their habitats have declined drastically since the second industrial revolution. This phenomenon is called 'colony collapse disorder.' Monoculture farming, mites, pesticides, electromagnetic waves, and the desertification of half our planet have all accelerated the extinction of the bee."

The crowd is silent. The speaker swallows, then proceeds.

"What is the solution? There are things you all can do to help. You can plant flowers outside your homes, for instance—small gestures like that. Of course, practicing eco-friendly agriculture in production can be considered a fix. And some say urban beekeeping is one part of the cure."

Photos appear to match what the speaker is saying: a flower garden, an urban hive, an X'd-out can of pesticides.

She continues. "But these are tasks for everyday people and bee-keepers. We bioengineers propose a different solution."

The speaker turns to the screen, now cleared of all photos except for a single image in the center: a vibrantly colored bee with large wings. The speaker turns back to the crowd, her tone serious.

"That solution is none other than the creation of an artificial breeding program for rearing super bees. These bees are born stronger, healthier, faster, more robust, more alluring, and smarter than any bees that have ever existed before."

The boats anchored at Daepo Port were as silent as birds returning to the nest after a hard day's work. The evening was still young, but one of the boats already had its lights on and was rocking anxiously in the harbor. Nervous, Chanmin checked his watch. It was past the agreed-upon time. He looked up toward Jusangjeolli Cliff, but there wasn't a trace of anyone near the dark rocks.

The men in black suits were whispering among themselves. Even in their conference attire, who would believe they were beekeepers, as brawny as they were? Chanmin tsked. Even back at the conference hall, the men had gone around as a pack, drawing attention. He had told the boss there was no need to come in person and certainly hadn't expected him to come this far and with this large an entourage. Now, it was getting late, and the boss wore a look of displeasure that seemed doubly upset on a face twice as wide as the average person's.

An assistant with a deadpan expression and the build of a physical trainer approached Chanmin.

"Dr. Yang, what's going on? What time did you say the handoff was happening?"

"Soon."

"Did you call?"

He had, but the call hadn't gone through. That was the first sign that something was wrong. He tried not to let it show. "I did call, and that's what I was told," he said.

The assistant gave him a doubtful look and returned to his boss to whisper something in his ear. The boss made his way over to Chanmin, tottering as the boat swayed. His assistant hurried after him.

The boss stood before Chanmin with his chest puffed out, wagging a finger in his face and saying something while pointing toward Jusangjeolli Cliff. The assistant quickly interpreted.

"He said you should go over there yourself and get us the product."

"Me? Even if I went, I wouldn't know where—"

The assistant cut him off. "We can't wait forever. We have a boat to transfer to at the Port of Jeju."

Chanmin sighed. There was nothing more he could do. He'd already received the deposit. The money was no longer even in his account. Seeing no other option, he headed toward the makeshift bridge connecting the boat to the dock. With a gesture from the boss, one of the men in suits rushed after him.

"What now?"

"The boss asked me to guard you," the assistant replied flatly. "It might be hard for you to get this done on your own."

It seemed more like this guy would be surveilling him, not guarding him. Chanmin raised his eyebrows but kept his mouth shut. He wasn't the type to get into unnecessary emotional disputes. He still believed that about himself, though it had been a long time since that cool, calm image of his was shattered. He stepped onto the dock and headed toward the parking lot, knowing that the man in the black suit was hiding something that bulged in the front pocket of his jacket, but he didn't have the energy to point it out. It was fine. Everything would be fine. If it wasn't, Chanmin was in for a world of hurt.

Black cliffs shaped like hexagonal pillars continued off to her side. How long had she been running? Twenty minutes? Thirty? She couldn't tell whether what she was hearing was the sound of the waves or the wind. Either way, she had the feeling both were growing harsher. Romi knew she should be running toward where she could see lights. But she'd taken off into the dark woods to escape Pilhyun and ended up lost. The more she ran, the farther away she could tell she was getting from any other people. She had narrowly escaped the woods, and now all she saw were those black pillars that stood facing the sea. Even if she wanted to get back on the path she'd been on, she had no idea where it was. Somehow, she had to find someone and call the police. Dizziness and nausea flooded her senses. She needed to snap out of this, fast.

Sensing that someone was approaching her from behind, Romi gripped the bag tighter and took off running again. If only she could come across one person—just one. But even the Jeju Olle Trail that was usually packed with people was empty. She truly regretted having left without her phone. In this day and age, wasn't going out without a phone no better than setting down your weapon and heading onto a battlefield? Actually, this was worse. More like rushing into battle without a ballistic helmet or anything for protection as the bullets rained down. Was Sumi all right? She had put herself in harm's way to save Romi, yet Romi still hadn't been able to report what happened to her to the police. She was about to burst with rage from how sorry and pathetic she felt.

Romi continued downhill, not knowing what direction she was headed in. Following the trail, this was the only way she could go. But the path led to the shore—from there, she wouldn't be able to go any farther. The ocean was a gray blanket spread out under the purple twilight.

She was about to turn back when she spotted Pilhyun in the distance running toward her. Romi took off at full speed only to come face-to-face with those rock cliffs yet again. There was nowhere else for her to go.

Pilhyun caught up to her, clutching his knees and gasping for breath. "Damn, you ran awfully fast for someone who didn't know where the hell she was going. You would think the effects of that drug would have kicked in by now."

Romi thrust the bag out like a shield between them. "No wonder I've been so dizzy! You spiked the yogurt!"

Pilhyun straightened up and burst out laughing, incredulous.

"You just realized that? Are you dense? Is that why the drug's been slow to take?"

"How would I know!"

There was no need to tell him that she'd only pretended to drink the yogurt, sipping a little because her mouth had been so dry and dumping the rest. Considering even that tiny amount had been enough to make her this dizzy, she wondered how potent the drug was.

"Why are you doing this to me? You're the one who's been stalking me, aren't you?"

Romi put all the strength she had into shouting. She had to buy herself some time.

Pilhyun took another step toward her, grinning. It was a grin that set off goose bumps on her skin.

"Do you remember now? Who I am?"

"We've met before?" Romi asked, seemingly genuinely surprised, but Pilhyun clenched his fists and exploded with anger.

"You're pissing me off! How can you not remember me? I've been to so many of your exhibits and autograph events!"

"You came to those?" Romi's narrowed eyes widened as she studied him. He looked so vicious now that it was hard to recognize him by his features, but even when his expression had been neutral, she couldn't say she remembered him. "I'm really not sure who you are," she said.

"You don't recognize me, yet you come all the way to Jeju to find some guy you met once or twice! I can't deal with this!" Pilhyun stomped his feet. "This is your fault!"

As his expression grew more menacing, Romi considered that she should apologize, but even that much empathy would be wasted on a stalker like him. She felt her anger skyrocketing to match her fear.

"So what if I can't remember you! So what if my memory is terrible! And so what if you managed to leave no impression whatsoever on me!" *I can't help that I don't find you attractive,* she almost said, but held back, swallowing the words hard. She was afraid to go that far. Besides, it wasn't like she could remember people she *did* find attractive either. *Look at me,* she thought. *I couldn't even recognize the guy I thought I'd fallen for.* Was she in the wrong for not remembering? Memory emerged somewhere in the interaction between a person's innate capacity to remember and their relationships with other people—but did anyone have a responsibility to remember? Regardless, no one had the right to force another person to remember them. From the moment coercion entered the equation, the whole thing became an act of violence. Romi had a lot to say, but she couldn't shape her racing thoughts into sentences. The world was spinning before her eyes, and she had lost all strength in her legs. As she watched everything around her swaying, Pilhyun broke into another broad grin.

"But now all that is over. I won't let you slip through my hands again."

Romi lifted her head to look him squarely in the face as he came closer, but she couldn't see well in the dark. Even if she had a sharp mind, she would hardly be any match for a man as evil and extreme as this one.

"What's going to happen to me?" Romi asked.

Pilhyun's voice sounded like a slowed-down tape playing in her ears.

"Yooouuuu'll juuuuuust haaaave to waaaaait and seeeeee . . ."

Romi took a step back, but there was not much room for her to go any farther. What was she going to do? She'd wanted to tell Kyungwoon one last thing before the trip was over . . . Pilhyun reached for her. Romi wildly brandished the bag she was holding.

"Don't come any closer!"

The moment Pilhyun's hand touched the bag, out came what sounded like the fluttering of thousands of wings at once, and suddenly everything went black. There wasn't even time to think, *What's going on?* as thousands of bees surrounded them. The powerful roar of wings made it hard to hear, and it was impossible to see anything properly.

"Ack, what is this!"

Several bees homed in on Pilhyun in his blue polo shirt. As he swung his arms around, struggling to chase them off, he staggered back.

"Argh! Go away!"

But most of the bees were circling Romi. Pilhyun had no choice but to back away from her slowly. Romi, too, could only take a few steps back, toward the sea.

Suddenly, someone shouted from the direction the bees had come from.

"Romi!"

Romi looked around, trying to orient herself toward that voice. She couldn't see much at all with the bees obscuring her view, but she was certain the person running toward her now was Kyungwoon.

"Kyungwoon? Kyungwoon!"

Even with the bees around her, Romi waved her hands. Kyungwoon was holding a can of repellent spray as he made his way to her through the swarm.

"Romi, throw me the bag! Throw it!"

"What?"

She couldn't hear a thing over the buzzing. She started to run toward Kyungwoon, but Pilhyun reached into the siege of bees and grabbed her by the arm.

"Let go of me!"

While they struggled, the buzzing of wings grew louder. The bees rushed toward Romi again, and Pilhyun ultimately had no choice but to release her. The noisy droning of the bees spread to fill the night. The sound seemed endless. But just then, an even louder sound rang out from the beach and drowned out the buzzing.

Bang.

The gunshot didn't seem to concern the bees in the slightest, but everyone on the beach froze. A man in a black suit had one hand raised high in the air. In that hand, he held a smoking gun.

The man in glasses next to him shouted at Black Suit in utter disbelief. "Are you insane? Why would you fire a gun here of all places?"

Black Suit seemed not to have understood him. The man in glasses waved his hands and shouted again, in English, "No! Don't shoot!"

Romi recognized him—finally, a face she knew at first glance. It was Chakyung's fiancé.

Chanmin tried to approach Romi and Pilhyun, but because of the swarm, he hesitated, reaching out with only his hands.

"Just my luck," Chanmin said. "What do you think you're doing? Hand over the bag, now."

Kyungwoon stepped in front of Chanmin, blocking his path. "What's going on here? Why does he have a gun? Tell him to get rid of that thing, fast! This is dangerous!"

"You'd better move, before things get even more dangerous."

Chanmin's words were brazen, but his hands were trembling as he shoved Kyungwoon back. The military was one thing, but none of them had ever seen someone fire a gun in real life. Kyungwoon moved to block Chanmin again. The two of them glowered at each other.

The situation on the beach was already growing thorny. Romi was surrounded by a swarm of bees; Pilhyun couldn't get to her easily because of the swarm; Chanmin and Kyungwoon were midstandoff; and the man in the suit was still holding the gun. To complicate matters further, another cry went up from a new arrival at the beach. It didn't sound like one person, either, but dozens of women shouting. Between the buzzing of the bees, the firing of the gun, and the cries of the human horde now on its way, the beach had become the site of sheer chaos on what would have otherwise been a quiet night.

"Goodness gracious!"

"I'll say! What's with the gun?"

"What's going on here?"

The crowd of middle-aged and elderly women who had carefully made their way down to the cliffs came to a stop at the sight of the man holding the gun and immediately started buzzing with chatter. But they seemed to have no intention of turning back.

Chakyung made her way to the front of the crowd. "Give it up, Chanmin!" she shouted. "What are you doing?"

Chanmin turned to her, his face going pale. But he couldn't move. Because right then, Black Suit fired into the air again. At the sound of the gunshot, everyone ducked. Chakyung slowly got back up from where she had crouched, mustering all her strength to shout again.

"Chanmin, get back! Help Romi first, then talk!"

"You get back!" he shouted. "This guy is dangerous—you're going to get hurt!"

If he knew the guy was dangerous, why had he come here with him? Chakyung felt pathetic, almost dumbstruck. She hadn't known he was that much of a blockhead. Perhaps he hadn't known that himself. But she knew it was impossible to back down in a no-win situation like this. For now, she had to try to keep everyone calm.

"Chanmin, it's not too late to turn this around. It's all right."

Black Suit aimed his gun at Chakyung and shouted something at her. Chakyung raised her hands, speaking calmly.

"It's all right," she said. Then, in English, "You don't have to do this. Please. Put the gun down."

Those in the crowd of haenyeo crouched behind her whispered among themselves in the Jeju language.

"Goodness, that bride-to-be from Seoul really has no fear, huh?"

"You can say that again! Where'd she even learn a whole other language? Small but powerful, that one is."

"What should we do? Can't we help her?"

"There are more of us—if we work together, we could lift him up and toss him."

"Oi, don't get ahead of yourself."

Black Suit was clearly hesitating. This wasn't a situation he could resolve by shooting any one person, and it was written on his face plain as day that he was growing more and more disoriented in the midst of all this chatter he couldn't understand.

Chakyung knew she needed to buy herself just a little more time. She took another step forward. Black Suit's hand was shaking. Behind her, someone shouted over the heads of the haenyeo. "Chakyung, wait!"

Even at the sound of Soo-eon's voice, she didn't look back. She knew that if she did, she would be giving Black Suit the space to act rashly. She had to be calm. But Black Suit's focus was wavering. He shifted his aim, pointing the gun in the direction the shout had come from. Once again, the haenyeo cried out in protest.

Chanmin also shouted at Black Suit behind him. "Leave her and the rest of them out of this! Go and search that bag!"

While this tense moment was playing out in front of him, Pilhyun saw an opening. He approached Romi and grabbed her by the arm, trying to drag her toward him. He figured while the others fought among themselves, he could get her to toss him the bag and run. He could withstand a few stings from the bees.

"Throw the bag! Let it go!"

Romi had the feeling all this trouble was because of this bag. What in the world could be inside it? Still, seeing as Sumi had risked everything to save her, Romi couldn't turn the bag over that easily.

"No! Get lost!"

She snatched the bag from Pilhyun, losing her balance. She had been standing on a rock that was more like a low cliff when she began tipping backward. Pilhyun tried to grab her, but she slipped from his grasp. Without a moment to process what was happening, Romi fell past the rocks and into the ocean with a splash. A huge spray of water went up. The bees that had been hovering in the sky above Romi's head now rushed out over the sea.

The scream everyone let out in unison rang out over the ocean at night.

One Hour Earlier

The road leading to the outdoor exhibition area had begun to feel incredibly long. Not only was it her first time here, but the dusk settling over everything made the place feel even more desolate. She hadn't been running for long, but Hadam was already out of breath. She had lost sight of Kyungwoon as he rushed ahead. Behind her, Jaewoong was struggling to keep up, hauling the huge bag with the drone inside.

"What's going on? Did something happen to Romi?"

Gasping, Hadam gripped her knee with one hand and pointed to the shade beneath a tree with her other. "Isn't that the car Pilhyun drove here?"

Jaewoong squinted. There was a black SUV parked where Hadam was pointing. "I think so. I don't know if that one's his, but it's the same model."

"Then we'd better hurry."

Having caught her breath, Hadam made to start running again when Jaewoong grabbed her arm.

"Why are you in such a hurry? You need to know what you're looking for to find it."

She was annoyed at his timing, but she figured it was best to answer him, fast. "Romi . . . was kidnapped . . . by Pilhyun."

"What?"

"She might be in danger."

"What are you talking about? Why would Pilhyun do that?" Jaewoong's narrowed eyes went wide. He seemed to be in genuine shock. Hadam didn't have time to concern herself with his feelings.

"He's Romi's stalker," she answered bluntly. "There's also the matter of the sexual assault . . . what you told me about Hwayoung . . ."

Hadam started running again. Jaewoong, still seemingly at a loss for words, fell into step with her.

"What about Hwayoung?"

"Hwayoung made a post on Facebook. Saying the person who assaulted her nine years ago was Pilhyun. And that she was sorry for not clarifying sooner."

She could sense Jaewoong's astonishment even in the darkness. He stopped short, still lagging behind her. "No way. Sunbae would never . . ."

Hadam shot him an icy look. "We were wrong to believe he wasn't that kind of guy."

She had no interest now in Jaewoong's shock. He was an adult, and he had to sort out for himself the disillusionment brought about by his own misconceptions and false beliefs, just like Hadam had done when it came to her beliefs about him. Right now, the most important thing was rescuing her friend.

When they reached the outdoor exhibition area, Kyungwoon was kneeling with his back to some sort of container and the body of someone passed out on the ground in front of him. Hadam's heart sank. Were they too late? Had something already happened?

"Romi! Romi!"

Up close, she could see that the container was a beehive. The person lying passed out in front of it had swollen eyes messily covered by hair. It wasn't the familiar blond hair Hadam had been expecting. It was brown. A pale face. Split, bloodied lips moving slightly.

"Hadam."

"Sumi, what happened? Who did this to you?"

Sumi pointed to the sky where the sun was setting. "Romi's in danger . . . the bees . . . follow the bees."

Hadam couldn't grasp what she meant. Romi was in danger, but follow the bees?

"Romi? Sumi, did you see her? Did Pilhyun drag her off somewhere?"

They had to call the police. As soon as Hadam took out her phone, Kyungwoon told her, "I called an ambulance. And the police. But a fight broke out among the members of a huge gang at a resort in the area, so all the officers at the nearest police station were dispatched there. They said it might take a while before anyone could come."

He looked up at Hadam, pale lips trembling.

"Could you stay here and look after Sumi until Jungmoon hyung gets here?" he asked. "I have to find Romi."

Hadam nodded. "Your husband should be here soon, Sumi, so don't worry. I'll . . ."

Sumi suddenly grabbed on to Kyungwoon's arm again. "Follow the bees. The swarm."

He also seemed confused about what she meant. Was she imagining things, still in shock from the violence?

Hwachul, who had been examining the beehive, turned to the rest of them and somberly announced, "There's not a single bee in here. They all escaped."

Kyungwoon rushed over and checked inside himself. When he turned back to the others, he wore a look of disbelief. "They can't have . . ."

Jaewoong, a silent spectator until then, commented, "It's almost nighttime, though? Bees don't fly at night, do they?"

Hadam had never thought about it, but she knew that bees relied on the sun to find their way. She had never actually seen any at night, but . . .

"These bees do," Sumi eked out with a groan, the words rising up into the cloudless sky so much like bees themselves. "These bees can fly at night. They follow their queen . . . everywhere. I gave the queen bee to Romi. In that bag."

She was going to say more, but at that moment, someone came running toward her, shoving the others aside. Hwachul grabbed on to Hadam to stop her from falling over.

"Sumi, darling! What happened?" Sumi's husband shouted, taking her face in his hands. "What jerk did this to you?"

Before anyone could answer, Jungmoon looked up and shot a glare at everyone else there. "And what are you all doing? Standing around and not rushing her to the hospital when you can see she's hurt!"

Jaewoong looked dumbfounded as he tried to piece together a response, but Sumi raised a hand and gestured to her husband to come closer. He leaned over, bringing his ear down toward her lips.

"What's wrong, honey? What do you need?"

Sumi's lips moved slightly. "You . . ."

"Yes, I'm right here! Just tell me!" He grabbed his wife's hand.

Drawing on a rush of strength that came to her out of nowhere, Sumi shook his hand off hers. "You talk too much," she said. "Shut up."

The wail of the ambulance siren was a signal to onlookers to congregate. Just a little while earlier, not a single person had been passing through the outdoor exhibition area, but now a crowd was forming. The EMTs loaded Sumi onto a stretcher and into the ambulance. Her husband followed after her, slouching petulantly. The police still hadn't arrived on the scene. Hadam didn't know what exactly the deal was with the other big incident that had taken place, but she hoped they would move as fast as possible to save someone who was in danger. She would be furious if they left her hanging in the wind like this. Jaewoong had left his bag with her and said he was going to look around. He seemed to be feeling guilty for ever having brought Pilhyun along. But his guilt was unnecessary. If Pilhyun truly had been Romi's stalker all along, he would have found some excuse to approach her regardless. When she thought of it that way, Hadam realized *she* was the reason he'd had even easier access to Romi this time around. Once again, she tried to tamp down the guilt standing in her way. Now was the time to use that guilt not as an excuse but to solve this crime.

Kyungwoon and Hwachul returned, drenched in sweat. There were no witnesses nearby, and they couldn't tell which direction Pilhyun and Romi might have taken off in.

"There are thousands of bees, so we should be able to find them, but it'll be dark out soon. Things could get dangerous, so every minute counts," Kyungwoon said.

His face seemed to have grown even more gaunt in the span of fifteen minutes. Nonetheless, Hadam admired the fact that he hadn't lost his composure. But enough of that—every minute truly did count, and they had two people to find. This was Romi they were dealing with, though. They couldn't even begin to guess where she would have headed—after all, she had no sense of direction.

"Let's split up and look again," Hwachul suggested. Could they find her if they searched in teams? They didn't have much time.

Hadam phoned Jaewoong, who had gone back to the convention center.

"Yeah, she's not here," he reported. "I'm taking one last look around and heading back your way now."

"No witnesses?"

"None—everyone here says they didn't see anything. I confirmed from the CCTV footage that two people went toward the outdoor exhibition area on foot, but they told me the next-closest security camera is under the jurisdiction of the police."

Hadam was so mad, she almost kicked Jaewoong's bag where it sat at her feet. Luckily, she stopped herself, her foot and her gaze lingering over it. What had Jaewoong said earlier . . . ?

"This drone you brought—is it good for night shoots?"

Jaewoong seemed to catch on to what she was thinking.

"It should be able to function without crashing headfirst into any-thing if there's a good amount of light. At least fifteen lux. But even in low light, it works fine. As it should, considering . . . I had to splurge a bit to rent it."

Even the camera lens on a specialty drone must have come at an exorbitant fee. It wouldn't have been easy to rent something like this from anyone. To own one of these, you had to be intensely passionate about filmmaking.

"What's the flight time on it?"

"Around twenty-five minutes, at the most."

"Got it. Hurry back."

Hadam ended the call and turned again to Hwachul and Kyungwoon. She had no choice but to step up as the director for the shoot they were about to do. The name of the project was *Rescuing Romi*. Until the police got here, she would have to be the one putting all the pieces into place to find Romi, Pilhyun, and the swarm of bees, fast.

She did not think this so-called drone, shaped like a tiny helicopter and meant for filming, resembled a bee at all. But once Hadam mounted a tablet to the master controller and plugged in the cable, she found herself hoping the drone would track down the swarm like a real bee. If Pilhyun really had gotten his hands on Romi, there was no time to waste. The drone's limited flight time was twenty-five minutes, and even less time remained until the light of day vanished and plunged them into darkness. Beside her, Jaewoong finished adjusting the camera settings on the drone and took over the secondary controller. Once he got the app working, the drone hummed to life with a sound like an actual bee and began to rise, opening its wings. It soon disappeared above them, and the footage of its surroundings appeared on the tablet screen. Kyungwoon and Hwachul had already set off.

The video on the screen showed the ocean blanketed in the purple light of evening, the mountain forests, and the sea at a glance. The drone was too far out to discern exactly what things were, so Hadam slightly adjusted its location. Just then, she picked up a phone call ringing in her Bluetooth earphones.

"Hello?"

"Hadam? Did something happen? I just heard from Soo-eon that a woman from Seoul was injured. And I saw you running around earlier. Is Romi all right?"

Chakyung sounded anxious. Hadam could hear loud chatter from other people in the background. She must have still been at the conference hall.

Eyes still on the tablet, Hadam explained the situation in the simplest terms. Chakyung seemed shocked, but she quickly regained her composure.

"Is there anything I can do to help?" she asked.

"Maybe you can follow after Kyungwoon and Hwachul and keep up the search until the police get here. You could also be the point of contact for—oh!"

"What is it?"

"I just saw something on the monitor. There's a swarm of bees flying over the beach!"

"Bees?"

"Yes! We're supposed to follow the bees to find Romi!"

Chakyung couldn't understand that logic. But she didn't seem at all flustered. Rather, it was exactly her nature to grow calmer the wilder the situation at hand became.

"Where is it? That location, roughly?"

"It looks like it's somewhere on the walking trail leading away from the hotel."

Someone in the background was shouting. "These waters . . . our hands . . ." Hadam couldn't make out the entirety of what was being said.

"Chakyung, let's hang up for now—"

Then came another shout on the other line. "Hadam, there are some locals here, haenyeo divers who say they want to help with the search," Chakyung said. "They say they know this area really well. We'll probably have an easier time finding her with more people on board. We should stay on the line, and you can let me know what you see on the monitor, describe for me the landscape or the bees' surroundings. Then the divers should be able to tell us where we need to go."

Hadam gripped the controller tighter. She had done film shoots countless times before, but never had her work felt as important as it did now. This was her first time filming something to save a person's life.

Back to the Present

The water shot about three feet into the air where Romi fell into the sea, and the bees immediately rushed toward that spot and gathered overhead. The swarm blacked out the sky. The shore was equally buzzing with noise.

Chanmin shouted to Black Suit, "What are you doing? Hurry up and grab that bag!"

Seeing that Black Suit didn't seem to have understood, Chanmin pointed and took off running toward the spot where Romi had fallen in, staring down at the rocks below. It was somewhat high up, and he could see even Black Suit hesitating. A man with a gun was afraid of the water. Chanmin nudged the other man forward, urging him, "Hurry and jump in. Do you want the boss to kill you? Get that bag!"

As Black Suit turned to Chanmin in irritation, Pilhyun sneaked up beside them and shoved Black Suit, hard. He fell into the water and flailed around in place, unable to swim. While Chanmin knelt down to peer over the edge of the cliff, Pilhyun tried to make a run for it. But at some point, Hwachul had appeared behind him and now stood blocking his way.

"Move!"

Pilhyun tried shoving past him, ramming his shoulder into the other man's chest, but Hwachul stood his ground and sprayed Pilhyun in the face with bee repellent. Just as Pilhyun screamed and reached up to cover his face, Hwachul grabbed one of his arms and twisted it behind his back. Pilhyun cried out again in pain, but no one paid any attention to him.

Kyungwoon was already in the water. He tried to swim toward where the bees had gathered, but the tide swept him back. He wouldn't be able to locate Romi without diving. "Romi!" he shouted, but the drone of the bees' wings and the roar of the waves drowned him out.

Chakyung and her group had at some point congregated on the black rocks and were standing in a circle. Kyungwoon's head kept dipping under the water and resurfacing like a duck's. As he watched him struggle, Soo-eon's expression hardened.

"The flow of the currents is tricky here because of the landscape," he told Chakyung. "It doesn't look like Kyungwoon hyung will be able to dive in and stay under. We can't afford to wait for the coast guard either. I'm going to have to go in."

Chakyung grabbed hold of his arms, her eyes full of concern. This was their only option if they wanted to save Romi. But now that night had fallen, the sea was like another place entirely. The waves were rough and unpredictable, the depths impossible to fathom. Chakyung was afraid, but now wasn't the time for fear.

Soo-eon smiled at her with his eyes, a look that told her not to worry. Nodding, she let him go.

He had started to pull off his shirt, when someone next to him tapped him sharply on the shoulder. He turned in surprise to find one of the elderly women from the crowd sternly shaking her head. Another granny laughed so hard, she snorted. Another still was in the middle of dramatically removing her dark blue, sequin-studded outer garments. Three or four others were also peeling off their clothes or tying T-shirts around their waists.

The one who had tapped Soo-eon on the shoulder chided him.

"Don't you dare, kid. You trying to go out there and drown yourself?"

All forty or so of the grannies from the event booth earlier collectively tutted at him.

"The water here's dangerous—only our most expert divers should even consider going out there. If we sent out one of the average divers or the rookies all willy-nilly, it could be a disaster."

The most expert haenyeo were in their late sixties and early seventies. They were the ones who had giggled like little girls when they spun the wheel for cosmetics earlier. Now Chakyung saw on their faces the kind of confidence they could wear only if they were fully certain of their abilities. Chakyung bowed to them, then took Soo-eon's hand and pulled him aside.

Once they were all set, the haenyeo let out a spirited cry. "All right! Let's move!"

As Chakyung had already recognized and as it became increasingly apparent, the crowd headed toward the sea was not the same group of suntanned grannies she had first encountered earlier that day. These women were professionals whose bodies had been trained and cultivated in the ocean over the course of decades; they had memorized the depths and shallows of these waters, their dangers and reprieves.

They swam out to where the bees had amassed, heads disappearing beneath the water one by one. After an impossibly long three minutes passed and they resurfaced, there was one more head among them.

The collective breath everyone on the cliff had been holding was released all at once. Someone let out a sigh of relief, and those in the crowd began to applaud as if that were their cue. Just then came a voice from behind them.

"Um, if it's possible, could I have some help here too?"

Everyone turned.

Hwachul was red in the face from struggling to contain Pilhyun and barely managed to eke out the words, "Someone . . . please . . ."

Still holding hands, Soo-eon and Chakyung exchanged a look. Right away, they sprang into action.

THE BEES ARE
SLEEPING

The detective's face was completely blank as she took Sumi's statement. She offered none of the usual sympathetic remarks about how hard this all must have been on her, nor did she reprimand Sumi by asking how she could have done something so stupid. The detective simply told Sumi she would need to visit the police station once she was discharged. With only that remark and an order for Sumi to get well soon, the detective left the hospital room.

Sumi sighed, grimacing from the pain in her chest as she shifted to lie down again. The doctor told her she had broken a rib and would need to rest for a while as it healed. She held an arm up to her forehead and placed her head on the pillow.

She'd heard from Kyungwoon that the haenyeo had managed to fish the bag out of the water. Like the detective, Kyungwoon hadn't reprimanded her, either, even though he would now never know what had been written on the notes inside it.

"The police told me they were my wife's lab notes, plus reports she'd been sent from universities in the US. They decided to turn them over to a company working on the development of super bees."

Sumi remembered the day Hyeyoung had first told her about all this. It was spring, and the two of them were on Hyeyoung's bee farm, looking out at the blue ocean glittering beneath the sun. Breeding the super queen bee was a success, Hyeyoung said quietly. They had created a queen bee resistant to all pests, a queen able to rear bees that were faster and stronger than any others. *The experiment to extract her queen mandibular pheromone is also in its final stages,* Hyeyoung said, laughing a little shyly. *Am I about to become super famous? Will I win the Nobel Prize?* she joked. But she lowered her voice as she went on about how this super bee's pheromones could be used to create different medications. For the first time, it might be possible to use trace amounts of honeybee pheromones to produce powerful aphrodisiacs. It was a dangerous technology. Hyeyoung looked worried as she warned that it could be abused, that there'd be people chomping at the bit to get their hands on it.

Honestly, Sumi didn't fully understand everything Hyeyoung was saying. It was like listening to her husband ramble at length at every meal about the beekeeping classes he was taking. She'd never had the slightest interest in beekeeping. Or in her husband, for that matter. Whenever she was cleaning or doing laundry around the guesthouse, Sumi gritted her teeth and thought about how she should have divorced him when he quit his job in architecture and urged her to leave her job at the bank so they could move to Jeju. At that time, though, she couldn't even consider divorcing him for that reason. There was no sense of newness in their marriage, and they'd hoped the move to Jeju might break them out of that rut once and for all. Their friends in Seoul always talked about how nice it must be to live on Jeju, but their wistful fantasies only went as far as going on a trip or spending a year there—none of them wanted to live there for the long term like Sumi. Never mind what they said about the famous Jeju lifestyle on TV or in articles filled with beautiful words—nothing about her day-to-day life on Jeju was all that enjoyable. She hated the humidity that dampened the pages of all the books on her shelves even with the dehumidifier running, and she hated all the bugs that found their way in through the windows in the summers. Sometimes she took comfort in watching the spread of soothing colors as the sun set beyond the mountains, or else in looking out at the ocean alone and listening to the tranquil early-morning waves.

She met Kyungwoon and Hyeyoung through a local meetup. They seemed much different from Sumi and her husband. They were good colleagues, and Kyungwoon was a good husband. Sumi didn't think people needed to have a shared passion for something in order to get married, but she realized that a shared passion was important for maintaining a marriage. When Sumi met Hyeyoung, she understood this for the first time—that love was wanting to share in passions you had never wanted to share with anyone else before.

For a while, Hyeyoung was just the wife of an acquaintance of Sumi's husband. Then five summers ago, there was an incident. One day when Sumi's husband wasn't around, an out-of-towner came to the guesthouse, found Sumi alone in the kitchen, and started making a move on her. At first, the man pretended to be a guest, but he changed his tune when he realized no one else was around. If Hyeyoung hadn't stopped by to meet up with her husband, who knows what might have happened? Hyeyoung chased the man off with her screaming. Then she went over to comfort Sumi, who was sitting there crying and in shock. It was the first time since Sumi had come to Jeju that someone had held her hand. Hyeyoung's hands were as rough as Sumi's. But for Sumi, the feeling of those hands on hers was the gentlest feeling in the world.

Now, when an urgent "code blue, code blue" sounded over the intercom outside her dark hospital room, Sumi heard hurried footsteps disappearing down the hall. This meant someone in the hospital was knocking on death's door. After Hyeyoung passed away, Sumi found herself thinking about her final moments whenever she read or watched news stories about accidents. Even as she lay in bed at night beside her husband, it was the outline of Hyeyoung's face she caught herself tracing in the dark. There wasn't a corner of her heart that didn't hold remnants of the other woman, but weirdly, it was only the memory of her face that had begun to fade.

That was why Sumi decided to get back in touch with the person who had reached out before with an interest in Hyeyoung's research and attempt to make a deal with him again. It was the first time in her life she'd been proactive about something. Three years ago, she and Hyeyoung had been planning to start a new life overseas and needed money. Hyeyoung wanted to protect her research, but at the time, she had no other options. She was still on the fence until the very end, and Sumi reasoned with her. Hyeyoung hated breaking Kyungwoon's trust, but she wanted to be with Sumi. She said if they couldn't be together without betraying anyone, they shouldn't have started this new relationship at all. But it had already begun, the betrayal already committed.

The last day of her life, Hyeyoung had messaged her, saying she'd decided not to sell the research. She'd been admitted with a scholarship to a doctoral program in the US and invited Sumi to join her, said this could be their fresh start. She was planning to tell her husband the whole plan. But then Hyeyoung died, leaving nothing but that message behind.

In the three years since, Sumi had longed to leave Jeju before even more of her memories of Hyeyoung faded. Every day was hard to bear. There was nothing she could do. Fortunately, or perhaps unfortunately, the man who had reached out three years earlier about the research was still interested in the deal. Sumi also considered Kyungwoon's amnesia to be a lucky break, as it meant he couldn't remember the details of Hyeyoung's work. The buyer had requested a queen bee from the hive as a sample, and Sumi knew the bees Hyeyoung had reared were now living on that bee farm in the mountains. She thought everything was set. If only she hadn't seen the suspicious man hovering around Romi, and if only she'd left Romi with him regardless of what might have happened to her. If only she'd pretended not to notice that man's dark, dangerous gaze.

When she first learned about Romi and Kyungwoon's relationship, Sumi had despised Romi. It was a strange feeling. If Hyeyoung were alive and thought Kyungwoon was seeing another woman, she would have felt that loathing too. Even though Hyeyoung was the one who had left him first, she wouldn't have been able to bear it if he'd left her. The number of people in the world who remembered Hyeyoung was dwindling by the day, and Sumi hated the thought of someone else taking her place. She hadn't known why this dangerous man was approaching Romi, but she didn't even want to warn her at first. Still, when she saw her at the outdoor exhibit, she couldn't simply look away. Not while knowing Romi would be in danger if she did. For some reason, when she thought about how Hyeyoung had helped her, she couldn't pretend not to know what was going on.

When the code blue was lifted, the hallway outside her room fell silent again. What did that silence mean? What had happened to the patient in danger? The crisis could have ended in either life or death. Sumi thought about that fine line. She had ended up on one side of it, while Hyeyoung had ended up on the other. Those lines weren't parallel. Even if they walked along what they thought were separate paths, they would meet again, Sumi thought. Whenever she was lying in bed, eyes wide open in the dark, she ended up imagining Hyeyoung's face again, as always. She realized she liked certain memories once she found that remembering them was painful. No matter how much it hurt, she still hoped those memories wouldn't completely disappear. Sumi remembered the day Hyeyoung had told her about the bee farm for the first time, how she felt she had accomplished something huge. She remembered the sunlight glittering on the rolling sea like pearls spilled from a snapped necklace, the sound of the bees like music, the day Hyeyoung had come to her carrying that paper moon and yellow lantern—she remembered them all. She recalled Hyeyoung's face in that light, the sound of their laughter spreading into the night sky. These memories, too, might end up coated in dust like that lantern, which Sumi kept in her living room now, but they were memories in which the two of them could be together until their lines met again.

◆ ◆ ◆

Project: *Searching for Honeyman*

Day Nine, Night, Seogwipo

"Chanmin ended up confessing. Said he'd planned to sell off the super bee sample and the results of the breeding experiments. Turns out he'd presented Kyungwoon's wife's findings under his own name and gotten academic acclaim for them, then bought her out. This was apparently a revolutionary breakthrough that would solve the crisis facing the modern beekeeping industry. That didn't seem to be the main draw for the foreign gang that wanted in, seeing as they sent a guy with a gun to pass himself off as a beekeeper. But if there was more to the deal, I doubt anyone will say."

When he was first taken into custody, Chanmin had tried to refuse to give a statement. But when he learned that Sumi had already confessed, he gave up. Sumi's motives were unclear, but she claimed to have been close to Kyungwoon's wife and to have already known about the existence of the super bee for a while. Now, three years later, when Chanmin attempted to make this deal again, Sumi accepted. Kyungwoon's amnesia had worked to their advantage. The plan was to steal the queen bee first and induce the swarm to follow her to a new hive hidden nearby, then contact Chanmin to coordinate the drop-off. Chanmin was then to hand over the hive to a third party that would be on standby on a boat. Sumi hadn't anticipated anyone getting hurt. Instead, with Kyungwoon unable to remember anything, she'd planned on tweaking the experiments and slightly altering the lab reports, keeping the author's true identity hidden forever. If the man in the black suit hadn't shown up with a gun, things wouldn't have gotten so out of hand. Seriously, why would someone bring a gun to a honeybee theft? Chakyung felt sorry about how it all had gone down, but this wasn't her business to meddle in. She hadn't even known about Chanmin's hundreds of millions of won in gambling debts, nor about the hardships his father's company was facing. They had been planning to spend their lives together, but they hadn't even been able to share their troubles with each other. Chakyung felt like she was only now discovering who Chanmin truly was. Certain discoveries could completely erase the person you thought you knew. The Chanmin she had known in the past was being wiped away. Their relationship aside, it was a shame to see a person's life go so far off course.

Chakyung didn't want to tell Romi all this. When the haenyeo pulled Romi from the water, Soo-eon had performed CPR to save her. The police arrived immediately afterward, and though she was rushed to the hospital, her condition wasn't critical. Once she gave her statement to the police, Romi had insisted on going straight back to Nol. Now she was lying in bed in their room, listening to the whole story. She said she was feeling fine and planned to head to Seoul the next day with Chakyung and Hadam. But as far as Chakyung was concerned, it might be a while before Romi was truly okay.

"Luckily, Hadam managed to track the guy who was with Chanmin—the one who had the gun—and record everything, so the investigation is going smoothly," Chakyung said.

The drone had been filming in the dark of the evening and from a bit of a distance, but it had captured scenes that were at least recognizable in places. It had been a long time since Jaewoong had filmed anything, but he'd managed to get some good footage.

"Romi, what can I say? I had no idea my sunbae—no, that asshole Pilhyun—was the stalker who'd been terrorizing you for years, and I kept bringing him around," Hadam said. She gripped her knees and bowed her head in apology.

Romi waved her hands. "What are you talking about? He was terrorizing me way before you introduced us, Hadam."

"He's in custody and under investigation for the assault and kidnapping here, but I heard they're looking into other crimes he committed in Seoul as well."

Factoring in the past charges brought forward by Hwayoung, the situation grew more complicated. After hearing Kyungwoon describe a suspicious car following him around from the bee farm a few days earlier, the police decided to look into the dashcam footage. Either figuring he would be found out soon enough anyway or else having given up hope entirely, Pilhyun also confessed he'd been at the site of the accident three years ago, chasing after the car Kyungwoon and Hyeyoung had been in that night. He hadn't known which car the man who'd gone to see Romi was driving, so he took out his anger by trailing Kyungwoon's car, not knowing they would end up in an accident. Thinking he'd be questioned for his connection to the crash, he'd fled Jeju. He didn't know Kyungwoon had lost his memory. Hearing all this, Kyungwoon woefully remarked, "I guess Sumi ended up avenging Hyeyoung after all."

At Kyungwoon's request, Hadam didn't tell Romi this part of the story. Relaying these facts and resurrecting these memories were his decisions to make. He said he would tell Romi when he felt she was ready to accept it. It was too cruel for both of them to harbor guilt all this time later over something neither of them could have prevented. And if they still felt guilty nonetheless, it was up to each of them to determine their share of that guilt.

"I didn't know he was that kind of person," said Romi thoughtfully, "but that's because I had no reason to look too closely into who he was deep down. I just hope everything he's done gets brought to light."

"He's a standard-issue stalker who obsessively follows around the woman he's interested in and, when she shows no interest in him, channels his anger into violence. He's probably committed lots of other crimes."

Hadam had no idea how she could describe so dryly this person she thought she'd known for so long. But she couldn't say she'd known him all that well. Everyone lived their lives loosely connected to people they hardly knew at all. Still, you believed you knew them based on nothing more than those loose threads.

"There was no interest I could have shown in him," Romi said, sounding somewhat tired and completely indifferent. "You have to know someone exists to have an interest in them in the first place."

This would have been a stalker's berserk button, Hadam knew. They were self-contradicting monsters who lurked in the darkest of shadows yet longed to be discovered. But no one knew them. No one wanted to know them. They were insignificant to others no matter how violent they became trying to prove their own existence.

There was a knock on the door. Chakyung went to see who it was.

"Romi, it's Kyungwoon," she called, casting a glance at Hadam from the doorway.

Hadam stood up. "We'll leave you two alone to talk."

Kyungwoon stepped aside so the two women could pass. Meanwhile, Romi quickly smoothed down her hair and sat up straighter. Kyungwoon bowed in greeting and approached her cautiously, looking awkward as he took the seat Hadam had been in earlier.

"How are you feeling?" he asked gently.

"I'm perfectly fine—so fine I feel embarrassed about cosplaying as a hospital patient like this." Romi lifted her hands in a gesture meant to show off her strength, but that only made the mood more tense. Neither of them could look the other in the eye. Romi folded her hands and fidgeted with her clasped fingers.

"I heard you jumped into the water to save me," she said.

"But I couldn't save you in the end," Kyungwoon said slowly.

"Still, I'm sorry. For causing you so much trouble."

"No, no. I'm the one who's sorry. It was because of my bees that everything got so out of hand."

"No, it's not your fault. I should be the one to apologize. I'm the reason the queen bee drowned and everything," Romi said, waving her hands.

A thin smile appeared on Kyungwoon's lips. "Don't worry about that," he said.

"But I caused problems for everyone, and it's not the first time I've done that, but it's so embarrassing."

As the words came rushing out of her and she continued waving her hands, Kyungwoon's eyes softened slightly, the tension in them easing up.

"Why do we keep apologizing to each other?" he said. "We're not the ones who did anything wrong."

"You're right. I'm a victim here, but I can't think of anything to say right now except that I'm sorry." In the heat of the moment, she'd ended up spilling all her feelings. Their eyes met. They burst out laughing.

"Not that I'm complaining, but what brings you here? Did you come to take back the royal jelly?" Romi asked, picking up the shopping bag on the table.

"I came to ask you something." Kyungwoon unclasped his hands and placed them on his knees, then leaned forward. "Why did you come to the convention center, to the exhibit, last night?"

Kyungwoon always spoke seriously, but something about him, his expression, seemed noticeably different today.

Why had she gone there? Romi thought back to her feelings at the time. It had seemed so urgent then, but now she couldn't verbalize what she'd wanted to tell him. She knew in her heart what she wanted to say, but the words just wouldn't come out.

"I can't really remember."

Kyungwoon was so close to her that her heart began to race like it was aiming to set the hundred-meter world record.

"I see." Kyungwoon pulled back again. "You should get some rest."

As he stood, Romi bolted upright and grabbed ahold of his arm.

"What are you doing? You're leaving, just like that?"

Romi could feel the muscles in his arm tense under her hand. Why was he acting like this all of a sudden? It wasn't the first time they had touched. But this time felt different. When he sat down again, his voice was even lower. "Should I not?"

She hadn't prepared anything to say, but she didn't let go of him. "We should—we should talk, shouldn't we?"

"About what?"

"I don't know! Anything."

"Mmm."

Kyungwoon reached across himself and took Romi's hand, still clutching at his arm, in his own. He lowered their hands, gently interlacing their fingers.

"Actually, there is something I wanted to say to you. It might be awkward, but . . ."

Romi's eyes widened, ears perked up to listen.

"I don't know if it's all right for me to tell you this given my situation."

Romi didn't know what he was trying to say, but she nodded eagerly. "Of course it is!"

"Some of my memories are starting to come back to me," Kyungwoon said softly. Romi's racing heart started to press on the brakes as if it had come to a yellow light.

"I remember bits and pieces of my wife's face, the accident, what happened that day."

"I see."

"Romi." He squeezed her hand. "The day of the typhoon, you remember what you said, right? That you'd come all this way to find me."

Her heart had pulled up to a stop sign now. Romi lowered her head, feeling drained. "But I was actually mistaken the whole time."

Kyungwoon shook his head. "I know there's no turning back time. The more I learned . . . the truth . . . about my wife, the better I was able to understand her. The more memories I recovered of her, the more easily I was able to let her go. And the more easily I was able to break free of the past."

"You lost her queen bee because of me."

"Another one will be born," Kyungwoon said. "When the season comes, another queen will hatch. I didn't even know there was such a thing as a super bee—how could I have lost something I didn't know I had? I can raise a new colony of them. If it hadn't been for you, I might never have known they existed." With that, Kyungwoon let go of her hand and looked her in the eyes, then bowed his head in gratitude. "So thank you. For finding me, even though it wasn't me you were looking for. For helping me to move forward."

When he looked up again, there was a brief silence. Like the pause when several cars came to an intersection with no traffic lights and the drivers were all trying to decide whether or not to floor it.

"I'm glad my terrible memory could be helpful to someone," Romi said. Ironically, though, she didn't feel 100 percent glad. "And I have something to thank you for too."

"What is it? Don't tell me it's the royal jelly?" Kyungwoon pointed to the shopping bag she was holding, his voice teasing.

Unlike her usual self, always the first to laugh, Romi was the picture of solemnity.

"Before, whenever I wanted something, I used to wait for someone else to bring it to me. Just sit around and wait for someone else to reach out first. But now I know. I can only get what I want if I set off in search of it." Something caught in her throat, making it hard for her to speak. "But when I did set off to look for it," she said, "I couldn't find it."

A shadow passed across Kyungwoon's face. "Romi, I know I'm not the person you wanted, but—"

"But even though I couldn't find what I wanted, I found something different. Something I hadn't expected at all. Something better."

Romi gathered her courage and looked up to meet his eyes. But before she knew it, her own eyes filled with tears, blurring her vision.

"Geez, what's wrong with me? So embarrassing. I always get like this."

Kyungwoon reached up and brushed away her tears with the back of his hand. "There's no reason to cry," he said.

The tears began to spill nonstop and turned into full-on sobs. "I know. I'm happy, so why am I crying? Maybe it's because today's my last day here on Jeju."

"Today's not your last day," Kyungwoon said quietly, lowering his hand.

"I leave for Seoul tomorrow."

"Even if you leave, that doesn't mean it's the end here. Not if you don't forget about me once you're there."

She couldn't tell whether his voice was wavering due to laughter or nerves. She sucked up her tears as suddenly as they had begun to fall. She rubbed her eyes and looked at him straight on. Once again, he was watching her, his face unfamiliar. But that was fine. Romi had come to love every moment she'd spent observing this stranger. All those lovely moments of unfamiliarity had come together to make him familiar to her at last.

In all seriousness, she told him, "That would be impossible."

A smile she had never seen from him before appeared on Kyungwoon's face. It was gentle but strong, a smile with a sort of determination to it, one that made his face unfamiliar yet again. "How can I trust that you mean that?" he asked.

"Should we kiss?" Romi blurted out, flustering even herself. "I mean, there's no way we could forget each other if we went so far as to kiss, right?"

"If you think so, I suppose we could try it," said Kyungwoon, bringing his face close to hers once more.

Just as their lips were about to touch, Romi murmured, "I'm not sure just a kiss would be enough, though . . . considering how terrible my memory is."

His breath grazed her lips as he laughed. "Then we'll have to do whatever it takes to make sure you don't forget."

◆ ◆ ◆

"The moon today is like a yellow French manicure." Chakyung gazed at the sky, then lowered her eyes again. "Now that I think about it, I'm overdue for a manicure. My nail polish is chipping."

Hadam examined her own nails. "I should probably get mine done, too, once we're back in Seoul. I never could while I was at my old job. Long nails would have just gotten in the way."

Even the French tip moon seemed to tremble as the wind blew through the yard where the two of them were sitting on a bench. Hadam shuddered a bit.

"When did you want to head up?"

Chakyung mulled over the question. "I was wondering whether we should head to a hotel and leave the two of them alone to talk through things."

"We still have to pack, though," Hadam pointed out.

"You're right—we do." Chakyung took her phone out of the pocket of her hooded jacket. "Then I'll give her a call and see if I can suss out the vibe—"

Right on cue, her phone pinged in her hand.

"Is it Romi?" asked Hadam, excited.

Chakyung scrunched her nose, as was her habit when she encountered a headache waiting to happen. "No," she said. "It's my job."

"At this hour? Don't tell me it's Director Dim?"

Chakyung sighed. "I don't think so."

Once he was all done with golfing, Director Dim should have gone back to Seoul, but it seemed he'd used the typhoon as an excuse to extend his vacation and even dropped by the event hall to pretend he was working. Earlier that morning, he'd kicked up a huge fuss over the phone, accusing Chakyung of dragging out the part-timers' shifts into overtime on a whim in a pointless act of kindness. As Jeju news outlets reported on yesterday's incident, they mentioned the haenyeo who had been taking part in a "cosmetics event" nearby when they rushed into action to save a life, and it seemed the story had rubbed Director Kim the wrong way. No matter how many times Chakyung tried to explain that this was a good thing, he lashed out about the company having been mentioned in connection with an ongoing criminal investigation. Growing fed up, Chakyung said she would take full responsibility for the situation. But she couldn't hold her tongue at just that.

"I'll cover the part-timers' overtime fees out of pocket. And I'll submit a written apology as well. But I must say, Director Kim, I had no idea you were so sensitive about overtime work."

Naturally, he lashed out again at that, but Chakyung—who had spent her entire life molding herself to be in harmony with the collective, putting the company's needs above her own—finally did away with any intention to compromise. The glass had already been knocked over.

"I suppose I'll have no choice but to write a report outlining my own overtime work," she said, "as well as the personal errands you've sent me on. There's quite a lot to cover if we're taking into account the last few years."

She hadn't even brought up the fact that he'd used a business trip as a pretense to golf, or that whenever they had a workshop, he went way overboard on comments that constituted sexual harassment. Chakyung ended the call with gritted teeth.

The message she had just gotten, though, wasn't from him but from a junior director at her company, Yoon Kyungwon. After Chakyung had declared war on Director Dim, she had reported him to Director Yoon, who was next in line for a promotion to senior director—in the event of a vacancy. Whatever her motives, Director Yoon would support Chakyung. But even with Director Yoon by her side, there was no way the company would look favorably at an employee who turned against an executive. Even before she saw Director Yoon's concern-laden message, Chakyung had braced herself for that.

Just as she sent a reply, Hadam tapped her on the arm. Chakyung looked up from her phone, following Hadam's finger toward where it was pointing. Through the lit window looking into the kitchen, she spotted Soo-eon sitting at the table and playing with the dog.

"Go," said Hadam gently. When Chakyung hesitated, Hadam got up from the bench first. "I was just thinking of going for a drive anyway."

Soo-eon wasn't surprised when Chakyung came in from the courtyard. Already, it was clear they couldn't part ways without saying their goodbyes.

Chakyung hurried over to the table where he was sitting. Her heart was racing even more than it had been when she'd filed the complaint against Director Dim.

Soo-eon looked exactly the way he had when they'd first met. But now she knew him better, in more detail. Eyes that smiled even when he was sitting still, a high but rounded nose, a jawline that had angles but wasn't sharp. Over the past nine days, his face had been strange in some moments, familiar in others, and always new to her. He was someone she'd gotten to know over so little time that parting ways here and now would make them strangers again, yet enough time that carrying on the way they were now could only make them closer.

Chakyung had already thought about what she wanted to say ahead of time. She felt such a sense of urgency that the words spilled out of her without any sort of preface.

"I can't bring Gnarly with me," she said.

The dog, as if already used to his new name, perked up his ears at the sound of it. Soo-eon's expression clouded over. He rested a hand on the dog's head.

"I see. In that case, I can—"

Chakyung raised a hand to stop him. "Hold on. Hear me out. What I mean is, I can't bring him with me right away."

Soo-eon looked at her wordlessly. Both his and Gnarly's eyes were fixed on her.

"I'm asking you to look after him for the time being. You told me if I take the future seriously but not the present moment, I'll never be able to move forward." Since that night, the words had embedded themselves in her heart like chunks of ice. Now, she could pull them out. Her heart had warmed enough to melt them. "So in the spirit of being faithful to the truth of this moment, I'm trying to make plans that will hold true in the future as well."

No one can be in a relationship that forces them to deviate from their nature. Chakyung was the same way. Her feelings at the moment were burning hot, but she couldn't proceed without a plan. She'd lived her entire life that way, planning for what she wanted. She could always revise the ones that went awry later. But she liked even the process of planning. It was something she'd always done. Even now, that hadn't changed.

"Here's my plan. Step one: I'll move out. I—I thought I was getting married and was planning to live with my parents until then. Now I have to explain to them that I'm not getting married after all. Of course, everything that's happened will make that easier to explain. I mean, it's not a good thing Chanmin turned out to be this kind of person, but it's no skin off my nose. Anyway, that's not what matters. My family has allergies, so I can't bring a dog with me right away. Which means I need another plan. Step two: I'll look for a place in Seoul. If Seoul's too expensive, then Gyeonggi-do. That should take a month at the most? Then Gnarly and I will have somewhere comfortable where we can live. I have to find a place that allows dogs, of course. Step three is about my job, and this is a problem. At the moment, I don't know what's going to happen at work, but I'll figure that out too. Gosh, why am I rambling like this? It feels like the biggest mess of a presentation I've ever given."

Chakyung had never babbled so much in her life. She'd worked so hard to prepare a clear and organized pitch. But as she laid out her plans, watching his face for a reaction, her words got tangled up in her emotions. Even more than any of the clients she'd had up to now, she couldn't guess what Soo-eon had thought of her spiel. He lowered his head for a moment, then looked up again, placing a hand on his chest. He let out a breath. Then he stood up. "You're fine," he said. "This is honestly the best presentation I've ever seen."

Now, Chakyung had to look up at him. She remembered the first few times they'd come face-to-face and the emotions she'd felt then. She'd enjoyed every one of these encounters. She was speaking with the present and the future in mind when she said, "I'll be back. I'll bring Gnarly with me, and we'll talk about what's going on with us."

When Soo-eon took her wrists in his hands, the corners of his eyes gently crinkled. "Okay," he said.

"I'd love for you to come with me too. That is, if you want to. If I have to go wherever you are, I'll just need to know what to prepare . . ."

Soo-eon raised a hand. "You can end your presentation there." He leaned down and peered into her eyes. "I also have to think hard about this. About what I can do. I have to leave again so I can graduate, finish up my studies."

Chakyung stumbled back in surprise. Now that she thought about it, they hadn't had much time to hash out these sorts of particulars. "Your studies? Don't tell me you're a student. An undergrad?"

Soo-eon's eyebrows shot up playfully. "No, I'm a grad student—in oceanography at the University of Hawaii. I'm on a leave of absence at the moment, but—what's wrong? You have something against students?"

Chakyung let out a sigh of relief. "Oh no, that's fine. I was just a bit shaken up at the thought of dating an undergrad at my age . . . though, of course, it wouldn't matter either way."

Soo-eon took another step toward her. "So we're dating?"

Chakyung realized she hadn't used the word "dating" since she herself had been an undergrad. But she didn't have a better word for this. The word alone still made her heart race the way it had in her college days. "We are," she said, "if that's all right with you."

He leaned in closer. "It's been all right with me since the first time I saw you."

"When I was passed out and looking like a total wreck on the plane?" she said, her hands coming around his waist.

Soo-eon placed a hand on her neck and the other on her back. His nose grazed her cheek. "I don't remember you ever looking a wreck. And I doubt I ever will." Gently, he pressed his mouth to hers and said into her lips, "But let's stay together long enough that I get to see that side of you too."

There was no need for Chakyung to reply. Because a moment later, his lips were on hers again, and she couldn't have said a word anyway. Gnarly, who'd been watching the two of them from afar, hurried over and squeezed himself between their legs to have a seat.

She'd come to Jeju and seen more than enough of the sea—the sea that took on a different appearance every time she looked.

Hadam leaned up against the car and counted the lights from the fishing boats. One, two, five—seven, if she counted the ones all the way out in the distance. What had the haenyeo said again? In Jeju, the near sea was "apbareu," and the distant sea was "nanbareu." But until what point was the sea near, and from what point on did it become distant? Hadam wondered whether there was a way to determine this with certainty and thought to look it up. But even searching for how to determine what was near and what was far in relation to the distance between people yielded no clear consensus.

On her way to the docks, she had gotten a message from Jaewoong. Think about it. I'll wait. She hadn't stopped here to call him back. She'd stopped because, before she thought about anything, she knew she needed to stand still.

When she came out of the police station after giving her statement, Jaewoong was waiting. They each rode in their own car to the nearest Starbucks to talk.

"I think she and I will manage to sort everything out," Jaewoong said. "I'm taking full responsibility. And when it's all over, I'm going to pay both our families a visit to apologize."

His expression was hard, but his eyes wavered with emotion. Hadam hemmed and hawed for a bit before saying only, "I see."

She still was firm in believing this wasn't her fault, that the problem lay with Jaewoong and his fiancée. She'd already said as much before, though, and didn't feel the need to bring it up again.

What Hadam couldn't stand wasn't just the fact that Jaewoong had been silently deceiving her the whole time. It was the fact that because of his silence, he'd put another woman in a position to be hurt. Never mind whether he intended to or not. Even if it meant hurting someone else, he should have let Hadam make her own judgments and choices. He hadn't even given her that opportunity. He hadn't asked her what she thought at all.

"I hope you don't think I was just momentarily swept up in those memories or looking for a cheap thrill before the marriage. Seeing you again made me remember who I was. I thought I could live like the old me."

Strictly speaking, Jaewoong hadn't lied. But he hadn't told the truth either. And because the truth had been kept from her, Hadam couldn't say the feelings she'd had for him were real. They existed only in a fantasy world where he wasn't already betrothed to someone else. Once that realization settled over her, Hadam found she had nothing to say.

"I'll wait for you," Jaewoong said. "This time, I'll wait."

She couldn't remember the last time she'd heard someone say something so heartfelt. All her life, she'd thought she was the earnest one. But now that someone was showing her that same earnestness, she didn't feel happy or ecstatic. In fact, she felt somewhat sad.

All she said in reply was, "Thanks for helping us find Romi. As for everything else . . . I don't know."

This was the truth. Aside from her gratitude, she didn't know what else there was.

It was a night when even the cars were racing full speed ahead. No matter how hard she stared out at the darkly swaying sea, no thoughts bubbled up in her mind like the sea-foam on the crests of the waves. In this case, though, the thoughts wouldn't be coming from her head—they had to come from her heart.

First, she had to leave. There were some truths that could only be learned with distance.

On her way back to the car, her phone pinged with another message. She glanced at the screen. This time, it wasn't Jaewoong.

> I heard you're going back to Seoul tomorrow. It's too bad we didn't get a chance to say goodbye. If you ever need anything from me, please be in touch.

Hadam thought of Hwachul's round face and gentle appearance. Only later had she noticed his strong arms, which had carried her when she passed out. Just as Romi had been searching for her own Honeyman, Hadam might have also found hers. But . . .

She messaged back: Thank you so much for so many things. I'm sure I'll be in touch to consult with you about bee farming for the documentary. I'll message you later on.

The reply came while she was still holding her phone, debating whether or not to wait for it: Yes, let's talk soon.

With that, Hadam put her phone back in her pocket.

Not every trip had to end with a romance. And not every story had to end with a couple kissing, the camera spinning around them a full 360 degrees. Just because a lot of people made that their ending didn't mean she had to. What was a romance to some people could be a documentary to others. The same scenery did not make for the same footage in everyone's eyes. That was what editing was for. While it would be nice if she could leave her life in the hands of a more capable editor, Hadam didn't have too many regrets.

She got in the car. It was time for everyone to head back to where they belonged. But maybe she could go for one last ride along the coast.

Once she started the car and her phone automatically connected to the Bluetooth speakers, rich sound poured out. The playlist she had been listening to earlier came back on. Coincidentally, the song playing now was the one by the famous singer she and Jaewoong had been listening to when they were trapped in the car during the typhoon—the song about welcoming in the summer. After that day, she'd searched for it on YouTube.

The lyrics described a summertime reunion of two lovers. Why had they listened to a song like this? Did everyone have the same anticipation that when they set off on a trip alone, they would come back coupled up? Hadam thought about it and decided this hope wasn't a bad thing in itself. Everyone pretending to imagine the same possibility whenever they went somewhere new—that was what made travel fun. But on this trip, Hadam felt no need to lament that this hope hadn't come to fruition. You expected your life to change, then felt frustrated with yourself for expecting so much, but the good thing about traveling was that you could step right over the remnants of those toppled hopes and leave them all behind.

Hadam tapped her phone screen to skip to the next song. The sounds of the guitar and bass eased into a steady rhythm that flowed from the speakers.

The song's title slowly came to mind: "Summer Plumage," referring to the feathers of a bird said to grow right as the season shifts from late summer to fall. Their plumage was the most beautiful during this time of year for the purpose of mating. The summer passes by. People pass by too. Even memories eventually fade.

Hadam found the lyrics asking the listener to sneer at the singer's botched work of art especially piercing. No, she thought, shaking her head. Maybe her Jeju romance had been botched, but the project hadn't been. Not yet. She had tons of stories to tell, one for all the many things that had happened. She hadn't planned for the *Searching for Honeyman* story to end simply with them either finding Honeyman or not. It was a project she'd started with the desire to make a film about several people's ongoing searches for their own Honeyman. She was still searching. She was still making that film.

So long to the summer, and on to the fall. Listening to the guitar riff coming through the speakers, Hadam got back on the road, leaving the sea behind. For the first time since she'd come to Jeju, she drove with no destination entered into the navigation system. She didn't know where she was headed just then, nor did she know what awaited her, but in that moment, this felt to her like the perfect ending.

ABOUT THE AUTHOR

Born in Seoul, South Korea, Hyun-joo Park is a novelist, essayist, translator, and critic. She studied English language and literature in college in Korea and graduate-level linguistics in the US. While a graduate student, Hyun-joo began work as a translator of English literature and a literary critic focusing on mystery and romance novels.

Returning to Korea, Hyun-joo continued her work as a translator and critic. She also began to write books of her own, including an essay collection, *The Romance Pharmacy*, and the two-volume novel *My Occult Days*. *Romancing on Jeju* is the English translation of her second novel, *Searching for Honeyman*. In 2023, Hyun-joo published *At 2 a.m. Laundromat*, a sequel to *My Occult Days*.

Hyun-joo hosted a podcast called *The Drama* from 2017 to 2018 and appears regularly on a TV critic program aired nationwide in Korea.

ABOUT THE TRANSLATOR

Paige Morris is a writer and translator from Jersey City, New Jersey. She has translated works by Pak Kyongni, Han Kang, Ji-min Lee, and others. A lover of love stories with perpetual wanderlust, she now divides her time between Korea and the US.

Photo © Yvonne Bramble